THE CAVERN

Utopia Press 2014

Book design by Stephen Gullette

First Edition

ISBN-10: 0990846407
ISBN-13: 978-0-9908464-0-6

© Utopia Press 2014

Utopia Press
2740 Oxford Village Ln.
Georgetown, KY 40324

www.brucewilliam.us

THE CAVERN

for Cary, Chris and Mildred

Prologue

Small rocks cracked and rattled down the steep slope as Pire struggled up the stone face of the cliff. The sharp sound was swallowed by the dense vegetation that clung to the foot of the mountain. Out across the distant plain, flames were darting from between the leaves of the Galba trees. Thick, black smoke snaked skyward causing the distant stars to flicker and disappear. The battle for the rebel camp was winding down. The sky above the mountain was lightening. Wispy clouds settled on the tops of the trees joining the silver webs of the saber moths. The staddich, the brief Osstarian night, was ebbing.

Pire crouched amid the rocks, exhausted. He was weary of the clinging dampness and the constant muggy breezes of the jungle. He thought of his home nestled in the cool, crisp air of the Northern Islands and of his friends. It was a distant memory now, more like a dream. For both Faceer and Stoma the worst had happened. The peace between the two species … peace that had lasted for thousands of years … was dissolving like the morning mist.

He gazed up at the few stars that remained in the lightening sky and watched as a brief burst of meteorites romped through the vast aerial plane between Rebal and the deep of space. "Star riders" the Faceer called them, and wondered if they could see the chaos that was unfolding on his planet. Resting his head on his knees he stared into the distance. A moist breeze blew across his face bringing the scent of priot flowers. Just over his shoulder a vine was in full bloom, its thick, jointed stems drooping almost to the ground. The beautiful red flowers that covered it announced that it would soon bear fruit, but there was no joy in that thought for Pire. He knew that ultimately the fruit would be processed into katoc, a sinister drug. As the giant red star Zenos made its way back from its exile on the far side of the planet, the tips of the flower's petals glowed in its faint, pink light: "is there such beauty that it can hide the evil heart?" The words of the old Faceer poem ran through his mind as he reached out to touch it. The sky gradually grew lighter and a new day began. But for the inhabitants of Osstar the world it illuminated had changed — perhaps forever.

CHAPTER 1

Pire glanced up long enough to see Diell making his way deftly through the clutter of the analyzer room. The exposed, bony ridge of spine, a remnant of some ancient reptilian ancestor, showed through his tunic. He knew by its flattened appearance that Zenos was high in the morning sky. Diell moved behind him and stood looking at the sheets of paper spewing from the printer attached to the bulky machine. The analyzer was one aspect of the Trague Center indispensable to the Faceer scientists lucky enough to have access to it. A massive array of conductors and optics tied to a central processing unit, it formed a bulky but effective information analysis system. It was considered quite advanced for a society that was only now moving from an agrarian economy to a technology based, industrial one. Pire's attention was not on the machine, though, but rather on what was coming from it. Diell could read the expression on Pire's face — and perhaps a bit more.

"How was the equatorial trip ... bad news?"

"Not really bad, just unexpected." Pire glanced up at him, forgetting his task for a moment. Diell was young and fresh-faced, with a curiosity considered intense, even for a Faceer. Pire had chosen him as his assistant at the urging of his Uncle. Diell was a Somacee, a member of Pire's blood-clan, and a distant cousin. He admired his curiosity, but his inexperience sometimes proved distracting. Pire was beginning to wonder if he had taken him in too soon. He studied the dark, curly hair that covered his rounded head. He had a lot of hair for a Somacee.

"The temperature is going up, isn't it?"

"Up? Yes, yes it's going up." Pire went back to the data. "I'm now certain that the average temperature on Osstar has risen almost 7 degrees since we began keeping records some thirty years ago."

"Seven! Did you have any idea that it would be that much?"

"I had calculated it to be a bit smaller — but only a bit. The statistics on agricultural yields, the instances of extinctions and the reduction of the ice caps had all pointed to dramatic increases. Still,

I haven't done the research necessary to pin down the problem. I'm hoping that this data will help me make a case to Dr. Lateer for the funding of a large-scale study."

Diell wasn't listening. He was rummaging through the drawer of a side desk, his arm up to his elbow inside it. His hand finally emerged with a treasure, a crumbled piece of paper containing a lump of keesa cheese. His speech was garbled as he spoke while he ate. "What if Lateer doesn't agree? He's controlled by the Stoma High Council you know."

Pire flipped the printout onto the desk and made his way to his cup of now cold chee. "Yes, I know, but surely the magnitude of this problem will overcome even the Stoma's short-sightedness. At any rate, I have a fall-back position if needed."

Diell cocked his head in the unique Somacee fashion and waited for the rest. Pire poured the thin, cold liquid into a pot sitting on an ancient electric burner and frowned at the pieces of keesa now covering his work table "... a less complex research project that should give me some answers even without a full-blown project. I'll go for the full project first, of course, but if I'm turned down, I'll still be able to do something." Pire swatted at the crumbs and frowned. "Would you like some chee to help finish that off?"

Diell ignored the sarcasm. He was picking up subtle energies from Pire, energies given off in a particular manner by each Faceer blood-group. "You're concerned about this aren't you?"

"Yes, I am concerned. Something's happening to this planet's climate that could have dire consequences for all of us, Stoma, Faceer and every other living creature on Osstar."

"So we've over-built a little, there's no reason we can't cut back on our polluting industries, clean up the land."

Pire resisted the soothing effects of the energy flowing from Diell. He returned to his work table and sorted through the reams of paper. "I suppose."

"What is it, Pire. What's troubling you?"

He answered without looking up. "If my assumptions are correct, my young friend, it is through no fault of our own that the temperature is rising. I fear that there may be something happening to Zenos."

His footsteps echoed against the polished stone walls of the Trague Center as Pire made his way to the front of the building. He peered into the empty offices as he passed, all arranged in the orderly fashion of the Faceer. The other, less enterprising, researchers had long since left for the comfort of their cozy homes carved into the face of the surrounding hills. He had spent the day going back over the figures, trying to find some mistake some procedural flaw that would prove them wrong, but the calculations had held true. The numbers stared from the pages of the report, cold and unsympathetic. "The data manipulates the scientist, not the other way round." The words of his father filled his head as they always did when he was anxious.

Outside the Center the last vestiges of twinight was clinging to the tops of the tall peaks of the northern mountains. Slender laange trees leaned outward in sharp angles seemingly suspended from the rock cliffs. Pire paused to look up at the statue of the great Stoma military leader Trague-Denard pompously guarding the entrance. He clinched the enameled teeth plates in his mouth and snorted in mock-contempt. How typical of the Stoma to make sure the name of one of their heroes adorned the facade of the largest and most ornate building in the Northern Islands. It was made even more ridiculous by the fact that it was a science center. The fields of science and technology were almost entirely the purview of the Faceer. Yet, ridiculous or not, without Stoma financing and political support there would be no facility and very little scientific research.

As the staddich approached stars began to appear in the Osstarian sky. In Stoma legend they were said to be sparks thrown off by fires raging on the surface of Rebal, their giant celestial companion. In the early days of the "Inclusion," when the Faceer were being integrated into Stoma society, the great Faceer scientists Tyard-Ming and Traag-Lucaar had been tortured and killed by Stoma priests for saying otherwise. It was an incident known to every Faceer, but never mentioned in the official histories. The Faceer had a saying: "The Stoma gave Osstar civilization, the Faceer its place in the universe."

Pire made his way down the paved avenue to the transport station located near the main dwelling of the House of Klut. The massive stone wall surrounding the shallow sea-water pool marked it as the abode of a powerful member of a very substantial House. It was, in fact, the second most powerful of the twelve great Stoma Houses on Osstar. As the delicate leaves of the spindly lapis trees growing at the edge of the front gate swayed in the moist breeze, he could see individual apartments sloping in circular terraces down to the sea. The Stoma lived in family groups. The location of the apartment indicated the rank of the family member with the lower levels, those closest to their beloved sea, going to the higher rank. The meticulously manicured grounds blended the vegetation with the dwelling areas so expertly that it looked as if the two had sprung simultaneously from the rich soil.

Like all Faceer, Pire had complex feelings in regard to the Stoma. He disliked their vanity, but at the same time admired the great dignity with which they conducted the affairs of the planet. In spite of the natural tensions between the Great Houses, there had not been a serious conflict on Osstar in living memory. They could be haughty and insensitive to what they considered an inferior species and yet they were often kind and magnanimous to their long-time companions. They were technologically less adept than the Faceer, but artistically much the superior species. The design of their dwellings and of their great cities set the standard for grace and beauty.

The Great Houses of the Stoma had ruled Osstar for fifty thousand years. They had directed the Faceer's early development, learned to communicate with them, finally bringing them into their households as companions during the period known as the "Inclusion." For thousands of years it had been a cozy and beneficial arrangement for both species, but always controlled by the Stoma. Now Osstar was changing. An agrarian society, embodied by the huge Stoma estates, was becoming industrialized. A fast-paced consumer economy was putting pressures on the old social order. The need for better, more complex machines was creating a demand for scientists, engineers and technicians. The Stoma had attempted to train their own children to fill these jobs, but young Stoma were more concerned with family and status and disinclined to what they considered work fit only for Faceer.

The Faceer, on the other hand, were eager to expand their role in Osstarian society. The colleges and technical schools were teeming with them. Their talents were beginning to make them indispensable to the expanding Stoma industrial economy. It was an elevation of status not appreciated by many of the heads of the Great Houses. But one thing was abundantly clear; the Stoma held the vast share of wealth and power on Osstar and were not likely to give it up willingly.

The great red star Zenos slipped behind the larger disk of Rebal, Osstar's orbital companion. Osstar, rotating on its axis, then turned its western hemisphere away from both and out toward open space. The twinight surrendered to the brief, dark period known as "staddich." A transporter squeaked to a halt in front of Pire and its doors opened with a loud swoosh. Pire paid the attendant and made his way to a seat on the right side of the vehicle, the side where male Faceer of Pire's age traditionally sat. He did it more out of habit than anything else. Seating restrictions no longer existed — at least officially.

Pire pressed his face against the cool window of the vehicle. The soft glow of gaslight from the lamps lining the cobbled street melted into a shimmering, liquid strand as the transporter sped along the twisting roadway. For a moment he was back with his father, on their way to the museum or the library. He could hear his gentle voice instructing him, admonishing him to strive for wisdom above all else. "The light of knowledge enters through the eyes, but wisdom flows through the window of the heart." A sharp bump brought Pire back to the present. The transport had come to a stop in front of a colorfully lit building with a large metal door. Pire rose and exited the vehicle. The sounds of laughter and spirited conversation instantly surrounded him and began to transform his mood. He was greeted at the door by a rather large Faceer in a shiny black tunic.

"Ah, Nubin Pire, how are you tonight?" The door keeper greeted him formally, using Pire's full family name.

"I'm better now, Dace," he answered.

"She's only been on once," Dace said, anticipating Pire's next question. "She's due on again shortly and, if I may say so, she is looking extremely healthy this evening."

The loudspeaker system crackled to life as a Faceer voice announced the next act. "Faceer of all clans and lineage, we are proud to present for your enjoyment the incomparable singer of the Sonnage—Steera."

The thin veil that had partially obscured the small stage lifted revealing a lithe young Faceer female seated on a small wooden stool. A low, mellow tone began to surround her even though she remained perfectly motionless. Subtle waves of energy surged through the music. Pire let the complex tones flow through him. They seemed to soak into his skin, to fill all the empty places.

A waitress came by bringing a glass of dark, musky-flavored panta. Pire saw nothing but the supple form in front of him. His eyes followed the dark, flowing hair of her head down to the whisper-thin coat of golden hair that covered her body, ending in the tufts of soft fur on her tiny feet. Her sheer tunic enhanced the form of her breasts and clung to a waist as hard and flat as that of one of the prime athletes of the Triall Mountains.

Steera was, in fact, a Triall Mountain Faceer, a Veertal, not a coastal Somacee like Pire. Noted for their athletic builds and passionate personalities the Veertal had been prized by the Stoma as companions in the old times and were brought into many of the Great Houses almost as family members. Many Veertal incorporated a portion of their Stoma House names within their Faceer names, a tradition that was often resented by other Faceer. There had even been stories of sexual activities between Stoma and Veertal, but this was dangerous even to mention and certainly never brought up in polite conversation.

Looking at Steera, Pire could see why any species would be captivated by her. She was a vision of sensuality and "health" as the Faceer liked to put it. Still, there was something about her, a quality that was unsettling. He attributed it to having spent too much time among the Stoma. "Veertal are too trusting ... too naive," he thought. She had promised herself to him, but she was a Trial Mountain Veertal, a strongly clannish bunch. When it came time to form the marriage bond, would she find a Somacee acceptable?

A hard hand on his shoulder jolted Pire back to the moment. He looked up to see the unwelcome face of Prier Datar. "Well, the dedicated young Faceer scientist takes some much needed time off. What happened? Did the Stoma masters' leash break?"

"Take the rhetoric somewhere else, will you. I've had a rough day."

"We've all had a rough day, friend. Every day under the yoke of the Stoma is a rough day for Faceer ... although some have found ways to make it easier for themselves."

"What is it with you Datar, this thing with the Stoma?"

"Pitiful. You, a trained scientist, believe the Stoma lies. When are you going to wake up and look around you?"

"Well, hopefully it won't be until well after mid-Rebal tomorrow." Pire smiled.

Datar continued, ignoring Pire's sarcasm. "I doubt that you will do any dreaming while you are in sleep-stasis, because you already live in a dream world. Some day—and I believe that day is not too far away—your dream world will become a nightmare and your love for your Stoma masters will fade in the harsh light of reality."

"You're quite the orator, Datar. You should run for local council sometime." Pire watched as he took his traveling political commentary to the next table. One could discount Datar's oratory. He was a known instigator, a character always operating on the fringes of the law. But there were other Faceer on Osstar, more respected and well known, who were starting to say similar things.

Pire reached for his drink. He felt a different, gentler hand on his shoulder.

"Buy a Veertal a panta?" The sultry voice floated down from the soft overhead light. He looked up to see Steera's pale yellow/gold eyes, the eyes that had so captivated him at the Academy some years ago, meeting his own. The harsh light from the incandescent bulb gave them a slightly greenish hue. He felt a rush of blood to his head.

"I think I can spare the change." Steera glided into the chair beside him, popped a short, sticky-sweet "stalar" stick into her mouth and snuggled up to his arm.

"Nasty habit for an athlete," Pire said, never altering his gaze.

"And you're not very cool and collected for a Somacee," she replied, returning his stare. "Fighting with Datar again?"

"Oh, you know his usual anti-Stoma rhetoric. It seems that everywhere you go someone is lashing out against the Stoma. At the moment I'm too tired to worry about it."

"And my singing didn't help?"

"Oh, perhaps a little," Pire replied coyly, "in all, a pretty good sonnage. The tone was nice, but the frequency of the energy was too much Veertal and not enough Somacee."

"Let's see if we can get those Somacee blood cells moving." She leaned across the table and gave him a soft warm kiss on the corner of his mouth, a particularly sensitive area on a Somacee's face.

"I've missed you. How were things at the equator?"

Pire collected himself. "Boring, really, I didn't get to see much of it; the security was tight. I think the Stoma make up dangers in order to justify their going along on our expeditions. All I did was collect my readings and come back."

"Well?"

"Look, can we continue this somewhere else ... say at my place after you get off?"

"Pretty clever way to get me alone," Steera purred.

"Yes it is, isn't it? I just don't like sharing you with all these gawkers."

"I've only got one more song and then we'll go." Pire nodded. All eyes followed Steera as she once again moved to the microphone. Her last sonnage was as soft and subtle as coola down. The house erupted in applause as she finished. She exited quickly before her fans could interrupt her rendezvous with Pire.

"Want to take the transporter, or do you feel like walking?"

"It's a beautiful twinight." She smiled a soft sensuous smile. "Let's walk."

Pire smiled back at her and took her hand in his.

They strolled along the stream known as Ossgar. Formed from the melted snow atop Mount Sagar, its frigid waters tumbled down from the heights and emptied into the sea by the House of Klut. The great, round ball of orange gas that was Rebal tagged along westward like a faithful servant, lighting the path worn by years of footsteps through the lush forest. They came upon a small wooden bench set in a circular clearing facing the hills. Steera pulled Pire down and kissed him.

"So talk."

"About what?"

"About your trip, the research. Do you think that all I do is sing in lounges?"

Pire tried to focus. "Let's talk about us. Should we set a date?"

"A date! My, but the equator has lit a fire under you."

"I'm serious. I think that we've waited long enough. I want to get on with our lives."

"Why the rush? I've still got to finish my degree to qualify for a position at the Institute. You're the one who advised me ... remember? And besides, you haven't even met my family. What would they think?"

"They'd think that you made a wise decision taking a handsome Somacee over some muscle-bound, muscle-headed Veertal."

Steera smiled and ran her finger through the soft hair on Pire's forehead. "You are cute. I will give it my deepest consideration. Now, even though my course Veertal impulses don't exactly harmonize with yours, I can still tell when someone is keeping something from me. You've avoided talking about your findings.

"They're very preliminary."

"And ..."

"And not in any scientifically acceptable form."

"And ..."

Pire's eyes fixed on a small insect crawling across the footpath. He consciously avoided eye contact with Steera. Finally, he blurted it out. "I think it may be Zenos, Steera."

"Zenos!" What do you mean?"

"I think Zenos may be getting hotter."

Steera immediately grasped the gravity of Pire's statement. They sat in silence for a moment. Finally, she gained the courage to speak. "What's causing it?"

"I'm not sure. I'm going to need more data."

"You're concerned about this, aren't you?"

"I don't know." Pire looked directly at her for the first time. Rebal's soft light nestled in her eyes. She looked as beautiful as he had ever seen her. "I could be wrong, and besides we have time to think, and as long as Faceer have time to think, there is hope." They were his father's words. He took Steera's hand and they made their way up the long hill to her apartment overlooking the stream as Rebal fled westward from the approaching staddich.

CHAPTER 2

Pire played his fingers in-and-out through the pinkish-white Zenos light streaming through the small window in Dr. Lateer's waiting room. Particles of dust floated aimlessly, tracing lazy spirals in its radiance. It had a hypnotic effect. Faceer lived for the warm light of their red star. Their metabolisms were dictated by it. The small, bony ridge that ran down their backs was attached to thick muscles that could cause it to lie flat or stand out as much as three inches in order to catch more sunlight and warmth. It was a metabolic booster system, a genetic gift from a cold-blooded ancestor that made up part of their evolutionary line. As he watched the light from Zenos appear and disappear between his fingers the lines of an ancient Faceer poem ran through his head:

Where can you hide from yourself, young Faceer?
Where is the cave so deep,
That it can smother your thoughts in its blackness?
When the day does come,
Will you not be naked to the light?

The door to Dr. Lateer's office opened and his receptionist coolly bade him enter. Lateer stood next to a small stove, brewing a carafe of chee, the dark, syrupy liquid that was the morning drink of preference for most Faceer. He appeared nervous. Pire accepted a mug from Lateer to break the ice.

"Do you take your chee with lapis juice?" It was an old custom, mixing one of the Faceer's favorite drinks with one of the Stoma's.

"No thank you, this will be fine."

"So tell me, young Pire," Lateer used the form of the word that a kindly old uncle might, "what exactly is all this about warming?"

"Well, I don't really have adequate data to make any definitive hypothesis. My sample is too small to be statistically reliable, but my preliminary data seems to show that there is a warming trend taking place." Lateer looked down his nose and snorted at Pire's pretensions.

"I suppose that you think this is somehow due to industrial pollution."

"It may be, but I'm not sure. That's why I need the institute's help in mounting a more extensive project."

"How large a project?"

"It would be to the North Polar Region. I would estimate that somewhere between 150,000 and 200,000 Kalar should do it."

"A hefty project indeed. Do you think the institute can find that kind of money?"

"I know that it is liberally funded by the High Council."

"And do you also know that those same Council members, the ones who so magnanimously provide us with funding, derive much of their wealth from the very industries that you are seeking to malign!"

"Dr. Lateer," Pire steadied his voice, "I'm after important scientific data, not on some crusade against industrial growth."

"And I, my fine young Faceer, am trying to maintain an institute that can support such research ... research into useful things, things that will help build Osstar, not divide it."

"I realize your position, Doctor, but the information gained may be of vital importance to the entire planet."

"Well I can tell you now that the institute will not go along with a 200,000 Kalar project, or even a 50,000 Kalar project aimed at causing trouble for Stoma industry!"

Pire tried a different tact. "I need a project to maintain my position and you need a project to justify the existence of the institute. Approve a project for 10,000 Kalar and I will produce the results you desire. Anyway, after some preliminary study of the little data that I have, I'm beginning to have my doubts about the pollution theory."

Lateer perked up. "Well now, I think we may be able to do just that. I'm glad you have some appreciation for the delicate nature of my position. I'll see what I can do."

"I can give you a list of the supplies that I will need, and, of course, I will need to take my assistant Diell ..."

Lateer stopped in mid-sentence. "We can discuss this after the grant is approved. Good day Nubin Pire." Dr. Lateer handed Pire his briefcase and hustled him to the door. "I'll be in touch," he said, and practically shoved Pire out of the office. The door had not been shut for more than a few moments when the receptionist gathered up her belongings and left as well, locking it behind her. Dr. Lateer checked the window curtain to make sure it was totally closed and made his way into his small inner laboratory. There, hidden in the shadows, sat a massive male Stoma.

Klut-takit was the government minister in charge of all research and technology on Osstar, and the probable successor to Klut-Prime, the head of the House of Klut. He was a formidable creature. His large, rounded shoulders flowed into two powerful, curved arms ending in huge hands. There was a hint of webbing between his four fingers and thumb, remnants of an aquatic ancestor. His head (completely hairless except for a rim of fuzz that formed a semi-circle around the back) seemed simply to emerge from his shoulders, curving gently forward and ending in a rather prominent nose. In accordance with an old Faceer custom, Lateer waited for Klut-takit to start the conversation. Klut spoke in a deep tone, one meant for the ears of Faceer.

"So, is this the young troublemaker?"

"Did you hear everything, Your Excellency?"

"I heard. Just because I don't have two hairy little appendages protruding from my cranium doesn't mean I am deaf. He sounded evasive. He knows something that he's keeping hidden. There are things taking place on Osstar, things that are of a sensitive nature. The High Council has reason to believe that there are subversive forces at work within the Faceer scientific community, a community that we rely upon a great deal. I want you to monitor him closely. I want reports of his activities, his movements. Do you understand?"

"Do you want me to cancel the expedition? I can if you order it."

"Absolutely not!" The forcefulness of Klut's response gave Lateer a start. "It is imperative that Nubin Pire be at the North Polar Station as soon as possible." Dr. Lateer cast his eyes downward and took a submissive stance. Klut's tone suddenly softened. "After all, we don't want to stifle legitimate research, do we?"

Klut-takit grabbed his cape and moved toward the door, signaling that the meeting was over. Lateer moved to the back wall of the small room and bowed slightly as Klut glided past him and out of the office. Only after he had been gone for several minutes did Lateer muster the courage to shut the door behind him.

CHAPTER 3

The clutter was rapidly disappearing from Pire's small laboratory as he packed instruments, warm parkas and supplies for the journey. The weather would be bone cold. The Faceer's hybrid metabolism, an advantage in warmer climes, would be a disadvantage in the high north.

A shadow floated across the writing board that adorned the rear wall of the lab. "Blast it, Diell. I wish you wouldn't sneak around like that."

"Sorry," Diell answered. "I've finished packing the plants and the tools, but what are we going to do with all that poly-sheeting?"

"You're going to see that all of it is packed onto the aircraft. This sheeting will be the only thing that stands between the plants, the polar winds and us. If we have to make a weight allowance in the craft, we'll leave you behind before we sacrifice one scrap of the poly-sheet." Diell's eyes dropped. "Come on, you young greel," Pire laughed. "I'll have need of you when we get to the pole. Go and recheck to see if we've inventoried everything. We don't want Dr. Lateer to accuse us of misappropriating his precious Institute funds."

Pire had returned to packing the second case when he again sensed a presence in the lab. "Is that you, Diell? You couldn't have checked the equipment that quickly." The scent and the vibrations reaching Pire didn't belong to Diell. "Steera!" He called her name even before he had turned to see her standing in the doorway.

"It's hard to sneak up on you."

"Impolite would be a better word."

"Looks like you're moving, going far?"

"Yes, as a matter of fact I am."

"You received the grant," she continued, "10,000 Kalar."

"It's also impolite to pry; how did you find out so quickly?"

"I have a few friends around here you know. And since we're discussing manners, what about someone who confides in you, and then tries to sneak out of town without so much as a fare-thee-well."

"I was going to tell you."

"When? Were you going to wire me after the plane had taken off?" Steera's hurt was tinged with anger.

"It's going to be cold, tiresome and maybe even dangerous." Pire went back to packing as he spoke, shoving winter clothing angrily into the case. "It's no crusade. It's a boring scientific expedition to go watch a thermometer in the coldest place on Osstar."

"I'm going with you."

"That's exactly why I didn't say anything to you. You are not going with me."

"It won't work, Pire. I'm a scientist, and you've whetted my Faceer curiosity. I want to know what's happening to Zenos just as much as you."

Pire stood firm. "You're not going on this expedition—period. It's too dangerous. I'm serious, Steera, this is not a place for amateurs." Pire wished he could have called the word back.

"Amateur! Amateur! We'll see who the amateur is." Steera pushed past him and out the door before Pire could catch her.

He looked at the crumpled winter tunic in his hands. "What a Zerrit brain I am. Now there's no telling what she might do." Diell reentered, looking behind him to make sure Steera was gone.

"Such anger, what did you say to her?"

"I said she couldn't go with us."

"Well I don't know how you said it, but it sure got her ridge up."

"I probably said it about as poorly as it could have been said," Pire admitted. "But it may have had the desired result."

"I wouldn't be so sure."

"What do you mean?"

"As she left she told me to purchase provisions for one more expedition member, a female ... should I?"

"We shall see, my friend," Pire sighed, "and soon I would imagine."

CHAPTER 4

It had been three days. Steera had not spoken to Pire or to anyone else for that matter. She had done what she always did when she was angry and hurt, locked herself in her room, closed out the world and read ... anything and everything that she could find. Only an appointment with her former mentor could have dislodged her from her self-imposed exile.

As she stepped off the transporter onto the rounded-stone surface of the street, the bitter taste of Pire's condescension was still in her mouth. "A lounge singer, that's all he thinks that I am. Well I'll show him." She covered the short distance to a pair of great, iron gates, jumped up and pulled the long chain that hung down in front. A loud ringing sound filled the air, and the retraction of the rope almost caused her to leave the ground. It was not designed for use by Faceer since they were usually obliged to use the rear entrance. Steera's close relationship with Family Klut gave her leave to use the front gate.

After a short wait, a young Faceer appeared. He seemed surprised to see another Faceer and a female at that.

"Veertal," he said under his breath.

"Thank you for pointing that out to me. I've come to see Klut-takit." Steera's tone was brusque.

"Oh you have, have you?" The young servant's voice mimicked her tone. "Well, His Excellency is in the feeding pool at the moment and is quite indisposed."

"Tell him that Dya-Klut-Steera is here to speak with him, and be quick about it." The emphasis Steera put on her Stoma sub-name produced results. The young Faceer made an abrupt about face and hurried off to the main shelter surrounding the central pool. He returned with a large metal key.

"Sorry for the wait," he said, breathing heavily. "I assumed that you were just another petitioner. His Excellency has had so many of them since yesterday."

"Since yesterday?"

"Yes, since his elevation to Klut-Prime." Steera smothered her reaction. She regretted her self-imposed exile for the last three days. The iron gates opened noiselessly and the two made their way down the wide stone walkway toward the entrance to the main shelter area. "Yes," the young Faceer continued, "tragic about old Klut. They say that no one in the air transport had a chance. At least the end came swiftly and painlessly."

"Yes, tragic," Steera continued calmly, trying to make sense of things. She took a chance "Have they identified the others that were with him on the transport?"

The young retainer complied. "Well, of course there were the four heads of the Security Branches and their retainers ... and poor Dr. Lateer. But I suppose this is old news by now."

"Lateer!" Steera could hardly contain her shock. She composed herself.

The young retainer gave her a curious look, "Yes, the poor fellow, was apparently a last minute addition to the flight. Bad luck, eh."

"Extremely bad." They reached the open portal leading into the main shelter area that covered the feeding pool. The great pool extended out over the cliffs above the Sea of Leeth, and commanded an unobstructed view of the promontory upon which the great house was built. Erected by Faceer engineers to Stoma designs, its foundation had been dug into the bedrock with the pool and terraces cantilevered out over the cliff using massive stone columns as supports. The sent of loris blooms and brackish water swirled in the warm breeze rising from the sea below.

The young Faceer asked Steera to remain there. As she waited, she pondered the shocking new situation. What was the old Klut doing on an air transport with all four Security heads? The Stoma hate to fly. And why did they bring Lateer along?

A large form abruptly appeared in the water and glided effortlessly from the central pool into the smaller, inner pool where Steera waited. In one fluid transition, the great Stoma rose from the water and walked to the chair in front of her. Steera could envision his ancestors making the same graceful evolutionary transition from water to land some ten million or so years ago.

Klut situated himself in the throne-like lounge chair and gave Steera an admiring look. "My, but you have grown into a prize specimen of Faceer," his voice was as resonant as a sonnage. Steera bristled at the old-fashioned use of the term "specimen." Klut sensed it immediately. "I mean to say that you have become a very healthy young Veertal female."

"Thank you," Steera replied. "But it is I who should be congratulating you on your elevation to Klut-Prime."

"You came all the way here to congratulate me, how thoughtful. It was, of course, a tragic way to assume the title."

"Yes, tragic," Steera replied emotionlessly, "the loss of so many great Stoma leaders."

"And of a great Faceer scientist." Klut made an awkward attempt at diplomacy.

"Were they on government business?" she asked innocently.

There was an awkward silence as Klut picked up an ornate shell and examined it intently. Finally, he responded. "As a matter of fact, they were. They were accompanying Dr. Lateer on an inspection tour of our newest research station in the North Polar Region. I suppose that the air transport had mechanical difficulty in the cold atmosphere. It's a tragedy." There was another uneasy silence between them. "Well, the Gods only know." The tone of his voice indicated that Klut wanted no further discussion of the matter. Steera politely complied and changed the subject.

"What a coincidence. The North Polar Region is the subject of my visit with you now."

"Then you didn't come just to congratulate your old mentor," Klut said, feigning hurt feelings.

"Of course I did, but I also needed to ask you a favor."

"There's been no end of that today; it would seem that they could give me a week or two to get my feet on the land, so to speak." His tone brightened a bit. "But, that aside, what can I do for my favorite Veertal?"

"Faceer," Steera corrected him, "we prefer to be called Faceer."

"Of course, I fear that it has been so long since I have been in the company of real Faceer that I've regressed. What can I do for you?"

"Have you resigned your position as Minister of Research and Technology?"

The question took Klut somewhat by surprise. "No, do you presume that I should?"

"I only thought that your new duties with the High Council would perhaps demand it." Steera regretted her impetuous nature.

"For your information, I intend to maintain the Research Ministry. It's vitally important to our development as a planet. I should have known it had to do with that young rogue." There was a sour tone in Klut's voice.

"What do you mean?" Steera asked, innocently.

"Nubin Pire, he's involved in some sort of research project funded by the Institute, I believe."

"Yes, a polar expedition. That's the favor I was talking about."

Klut feigned indifference. "We've already funded his project, what else does he want?"

"It's what he doesn't want that concerns me. He doesn't want me to go with him."

"He's madder than I thought," Klut's smile made Steera uncomfortable, "or he's spending far too much time in his laboratory."

Steera pushed on. "This is serious, 'Nye-Nye.' I need to be on this expedition if I'm ever going to be anything more than an ordinary lounge singer." Steera had taken a bold step by using the pet name she had given him as a youth. Klut reacted as she had hoped, and smiled warmly at her.

"I've heard you sing, little one. You are already more than just an ordinary lounge singer." Klut-takit sat staring at his former favorite. His mind was churning. Finally he smiled a strange smile and spoke "Well, I can't sit idly by and see my little Steera bullied by some half-baked young scientist. You shall have your place on the expedition or there will be no expedition. But, I will need a little something from you in return." Klut's words were slow and deliberate and his tone persuasive. "I will need for you to keep me informed as to what's going on up there. You know, more of a personal thing just between you and your old Nye-Nye. Oh, I could get reports from any of the other staff, but they are so dry and formal. I need to hear it from you, little one, so that you can tell me, in your own words, what is really going on. Do this for me, and I will see to it that your expedition is given top priority. So, now what do you think of your old Nye-Nye?"

Steera leaped to her feet and threw her arms around his thick neck. She caught herself and quickly broke the embrace. "I hope that wasn't inappropriate behavior toward a member of the High Council."

"What could be inappropriate between two old friends?" Klut laughed a fatherly laugh. "Go, and make your arrangements." Steera had turned to leave when Klut stopped her, "Oh, and Steera. Come back before you set out on your expedition. I will have a little gift for you ... RAS!" Klut bellowed for his retainer. Ras quickly appeared. "See my precious pet to the front gate." The form of the word "pet" caused Steera to lower her eyes to the Faceer retainer. Klut gave her an affectionate kiss on the forehead, then quietly slipped back into the pool and disappeared.

CHAPTER 5

"Put the sheeting and the supports for the greenhouse in the same case. We'll put the shelter supports in a separate one. How many cases are there?"

"Seven so far," Diell shouted back.

"Seven! Why so many? How many are you packing for anyway?"

"For three," Diell replied, "just as instructed."

"Yes, instructed by Steera!" Pire grumbled. "Do you still believe that she's going with us?"

"I would never underestimate the power of a female of Steera's caliber."

Pire turned on the table radio in disgust. The broadcasts that day had been speaking of nothing but the tragic crash of the air transport and the deaths of the old Klut and the other heads of the Osstarian Security Bureau. While the broadcasts gave only brief mention to Dr. Lateer, the subject of his death was the main topic in Faceer society. Faceer loved a mystery. What was the purpose of the trip to the Northern regions? Why were the Security heads involved? And the old Klut himself, second in seniority on the High Council, why did he risk such a trip? There was only one transport landing strip in the entire North Polar Region, and it was notoriously treacherous. It made no sense. Pire stacked the last of the cases in the hallway and saw to his personal pack. He hoped that they would be able to learn more about the purpose of Lateer's trip when they arrived at the North Polar Station ... if they arrived.

Steera straightened her tunic and stretched to ring the great bell at the front gate of the Klut estate. This time the ring was answered promptly and the Faceer retainer proved the model of politeness.

"It's very nice to see you again so soon," he cooed. "I trust you are here to see his Excellency."

"Yes, as he asked me to do. You are Ras, then," she asked, trying to put him at ease.

"Yes," he replied awkwardly, "I hope I haven't offended you in any way."

"Not at all." Steera studied the demeanor of this Faceer. No doubt he was a most trusted and highly regarded retainer.

Ras escorted Steera to the main shelter where she found Klut deep in discussion with a group of Stoma security officers. Two of the younger Stoma looked up in surprise as they noticed Steera. Klut seemed momentarily startled but recovered quickly.

"Ah, my little Steera, you've come for your gift."

"Yes, Excellency." Steera took pains to show the proper respect in front of the unknown Stoma.

"If you will excuse me for a moment, I must attend to something." Klut led Steera out of the large hall and into a small side room. There, on an ornate table carved from solid Darma-shell, sat a pair of boots. They were hand-crafted from pure sto-metal, a silvery, metallic fabric that was flexible yet as strong as taanar hide.

"I hope these will serve you well on your trip, little one. I've ordered the air station to give your transport priority status. I assume that will help you smooth things over with your impetuous young friend."

"Thank you so much Nye-Nye," she replied. "I'm overwhelmed by your thoughtfulness."

"Think nothing of it. As Minister of Research I'm simply doing my duty in supporting useful investigation." Klut lifted the boots off the table and shook them a few times in the air. "As light as a scal feather," he bragged. "These will keep those furry little feet warm in the coldest of climates." Klut knelt down in front of Steera and placed them on her feet. It seemed to take him an inordinate amount of time to fit them. "Now I want you to wear these at all times. As you wear them, they will better conform to your feet. They'll be more comfortable that way."

Steera was embarrassed at the sight of a member of the High Council groveling at her feet. "Thank you again."

"So," Klut said, straightening up at last, "be off with you now. I've important Council work to attend to." He turned to leave and then turned back to Steera. "Oh, and by the way, my dear. It's about that little report. I'd appreciate it if you would give it to the captain of the security guards after you've been there a few days. His voice grew stern, "give it to no one else." It softened again. "Tell him it's a letter to your Nye-Nye, he'll know who that is." Klut exited, leaving Steera to the care of Ras who had reappeared as quickly as he had left.

"Nice boots!" he said admiringly.

"Yes," Steera said, gazing down at them. "They are, aren't they?"

To Pire's amazement, two official vehicles were waiting at the front gate of the air station to escort him and Diell to the waiting transport. Before they could raise a finger, several strong young Faceer began hauling the cases of equipment to the cargo hold of the airship. As the workers finished loading the three-engine transport, a large government vehicle screeched to a stop in front of the ladder leading to the cockpit. Pire watched as a shapely pair of legs emerged from the rear seat sporting shiny silver boots. Pire recognized the legs.

"I take it that we're looking at an official expedition member," he said as Steera exited the vehicle.

"How did you ever guess?" she replied, a tone of triumph in her voice.

"One doesn't buy a pair of boots like that for a stroll in the foothills."

"I didn't buy them, they were a gift."

"Pretty impressive. I assume they're from the same individual that provided the government escort?"

"...and the transport...and the loaders." Steera had made her point.

"In truth, we do welcome the help. Diell may be a decent scientist but he's a bust when it comes to packing."

"Well then, let's just say that I'm along to provide a little technical support and leave it at that." Steera moved a little closer to Pire and his resolve quickly dissipated. She put her arm on Pire's shoulder and whispered into the fur around his ear-hole, "Forgiven?" The combination of Steera's soft breath and the low vibration of her voice caused electricity to shoot down Pire's spinal ridge. Steera felt the sudden surge of current. "Oh my! I suppose that was a yes!"

"I'm glad you're going to be with me. Forgive me for being so hardheaded."

The reunion was interrupted by the high-pitched whine of the transport's engines as they started to come to life. Pire helped Steera into the cramped, passenger area of the craft. Faceer were better flyers than Stoma, but only slightly.

"It's a good thing we Faceer like snug places," he laughed, trying to break the tension. Diell finally made an appearance as the sound of the engines reached its peak. The cumbersome transport lumbered down the runway and floated skyward.

The atmosphere of Osstar thinned so dramatically at higher altitudes that aircraft had to be designed with air-tight cabins and wingspans long enough to provide sufficient lift in the unpredictable pockets of low pressure. Combustion gases were also stored on board to supplement the available oxygen when the craft reached altitude. This left precious little room for anything else.

Pire settled into a space just in front of two cargo cases and pulled out the insulated flask of chee that he had stuffed into his parka. The steam from the thick liquid hovered in the cool, thin air. He poured a small amount into the attached cup and offered it to Steera.

"How about a little warmth before the real cold sets in?"

"No thanks," Steera answered. "I'm going to try and get used to it now, before I have to step off the transport into that polar wind."

"Suit yourself, but I can tell you from experience that you never get used to the polar wind." Steera shifted uncomfortably in her seat.

"I'll have some," Diell chimed in.

"You'll always have some of whatever it is," Pire kidded. He squirmed back against the airship's bulkhead, trying to get as comfortable as the cramped space would allow. Sipping on his hot chee, he spoke to Steera. "Do you expect that there will be someone waiting for us at the polar station?" "Somehow I think so," Steera answered. "Klut has certainly taken an interest in this expedition."

"Klut, himself!" Now I know how you managed to pull all of this off, and it explains the boots. But why is the big Klut so interested? Is it his natural loyalty to a Klut family pet?"

Pire's sarcasm was irritating. "You Somacee can't stand our relationship with the Stoma, can you?"

"I just find it a bit naive."

"It's practical, that's all. The Stoma have always been very supportive of our group, and we see no need to jeopardize that support."

"Regardless of the cost?"

"What cost?" The Stoma have never asked a thing of us."

"Just unquestioned obedience," Pire shot back. "When the Somacee agitated for better equipped schools and more qualified teachers, where were the Veertal? Protecting your cozy little relationship with the Stoma, that's where. The Stoma support you because you don't cause them any trouble. Try and upset their power monopoly and see how supportive they are."

"You're sounding like your friend, Datar. I didn't come on this expedition to discuss politics, Pire; let's change the subject."

"Steera, I need to know what interest Klut has in this expedition and why he went to the lengths he did to get you on it."

"He's the Minister of Research. He put me here because I asked him."

"It just seems odd, the expedited transport, the loaders, and the priority runway, that's a lot of trouble for a Stoma to go to for a Faceer friend. It's even stranger when you consider the events of the last few days. Do you think that the old Klut and the security chiefs were taking a polar holiday? It seems very convenient for Klut-takit, removing all of his major competitors at one time."

Steera twisted away from Pire and ended the conversation. She sat with her hands clasping her knees, staring at an exposed rivet on the bulkhead. She was feigning indifference, but her mind was racing. Pire had raised some very good questions. Maybe she was naive. Maybe Klut was using her. Pire was having thoughts of his own and they were not pleasant. How close were Klut and Steera?

The airship reached altitude, bouncing and swaying with each passing cloud. The dull drone of the engines had a hypnotic effect on the passengers in the cramped cabin. Steera felt herself slipping into sleep-stasis. The last thing she remembered was putting her head on her knees and looking down at her shiny new boots.

CHAPTER 6

A strong bump heralded the transport's arrival at the North Polar Station. Pire used the cargo cases to pull himself up and look out the small round window at the top of the passenger area. It was almost completely frosted over. Outside, he could see dark figures scurrying about, moving against a stark white background of snow. Uniformed Stoma security officers toting long-barreled gas rifles were everywhere.

"Look at this," Pire said to Steera over his shoulder. "I've never seen this much security in one area." Steera pushed against a cargo case and partially climbed Pire's back to see.

"Neither have I. I wonder what's up." Before she could finish her thought, the long metal walkway lowered at the side of the craft and a rather handsome male Faceer stuck his head inside the cabin. The clump of yellow/gold hair sticking out from around the hood of his parka and the matching hue of his eyes gave away his blood group and clan immediately. This was a Veertal, a Triall Mountain Veertal.

"Many greetings." He grinned as he used the formal Faceer salutation. "Welcome to the coldest place in the universe." Steera couldn't believe her eyes. She felt a lump the size of a priot fruit form in her throat. She composed herself.

"Hello, Seelar," Steera answered.

Pire stared at her. "You two know each other."

"Very well," the greeter answered with a wry tone. Steera remained silent. Pire's body tensed inside the cramped cargo bay. Seelar sensed his anxiety.

"Please, come with me to the reception area." His voice was soft but compelling none the less.

"But my equipment!" Pire protested.

"Your equipment is already being unloaded and will be properly stored. I suggest a warm cup of chee in the reception area and then we will be able to talk." The Young Faceer reached out his hand to Steera and led her down the metal steps. "Forgive the confusion; we have had quite a bit of new activity up here in the last few days." His tone was too familiar for Pire's taste. In the distance, Pire could see a line of heavy vehicles heading toward a building that was being constructed into the side of a large snow bank. The polar wind whipped under his Kaba-fur hat and small crystals of ice, like bits of blowing glass, stung his face. The three reached the shelter of the reception area and shook the snow from their clothes.

"So, your flight was uneventful?" Seelar spoke exclusively to Steera.

"I suppose so," she answered, "I remained in stasis most of the way."

"Where are you putting my equipment?" Pire was irritated. "The plants I brought must be protected from this cold!"

"I assure you that your equipment is receiving the best of care," Seelar replied. He turned his attention back to Steera. "So, how have you been? The last I heard was that you were performing as a sonnage singer in the North. Are you still living with Klut?" Steera bristled at the tone of condescension in Seelar's voice.

"I'm living on my own and doing quite well, thank you."

Seelar glanced at Pire. "On your own is it?" Pire could feel the hair around his ear holes start to stiffen, a sign of intense displeasure. Seelar changed the subject. "I work for Druk-Klat-tasis, the new security chief of this facility and of the new government research facility that is being constructed here at the pole."

"As a Veertal familiar?" Pire sneered. Steera was surprised at Pire's tone.

"I won't be antagonized, Nubin Pire," Seelar snapped.

"How do you know my name?"

Seelar pushed the question aside. "I don't have time for this." Seelar turned and quickly made his way out of the reception area before Pire could fire any more questions at him.

"Well done." Steera broke the silence. "Why didn't you just invite him outside for a contest with blinding sticks?"

"I don't like him."

"Really, I thought you two hit it off quite nicely."

"What's your connection with him?"

"Family friends; we went to basic school together." Steera answered in as matter-of-fact a tone as she could muster.

Pire didn't believe her, but he let it drop. He went to the window and watched the lines of construction vehicles snaking their way up the side of the huge snow dune. Their tracks were covered by the blowing snow almost as they ascended the dune. "Hand me the distance glasses. I think that they are in my pack." He raised the long glasses to his eyes and flipped down the light filter to combat the glare coming off the snow. The new building was going up in a hurry, but it didn't resemble any type of scientific structure he had seen. "It's too small to be a major research facility, and the construction is too flimsy to last in these conditions. It looks like a temporary structure to me."

Two hours passed. No one at the facility had made any attempt to instruct Pire and Steera. They were still waiting in the reception area.

"I'm going to try and find someone. It's seems that we have been forgotten in this sea of activity." Pire started toward the door just as a squad of Stoma security guards were entering. In their midst was a stocky Stoma in a huge Kaba-fur parka. The Stoma officer stood for a moment staring at Steera and then spoke, "Welcome to the Osstarian Northern Polar Research Center, my young Faceer friends. I trust you have been treated with deference by my staff."

Druk-Klat-tasis was a second level male of the House of Druk. The Klat sub-name indicated the female line of his family. With only twelve Stoma houses on Osstar, many Stoma had the same names and sub-names. Druk's identifier or "image" name, "tasis", came at the end of his sub-name. It was employed to lessen confusion. In normal conversation the female line surname was dropped.

"We have been treated kindly, sir," Pire responded.

"And you, my dear," Druk-tasis turned to Steera. "I trust you are adjusting to our lovely climate."

"I am familiarizing myself, Your Presence, but this is certainly not my idea of a lovely climate." Druk-tasis smiled at Steera, acknowledging her address (that of a retainer to a superior) as a sign of courtesy and respect. "Come then, I would have a word with you. Let us go some place we can get rid of this heavy attire." He turned to the seven security officers who were still hovering nearby and dismissed them. "We'll be meeting in the inner chamber. I don't believe you'll be needed any longer." The officers looked at each other uneasily for a moment and then melted away, one-by-one. Druk-tasis led Pire and Steera into a small antechamber and closed the door. Steera and Pire sat down in a pair of Faceer-sized swing-back chairs while Druk-tasis leaned against the small dining table. "So," he said to Steera, "you are a lounge singer." Steera started to protest, but simply nodded. "And you are Nubin Pire from the Trague Center?" Pire did likewise. An uneasy silence ensued. "So, what brings you here?"

Pire was the first to speak, "I would think that you would know that already."

Druk-tasis smiled. "Ah, Faceer, analytical and straight-forward, I like that. I can be straight-forward as well." He put one of his stubby fingers to his lips, indicating that they should not speak. Moving around the room, he came to a small light fixture protruding from a corner of the wall. Reaching behind it, he extracted a crude circular microphone. With a flick of his finger he severed the thin wire affixed to the coil.

"There," he said, his voice showing signs of relief, "now we can talk." Pire and Steera stood in stunned silence, not knowing what to say. "I can assure you that you've nothing to fear from me." The two remained silent. "I wish that I had more time to explain, but time is a precious commodity these days. We can't stay here too long; we will raise suspicions. I will only say that this is no research station and you're not here to do an experiment." Druk-tasis peered out the small pinhole in the door to make sure the security officers were gone. "You will dine with me tonight in my private chambers, where we can talk. Until then I would suggest that you say very little to anyone here." A loud knock interrupted the conversation.

"Sir, are you all right?"

"It didn't take long for them to discover the broken microphone. That means that they were listening. You see, even the head of security is not exempt." Druk moved to the door. "Yes, I'm fine. I was just leaving." He turned back to the two confused Faceer. "Tonight we will talk of many things. My private chamber is the one place they aren't monitoring—at least not yet."

Druk opened the door and disappeared. Steera rose from her chair and walked over to Pire. They embraced.

"I'm sorry for not listening to you. I didn't realize we were going into such a situation."

"Nor did I," Pire said. "This is unexpected. "Well, we have no where else to go tonight—unless of course you have made dinner reservations at the North Polar Restaurant."

Steera smiled and kissed Pire. "I'm glad I am with you, whatever may happen."

A Stoma guard entered and escorted them through the lobby and out into a hallway that connected several small sleeping rooms.

"You should be comfortable here," his voice was devoid of emotion.

"Both of us?" Pire asked.

"You have adjoining rooms as befitting your partnership status." The guard wheeled and left. Pire and Steera retired to their rooms to await the next surprise.

At approximately three hours past Rebal-wane four security guards showed up at the door to Pire's chamber and, collecting Steera as well, led them through the main lobby to the far end of the second corridor and into the waiting area of a comfortably appointed room. Druk-tasis emerged from the doorway to his chamber and bade them enter. Once inside, he seated them at a plain Stoma eating table, adjusting the height of their chairs to accommodate Faceer. He studied them for a moment, wondering how to start the conversation.

"Straight-forward," he finally said aloud, "a favored Faceer trait. I felt I could trust you two the moment I laid eyes on you. So, I will get right to the tale." Druk-tasis rose and walked toward a large side window. Gazing out across the vast expanse of featureless snow, he began. "Five months ago, a small drical mining unit got a strange reading on its detector while exploring a snow dune. Approximately two hundred yards into the side of the dune, they uncovered something. It wasn't a drical vein. It was a metallic cylinder about the size of a drum of aircraft fuel. At first that's what we thought it was. The metal was shiny and bright as if it had only been buried for a short time, but it was encased inside ancient ice. The cylinder also had strange markings etched around the outside."

"What sort of markings?" Pire asked, his Faceer curiosity fired.

"Like nothing I've ever seen. They were arranged in rows and many of them were repeated again and again."

"Like writing," Steera said.

"Exactly, but not in a form any of us had ever seen. We decided to call in an expert on primeval languages so we arranged to have Tyyard Soung brought up here from the Luut institute in the Lower Midlands."

"Tyyard Soung!" Steera interjected. "I studied languages under him at the Academy."

"Let him finish."

"Yes, our time is limited." Druk returned to the table and poured warm chee in three cups. "Soung didn't discover anything. He never made it here. It seems that one of the miner's family members was a Stoma security officer. Secret photographs of the cylinder were taken to a facility in Prass. Shortly afterward, the executive committee of the High Council met and selected Dr. Lateer to take Soung's place. Klut-prime was chosen to lead the expedition. You, of course, are aware of their fate."

"But I don't understand," Steera said. "Why should there be such interest in an archeological discovery?"

"Because it poses some threat to the power of the Stoma," Pire said. Steera shot him a dagger-like look. He wished that he had been more tactful. "Forgive me, Your Presence. I jump to conclusions."

"No offense taken, young Faceer," Druk-tasis said calmly. "You are correct." The three were silent for a long moment, an unspoken question hanging in the air. Druk responded, "I'm taking the risk of telling you this, because I need you to know what it is we are dealing with. I'm not sure the average Faceer knows much of planetary politics, but all is not the harmony and unity of purpose in the High Council that is suggested by the daily broadcasts. There have been heated debates going on for some time as to the future of Osstar and of our two species. There is a faction within Stoma leadership that believes we are in danger of becoming subservient to the Faceer, particularly in light of our growing reliance on your technology. Many of the older Stoma Houses see this as a threat to their security — and they have a point. There is another faction that sees a stronger role for Faceer in our economy as inevitable and mutually beneficial if an understanding is maintained between the two species."

"You are a representative of the latter view," Steera said. "I sensed something about you from the beginning."

"A charming Faceer talent," Druk-tasis replied. "Yes, I believe that the future of Osstar is bigger than any one species or even any one philosophy of life. If Osstar is to progress, we must evolve beyond clannishness and cultural prejudices. But a new threat to that evolution may have been unleashed by whatever it is that we have found in that little hole in the snow." Druk-tasis hesitated for a moment. "Have either of you heard of the Stomari?"

Steera and Pire looked at each other. Pire spoke, "There is talk among some Faceer of an organization of Stoma dedicated to keeping Osstar a Stoma-ruled planet."

"That is the Stomari, but it goes beyond simply keeping Osstar under the control of the Stoma. Its aim is to make sure that any threat to Stoma rule is not just controlled ... but eliminated." He let the impact of that last word sink in. "The security officers you see around you all carry a small red circle with a black center just behind their left ear holes. They are all Stomari."

"All of them!"

"As far as I can tell," Druk-tasis answered. "They arrived on a separate air transport the same day that the one carrying Klut-Prime and Lateer went down."

"So you don't think the crash was an accident?" Pire asked cautiously.

"The leader of the peace faction within the High Council, the leader that opposed the Stomari, was the old Klut. You two are not here by chance. The first act of the new Klut-Prime was to see to it that the institute authorized your trip. He wanted you here."

"Then he had set it up before I even met with him ..." Steera caught herself.

Druk-tasis stared down his prominent nose at Steera and then turned to Pire. "We cannot stay here much longer. Everyone at this station is under intense scrutiny, including myself. Meet me by the main hangar, the one just outside the compound, at one minute past Rebal-wane. As Druk was finishing, the sound of boots could be heard thumping on the stone floor outside the chamber, getting progressively louder. Druk looked Pire directly in the eye. "You'll have to trust me or we are all done for." Someone pounded at the door. Druk opened it. A large Stoma trooper stuck his head in. "Yes, sergeant, I must have forgotten the time.

"We have orders to see that all non-essentials are in quarters by Rebal-rise. They are your orders, sir."

"So they are. Then see to it that they are taken there immediately." Pire and Steera were surrounded by security. "And sergeant," Druk-tasis' tone turned serious, "see that they are treated with courtesy."

The sergeant scowled and ordered his troopers to escort the two Faceer to their quarters. Pire looked back over his shoulder at Druk-tasis as they were leaving and noticed a worried expression on his face. Steera noticed something else. Druk-tasis walked with a distinct limp.

CHAPTER 7

Pire and Steera's were escorted back to their rooms. The troopers left them, except for the officer who lingered a moment, eyeing them curiously.

"I trust you will be comfortable here," he said frostily, "and I believe you can say that you've been treated with courtesy."

"Yes we have," Pire agreed. The sergeant made no move toward the door.

"I suggest that you confine your movements to this building. There's a lot of construction work going on and we wouldn't want any accidents to mar your visit with us." He cracked a wry smile and started to close the door behind him. "Be safe and well." The door closed with a loud bang.

Pire shrugged it off. "I'm going to clean up. I'm a wreck after that long flight." He put his finger to his lips and motioned toward the ceiling. Steera followed him into the bathing chamber. As soon as he was inside, he turned on the large, thick spigot and icy water thundered into the polished Darma-shell tub. "I think we'd better do our talking in here. We have to assume that there are listening devices everywhere." Steera nodded and sat on a small stool as close to the spigot as possible without getting wet.

"Are you going to meet with him tonight?" she whispered.

"Do you think I should?" Pire was very interested in Steera's answer.

"I don't know what to think. Everything I believed to be true is suddenly in question. If the Stomari arranged the murder of old Klut-Prime ..."

Pire finished the sentence in his head and broke the silence. "I suppose there are no options. I will have to meet with Druk-tasis tonight and at least see what this cylinder thing is all about. I hope I can trust him."

"I believe that you can," Steera said. "I sense a good spirit in him."

"I thought it was the Somacee who had the more heightened senses." Pire smiled at her and reached out to stroke her hair. "I too liked him from the beginning. There's a quality about him, almost Faceer-like. But, in any case, I've got to risk it. I don't know about my senses, but my logic tells me that we're safe here as long as we serve some purpose to the Stomari. What that purpose is I don't know."

A loud knocking interrupted the conversation.

"I'll get it," Pire whispered.

"Be careful."

Pire turned off the now-warm water and quickly made it to the front door, which was still under an assault by whoever was entreating entrance. He turned the latch and a parka-clad figure lurched through the portal and flopped onto the floor. Pire jumped back in astonishment. A familiar face slowly emerged from the furry hood.

"Diell! Where in the name of the polar winds have you been? I trust that you got all of our gear off the transport and into the tracked vehicles for the trip north?"

Diell struggled to adjust the parka so that he could speak. He righted himself and sat up in the middle of the floor, assessing his surroundings. "As a matter of fact, I didn't."

"You didn't? Why not?"

"Ask your security officer friends," Diell replied. "I tried to unload the cargo hold but before I could do anything six of the big oafs took everything out of the transport and whisked it off to the main storage building. When I protested, they said to take it up with the facility head. What's going on, anyway?"

"We're not sure. By the way, what happened to our personal packs?"

"I have them with me. It's the one thing I managed to wrestle away from them before they took everything to the storage facility."

"You did well, young Faceer." Pire's voice turned to a deep

mock seriousness. "Guard them with your life. Keep them with you at all times."

"Why, what's so important?"

"Because, we may have to leave on short notice."

"Short notice?"

"Yes, there's a rumor that a blizzard is heading this way." Diell looked puzzled. In the corner of his eye, Pire saw Steera muffling a laugh. "Now take all these things to your room and wait for us." Pire helped Diell to his feet and pushed him out of the door.

Diell yelled back at him as he stumbled down the hall. "But this is the North Pole, there are always blizzards here."

"Go," Pire laughed, "...and keep those packs with you."

Pire cocked his head and listened as the mechanical clack of his timepiece counted down the seconds. The multiple dials on its face calculated the complicated rotation of the three prominent orbs of his universe. It was almost one minute past Rebal-wane and he had yet to figure out a way to slip past the security officers and keep his appointment with Druk-tasis.

"Perhaps I could just nonchalantly stroll out the front door?" he said to an anxious Steera.

"You heard the security captain," Steera frowned, "we're confined to this building."

"Well I've got to do something!"

"What if I suddenly became ill?" Steera asked.

"These are well-trained security officers; they would never go for it. Besides, that handsome retainer might come to your aid." Pire looked for any reaction on Steera's face, there was none. "I can't believe that Druk-tasis would give me an impossible task. I think that I'm just going to go down the corridor and see if there's a way out of here."

Before Steera could protest, Pire had pulled on his parka and heavy gloves and started down the long corridor toward the side entrance that faced the large aircraft hangar. His timepiece now read three minutes past Rebal-wane and his search for a safe exit took on an air of urgency. He reached the silver metal door to the exit and noticed something strange; there were no security officers to be seen. He looked back over his shoulder in both directions and saw the same thing—no one. The doorknob was freezing cold. He pushed the door open about a quarter of the way and cringed, waiting for a loud alarm to go. No sound came, only the frozen silence of the polar twinight. "He's either arranged this quite well, or this is a trap," Pire thought.

Pire slid out of the door and hugged the side of the metallic/stone building, moving ever-so-slowly northward toward the large hangar. The polar wind sliced through his parka as if it were made of paper. As he reached the end of the building, he looked both ways and made a mad dash across the open space. He reached the small entrance door beside the larger hangar door. His foot caught an invisible clump of ice and he soared skyward, landing in a heap of powdery snow. Jumping up he lunged forward, fearing his spectacular fall had caught the attention of every security officer in the compound. To his surprise the door swung open with only slight pressure. Standing just inside was a figure wrapped in a Kaba-fur parka.

"Quite an impressive entry," Druk-tasis said with mock approval. "Were you being pursued by a cather-cat?"

"Amusing," Pire said, brushing the ice and snow from his parka, "I suppose you would have preferred that I stroll through the center of the compound?"

"It would have made no difference," Druk-tasis replied, "all security officers are in a special training meeting in the main administration building. Rank does have its privileges you know. We must be brief," Druk-tasis continued. "As I told you earlier, you aren't on this expedition by chance. The Stomari picked you to help them do something that they haven't been able to do themselves. They need you to open the cylinder."

"Open it! You mean that it's hollow?"

"Definitely."

"But why me, there must be a dozen scientists more qualified to deal with this sort of thing."

"Lateer had told them of your earlier research in regard to the nature of light. On first inspection, the cylinder's top made a slight movement when an electric torch passed near it. It is believed that the triggering mechanism works on a light principle. They wanted this done as quietly as possible in order to avoid engendering any suspicion from 'unfriendly' elements. A separate expedition would have raised questions. So, since you were already scheduled to come here, you were the obvious choice. Steera, however, is another story. It's unclear why she was included. Perhaps it was her relationship to her old mentor."

"You know about Steera and Klut-takit?"

"Yes I do, and I found it interesting that she didn't reveal that to me when we talked, earlier."

Pire felt a dull ache in the pit of his stomach. "You don't believe that she's in on this, do you?"

Druk-tasis shifted his gaze. "I'm not sure. She is Veertal, and has family ties with the new Klut-Prime."

"She knows your assistant, Seelar as well," Pire said, almost apologetically.

A cold expression crossed Druk-tasis' face. "I don't want to jump to any conclusions, but she is a typical Veertal, naive, trusting and therefore susceptible to being manipulated. My advice is to keep an eye on her."

"So what is it that I am to do?"

"You're going to open the cylinder; I believe that you can do it. But not tomorrow as the Council planned. You're going to open it tonight, in one hour as a matter of fact. The Stomari fear that it may be a relic of an ancient civilization that flourished millions of years before the Stoma left the warm waters of the early oceans, a civilization perhaps even more advanced than our current one."

"What does it matter if it's an earlier civilization? It would seem a perfect opportunity for them to study and learn from it."

Druk-tasis cocked his head and starred at Pire. "Ahh, the Faceer dedication to logic. You make excellent scientists, but not very good politicians, but you're making a most unscientific assumption. You're assuming the civilization was Stoma. What if it weren't?

What if the rulers of Osstar found that there was an older, more advanced civilization that was not Stoma but Faceer? Every Faceer has heard the legends of "the old ones," an ancient Faceer civilization that had flourished in the high mountains of the North. What if it were true, and what if they were far older than anyone thought?" Pire began to realize the stakes of the game in which they were involved. "That's why we must see the contents of that cylinder first. The Stomari have come out from behind their veil of anonymity and are making their move for control of Osstar. This is bad news for Stoma like me, and even worse for Faceer. Now, return to your quarters and say nothing about this. There is a security check every forty-five minutes. You must be in your room for it. Then, in exactly one hour, and I emphasize the word exactly, you will go to the hygiene room at the north end of the building. You will see that one of the windows has been left unlocked. Exit through the window and make your way to the rear of this hangar as best as you can. There will be officers on duty. I couldn't fix that; it would have appeared too suspicious. When you get to the rear of the hangar there will be a snow vehicle waiting. Get in, and you will be brought to the cylinder. Say nothing to the driver."

"What do you want me to bring?"

"Bring that famous Faceer curiosity — now go!"

"But how will I get into the building?"

Druk-tasis hurried toward the front entrance of the hanger, calling back to Pire over his shoulder. "You're Faceer, figure it out." He paused. "And Pire, don't say anything to Dye-Klut Steera." The message was clear.

CHAPTER 8

The door from which he had exited was still ajar. Pire pushed his way back inside the long corridor that led to his quarters. It was empty, but he took no chances, moving the distance to his room as quickly as possible. No sooner had he turned the opener than he heard the heavy footsteps of a security contingent heading in his direction. He fell into his room and hurriedly shut the door behind him. Steera was sitting on his cot. Pire noticed that a chair had been pulled up to the small, round window that looked out on the compound. Steera had obviously been watching for his return.

"Well, what's the plan?"

Pire felt a twinge of uncertainty, but he was bursting with apprehension. "The cylinder is hollow," he blurted out. "They want me to open it."

"Why you? Your area of expertise is climatology."

"Apparently someone has discovered my early work on the nature of light and electricity. I was working on an experiment to show that light could be shown to have both wave and particle properties. The Stoma believe that the covering on the cylinder is operated on some sort of light wave principle."

"So when are you going to open it for them?" Steera asked.

Pire hesitated, "Oh, tomorrow ... sometime ... I'm not quite sure when."

"And after you've opened it, what then?" Steera's questioning was methodical and logical. It was forcing Pire to a decision.

"Steera, do you trust me? Because I trust you." Pire bit the inside of his cheek at his awkward statement.

"Of course I do. What a silly thing to ask."

"There's something I have to do." He stopped again.

Steera sensed Pire's uneasiness. "If there is something you need to do then go and do it," she said.

Pire picked up his coat and moved toward the door. Steera followed. As he opened it to leave she grabbed his arm.

"We are Faceer, and as long as Faceer have time to think, there is hope."

Pire started to speak but didn't. He edged out into the hallway and watched as Steera closed the door behind him. "If this was the voice of a collaborator, he thought, there truly is no hope for Os-star."

Pire wadded his bulky parka into a ball to make it appear to be an exercise suit and carried it under his arm as he made his way down the hall to the hygiene room; this rendezvous with Druk-tasis would not be as easy as the last. The security count had come precisely as Druk-tasis said it would, which gave Pire a degree of confidence. The passage to the hygiene room was made without incident, and he found the door open and the room empty. Entering, he made straight for the window. It was open. Pushing his parka in front of him, he slid out head-first, landing in a pile of snow.

The frigid air burned into his flesh. He could feel the automatic retraction of his spinal ridge as the bitter cold enveloped him. He quickly latched his parka and began making his way toward the large hangar on the western side of the compound. A low-pitched, rumbling sound announced the arrival of a tracked snow vehicle. With it came another, more disturbing one — the sound of a Stoma voice.

"What's this vehicle doing here?" Pire couldn't hear the driver's response. He was crouching in the snow not twenty feet from the dark form of the security officer, trying not to breathe too heavily. He watched as the officer walked around the vehicle to the driver's side and stood looking at a handful of documents the driver had thrust out the open window. The officer studied them, handed the papers back and instructed the driver to move on.

Pire was in a quandary. Should he run toward the moving vehicle and risk being seen? He heard a familiar voice in his head. "Things are hidden best when hidden least." He decided on a bold move. He stood up and began walking purposefully toward it just as the security officer wheeled and headed in his direction.

"Oh storms of Rebal!" he thought. What do I do now?" As if in a dream, he continued toward the slowly moving vehicle. The security officer marched right past, giving him only a cursory glance. His heart rate began to slow but the pace of the snow vehicle did not. Practically sprinting, he grabbed the frigid handle of the vehicle's door and threw himself into the front seat. Pulling back the hood of his parka, he started to speak. The words froze in his throat at the sight of his chauffeur. In the driver's seat of the snow vehicle sat a fully-uniformed Stoma security officer. The driver sat stone silent as the vehicle continued its steady pace toward the building in the distance. As Druk-tasis had instructed, he made no attempt at conversation.

The makeshift building that protected the Stoma's great discovery drew nearer, and still the officer said nothing. The vehicle was moving forward, but seemed to be getting no closer to the entrance. As they cut around the last large snowdrift, Pire realized that the driver had no intention of stopping, or even slowing down. Without thinking, he pushed open the vehicle's side door and jumped. Landing squarely on the seat of his insulated pants, he watched as the snow vehicle disappeared into the snowy polar twinight.

The frozen surface was so cold that it quickly returned Pire's attention to the task at hand. He had to get into the building. He now realized that the security officer had dropped him behind a drift that shielded him from the main entrance. He rose slowly and saw what he had hoped he wouldn't: three security guards standing at attention in the entranceway. Going in the front door was no longer an option. A quick survey of possible alternative routes pointed to the circular wall closest to him. A section of the wall curved away from the front entrance and from the guards. Crouching low, he covered the short distance between the drift and the wall. He pressed against it tightly as he caught his breath. The chill of the meta-stone alloy soaked through his gloves and his fingers started to go numb. This was cause for concern. Faceer reacted to extreme cold by shutting down external systems and shifting heat to the internal systems and to the head. A small internal organ, situated on the main artery from the heart, regulated the blood's temperature before passing it to the rest of the body. This blood temperature stabilizer would stave off death until the individual could get to a warmer place. Unfortunately, it had evolved in a less severe climate. Numbness of the fingers meant that the level of internal heat was becoming insufficient. Pire was reaching the end of his metabolic tolerance to this severe cold. He had to move, and quickly.

He had progressed about halfway down the length of the wall when he noticed a small hole at its base. As he bent low to investigate, he heard the sharp report of a gas rifle. An instant later, a shell exploded on the wall above his head, showering him in shards of ice and stone. Holding his arms out in front of him, he leapt headfirst into the hole. It proved larger than he had estimated. His entire body fit easily inside. Outside, muffled voices were laughing as stray rounds thumped into the frozen wall.

As he moved farther into the tunnel he began to realize where he had landed. The soft fur lining the walls of the tunnel marked it as a polar cather-cat den. The Faceer and the cather-cat had a long and antagonistic relationship. The joke among Stoma was that the Faceer had come to live with them to escape extinction at the hands of the intellectually superior cat. The cats of the temperate areas once preyed extensively on Faceer. Polar cathers were large, subsisting on a diet of artic hircus, fish and some larger migratory birds. But he assumed that it would be easy for them to develop a taste for Faceer flesh in short order. He racked his brain to try and remember his classes on cather-cat habits. How were their dens laid-out? Where in them could they usually be found? What were their eating and sleeping habits? He knew that they liked to dig deeply but in this perpetually frozen climate he wondered just how deep they could go.

Pire continued along the tunnel until it opened into a large chamber. It was apparent that the builders had inadvertently intersected the den when putting in the foundation. "How nice for this cat," he thought. "They've added a room at no charge." He began looking around the top of the den for any sign of a breech that would lead into the building itself. Just above a ridge of rock he saw a shaft of soft light. Upon closer inspection he made out the rounded shape of a ventilation grate that could provide an entrance.

Pire was basking in self-congratulation when he flinched at a sharp pain in his left foot. Panic gripped him. He spun around to see a small furry creature gnawing playfully at his boot. Lifting the tiny cat into the air, he nuzzled it with his nose. "Well, little fellow," he cooed. "What do you think you're up to? Going to make a meal of your first Faceer?" He heard a second squeaking sound. "Another one! Someone's been pretty busy." Then it hit him. Where there are babies, there are mothers. Suddenly the little balls of fur didn't seem so cuddly. Pire gingerly sat the little cat down and moved toward the grate. He reached up to get a handhold on the rim of rock directly below it and put his left foot squarely in the center of yet another mound of fur. This one, however, made a deep groaning noise. In front of the wall of rock, there lay a full-grown, female cather-cat, almost as large as he was, and he had just put his foot in the middle of her stomach.

Pire dug his fingers into the rock and, using all of his strength, pulled himself onto the ledge just below the ventilation grate. He fully expected to see the large predator clawing her way up the wall after him, but he heard no sound. Could she be dead? He remembered his earlier studies of Osstarian predators. Polar cather-cats alternate between periods of activity and periods of heavy sleep to conserve energy. She was, most likely, sound asleep.

He took a deep breath and, arms extended over his head, pushed against the heavy metal grate. It made a scraping noise and came free. He jumped up as far as he could and used his arms to pull himself through and into a dark room full of pipes and motors.

The light in front of him was filtering through a crack in a tall, slender metal door. Pire put his earhole against the door and listened—nothing. Finding no sort of handle or latch, he leaned against the door. It opened, slightly. Pire could see that the door led to a circular hallway. Across from it stood a slightly smaller door and, a short distance down from that, another one of identical size.

It was the Stoma way of building—circles within circles. The cylinder would most likely be in the inner-most circle. A dark shadow floated silently past the door. Pire froze. The door opened in such a manner that a guard couldn't see in unless he was traveling in the opposite direction. He gently closed it and remained absolutely silent, checking his timepiece as he waited for the return of the guard. He heard the clack of Stoma boots on the hard floor. "Five minutes to make the circuit. I'll give him two-and-a-half minutes and then I'll go for it." At the appropriate moment he launched himself across the hall and burst through the door on the opposite side. It really didn't matter now if the entire Stomari security detail was waiting for him, there were no options left.

It was, however, only ghostly silence that greeted Pire's crude entrance. His eyes adjusted to the dim light. He stood at the edge of a large room, much larger than one would have guessed possible from the exterior of the building. It had been excavated to a depth of some thirty feet. Overhead hung various types of scientific equipment: scanners, alpha ray machines for seeing inside of things and data monitoring machines. In the center of the room, on a large metal table, sat the object of the Stomari's fears—a sleek, silver cylinder.

Pire took care not to make a sound as he approached the cylinder. It was about half his height, constructed of a metal alloy that showed no signs of wear or corrosion. The delicate nature of the symbols surprised him. The detail was Faceer-like. Yet, the soft, circular curves of the symbols were like none Pire had ever seen.

"Hard to put into a category, isn't it?" The voice was that of Druk-tasis. It came from the shadows on the opposite side of the room. It hardly registered with Pire, who stood entranced by the object in front of him. His scientific curiosity had overridden his wariness.

"Definitely not Stoma," Pire said, running his hand along the cool, metal exterior. "Yet, not Faceer, either."

"My analysis as well." Druk-tasis emerged from the shadows.

"I see that you made it in one piece."

"No thanks to you. You could have provided a bit more detail."

"With this level of security, and not knowing who is friend or informer, the less said the better. But I knew that I could trust the Stoma to shoot at anything that moves, and that a Faceer would be unable to resist a hole in the ground."

"A cather-cat hole!" Pire complained.

"Well, as the old Stoma saying goes 'let sleeping cathers lie.'" Pire suppressed a smile. He had never encountered a Stoma with a Faceer sense of humor. "Let's get to it. We've got to be out of here in twenty-five minutes or you'll never make it back to the residence building."

"How should I proceed?"

"When we first examined it, a beam of light from the alpha ray machine's electric aiming device fell on one of the symbols, just here." Druk-tasis pointed to an area on the cylinder. "There was a slight movement of the cylinder top. It gave a quick jerk and then it stopped."

"It must respond to the wavelength rather than the intensity of the light. Different colored light is produced by the differences in the length of the waves. Since the light produced by the aiming device was white light, it contained all of the wavelengths mixed together. One of those wavelengths caused the lid to move, but it wasn't pure enough to open the cylinder top."

"Yes," Druk-tasis agreed, "that would explain why merely making the light brighter didn't do anything. So, what do we do?"

"Perhaps there is a simple solution," Pire said confidently. "A piece of triangular-shaped glass will separate a stream of white light into its component colors. If we could find something like that around here, we may be able to find the wavelength that triggers the mechanism.

They immediately began to scour the area. Pire thrust a hand into a box containing electrical insulating parts and drew out a thick, glass insulator. He placed it into a vice attached to the table and gave the handle a turn. With a loud crack, the insulator broke into several pieces. Pire began sifting through the debris. After a short search, he held aloft a piece of insulator residue with a triangular shape. "We'll see how sensitive this thing is," he said. "At any rate, if it doesn't work tonight, it probably won't work tomorrow either and we'll have to send back for a proper diffusion lens."

Pire positioned the alpha ray emitter so that the light from its aiming device would fall just in front of the area on the cylinder identified by Druk-tasis. He held the piece of glass level and switched on the light. The beam hit the glass insulator and bounced onto the surface of the cylinder. As he had hoped, Pire saw the familiar colors of the Osstarian rainbow wash across the side of the cylinder.

"It works!" he nearly shouted. "Now to see which wavelength tickles its nose." He slowly moved the light source and the diffracter along the light sensitive area of the cylinder: violet... blue... green... yellow. Suddenly, at the beginning of the red spectrum, he heard a faint whirring noise. As the light moved squarely into the red, the top of the cylinder shuttered and swung round as if on a hinge. Druk-tasis and Pire looked at each other in amazement.

Druk-tasis broke the silence. "You opened it, you have the first look."

Pire leaned over the top of the cylinder and peered in. The inside of the cylinder was smooth, covered in soft, crimson-colored cloth. It appeared to be layered. A metallic disc lay atop the first layer. Pire removed the disc. It did not feel cold to the touch, even though the temperature inside the building was near the freezing point of water.

Pire used the light from the aiming device to illuminate the inside. A glint caught his eye. Letting his curiosity overcome his fear, he reached inside and withdrew a shiny, metallic instrument. As he examined it, his fingers slid along the unmarked side of the smooth handle. Suddenly, a sharp shaft of blue light shot out from a small opening at the top of the instrument. A blue glow filled the room. As he ran his hand back-and-forth across the handle of the device, the light narrowed and intensified. Druk-tasis couldn't' stifle his cry. "Look at the cylinder!" The point where the light struck the side of the cylinder was beginning to glow a deep red/orange. "It's burning it!"

Pire, lost in the strange spectacle, accidentally let the fingers of his other hand pass through the beam. He recoiled in horror, expecting to see half of his hand missing, but there was no damage. He waved his hand through the light again, nothing, no heat at all. Yet the point at which the light struck the cylinder was beginning to glow white hot. Pire ran his finger down the other side of the handle and the light shut off as abruptly as it had started. He reached out and held his fingers above the spot on the cylinder that had been the focal point of the light. He felt no heat. He touched it. It was cool to the touch. "Well, so much for the primitive culture theory," he said looking at Druk-tasis.

His curiosity now fully fired, Pire lifted the next separator and found another metal disc engraved with both symbols and what appeared to be drawings. The markings were delicate and precise. They formed the image of a large sphere divided into many sections by a series of intersecting lines. Within three of the sections were smaller circles, each divided into four equal segments. "This looks like some sort of reference table," Pire said. "Perhaps we had better hang on to this."

"I agree," Druk-tasis answered. He pulled a small cloth pouch from under his parka and tossed it to Pire. Pire stuffed the disc into the pouch and turned his attention back to the cylinder. He estimated that they had been in the room for more than twenty minutes, and each passing minute brought the risk of discovery. The next several layers held different, unique objects: patches of shimmering cloth that one could squeeze into a ball only to have it spring back to its original condition without a seam or wrinkle, pieces of a glass-like substance in the form of cups and bowls, and several covered bowls containing a variety of grayish powders. Pire thought that it might be important to analyze the powders to see if they could be identified and perhaps dated, but Druk-tasis spoke before he could make the suggestion.

"Let the Stomari have that stuff. Eating utensils are something they can understand. Is there anything left?" Pire cleared away the last of the utensils and lifted the final covering. There, nestled in the soft, red cloth, lay a rectangular object with large red and gold symbols etched onto the front plate. Pire lifted it carefully from the cylinder and examined it.

"It appears to be a book. The symbols match some of those on the cylinder." He opened the front cover. On the first page, engraved in bright colors and printed on what appeared to be the same wafer-thin flexible cloth was the image of a terrifying creature, unlike anything Pire had ever seen. It was huge, with long claws and a mouth filled with menacing teeth. Fire was spewing from its nostrils. On the next few pages were more symbols, and then came another image. This one caused a bolt of electricity to shoot down Pire's spinal ridge. "You need to see this." He handed the book to Druk-tasis.

Staring at him from the page was an illustration of a small being dressed in short trousers and a tunic. Strapped to its side was a short, shiny knife, not unlike a ceremonial Faceer stabbing knife.

The being's face was smooth, his ears had two rounded lobes cupped on the outside, and there was a prominent nose. But Pire and Druk-tasis' attention was drawn to the bottom of the page. There, sticking out from inside a pair of loose fitting sandals were two completely normal feet—Faceer feet—with their long toes and tufts of fine hair covering the tops.

"This is what the Stomari fear," Druk-tasis said, "evidence that the Faceer had a civilization older and more advanced than the Stoma. You must take this with you. It is the key to your future." Druk-tasis hastily stuffed the book into the pouch with the metal plate and a few of the vials of powder. "Leave the instrument; it will give the Stomari something to chew on. These other items you must take with you and guard with your life. It is not only your future that you protect, in it may lay the key to the future of Osstar. If the Stomari see it they will never let it become known outside their circle."

"Take it with me to where? Even if they don't know of its existence, they will never let me away from here with any knowledge of the cylinder," Pire replied. "I realize now that I will never leave this place alive."

"Don't give up so easily my young friend. We have prepared for certain contingencies. What the Stomari will learn when you open the cylinder for them tomorrow will confirm nothing. The most dangerous pieces of evidence will have been removed. Now, I must ask you to do something that I know will go against your logical Faceer instincts."

"And what is that?"

Druk-tasis drew back his muscular arm, and made a fist. "You must trust me," he said, and unleashed a blow against the side of Pire's head.

CHAPTER 9

Pire's eyes were beginning to focus. Vague objects were cutting erratic orbits in the air just above his face. He reached up to swat away what he thought were seedge flies.

"Doctor, I think he's coming around." The voice seemed to float from out of the fog. Another object moved into Pire's view. This one had a blurry Stoma face attached to it.

"Just take it easy, young Faceer," the voice said, "you've had quite a jolt. Do you remember anything?" Pire started to call for Druk-tasis out of the fog in his head, but caught his words in time.

"No," he said groggily, "what happened?"

"We're not sure. We found you in a snowdrift just outside the residence building. Snow vehicle tracks were near by, so we assume that you were struck and knocked into the snow. It's a good thing that our security officer found you when he did ... few last the night in the polar cold."

"I remember going outside to look around the compound. A snow vehicle approached me, and then nothing. I had some personal belongings with me in a small pouch ... did they find anything like that with me?"

"You'll have to ask security about that. I'm just responsible for getting you in shape for something they need you to do tonight. You seem to be a pretty valuable little Faceer." Pire could hear the condescension in his voice. This was most certainly a member of the Stomari. He decided to end his probing about the pouch. "We'll let you rest for a little while longer and then you can return to your quarters. And I advise that this time you stay there until you are summoned. That Faceer curiosity will end up getting you all killed." The tone was menacing.

"This is no house of healing," he thought. "This is a Stomari interrogation center."

Pire laid his head back on the hard pillow and closed his eyes. He tried to remember the wondrous things he had seen in the cylinder. What a wealth of knowledge they could impart if they could be freely studied. But the little creature in the book would most likely make that impossible.

His thoughts drifted to the sunlit meadows of the Northern Islands. Home and family meant a lot more to him than they had only a few weeks ago. He began to wonder if he would ever see them again? He thought of Steera. He now knew that the Stomari were real, and worse than that, they were frightened. They would rather rule a dying planet than share an evolving one. His eyes closed and the calm of sleep-stasis engulfed him. His father's voice filled his head.

"Rest, little one ... tomorrow's a busy day."

Sitting on the large, rigid, plastic cot that the Stoma felt would pass for a cozy Faceer bed, Pire wondered about Steera and Diell. Soon after being pronounced well enough to walk, he had been escorted back to the residence hall by armed guards, and deposited in a new room. He had not been allowed to leave it or to have any visitors. All he could do was sit and wait, holding out the hope that Druk-tasis would protect them.

The frozen quiet of the polar twinight was interrupted by a thump against his door. Pire rose to his feet and watched as the metal door swung open under the force of a Stoma forearm.

"You're to come with us," a gruff voice barked. It was the sergeant of the guard that he had met earlier. He was in no better a mood.

"Where am I going?"

"Wherever I take you," the sergeant snarled.

"Listen here. I'm a free citizen of Osstar and I demand to know where my friends are." Two officers grabbed him by his arms, lifted him into the air and carried him down the hallway. His feet did not touch the ground until they came to the main door. There Druk-tasis met them, dressed in a heavy parka.

"Put him down," he said, gruffly. "I don't want him harmed — at least until after he has accomplished what we need for him to accomplish. Now, young Faceer," he spoke directly to Pire. "You will come with me." He loaded Pire into the back passenger compartment of a snow vehicle and ordered the driver to take them to the research building. The snow was blowing in vicious circles around the small transporter.

"You can speak now," he said to Pire as the vehicle's motor roared to life.

"What about him?" Pire pointed to the driver.

"You've already taken a ride with him. He's the one who took you there last night."

"Steera and Diell?" Pire asked, not wasting precious time.

"They're safe for now. There's no time to explain. You're to open the cylinder just as you did last night. Afterwards you will be taken to a holding cell in the administration building. The guard there is sympathetic to our cause. When he tells you to go with him, go and ask no questions! You will be flown from here in a cargo transport to a place beyond the reach of the Stomari. Others will then see to your welfare."

Pire looked long and hard at his Stoma friend. The stern mask of a Stomari security officer had melted away. "Why? Why do you help us at such a risk?"

"Remind me some day to tell you the story of a little Stoma with a misshapen foot that was such an embarrassment to his important family that they left him on a cold mountainside to die." Pire looked down instinctively at Druk-tasis' boots. He noticed for the first time, that one was considerably thicker than the other.

"You are that Stoma."

"Yes," Druk-tasis replied. "I was cast out by my own kind and doomed to a lonely death on a cold dark mountain until a family took me in and raised me as one of their own ... that family became my family, and they were Faceer not Stoma." Druk-tasis reached out and grasped Pire's hand. "It is so easy to give in to the forces of fear and hatred; it takes real courage to stand against them. This planet belongs to all of us my friend, and we must all do our part to save it." Druk turned to gaze silently out upon the blowing ice and snow. Pire pondered his words as he cradled the pouch inside his parka. The simple life of a scientist was becoming a dream as distant as his home in the Northern Islands.

CHAPTER 10

The envoy didn't bother ringing the front bell. He opened the gate himself and brushed past the nervous Faceer retainer guarding access to the reception area. Klut was seated at a large desk having just put down the receiver of the communicator.

"Your Excellency," the envoy was breathing heavily.

"You have news of the expedition," Klut asked.

"Yes sir, I have two packets for you."

Klut pushed aside the other papers on his desk and opened the first packet. He quickly read the report of the contents of the cylinder and the rather tersely written analysis of the nature of the contents. His eyes found the bottom of the report and saw the name Druk-Klat-tasis. He had always had misgivings about Druk-tasis, having spent so much of his early life with the Faceer. The story of his capture and imprisonment at the hands of the Faceer, after having been tragically lost on a family trip, was a common tale in Stomari circles. "The unfortunate Druk," he thought.

Klut fumbled through the second report, which had been prepared by his own, hand-picked captain of Stoma security. The tone of this report was vastly different from that of Druk-tasis'. Klut's eye ridge wrinkled as he read of the advanced cutting tool. He wondered why it had been included with something as mundane as eating utensils. Why didn't these ancient Stoma ancestors — if that was indeed whom they were — leave something that could have been used to identify them? He felt there was something missing from all this.

"Are these all the reports?" he asked.

"Yes sir," the envoy answered.

"No other mail ... perhaps a letter from a young Faceer female?"

The envoy looked perplexed, "No sir, that's everything."

Klut was worried. Something was not right. Above all he had

expected a letter from Steera. He scratched out a short, hand written note on a piece of paper, sealed it and handed it to the envoy. "Give this to the sergeant of the security contingent at the polar station. Give it to no one else; is that clear?" The envoy almost lost his balance as he wheeled to exit.

Klut sat alone in the reception area, staring at an old photograph of his father, turning it over-and-over in his hands. Finally, rising from his chair he made his way out across the courtyard to a part of the main wall that jutted out over the harbor. The sea foam breaking on the harbor rocks far below left a crusty ridge at the water-line of the sandy beach. Coola birds darted in and out of the surf, tiny fish wriggling from their sharp beaks. His world was changing. He sat on the wall and let his nostrils fill with the smells of the sea. Looking out across the harbor, a feeling of abject loneliness came over him. "So it begins," he said sadly.

Time limped by in the dark, sparsely furnished room that had become Pire's holding cell. He had no way of knowing just how much had passed. He was worried. The pouch with the objects from the cylinder was missing. He could only hope that Druk-tasis had taken it for safe keeping, until such time that they could be spirited away from the Polar Station. There had been a lot of activity at the research station since he had opened the cylinder. Security guards bustled up and down the halls of the administration building. Outside, the drone of transport engines had become almost continuous. There was no sign of his rescuers. He studied the face of every security officer who came near the small window, his only opening on the outside world, and tried to watch for any subtle sign or signal. He had faith in Druk-tasis, but it would not last forever.

He had just sat down on the cot to catch a little nap when he heard the soft scratching noise of a key in the lock. The door to his room opened cautiously and a smallish Stoma security officer stuck his head inside.

"Five minutes," he whispered, "get sick and beat on the door in five minutes." Before Pire could reply, the officer disappeared. Pire knew that he didn't have a lot of options. Sooner-or-later he would have to trust someone, so he counted down the minutes. After the suggested interval, he rose to his feet and began to pound on the metal door.

"Please!" he shouted. "Please help me! Someone help me!" He waited a moment and shouted again. "I need help ... please some-one!" Pire dropped to the floor. He had barely hit the ground when the door banged open and three security officers rushed into the room. An officer knelt down and examined him. Pire recognized him as the one who had told him to feign illness.

"Looks like he's gone into some sort of coma," he said, putting his stubby Stoma fingers on Pire's neck. "You know how these little hair balls are when they get a little cold, they freeze up like an ungreased dung-wagon." The comparison brought hearty laughter from the other two officers. "Get a cart and I'll take him over to the infirmary." The two left briefly to get the cart. Pire cautiously opened one eye.

"How am I doing?" he asked the Stoma officer, hoping upon hope that he had been sent by Druk-tasis.

"Quiet!" the officer snarled. For a moment Pire thought that he had made a terrible mistake in trusting this Stoma, but the officer again spoke. "I'm taking you to a waiting transport. Don't make a move or a sound, or you will end up in the interrogation room with a far less sympathetic Stoma audience."

"Where am I being taken?" Pire whispered.

"I don't know and frankly I don't care. I'm helping out an old friend — and doing so at great risk to my career, I might add."

"I appreciate your help," Pire said.

"I told you. I'm not helping you, I'm helping him," he snapped. "I don't particularly like Faceer. We give you everything and you repay us with treachery. This was our planet long before you got here. We took you in when you couldn't make it in the wild. We clothed you, taught you, and civilized you, and now you turn that knowledge against us. Well, I can tell you that we will not give up Osstar easily. Your ruthless Faceer Ka will have a fight on their hands. We may be thousands of years more civilized than you, but we haven't forgotten how to defend ourselves."

Pire could hear the pain and fear in his voice. "All Osstar is in a struggle, my friend," he said, using the most intimate Osstar-ian word for friend. "We struggle against the forces of hatred and fear." The Stoma gave Pire's hand a slight squeeze. The two officers returned with the cart. They scooped Pire up and placed him on it, strapping him on tightly and covering him with a thick blanket.

"I'll handle this from here," the officer said, and rolled Pire out of the room and down the long corridor.

Pire's cart hardly slowed as he passed the final checkpoint in the administration building and rolled out onto the long, stone walkway that led to the infirmary. From under his blanket he could feel the change in vibration as they transitioned from the smooth, polished floor of the building to the rough surface of the walkway. The icy breeze that slipped up under his covering confirmed that they were outside.

Suddenly, the cart shuttered, lurched to the left and briefly stopped. Pire heard what sounded like a scuffle. It ended abruptly, and the cart lurched forward again. It now seemed to be going in a different direction. Pire tried desperately to see from under his thick shroud, but couldn't. He began to panic. Then he heard it—the sound of air transport engines growing louder and louder. He relaxed a bit. Apparently, the plan was working. He was being taken to an aircraft, which meant that he was leaving the polar station. No matter what happened, that could only be good.

The cart stopped a final time, directly beside the big transport, and several sets of hands began freeing Pire from his straps. He was lifted from the cart and heaved into the cargo bay like a sack of dried hircus. As he looked back at his rescuers he was amazed at what he saw. Instead of Stoma security, he saw only Faceer. They were working feverishly and exiting the area just as soon as their tasks were completed. He had had no idea that there were so many Faceer at the station.

The increasing pitch of the engines began to make it difficult to think. Pire found a comfortable spot in which to spend the duration of the journey. The large craft lumbered down the strip and rose slowly skyward, its wings cutting looping spirals through the swirling snow. With no windows in the cargo section, Pire did not see the scurrying of security officers on the ground or hear the whiz of exploding bullets as they passed near the transport. As far as he knew, the most perilous part of the journey was over. He formed the edge of his blanket into a crude pillow and let the dull, continuous drone of the engines lull him into sleep-stasis.

Diell's smiling face appeared in front of Pire as if from a dream. For a moment he thought that he was back at the Trague Center, delivering a lecture to a group of over-eager Faceer students. He looked up, smiled a groggy smile and then regained his senses.

"Diell, It's you ... you're alive!"

"Of course I'm alive. Now, just where the sparks am I, and where am I going?"

"Steera," Pire asked frantically, "where's Steera?"

"She's over there in the corner, still in stasis," Diell answered. "She hasn't gotten much rest lately worrying about where you were and what had happened to you."

Pire was relieved knowing that she was all right. He decided not to wake her. "How did you get here?" Pire asked.

"We were put on this transport early this morning and have been stuck in here since."

"Did any of the officers that brought you here look familiar to you in any way?"

"That's the curious thing," Diell said. "We weren't brought here by Stoma security."

"You weren't?"

"No. Last evening, just after Rebal-rise, someone knocked on our door. A Faceer dressed in an over-sized, white parka, and looking very nervous, told us that we were being transferred the next morning and that we should be ready to go just before Zenos rise."

"Did you recognize him?"

"No. He appeared to be Somacee, but I saw no other identifying marks or apparel. He had on standard issue Polar Station parka, so it was hard to tell."

"Did he mention Druk-tasis at all?"

"No, he just said to be ready to go and he handed me this." Diell pulled out the cloth pouch that contained the artifacts from the cylinder.

"Oh Gods of Leeth!" Pire exclaimed. He grabbed the pouch out of Diell's hand. "I was wondering if I would ever see this again."

"I ... I didn't have time to open it. What's in it?"

Pire gave Diell a wry look. "You've been in this aircraft since Zenos rise and haven't looked into the pouch?"

"Well, maybe just a peek."

Pire laid his head across his shoulder and smiled at Diell. It was a gesture that needed no explanation for a Somacee. "We'll need that famous curiosity, and soon I would imagine." He took the book from out of the bag and began looking over the thousands of symbols, wishing silently that the authors had put in more illustrations. Diell grabbed the metal disc and turned it over-and-over in his hand, unable to make any sense of it. Steera stirred slightly in her corner of the cargo bay, announcing that she would soon be emerging from stasis. All the while the engines droned on as the transport continued to fly southward, over the blue sheets of ice that covered the northern sea.

CHAPTER 11

The cramped trio had been flying for over three hours. The crisp, white snowcaps of the polar mountains had gradually given way to the dull green of the deciduous forests of the Northern Islands. Pire had been studying the metal disc without much success. His concentration was interrupted by movement from the corner of the cargo bay. "Well, have a nice beauty sleep?" Pire helped Steera extricate herself from her heavy parka. "You won't need this. We're already hundreds of miles away from the polar winds."

"Hundreds of miles," she replied sleepily. "Where are we?"

"You know as much about that as I do," Pire replied. "Diell, help her up. I need to fill you in on what has been happening so far." The three arranged themselves in a rough circle in the center of the cargo bay. Pire produced the pouch and took out the metal plate. He passed it around to let them see it.

"The night that I left you, I went to the research station and opened the cylinder. It contained the most incredible things that I have ever seen: an instrument of some kind that with only a beam of light could cut through the thickest metal and yet not burn a hair on your hand if you passed it through the beam, and a metal plate—a disc—etched with a degree of precision that would be impossible for our best craftsman."

"So the old stories were right," Steera said. "An ancient, race of Faceer did exist on Osstar prior to the reign of the Stoma."

"It may have been a Faceer civilization," Pire said, "or there may be other explanations."

"What other explanation could there be? Only the Faceer have exhibited anywhere near the technical skills to produce the things that you describe."

"We found one other item." Pire took the book out of the pouch and handed it to Steera. Diell crowded over her shoulder to get a look. Steera's fingers ran over the raised figure of the great beast on the front of the book.

"What in the winds of Aldor is it? I've never seen anything like it."

"Nor have I," Diell said, "except perhaps for the legend of the great Zarn fishes that ate entire sailing ships."

"That's no Zarn fish," Pire said. "Keep turning the pages."

Steera turned the thin, flexible pages until her gaze fell upon the image of a small, stout being in a remarkably Faceer-like tunic. He was clutching a stabbing knife in one hairy hand. The small, bulbous nose, rounded semi-circles of flesh guarding the ears, and the pale, flexible skin on the exposed hand seemed more Stoma-like than Faceer. But it was the feet that captured her attention. The feet were covered in soft tufts of hair, just like her feet. "What are they?" she asked. "Who are they?"

"That's the question we must answer," Pire replied. "And we must try and do it before the Stomari erase every trace of the cylinder and its secrets."

"But what does this all mean?"

"I'm not sure," Pire admitted. "It could mean that the Faceer had a distant, more highly civilized ancestor, one that existed before the emergence of the Stoma, or it could mean that we have a common ancestor with the Stoma."

"A common ancestor with the Stoma?" Steera mused. "That could explain some of the physical similarities."

Pire paused for a moment, pondering his next words carefully. "There is another possibility," he said.

"What other possibility?" Diell asked.

"It is the possibility that at sometime in the distant past Osstar was home to a race of creatures that were neither Faceer nor Stoma, perhaps not even native to our world."

"I find that difficult to believe," Steera said.

"I do as well," Pire answered, "but I find it just as difficult to believe that anyone could dream up a creature like that."

"But we do have mythical beasts in our old stories."

"That's the point. We have stories of mythical beasts and pictures of mythical beasts from almost every period of Osstarian history. Yet no one has ever seen a beast like the one on the front of that book. Whatever its origins, it does not serve to support the Stoma's claims to sovereignty on Osstar. You can wager that the Stomari will be doing everything in their power to suppress this discovery."

The slowing of the transport's engines interrupted their conversation. Pire looked out the craft's small window and saw the green landscape of the Upper Midlands drawing nearer. Far below, he could make out a strip of clear soil cut into the vegetation and dark specks moving around two small buildings at the end of the landing strip. The transport made a delicate bank to the left and dropped gently onto the crushed stone of the landing strip. After a few minutes, the cargo door opened and a Faceer dressed in a light-blue, one-piece uniform motioned for them to get out.

"Where are we?" Steera asked. The uniformed Faceer said nothing. He led them into the side door of the small, building closest to the aircraft. Inside, they found three uniforms of the type worn by their escort.

The wind blowing across the landing strip was still cool, but much more pleasant than what they had experienced at the pole. They gratefully exchanged their heavy attire for the lighter garments. Pire ran his fingers over the large round emblem that adorned the left front side of the uniform. It was a beautifully embroidered open globe of Osstar, showing all the major land areas. He stared at the emblem. There was something about it, something that he couldn't quite grasp. In the corner sat three pairs of light-weight boots. Diell and Pire immediately shed their heavy, insulated polar boots for the lighter versions. Steera, however, hesitated.

"Come on, Steera. You'll be sorry you didn't change your boots if we go farther south."

Steera remembered Klut's admonition to keep his gift with her at all times. "These boots are far superior to those flimsy things," she replied. "You take your lightweight boots. I want something that's going to hold up if we have to do much walking."

"Suit yourself." Out of the corner of his eye, Pire watched Steera change into the new uniform. He noticed Diell watching as well, and gave him a frown followed by a quick wink. They finished changing and waited. When the door finally opened again, the same uniformed escort handed them each a flask of keera water and silently led them back to the refueled transport.

Pire turned before getting back on the craft and spoke to the escort. "Thank you for the keera water. Any idea how long a flight it will be?" The escort shoved him into the cargo bay and slammed the hatch behind him. The three Faceer shared an uncomfortable silence.

Steera finally spoke. "Did you notice the symbol on their right hand?"

"I didn't get a good look at it."

"Three lines coming from a central point with a star shape at the end of each line."

"A tycor? The throwing weapon our ancestors used against Cather-cats?"

"That's what it looked like," Steera replied

Diell had finally latched the last hook on his new boots. "Who do you suppose they are?"

"I think it safe to say that they are not in league with the Stomari, beyond that I am reluctant to guess. I have, however, seen the symbol of the tycor once before. It was on an official report sitting on Dr. Lateer's desk that dealt with some problems they were having at a research facility near the equator. They were experiencing a lot of disruptions, communications being cut, research teams disappearing, and things like that. I flipped a few pages and saw the drawing of the tycor. Lateer returned before I could learn much more, but before I closed the report, I noticed a word scribbled into to the margin just beside the symbol. It was in Lateer's hand writing."

"What did it say?" Diell asked, impatient with Pire's deliberate pace.

"It simply said: *Faceer Ka*."

Pire leaned back against the bulkhead wall and opened his

flask of keera water, letting the cool, sweet liquid run down his throat. The hum of the idling engines vibrated down the curved, metal spine of the cargo bay, massaging Pire's stiff back. The three companions were soon feeling better. The engines on the transport reached full power and in a few minutes they were airborne again and heading farther south.

T hree weary Faceer whiled away the time in the cramped cargo bay the way Faceer always do, by thinking. How could they have lived so long on Osstar and been ignorant of the underlying turmoil that existed. It had become evident to them that the Stomari movement was far more powerful and widespread than they had ever imagined, and may have reached even the highest levels of the planetary government. The Faceer Ka were thought to be more legend than fact by most Faceer. Could they be real as well?

"We've been living in an academic vacuum," Pire said to no one in particular. "I do research for the Stoma as do a great number of Faceer, but do we really know why they fund it? What are these research facilities really? How many have the Stomari set up across Osstar?"

The report on Lateer's desk suddenly began to make more sense. The Faceer Ka sabotaging a true research facility would be the work of mindless anarchists, but the Faceer Ka attacking a government intelligence operation; that at least had some purpose.

A chill ran down Pire's spinal ridge as he though of the ways he had possibly collaborated with the Stomari, collecting data and reporting on such things as climate and population movement. The Stomari always seemed more interested in population figures and demographics than they did in other scientific data, a fact that Pire had always attributed to their strong profit motive. But now he had to rethink all of his past activities at the institute and he was becoming uncomfortable with some of the possible conclusions.

Before Steera could join the dialogue, there was a loud thump at the pilot's compartment door. The three sat up against the bulkhead. The door jiggled for a moment, and then abruptly flew open wide. Aglow in the light from the instruments in the pilot's cabin and dressed in the same blue tunic, stood a familiar figure.

"Seelar!" Steera blurted out.

"At your service," he said and bowed as deeply as the doorway would allow.

"Then we were rescued by Druk-tasis!" Pire exclaimed.

"In a manner of speaking you were," Seelar replied, "although I doubt dear Druky would approve of your rescuers."

"But he told us that someone would come for us ... take us away from the polar station on a transport." Pire was puzzled.

"And he was, of course, correct. Someone did come for you, and you are indeed on a transport heading away from the polar research station. It's simply that you are on a different transport than Druk-tasis planned."

"Then if Druk-tasis didn't rescue us who did? You were one of Druk's assistants."

"That's what I meant when I said that in a way Druk-tasis did rescue you. You see, without my authority as his assistant I wouldn't have been able to commandeer this transport, and I would not have known the plan for your escape so that we could alter it slightly."

"We?"

"Your new friends and benefactors," Seelar grinned, "the Faceer Ka."

Pire couldn't hide his look of astonishment. "Where are you taking us?"

"You are going to Faceer Ka headquarters in the Equatorial Region. And after I tell you what has really been happening on your beloved Osstar for the last few years, it is my hope that you and your friends will join us in our cause." Steera and Diell looked at Seelar and said nothing. "But whatever your decision, you will make a full report to the council on the activities at the Polar Station." Pire gave a subtle kick to the pouch, shoving it under a discarded parka with his foot. Seelar noticed it.

"Interesting pouch. I haven't had a chance to look at is contents. Are they of interest to us? Those thick-brained oafs were guarding it too closely, or we would have commandeered the cylinder as well." Seelar's tone darkened and his anger increased. "Events are moving more quickly than you can know. The time for the pursuit of pure science is over. We must learn to fight. It's time to realize that there can be but one dominant species on a planet. There will be no turning back." He looked directly at the three astonished Faceer crouched in the cargo bay, "and there will be no place for weakness in regard to the Stoma. It is us or them." His rage subsided as suddenly as it had come. "The transport will be landing in about an hour," Seelar said, calmly. "You will be given more instructions at that time." The cabin door closed. Pire, Steera and Diell slumped down in the cargo bay. A flask of keera water was passed quietly between them. They spoke not another word until the engines of the transport started to wind down and the craft began its descent into the deep, damp green of the equatorial jungle.

CHAPTER 12

At the offices of the High Council, armed Stoma guards stood three-deep in the entranceway. The hallways were alive with activity after the news of the abduction of the Faceer scientists by the Faceer Ka. Couriers ran up and down with the latest reports on what was officially being called the "Insurgency." The news broadcasts painted the kidnappers as a band of rogues from the unincorporated territories and urged calm, but it was being suggested that members of the Stoma militias (organized two years earlier, after the first reports of Faceer Ka attacks on remote outposts) begin to assemble for "situational updates." It was also being suggested that only the oldest and most trusted Faceer retainers be allowed to stay in the main Stoma dwellings, and that information of any strategic value be closely guarded. Osstar was starting to come apart. The bond between Faceer and Stoma was being stretched and tested. A thousand years of peace was in danger of succumbing to fear and mistrust.

Klut sat nervously outside the office of the head of the High Council. As well as being the head of the most powerful House on Osstar, Takir-Prime was, as befitting his exalted position, one of the largest and most physically imposing specimens of Stoma on the planet. A long scar down the smooth skin of his forehead attested to his dedication to "zumatzz" the ancient combat ritual practiced by a handful of the most elite young Stoma at the Academies. The test of zumatzz was to absorb the most blows without being knocked off a small, square post. Takir's record (seventy-two) had never been broken.

Klut silently rehearsed what he was going to say, trying to get every nuance of language correct. Takir-Prime entered, accompanied by four heavily armed security guards, and spoke before he had even settled into his chair.

"Well Minister, what do you think of your little Faceer pets now?"

"I still have reason to believe that the uprising is confined to a small group of militants and is not yet a full scale rebellion."

"And what gives you reason to believe that? Are you aware that we lost twenty-five Stomari guards in the attack on the Polar Station, and that the Faceer Ka had over one hundred casualties! These are hardly the actions of a few fanatics!"

"Yes sir, but the polar attack was a suicide mission."

"And what prompted this sudden Faceer death wish? Perhaps we can find the source of it and spread it throughout the Faceer population." There was no jest in Takir's voice.

Klut changed the subject. "I must presume that you are already aware of the contents of the cylinder found buried in our North Polar Region?"

"I am aware through my own sources. I received no reports from your security Ministry."

"Things have been happening rapidly," Klut explained. "The great distances involved have made it difficult to keep everyone up to date." As soon as his statement left his mouth, Klut realized he had made a mistake.

"Everyone!" Takir roared. "I am the head of the High Council, Minister. I will be kept informed if I have to slaughter the entire Security Ministry to do it!" Klut was shocked and embarrassed by Takir's outburst and with his allusion to the transport crash. It was Klut who had arranged the "accident" on orders from Takir-Prime. Takir calmed down a bit.

"I am aware of the need for security, Minister. My sources have also warned of possible traitors in our midst, although how any Stoma could give aide and comfort to those little furry-footed computers mystifies me. Still, it is imperative that I be kept apprised of all movements of the Faceer Ka and their supporters, no matter how small a group of militants you estimate them to be."

"I have a full report here from Druk-tasis on the raid and kidnapping at the North Polar Station."

"Old news, Minister," Takir snapped back. "And what makes you think the three Faceer scientists were kidnapped? I'm assuming that they were part of the operation."

"One of the scientists was a Faceer female, a Veertal, with strong ties to my family."

Takir shifted uncomfortably in his chair. His tone became dark and sarcastic. "And of course a Veertal, the most prized of all the little Faceer companions, could never betray her host family. Wake up, Klut! What some of us have warned about for years untold is finally coming to pass. Your little familiars have outgrown their pens. They have looked enviously down from their holes in the hills upon our mansions and have decided that it is time we were pushed back into the sea from whence we came. And we have brought it upon ourselves; we have handed them power. This new machine age will be our undoing just as my father forewarned. But one thing has not changed and will never change. The Stoma have the rightful claim to Osstar. We gave the planet its culture, its government and a sense of order. We will not relinquish that claim just because a gang of house pets have developed an aptitude for tinkering."

"What about the contents of the cylinder? The instrument was very un-Stoma like." He saw the anger rise once again in Takir-Prime.

"The cylinder contained some ancient Stoma prayer books and eating utensils dated by our best archeologists to a very early and previously unknown dynasty. There was no magical instrument, or any reference whatever to the Faceer. Any reports to the contrary are false and dangerous to the peace and stability of Osstarian society." Klut knew exactly what that last phrase meant.

"I agree completely, your Excellency, and have made certain that all the Stoma present at the opening of the cylinder know the same. There is, of course, the problem of the Faceer scientist that opened the cylinder."

"Nubin Pire," Takir said, almost instantaneously, "...your choice to go in the first place."

Klut continued, brushing aside the comment. "Of the three Faceer at the station, he was the only one who could have seen any of the contents."

"And he is now in the possession of the Faceer Ka. What exactly are you doing to retrieve this valuable witness to our great discovery?" The sarcasm slipped back into Takir's voice, "... are you alerting your Veertal allies?"

"Through intelligence gathered by those allies, we have learned that he has been taken to a Faceer Ka encampment somewhere in the equatorial region. My sources also report something else, which, if true, could cause us a much bigger problem. I had one of my troopers watching Nubin Pire's room at all times. He reported that the night before the cylinder was opened, Pire was found unconscious in the snow outside the residence hall. He had been missing from his room for over five hours and the guard didn't know where he had been during that period."

"Get to the point, Minister."

"The point is that Pire's disappearance gives some credence to a rumor that we have been hearing ... a rumor that Pire had already opened the cylinder the night before, and removed some objects from it." Takir's brow furrowed.

"How reliable is this rumor?"

"It came from one of the Faceer working for the Station Chief, Druk-tasis."

"That's the unfortunate Druk with the deformity."

Klut nodded. "The rumor also says that the objects removed where of great value to the Faceer Ka."

"What sort of objects?"

"It is unclear right now, but it may be that they are being taken to the safety of the Faceer Ka camp in order to further analyze them."

Takir made a motion to the guard nearest him who immediately took a thick, stubby stalk of stalar from his tunic and handed it to Takir. Another trooper lit a faar-wood stick and thrust it under the end of the stalk. Great billows of acrid smoke rose and filled the room. Takir reacted to the soothing effect of the inhaled smoke. His mood changed perceptibly.

"Klut, it is important that we retrieve any of the Stoma artifacts that may have been stolen by the Faceer Ka. As guardians of the peace on our planet, we must not allow this persistent myth of an ancient Faceer civilization to incite the gullible."

"I reached the same conclusion a week ago," Klut replied.

"And what are you doing about retrieving these three dangerous criminals. I hope you are not relying on a few Veertal informers?"

"We are following them to the Faceer Ka encampment." The boldness of Klut's statement caught Takir by surprise.

"Following them! We've not even been able to discover one of their cells in the city. What makes you believe that you can find their headquarters in the heart of a dense jungle?"

"We are using this." Klut held up a tiny device. "It's the latest in Faceer technology, a tiny radio transmitter. It sends out a signal that my troopers, equipped with a proper receiver, can track directly to the source of the transmission. It's ironic that the Faceer should give us the technology to bring down the Faceer Ka."

"I'm not ready to bury the Faceer Ka quite yet. How did you happen to plant this little transmitter of yours in the Faceer Ka camp? Do you have an agent at that level of trust?"

"Trust is not an issue, as the agent is not aware of its presence. She is delivering the transmitter to the camp with the direct assistance of the Faceer Ka."

"She ... it's a female, then."

"Yes, a healthy young Veertal female. It is my former retainer, Steera. Before she left for the expedition, I made her a present of a new pair of sto-metal boots. The left boot had a hollow heel that contained the transmitter. I had planned to use it to track her movements at the polar station. As it turns out, the Faceer Ka's kidnapping has been most fortuitous. If we are lucky, it will lead us to their main encampment."

Takir-Prime eyed his High Council companion and smiled. "I am grateful that I can count on you, Klut. I was being cautious to this point. The halls of this center are filled with Stoma 'peace lovers,' well meaning but weak-willed. They are the real danger to Stoma society. I know — and now believe that you also know — that we will not be able to resolve this issue without bloodshed. The insurrection is much more serious than we have reported to the public. We have experienced attacks at seven of our major science stations in the last 30 days. The Faceer Ka are becoming bolder with each success. And, if they have indeed stolen something that can give some legitimacy to their claims on Osstar, we must deal with it now while they are still too weak to mount a full-scale revolt. We must not weaken or falter in our task. We must be prepared to sacrifice our lives, and the lives of others to be victorious. Our future depends on our resolve!"

"I understand, Your Excellency, and I agree totally."

Klut turned to leave. Sadness slowed his pace. He thought of Steera, remembering her in happier days. Perhaps she would escape the coming upheaval. Perhaps he would be able to save her. But he knew that Takir was right. It was no time for sentiment. It was now becoming a struggle between two species for control of the planet.

CHAPTER 13

Diell squeezed the trigger on the gas compression rifle and felt the slight recoil as the explosive bullet burst from its barrel. A moment later, the right shoulder of the Stomari security officer shattered in an explosion of steel and plaster.

"Nice shooting for a rookie," a voice said. The instructor examined the target, walked over to his newest pupil and put his arm around him. "It's a lot more exciting when it's the real thing," he smiled. "I hope you'll get to see for yourself soon enough." Diell accepted the congratulations of lieutenant Riatt. In the two weeks that he, Steera and Pire had been at the Faceer Ka camp, Riatt had become his friend and mentor.

"Do you think we may see action soon?"

"Soon enough, if our intelligence is correct. The Stoma are buttoning up their research facilities all over the planet, and they're making no attempt to cover up the expansion of security garrisons in every corner of Osstar."

Diell looked out over the central courtyard of the compound and watched as the Faceer Ka troopers transferred containers of arms, food and ammunition to the camouflaged storehouses on the perimeter of the encampment. "How many are there of us, do you suppose?"

"Only a few people know for sure," Riatt answered, "but I can assure you that it's a lot more than the Stoma think. They'll find out as soon as they make their move on our compound in the North Polar Region."

"How do you know that they will?"

"The best thing about the Stoma — especially the Stomari — is their predictability. We left so many clues as to the whereabouts of our polar camp that even those sensory-deprived fish will be able to sniff us out. Then they'll get their first big Faceer Ka surprise."

"An ambush!"

"The Stomari are predictable, young friend, the Faceer Ka are not. It's not an ambush; it's a trap! The Stomari will find no Faceer Ka at the compound, only about ten-thousand pounds of high explosive. It will give the Stomari a rude wake-up call and hopefully discourage them from further fighting." Diell smiled and held the rifle to his cheek. "Keep practicing, you're going to need it."

Riatt walked across the compound in silence. He had said his lines well. He had made the required impact on an impressionable young Faceer. He had begun the process of producing another young killer to fill the ranks of the Faceer Ka. His heart was aching. He was doubting the rhetoric that had drawn him to the movement some five years ago. The goal of a greater role for Faceer in the affairs of the planet seemed to be disintegrating into a cynical lust for power. He was no longer training the future leaders of a Faceer government; he was making mindless killing machines. A decision was coming, and it would be soon. He felt the solid heft of the gas rifle in his hand. He squinted down the length of the long barrel. The sight came to rest on a young female in a camouflaged tunic. This was what had become of his beloved homeland.

Pire had not seen or heard from Steera for almost three days. She had taken the book and gone off to try and decipher the writing. He was uneasy about her relationship with Seelar. She was drawn to excitement, and to anything or anyone interesting and perhaps a bit dangerous. Seelar fit all those categories.

He sat with his head against the wall of the small sleeping room and drew his knees to his chest, placing the cool metal disc on them. Setting it at a slight angle, the series of geometric symbols shone in the Rebal-rise light. There was something compelling, something strangely familiar about the disc. He leaned his head back and let the drone of the soft, equatorial rain wash over him. He realized that he had had very little time for relaxation of late. Outside, only the muffled sounds of the continuous stacking and loading of a military supply facility interrupted the soothing monotony of the rain — not one voice could be heard.

"Got it figured out yet?"

Pire almost hurt himself scrambling to his feet. Steera was standing in the doorway holding the book taken from the cylinder. "I'm afraid not ... how about you?" He decided not to press Steera on her whereabouts the last three days.

"I've been holed up alone for three days with this thing." She knew what Pire wanted to hear. "I can see some patterns in the symbols, but I'm not sure if they represent objects or sounds. I'm pretty well stuck."

"I know the feeling. I get a sense of familiarity when I study the drawings on this disc, but I can't quite place it. It's still hard for me to believe that a species as intelligent and advanced as these beings would leave such sketchy information. I feel that we haven't found all the pieces to the puzzle yet."

"I hope you're right. All I know is that I'm going to need more information than I have right now if I'm going to be able to under-stand this language." There was a long silence. Each was trying to find a way to steer the conversation in a more intimate direction. Just as Pire had finally made up his mind to speak, a handsome Faceer head popped through the open door.

"Well, there you two are!" Seelar chirped, "I was beginning to wonder if you had both slipped off to join the Stomari." Seelar's laugh had an edge to it. Pire looked deeply into Seelar's eyes; they were no longer the eyes of a Faceer. The little mischievous spark of light that had made the Veertal the favorites of their Stoma mentors was gone. In its place was the cool, emotionless leer of the cath-er-cat.

"When do we address the council?" Pire asked, matter-of-fact-ly.

"I'll come for you about mid-Ribal," Seelar answered, not tak-ing his eyes off of Steera.

"I'm afraid I'll not have much to say."

"That's good, because you'll not be there to lecture us. You'll be there to answer questions. And you my lovely," he purred, "are you planning to join us?"

"If it is requested," Steera answered, uneasily.

"Oh, but of course it is. I would never deny the Council the experience of gazing upon the loveliest Faceer ever to grace central headquarters."

Steera too began to notice his eyes. They were deep-set now, and jet-black. She recognized Seelar's condition. He had been taking katoc, a powerful drug once used only for war or hunting cather-cats. A Faceer under its influence was unpredictable and absolutely fearless. Legend was that after hunters had taken the drug and gone off to hunt, the entire encampment would pack up and move so that they could not find their way back until after the drug had worn off. Her heart sank at the sight of her old flame. The thought of any Faceer eating it in the present day was frightening. She glanced over at Pire, wondering what she should do.

"I don't particularly see what she could lend to a discussion of the cylinder," Pire broke in. "She is concentrating solely on the translation of the markings and as of yet has not made much headway."

"It doesn't surprise me that you couldn't see it," Seelar snapped, "for a scientist, you seem to miss a great deal." Pire let the insult pass. "And you, my sweet. I would like for you to come with me and discuss the translation problems in more detail." Seelar held out his hand. It was trembling slightly.

"I'm sorry, Seelar, but I'm many hours past a period of sleep-stasis. I need at least a half a day to be able to get my thoughts in order."

"Nonsense," Seelar barked. "The times call for extraordinary measures from all of us. You can catch up on your stasis after we have secured Osstar for our own kind." Seelar reached out and grabbed Steera's arm roughly. Pire leaped up and rushed toward him. Seelar threw Steera aside and wheeled to meet his attacker. "Come on, Somacee lap-cat!" he roared. "I've been begging for the chance to put you in your place!" Pire crouched in a defensive position and felt the wind from Seelar's errant blow snap over his head, he had raised himself and drawn back his fist to strike Seelar in the face, when he realized that Seelar's arms where still straight up over his head. "Let me go! That's an order!" he yelled.

"Not until you cool off a bit." Pire recognized the voice imme-diately—it was Lieutenant Riatt.

"This is a court-martial offense, Lieutenant; now let me go!"

"I'm sorry, sir. I'm just trying to keep you from doing some-thing that you will regret later. You're a little overwrought at the moment."

"You're the one who's going to regret it!" Seelar squalled.

"I don't think either of us needs to have this little incident ban-died about. Why don't you just relax and we'll all forget it ever hap-pened." Seelar calmed down as Lieutenant Riatt relaxed his grip.

"You're lucky he came in when he did, scientist. I would have enjoyed showing you a little Faceer Ka fighting technique." Seelar straightened his tunic, turned and stomped out of the room.

"Thank you, Lieutenant," Pire said, breathlessly. "That was a timely entrance."

"It was no accident. I saw him headed this way with trouble in his eyes—if you know what I mean."

"We do know," Steera said. "How much of that stuff is going around? I thought that katoc was a thing of the past."

"It was, at least it was until recently. The first recruits to the Faceer Ka movement were instructed in early Faceer culture, to give them a clear Faceer identity. One aspect they discovered was the use of katoc. It was found that normal Faceer became fearless and aggressive under its influence. Since we Faceer are non-aggres-sive by nature, the leaders of the movement saw value in it. The effect is more profound on some, than on others. There is, however, one effect that seems to be consistent. It is extremely difficult to give it up completely."

"Are you saying that there are a lot of Faceer Ka addicted to this stuff?"

"A great many," Riatt replied almost apologetically.

"What about you?" Steera asked without thinking. "You seem to be all right."

"It was only through a concerted effort on my part. The use of katoc is now mandatory for all Faceer Ka troops and is issued along with the daily ration. For several months I have been pretending to take my ration, but have instead been discarding it."

"Why are you telling us this? Isn't this dangerous?" Pire flinched, wishing that Steera could learn to be more discrete.

"Because I know who you are and why you are here," Riatt said directly.

"How can you know that?" Pire asked.

"Let's just say that there are factions even within the Faceer Ka."

"Then you're not really Faceer Ka!" Steera blurted out. Riatt put his fingers to her lips and looked around uneasily.

"On the contrary, I am Faceer Ka. The movement has changed, not I. New leadership has distorted its message. In the beginning, our purpose was to work for political equality with the Stoma. We had planned to use peaceful techniques: General strikes, civil disobedience and economic boycotts, to attain our goals. Out-and-out violence was never to be our main tool. Unfortunately, the pace of reform wasn't sufficient for many of our members, and talk of violence escalated. It probably wouldn't have gotten very far if not for the creation of the Stomari — and the reintroduction of katoc into Faceer culture."

"We only just learned of the existence of the Stomari," Pire interjected, "even though we have apparently been working for them for many years."

"Don't be too hard on yourselves; the Stomari have been brilliant in their deception. Most Faceer still have no idea of the extent of their involvement in the affairs of our planet. They have been slowly increasing their presence in government since the early days of the Faceer Ka movement, first in the intelligence and security agencies and then expanding into education and industrial development."

"I had no idea how much control they were exerting over the institute's budget until my polar expedition," Pire said in agreement.

"They were using the education and research infrastructure to establish intelligence centers all over Osstar. We began to realize it when we noticed so many high-level Stoma taking an interest in research and development. The crash of the transport and the death of the old Klut sent a strong message that the Stomari had taken firm control of Osstar."

"Then Klut-takit, the new Klut-Prime ... he's Stomari too!"

"One of the most powerful," Riatt answered. Steera felt her heart sink. "Don't worry, Steera," Riatt continued, "we know your relationship with Klut-Prime and believe it to be innocent ... at least most of us do."

"Most of us!" Pire leapt to Steera's defense. "What does that imply? I can assure you that Steera is no Stomari informant!"

"Informant is a harsh term. It could be, however, that her closeness to Klut-Prime may have been used to the Stomari's advantage."

"I don't understand."

"Did you have occasion to speak with Klut-Prime or any of his assistants before you left for the pole?"

"Yes, I met with Klut-takit shortly after he was elevated to Klut-Prime and again before I left."

"Did he offer you any advice or ask any special favors of you?" Steera looked at Pire from the corner of her eye.

"He did ask me to keep him informed of things as they developed at the pole."

"So, that's how you insinuated yourself into my expedition!" There was a tinge of anger in Pire's voice.

"It was not!" Steera snapped. "I know now it was because I was the best linguist available and the only one capable of deciphering the markings on the cylinder. Besides, he only asked me to write to him and let him know how I was doing."

"Why didn't you mention this to me?" Pire was obviously agitated, "how can you Veertal be so naive?"

Riatt attempted to calm them. "It doesn't really matter now. The Faceer Ka have made it all moot by bringing you here. You mentioned a cylinder, what was it exactly that you discovered at the pole?" Steera avoided Pire's glance and remained silent. "I understand your reluctance to talk. From what I have been able to glean from the gossip, it was a discovery of major significance."

"Yes," Pire spoke without thinking, "but significance to whom is the question."

"The conjecture is that it is evidence of a previous Faceer civilization." Riatt spoke calmly, trying to keep the conversation going.

"It's too early to jump to conclusions. The evidence points only to a hitherto unknown civilization on Osstar, one in our distant past. The Stomari have only one desire and that is to destroy any evidence of any civilization more ancient, and perhaps more advanced than their own."

"And what of this cylinder with the markings, where did you find it?"

"I should be saving this for the Council meeting." Pire knew he was getting too deeply into the subject. "I don't know why I'm telling you all of this. For all I know, you're a Stomari spy or the leader of some new sect of fanatics."

"That is a wise point of view, but it is dangerous to use the word fanatic here. You are in the heart of the Faceer Ka movement. This is the place of the Ka Warriors — the silent ones."

"The Ka Warriors?" Steera asked.

"The most dedicated and fanatical of the Faceer Ka. Fueled by their daily ration of katoc, they are fearless and totally dedicated to bringing down the Stoma. Have you noticed anything strange about this encampment?"

"The quiet," Pire answered without hesitation. "It's so profound that it's unsettling."

"Ka warriors make no sound because they can't. They have all had their tongues surgically removed." Steera was aghast. "They have done it so that they will not reveal the locations of Faceer Ka encampments — even under torture. They represent the new breed that has taken over the movement, a confederation of malcontents and drugged psychopaths. Once we had dreams of a great future for the Faceer and for Osstar, now we plan raids and ambushes with no real sense of need or purpose. In our zeal to stop the Stomari we have become just like them."

The pain in Riatt's voice was plain. "You say that your allies had spies at the polar station."

"Yes," Riatt replied, "we are gaining a significant following among the Faceer Ka. It grows with each atrocity we commit in the name of liberation."

"I can tell you that among the Stoma there are also those who abhor violence just as strongly as you. I am here, and in possession of the items taken from that mysterious cylinder, because of the courage of a Stoma security officer." Pire thought of Druk-tasis and hoped that he would not have to pay for his escape with his position, or worse, with his life. Pire extended his hand to Riatt, palm up in the Faceer fashion. "If we are going to save this little planet of ours, we will have to start by trusting one another." Riatt placed his hand over Pire's and squeezed, "sharing his heat" as the Faceer put it.

"Maybe we can start right here," he said.

"The beginning of a new movement?" Riatt placed his other hand on Pire's shoulder.

"Perhaps, perhaps the time has come."

"I know a Stoma officer with a misshapen foot who would be very happy right now." Steera moved to join them and they extended their arms to include her.

"Now," Riatt said, breaking the spell of the moment, "what about this cylinder? I have a little mystery to figure out, and your knowledge of these things may be helpful."

"It was discovered by a drical mining outfit, buried in a snow-dune."

"I had heard that, but it's good to have it verified by an eye-witness. What was its nature?"

"It was smooth and metallic, and it appeared to be hollow. I was brought there to open it for the Stomari after which I was to meet with one of their convenient 'accidents.'"

"Is this where the friendly Stoma officer comes in?"

"Exactly ... he arranged for me to be taken to the cylinder the evening before. Together, we opened the cylinder and stashed what we felt were the most important objects into that cloth pouch." Pire pointed to the pouch resting on a small table in the corner of the room. Riatt approached the table and took the pouch in his hands, handling it almost reverently. He could feel the rectangular shape of the book through the soft material and he marveled at how light it seemed for its size. He started to undo the drawstring, and then caught himself. He looked back at Pire, as if to ask permission. "Please," Pire said, "proceed. I suppose that we're all partners in crime now."

Riatt drew open the string, reached in and clutched the book. He slowly pulled it from its hiding place and ran his hand over the raised image of the creature on the front. "What in the name of Rebal is it?"

"We believe it to be the representation of an ancient, perhaps mythical, beast."

"But who made it?" Riatt asked, unable to take his eyes off the image.

"That, my friend, is the question of the millennium. But you haven't seen the best part. Keep turning the pages." Riatt turned the next few pages, scanning the strange symbols, until his eyes landed on a sight that caused him to catch his breath.

"This is absolutely incredible!" he said shaking his head. "This being looks somewhat Faceer, and yet is obviously not. I can see why the Stoma would want to suppress something like this. He looks much less like a Stoma. Do you have any theories?"

"We really can't theorize much until we learn how to decipher the symbols," Steera said. "And we can't do much of that until we can construct some sort of sound analog for each of them."

"And you say that this was all contained in the cylinder?"

"Yes. There were several glass-like vials with a common look-ing, grayish powder and some utensils, but the important items were this book, this metal disc and a truly amazing light instrument that could burn metal and yet not harm flesh." Riatt had walked over and picked up the disc. "And where is the instrument?"

"We left it; a little puzzle for the Stomari to work out, or per-haps a piece of support for our peace loving friends."

"Riatt turned the disc over in his hands, holding it to the light and examining it from several different angles. This is intriguing," he said and placed it back on the table. "What was the size of this cylinder?"

"About the size of a small drum of aviation fuel. Why do you ask?"

"Remember, I told you that I had a mystery to unravel. What you have just told me may help."

"How so?"

"Some sixty or sixty-five miles from here, in the heart of the equatorial jungle, there is a large colony of Zerrit Apes. It is, in fact, the largest Zerrit Ape clan on Osstar."

"I've never heard of a colony of that size in the Equatorial Region. How could it have escaped study?"

"Because," Riatt continued, "every group of researchers sent into that area came back badly mauled if indeed they came back at all. The colony gained attention about eleven years ago, when traffic into the interior started to increase." Riatt walked over to the small, dingy window and looked out across the assembly yard. Long lines of blue uniformed Ka Warriors were continuing to unload munitions and supplies from the four large transports parked on the airstrip. They moved in uncanny unison, as if every move had been pre-orchestrated, looking up only occasionally to acknowledge a hand signal given by one of their officers. Riatt continued speaking as he watched. "The equatorial interior is the only place on Osstar that the Priot vine grows. Katoc is made from the fruit of the Priot vine."

"Then the Zerrit Apes are protecting the vines," Pire said. "Is it possible that they also know about the use of katoc?"

"Perhaps," Riatt replied. "Or, perhaps they are protecting something else."

Steera sensed evasion in Riatt's tone. "You're not telling us all that you know," she said, bluntly.

Riatt regarded his new compatriots and wondered how much more he should divulge. He decided to continue. "A few years ago, we interviewed a group of Faceer whose clans have inhabited this area since the early times, long before the unification with the Stoma. They told us that the Zerrit Apes had some sort of temple or holy place in the heart of the jungle. Only one Faceer had ever seen it and lived to tell the tale, and that was many years ago. They told us that the Zerrits guard it with their lives."

"So what are they guarding?" Steera asked, still sensing evasion in Riatt.

"The story the Faceer told was that they have a God — or at least something that they worship as one."

"How did this Faceer know it was a God? A religion would suppose an intelligence level never before seen in Zerrits."

"He said he saw a crude stone temple carved out of the mouth of a great cave, guarded night-and-day by hundreds of Zerrits. Upon occasion, they would gather plants, stones and other items and take them into the temple. It had many of the aspects of a religious observance."

"So what were they worshipping?"

"I'm ... I'm not sure." He turned again to look out across the assembly grounds. "Those apes guard something in that temple, something quite unusual and perhaps very ancient. Have you come across anything that would fit that description?" He looked directly at Pire.

"The cylinder!"

"It's a possibility," Riatt answered, examining the metallic disc he had taken from the pouch. "Where did you say they found the cylinder?"

"In the North Polar Region," Pire answered.

"Be more specific. Here, show me." Riatt used his finger to draw a large circle in the dust covering a table and sketched in the basic land areas of Osstar. Pire took a small piece of wood and made a mark at approximately the area of the North Pole where the cylinder was discovered.

"Here," Pire said, "the cylinder was uncovered just about here."

"That's what I thought," Riatt replied. "You have solved my mystery, and now I may be able to solve one for you."

"What do you mean?" Pire was tiring of the riddles.

"Sometimes you academic types look at something too closely. You make something complex out of something simple. Take this for example." Riatt picked up the metallic disc and offered it to

Pire. "You have been examining this since you took it from the cylinder but you haven't gotten anywhere."

"It has been difficult. Steera has not been able to decipher the meaning of the symbols."

"Maybe you're looking at it the wrong way. Look at the disc." Riatt took the disc back and held it at arms length. The circles within circles flashed in the glare of the artificial light.

"It looks to me like a code, done in geometric signs and forms."

"You've said that something looks familiar to you. Open your mind, throw out all of your scientific training and just let your eyes see what they will see."

Pire took the disc from Riatt and tried to do as he had suggested. He let his mind relax and fixed his gaze on the disc. He was on the verge of giving up when, in a swirl of circles and lines, it started to come to him. Continents began to take shape, along with islands and oceans. It was there in front of him, as plain as could be.

"Osstar!" Pire blurted out. "It's Osstar!"

"Quite right," Riatt agreed. "Here are the Polar Regions," he pointed to the top and bottom of the disc; "this plateau must be the Northern Islands, and this large circle here on the very edge of the disc is the Circular Island Continent with the Equatorial Region stretched out along the center. The Upper and Lower Midlands are larger than actual scale, but they are evident none-the-less. It's unmistakable. Now," he continued, "take a look at the smaller circle at the top."

"It's at almost exactly the spot where we found the cylinder."

"Precisely," Riatt said, "now look at our current location." Pire looked at the central section of the disc and noticed a second small circle located at the equator not far from the position of their camp. He looked up at Riatt.

"Could it be another cylinder?"

"Perhaps. If it were, it would answer a lot of questions, wouldn't it?"

"We've got to get to that cave." Steera looked at Pire, there was a sense of urgency in her voice. "It may hold the key to deciphering the language."

"It may hold the key to a lot of things," Pire added. "Maybe the people who designed this mystery were wiser than we first imagined.

Riatt broke in, "but you haven't quite finished." He turned the disc over in Pire's hand. At the bottom, in the area of the Southern pole, was yet another small circle with intersecting lines. "It would seem that our ancient friends—if indeed they are our friends—had a taste for mystery."

CHAPTER 14

Thin, gray clouds hung just above the roof-tops of the Central Government Complex. Fall had come to the Stoma city of Prass in the Upper Midlands, or at least what passed for fall on Osstar, and the short, dull rainy-season was descending like an old overcoat across the central plateau. The mood at the Complex was matching the weather as reports of Faceer Ka attacks and raids came in from all over Osstar. On Mannot (the large central island in the Great Circular Continent) a Government broadcast station had been seized. Faceer residents were being urged to leave the cities and congregate in the mountains, where it was said that the Faceer Ka now had complete control. Supplies of fuel and food from the equatorial regions had been disrupted, and communications with Stoma Research facilities in the area were practically nonexistent. In the more industrial Southern Islands, production had been cut in half due to a lack of replacement parts for machines and clever sabotage at all points along the production line. The Stomari's worst fears were being realized. The Faceer's knowledge of the mechanics of Osstarian society was being held like a sword at the throats of the Stoma.

Klut paced the cold stone floors of the communications center, now transformed into a situation room after the incident at the Polar Station. He stared at the large map of Osstar on the back wall and frowned at the increasing number of pins sticking from every area. The red pins designated places where the Faceer Ka were suspected in attacks or sabotage against government facilities; the blue pins outlined areas of Osstar which were virtually in Faceer Ka control, and the yellow pins were for those areas still in Stoma control.

A slight grin crossed his smooth face as he noted the two black pins that had been placed on either side of a point just to the east of the polar research facility. His intelligence had been able to discover the supply base of the Faceer Ka. Even as he studied the map, two divisions of Stomari shock troops were surrounding the camp and preparing an attack. It would be a decisive Stoma victory, and one that would send a message to all Faceer Ka as to the Stomari's ability to defend their interests.

The sound of heavy boots on the stone floor woke him from his fantasy. A tall, slender Stoma Officer snapped to attention and waited for Klut to speak. Somar-Loors-denoth was a striking young Stoma. The son of a prominent family from the Southern Islands educated at the prestigious Sooth academy. He had achieved the rank of General in the shortest time in the history of the Stoma Armed Security. Hand-picked by Takir-Prime to head the elite Stomari Shock troops known as the Guards division, his loyalty to the cause was unquestioned.

"Do you have my information?" Klut snapped.

"Yes sir," the young General replied and brought out the rolled-up map clasped under his arm.

"Bring it over to the table." The two walked briskly to a large, empty table. Somar-loors spread the map across it and reached up to adjust the angle of the overhead light.

"The strongest signals are emanating from here," he said, pointing to a small area about twenty miles from the equatorial coast.

"Are you sure that this is the main camp? We cannot tolerate any missteps at this point. If we lose them here there is little chance that they will allow us a second opportunity."

"Our agents from the equatorial research station have been noting a lot of unregistered transport flights in the area. Mainly transports from the Faceer Guilds."

Klut bent lower to get a better look at the location. "It looks like a plausible site for a headquarters, but I want better confirmation than the word of an informer. Klut regretted his harsh tone, and placed his hand on the young Stoma's shoulder. "I know that you are doing your best. You must excuse my gruffness; it is the result of too many days at my post. I'm certain that with the help of commanders like you, we will be able to resolve this situation soon and get back to the business of ruling a planet. It is, after all, the Stoma birthright."

Somar-loors snapped to attention and saluted. "We will not fail," he said. Pivoting on his black, sto-metal boots, he marched confidently out of the room. Klut returned to his map, "only a matter of time," he thought, sticking a large black pin at a point some twenty miles from the coast of the equator. "I pray that there is enough of it left."

D ruk-tasis scanned the empty white expanse of the polar plain. The stiff, frozen fingers of his gloves made it difficult to focus his long-distance glasses. A frigid wind whipped small, stinging grains of powder-dry snow into every opening of his parka, and the bitter cold caused the lenses of the glasses to cloud as the heat from his face warmed the air around the eyepiece. He took the glasses from his eyes and quickly pulled the cover of his parka back over his exposed cheeks.

He had led two divisions of the best Stomari shock troops into the interior of the polar plains under orders from the High Command. He knew that should he return empty-handed suspicion would follow.

He waved his hand in the direction of the armored snow vehicles that were sheltering several hundred Stomari troops, and they began moving cautiously on a northerly course. Turning in the opposite direction, he made a similar motion to a more distant clump of vehicles. Dark forms could be seen moving against the glaring, crystal-clear pinkness of the polar sky. Slowly, as they approached what seemed to be a large snow dune, the glare began to subside a bit and the angular form of an entranceway began to emerge. "Damned clever," Druk-tasis said admiringly, "you'd never suspect it to be more than just another snow dune in a vast wasteland of identical dunes."

He waited until both units were in position on the flanks of the artificial dune, and then signaled the armored cannon to smash down the entrance. With a gigantic roar the heavy mobile cannon gained speed and hurled its enormous weight at the entrance to the

Faceer Ka outpost. The great door shuttered and gave way under the weight of the cannon, bursting inward in a blizzard of artificial snow. A great roar went up from the Stomari troops as they rushed into the breach. Wave upon wave poured into the heart of the Faceer Ka outpost, prepared to exchange fire with an enemy that they could at last fight in the open. But the onslaught quickly lost momentum and came to a stop. Druk-tasis motioned to his driver to follow the troops.

Inside, a facility that had served as a sophisticated raiding and intelligence post for upwards of three hundred Faceer Ka troops sat totally abandoned. He could sense the disappointment of the troops as they began to sift through the clutter the Faceer Ka had left. The evacuation had obviously been a hurried one. As far as Druk-tasis was concerned, the operation couldn't have gone better. He would be able to report to Klut that the outpost had been secured and he hadn't had to see a single life sacrificed on either side.

As he watched the advanced guard began moving systematically through the complex. An uneasiness overtook him. It was unlike the Faceer Ka to abandon a facility like this and make no effort to take furnishings and equipment. They had planned the abductions of the Faceer scientists so adroitly; why would they leave their headquarters in such a rag-tag fashion? Druk-tasis watched as the troops began to disassemble the equipment and load it onto the tracked transports.

"At least the equipment wouldn't go to waste," he thought. "The Faceer know that we can't resist pirating good equipment." The thought hit him with the impact of electric cannon. "They know we can't resist." He wheeled and shouted to the officer nearest him. "Get the troops out of here ... **NOW**!" The officer turned slowly toward Druk-tasis. A twisted smile momentarily crossed his lips. A second later, the walls reverberated with the sounds of a massive explosion. The last thing Druk-tasis remembered was seeing the smirk on the officer's face turning to a look of astonishment as his head separated from his body.

It had been more than three hours since Riatt had taken leave of Steera and Pire. The Council meeting was scheduled for early evening, one hour past Rebal-wane. Pire had thought the time strange for a meeting of such gravity, but he had come to expect the unusual when dealing with the Faceer Ka. He and Steera had been rehearsing exactly what they would and would not reveal to their hosts, who were looking more and more like captors as their stay at the camp continued. Pire picked up the pouch from the table and thought about trying to hide it. He realized that it was too late for that.

"I think that only one of us should talk at the meeting. If anything were to happen in there I'd rather it be me that they come after. Besides, it will make our story more consistent if only one of us talks." Pire waited for Steera's argument but it didn't come. Steera met his hand with hers and they exchanged a knowing glance. He was right of course. It would be the wisest way to proceed.

She watched him as he stood with his back to her, putting on a clean tunic, observing how well proportioned and muscular he was. His shoulders were broad and square for a Faceer, particularly for a Somacee. She studied the taut skin running down both sides of his spinal ridge and ending in well formed "hocks" as the common Faceer would refer to the buttocks. A sudden flush of breeding passion heated the skin of her face and moved slowly down her abdomen.

"Enough," she thought. "No time for this sort of thing now." It was too late. Pire's senses had read the strong message. He wheeled quickly and caught her in his arms, pressing his mouth against her cheek. His breathing was becoming almost frantic. The pressures and fears of the last few weeks melted in one great passionate kiss. Pire and Steera fell, entangled, onto the small cot in the corner of the room. For the next several minutes, the problems of Osstar vanished in a blur of motion.

Steera's heart beat a rhythmic pattern lay, as she lay, breathing deeply. Boom ... boom ... BOOM. The pounding grew louder, as if her heart was going to explode through her skin. Pire was motionless beside her. Emerging from her dream she looked up in time to see the door of the cabin fly open and four armed Ka Warriors burst in. Pire instinctively leapt to his feet in a fighting stance. The soldiers stood in their self-inflicted silence. Finally, one of them motioned Pire and Steera toward the hallway. Grabbing their discarded tunics in haste they stumbled through the door, dressing as they went.

Pire smiled softly at his lover. "Poor time to come calling." Steera smiled back and followed the lead of the guards to what she knew would be a far less pleasurable experience.

CHAPTER 15

Klut-Prime adjusted his officer's uniform and prepared to enter Takir-Prime's private sleep chamber. The Stomari guards assigned to his personal retinue were cold and impersonal to everyone, regardless of their rank or family position, and were particularly surly when it involved disturbing the head of the High Council's rest periods. Rest had a special place in Stoma ritual. The "Tiirra," the period of rest taken during the staddich, was the unique privilege of only the highest-ranking Stoma males. The rotation of Osstar, its angle of tilt in regard to both Rebal and Zenos, as well as its slightly elliptical orbit around both, made the staddich erratic—longer at some times of the year than at others. It was the one true period of darkness in the Osstarian night, and was believed to be when the spirits of the Stoma ancestors came out to commune with and advise the rulers of the Great Houses. Only the leaders of the Great Houses and the very young were allowed to rest during this time, all others were to be "on watch." Disregarding this custom was serious business. By interrupting his staddich, Klut was implying that what he had to say was more important than the wisdom of the ancestors.

Two Stomari officers with pained looks on their faces cleared the entry way to the bedchamber and bade Klut enter. Inside, sitting on the side of a huge, shallow pool of water, was Takir -Prime rubbing the sleep from his eyes.

"This had best be important, Klut," Takir growled, "I haven't had a decent Tiirra since this foolishness began."

"Pardon the interruption, Excellency, but I'm afraid I have some bad news to relay."

"Excellency!" Takir-Prime repeated the title with a mocking tone. "It must be bad to evoke such humility from a Klut." Klut-

Prime tactfully avoided the insult.

"It is, Excellency," Klut continued, "bad news for all Stoma and for Osstar." Takir-Prime drew himself out of the sleeping pool, letting the soft breeze blowing in from the sea dry him. He was worried by Klut's demeanor.

"Give me all of it, Klut," he said, slumping into the large chair next to the sleeping pool.

"A few minutes ago we received a faint message from our polar station." Takir-Prime sat upright in his chair.

"They failed to capture the Faceer rebels?" he asked.

"Worse, I'm afraid."

"What do you mean worse?"

"It appears that it was all a trap. When the troops reached the supply base, the Faceer had gone, making it appear as if there had been a hasty retreat. Then, as our troops were securing the base and its equipment, a powerful explosive device was detonated." Takir sat motionless as Klut continued. "It was either a remote detonation, or some sort of timed mechanism, but the results were tragic."

Klut waited for an outburst from Takir, but he said nothing. He sat quietly, staring out across the beach. The first rays of Zenos were glowing like small fires from the top of the dunes and the chatter of coola birds filled the soft morning air. Klut broke the brief, uncomfortable silence. "Our preliminary report is three hundred killed and over four hundred wounded." Klut paused again, giving Takir time to respond, but there was only a gloomy silence. "I have initiated a state of emergency in your name."

Finally, Takir spoke. His voice was subdued. "Who was leading the expedition?"

"The chief security officer was Druk-tasis; he is missing and presumed dead." Takir-Prime lowered his head for a moment, and then a transformation began to take place. He rose from his chair, his great voice filling the room.

"Captain!" he commanded, summoning his security chief. "I want you to notify Druk-tasis' next of kin, and I want you to do it in person. Do you understand?" The captain understood. "Klut, come with me." Klut had to run in order to catch Takir as he wheeled out of the chamber and into the small ante-room attached to his office. He closed the door and motioned for Klut to join him at a reading table located against the rear wall. "I don't need to impress upon you the gravity of this situation. The Faceer have struck us a serious blow. When word of this gets out, any lingering illusion that the Faceer are just docile little watchmakers, incapable of strategic thought, will be as shattered as the walls of that polar base. We need to do something now, something that will restore the people's faith in the strength of the Stoma government.

Klut paused for a moment and then reached into his tunic, withdrawing a folded map. "I may have just what we need."

The harsh light of the hallway faded as Pire and his guards made their way to the main meeting room. Ahead of them was a large chamber lit only by candles. Seated at a long table were ten or so forms silhouetted in the soft, smoky half-light. He had lost track of Steera. They had taken her elsewhere before he had been hustled into the main building. Before his eyes had time to adjust to the dim light, a sneering voice shot out from the shadowy figures in front of him.

"Report!" Pire still couldn't see much, but he recognized that razor-edged, cynical screech. It was Seelar.

"Report!" he repeated with greater urgency.

"I'm not sure what you're referring to." Pire played for time.

"Well, to refresh your memory and to bring the council up to date, I'm referring to the cylinder that you so adroitly opened for your Stoma masters. The cylinder that contained the evidence we need to end Stoma tyranny."

"I'm not sure we have that kind of evidence, at least from what we discovered from the Polar cylinder." Pire nearly bit his tongue in half. It was a most careless choice of words.

"Just tell us what you've discovered. We'll decide its importance to the cause." Seelar sneered.

"The cylinder was definitely not of Stoma design. Even the most advanced of the early Stoma cultures wasn't capable of that level of sophistication."

"Then it was of Faceer origin!" Seelar leaned forward, placing both hands in the center of the large table.

"Well, it's hard to say ..."

"Silence!" he roared. "If it wasn't Stoma than it must have been Faceer, proving what we have said all along, that the Stoma stole our culture and enslaved us."

"The contents didn't ..." Pire tried to continue, but Seelar was in a drug-induced fury. Looking to his left and right, he played to the rest of the Council.

"They enslaved us, and then rewrote history to make it appear as if they had helped us!" All around heads were nodding in agreement. "They executed anyone with knowledge of the distant past, and would have gotten away with it if it hadn't been for a few resourceful Faceer ancestors who had the foresight to bury the evidence before the Stoma could destroy it. Seelar glared directly at Pire. "You have something of great importance to show us, I believe." Pire unconsciously gripped the pouch. "Show us the evidence that have the mighty Stoma shaking in their sto-metal boots."

"The evidence won't be much good to you because we haven't been able to decipher its meaning yet. If we release it before we have authenticated it, the Stoma will be able to call it a hoax."

"Do you think the Stoma care anything about authenticity?" Seelar growled. "They will disavow anything we produce. But when the Faceer see it, it will start a chain reaction that will sweep Osstar and send the Stoma back to commune with their ancestors in the ocean. Now give me that pouch!" Seelar leapt from his seat and across the table, tore the pouch from inside Pire's tunic and held it high over his head. "Here, my brothers," he bellowed, "here at last is the true legacy of our ancestors—they make us a present of Osstar." Seelar slung the contents of the pouch across the great table for all to see. An eerie silence filled the chamber. There, on the table, lay an assortment of everyday items: a spoon, a bowl and a few wooden plates.

Pire stared in astonishment. "Riatt," Pire thought. "He's either a thief, or smarter than I imagined."

Seelar's rage reached a crescendo. "Treason!" he screamed, pounding his fist on the huge table again and again. "Someone will pay for this!" He pointed a finger at Pire. "You think you can make a fool of me, but I'll have the last laugh!"

Seelar again pounded the table, this time with a fury that startled even the others seated at it. But the sound was too loud to have been produced by a Faceer fist, no matter how enraged. Pire realized that it wasn't coming from Seelar's direction at all, but from behind him. Several more loud bangs echoed through the chamber and a blast of hot air spun Pire around and pushed him up against the wall. The room erupted in flame as Faceer scrambled for cover. Within minutes alarms started to sound all across the compound. Shouting mingled with the awful din of gunfire and explosions.

Pire managed to crawl about a hundred yards through the debris of what was once the main building of the complex. It had been reduced to rubble by the blasts. He reached a rock wall next to the building, and raised up just high enough to peer over it. What he saw amazed him. Stomari—hundreds of them—were pouring into the compound, laying down a withering fire. The Ka Warriors were putting up a valiant defense, but it was obvious that this was a well planned and coordinated attack.

Pire's thoughts went immediately to Steera. A salvo of explosive shells landed in a tight pattern only fifteen or so yards from the wall. The huge clouds of dust and smoke it churned up made breathing difficult. Pire realized the dire nature of his predicament. He scrambled down the wall to its farthest point and made a dash for the camp's southern perimeter. The cool twinight of Rebal's shadow was ebbing and the pink light of Zenos was returning. It was getting lighter by the minute. Pire knew he had only a few minutes if he were to escape the onslaught of the Stomari shock troops. He flung himself down a steep embankment as a shower of explosive bullets hissed and sputtered overhead. Running, stumbling and rolling over several times he finally landed, feet-first, in a large clump of Priot vines. He stood upright for several minutes, trying to get his bearings. The mass of vines in which he was standing suddenly seemed to come alive. He felt something, long and sinewy wrapping around his legs, as he bent down to untangle his feet, the lights went out.

CHAPTER 16

Steera protested loudly as the Ka warrior hustled her along towards the meeting chamber. Her complaints were ignored. Pire was already out of sight, and the guard assigned to her didn't seem to be in any hurry. Ka Warriors were, as a group, intimidating, but this one was particularly sinister. They were falling farther and farther behind Pire and the lead group. Pire's contingent rounded the stone fence that flanked the entrance to the building and disappeared into the covered entranceway. Steera's guard abruptly stepped in front of her and extended his long arms to block her way.

"What are you doing?" Steera protested. Not a sound passed the guard's lips, but a repulsive smile transformed his face. Steera immediately sensed a state of sexual arousal in the guard and tried to push her way past his extended arms. He caught her and spun her around before she could break free. "You'll get in big trouble for this. I'm a scientist, and very important to the Faceer Ka." By the sound of his breathing and the strong electrical energy he was giving off, she knew that he was not going to be distracted by threats. In one swift move he penned her arms behind her and pushed her into a small metal tool shed some fifty or so yards from the stone wall.

"Let me go! I am a personal friend of Seelar ... he will have you shot for this!" Steera knew that the guard was now beyond control. With a quick shift of weight, she managed to break free for an instant. She felt around frantically for anything in the shed she could use as a weapon. Her hands found the handle of a large chopping knife used to clear Priot vines. With all her strength she turned and swung the knife in one motion. The blade came to an abrupt stop, as if it had hit a stone wall. The Ka warrior had caught it in mid-flight. With a look of pure lust in his eyes, he pulled the knife away from

Steera and flung her to the ground. As he stood towering over her, his crazed expression suddenly turned to one of surprise. Standing immobile with his arms raised over his head, he toppled forward, missing Steera by only a few feet, and lay stretched out in front of her on the floor of the shed. Dark red liquid began covering the back of his neck, oozing from a hole the size of a priot fruit. Steera sensed another presence in the shed. Looking over her shoulder she saw the silhouette of another Faceer.

"You sure know how to attract trouble," the voice said.

"Diell ... is that you?"

"That's corporal Diell to you," he chided, putting his stabbing sword back into its sheath. "Now get out of here before any of his pals start to miss him."

"I could kiss you," Steera said, grabbing him around the neck.

Diell smiled. He grabbed Steera and pulled her toward the door. "We've got to get you and Pire away from this compound. I've heard discussions about what they're planning to do with you after Pire reports on the cylinder." Steera understood. There would be no place for non-believers on the new Osstar.

Diell and Steera slipped out the door of the shed and started for the thick undergrowth on the eastern side of the compound. It was strangely quiet ... almost too quiet. Diell noticed that even the high-flying coola birds seemed to be barely flapping a wing in the thin atmosphere. He watched, transfixed, as they floated downward in gentle circles. They seemed to be descending towards the center of the compound, yet something about them didn't seem right to Diell. They were coming down too quickly, and in too tight a pattern for birds. He squinted in the glare of the Zenos light.

He could now make out large, circular shapes against the high thin clouds. In an instant his brain made the connection. These weren't coola birds ... they were parachutes. Just as he and Steera reached the edge of the jungle, smoke and fire began to flash from the figures in the sky. Explosive shells spattered all around.

"What the sparks is that?" Steera cried.

"The coola birds have obviously acquired weapons, quickly, into the jungle!"

As they lunged into the thick undergrowth of the equatorial jungle, the compound exploded around them.

Pire's feet flew out from under him and his head landed roughly among the twisted priot vines. He kicked and struggled trying to free himself, but it was to no avail. Before he could manage a sound, he was bound and his head covered with a cowl of coarse cloth. He could feel hairy hands groping and grabbing him as he was hauled brusquely through the bush. He couldn't see anything, but he could make out faint grunting noises. "Ka Warriors," he thought.

Pire's abductors were moving quickly, and with little apparent effort, up a steep incline. He could feel their broad, muscular shoulders under him. They were very strong, more so than even the fittest of Veertal athletes. Then he remembered the hair. If they were not Ka Warriors then who were they? They were too short for Stoma, and their gait was too smooth.

The impact of being dropped to the ground jolted Pire back to reality. He had lost track of time, but could tell by the falling temperature that Zenos was waning. The jungle was become cool and damp and Pire could hear his captors rustling around in all directions. At first he speculated that they were gathering material for a fire. But that was not likely. While he couldn't be sure how far from the compound they were, he doubted they would chance a fire if they were being hunted.

A pair of large, hairy arms hoisted Pire into the air, unceremoniously depositing him into a pile of freshly picked priot vines. The vines had been skillfully woven into a soft bed. Stress had taken its toll on Pire. He began to slip into sleep stasis. As the inner lids of his eyes began to fold upward, a small hole revealed itself in the hood covering his head. He thought for a moment that he could see something outside. It was a face ... but a face unlike any he had ever seen.

Diell and Steera had waded for more than an hour up the ever-narrowing stream. The jungle vegetation was slowly strangling the meager flow of water. Looking upstream, Diell wondered how much longer they would be able to use the path that the stream afforded them. He thought it ironic that a Faceer would be wishing to spend more time in the water, but he knew that fighting their way through the thick priot vines would be far more difficult. Steera hadn't uttered one word of complaint, but he knew that she was becoming exhausted.

"We'd better see if we can find some sort of break in the jungle so we can make a place to spend the night." Steera only grunted a bit in agreement. "If anyone is following us through this they'll be as tired as we are by now."

Diell knew that he was talking to himself; Steera was exhausted. They wouldn't be able to go on much farther even if they wanted to. He noticed that the stream widened a bit a few yards in front of them, and formed a small pool over the large root of a galba tree. "There may be room for us to rest ahead," he said. He moved back toward Steera and put her arm over his shoulder. Steera made no protest, allowing Diell to more or less carry her the last few yards and lift her onto the solid base of the tree. Diell pulled himself onto the bank of the stream. The roots of the tree made a large, circular platform a few feet above the water. Steera had already pulled herself into a tight ball to conserve heat, and was entering a period of deep sleep stasis. Diell knew that, regardless of the threat of capture, they would be unable to go any farther until they had both had a chance to recharge. Too tired even to attempt to construct a bed from the surrounding vegetation, he leaned his head against the thick trunk of the tree and let himself begin to relax.

"I wonder what the great Nubin Pire would think of his addle-brained assistant now," he thought.

The great disc of Rebal peeked through a small break in the jungle canopy. Diell's eyes stared skyward, and then lowered, coming to rest on Steera. A feeling of tenderness came over him as he gazed at her. He had never seen her like this before, small and vulnerable. To Diell, Steera had always been the epitome of the strong Veertal female, well educated and well connected yet aloof, out of reach of an average Faceer. Diell wasn't feeling average. He was feeling proud. He had acted without panic or fear to rescue her from the Ka Warrior, and had gotten her out of the compound in the face of enemy fire. The image of Steera still in his mind, Diell let sleep overcome him. Their fate was, for the moment, in the hands of the Gods.

In the center of the compound the smoke and dust was beginning to settle, but fires and commotion still raged on its periphery. A squad of Stomari shock troopers prepared a make-shift internment area in the smoldering remains of one of the smaller buildings adjacent to the main hall. The first battered and bloodied Faceer Ka troopers were being dragged in and prepared for interrogation. Thus far, no one had seen a Ka Warrior among the captured. This didn't surprise the captain.

"Take that sub-Zerrit Ape into interrogation." The sergeant barked at a young Stomari trooper holding the limp form of one of the Ka soldiers. Turning to address the captain, the sergeant's eyes scanned the growing numbers being herded into the internment area. "They're not so tough, these Faceer rabble."

"I wouldn't be so sure," the captain replied. "They put up a pretty good fight once the initial surprise of the attack wore off, and you'll notice that of the forty or so of them that we've rounded up there's not a Ka Warrior among them."

"Even so, captain," the sergeant continued, "we've shown ourselves to be just as cunning as they and that will have an effect on any future moves they may be planning. All-in-all, I'd say this is a great victory for Stoma-kind. I'm optimistic!"

The captain shook his head and surveyed the battlefield. The bodies of five of his shock troops were being loaded onto a large, hand-drawn wagon. "You can afford optimism, sergeant. After the news of our victory is plastered across the papers, most Stoma will assume that this whole thing will be over in a few months. But from what I've seen here we had better be prepared for a long conflict.

Try and make an identification of every prisoner you receive, paying special attention to Group and Clan affiliation. Central Command is looking for three Faceer: a Veertal male of the Daas Clan and two scientists, a Veertal female and a Somacee male. There will be a rough time for us if they escape."

The captain turned to make his way to the far end of the compound area where a Cotaan (a large, round tent made from animal skins) had been set up to house command headquarters. Once inside he snapped to attention and saluted. His commanding office was setting at a small desk going over a series of photos. He held out one of the pictures to the captain.

"Seen this Faceer?"

"No sir"

"His name is Seelar. I'm not sure of his pre-name, but it doesn't matter. Very soon every Stoma on Osstar will recognize this face."

"Is he the leader of the rebellion?"

"Most likely. He must be captured. It's an order from the leader of the High Council himself."

"A personal order from Takir-Prime, he must be one dangerous Faceer!"

"Treacherous would be a better term. He did all this while posing as an assistant to the head of Stoma security at the station."

A coughing noise coming from the front of the cotaan diverted their attention. A Stomari officer in a blood-stained uniform stood at attention at the entrance. "General," he said, his voice heavy with fatigue.

"Yes Colonel."

"General, I'm afraid we have not had any success in locating the Faceer leader or the two loyal scientists." The General winced at the use of the Stoma word for loyalty. "We have interrogated over one hundred prisoners thus far and the most consistent story we can piece together is that the leader was wounded in the initial attack and hasn't been seen since."

"Not acceptable, Colonel," the General barked. "We must find this aberration and drag him back before the High Council in chains if necessary. He must be a lesson to any other Faceer who would stand against us. Now go back out there and turn over every rock and log and root out this little stroolworm." The General watched him hurry back across the compound shouting orders, sending troopers scurrying in every direction. He knew that Seelar had likely escaped him, yet he knew something else, something that only he and a few others knew. He knew that somewhere in a soft, sto-metal boot a small transmitter was still beeping away, sending out a signal that he could follow. General Somar-loors, commander of the most elite of the Stomari troops on Osstar, the hand picked instrument of Stoma superiority, may not find them all, but he was not going back to the High Council empty-handed.

CHAPTER 17

Pire's captors had fashioned a crude hammock from priot vines and two of them were now carrying him through the jungle at what seemed a greater speed than before. The swaying of the basket kept him constantly on the edge of nausea. In the distance he could hear the cries of Kaakalls. They intermingled with the muffled sounds of breathing from his still-mysterious captors. They had made nothing more than grunting sounds since the journey had started. Moving with speed and purpose, they seemed to have a destination in mind. They had to be Ka Warriors.

His speculation was interrupted by the impact of another rest stop. The basket was simply tossed to one side with Pire in it. He heard his abductors scramble away in different directions. The sound of an aircraft began to fill the air above him. It had come upon them suddenly, but was now lingering just above Pire's position. The engine noise identified it as a small reconnaissance craft, its undersized motors struggling to maintain altitude in the thin Osstarian atmosphere. The craft made broad circles in the air around them for about ten minutes, and then the drone of the motors began to recede. In a few minutes, the jungle was quiet again. Pire waited for the return of his captors, but could hear no sounds. "Cautious," he thought, "... like an animal."

The minutes continued to creep by. Pire parted the vines of his vegetative prison using his bound hands as best as he could. He had also managed to enlarge the small hole in his head covering, giving him the ability to make out form and movement in the dark jungle undergrowth. Peering out of his hammock, he could see that the once dense vegetation had given way to sparser foliage and rockier soil. He had been in the equatorial region before, gathering temperature readings, but had never seen this kind of desert-like condition. They were obviously high above the jungle floor.

The terrain continued upwards in the few yards ahead that he could see. He began to wriggle his wrists back and forth and felt the vine bindings begin to loosen. Within a few minutes he had managed to free his hands. He quickly untied his feet and removed his cowl. "Careful now," he instructed himself, "mustn't go too fast. They may be watching from the cover of the vegetation. This could be a trap."

He carefully parted the vines of his hammock. The jungle was indeed sparser, and the priot vines had given way to stunted trees and large feathery bushes like those found in the higher elevations of Pire's home in the mountains of the Northern Islands. Still, he could see no sign of his captors. He began working the vines of his hammock back-and-forth, using the same technique he had employed to loosen his bonds. Before long, he had made a hole in the basket large enough to squeeze through. Outside of his cage he saw that he was at the base of a large plateau. He made straight for the thickest area of vegetation. As he reached the base of one of the small trees, he saw two shadowy figures approaching his discarded basket. In the half light of Rebal-wane, he couldn't make out who or what they were. His instincts told him to forgo the identification process and get as far away as he could.

Pire squeezed into a gap in the trunk of a small tree that had sprouted on the steep bank of a dry streambed. Downstream, the jungle thickened and led back in the direction of the camp. In the other direction, the stream climbed toward the rock-strewn top of the plateau. The high ground would give him a vantage point from which to observe the movement of any troops in the area—Faceer or Stoma.

The dry, sandy bottom of the stream was crossed in several places by tracks. Some appeared to be cather-cat tracks, but the most numerous were tracks that were Faceer-like but wider, with toes spread farther apart. Rebal was almost completely gone, and the deep twinlight of the approaching staddich was settling in. The wind picked up and the temperature began falling.

Pire continued up the steepening slope of the dry streambed,

ever watchful for cather-cats. At the top of a ridge, the slope flattened out a bit and he was able to catch his breath. In the distance
he could see the outline of what looked like stone burial mounds,
the type that his early ancestors had constructed in the distant
times of Faceer pre-history. He could make out movement around
the stones. Pire's dorsal ridge was fully retracted in its heat saving
position and yet he was still cold. He remembered that he hadn't
eaten in over a week and had had precious little to drink, either.
Faceer were tough, but not indestructible. He decided to move forward to get a better look.

The streambed narrowed and deepened on the other side of the
ridge, and led directly to the stone pile. Following it, he reached the
level of the base rocks. He had extended his hand to grab the top
of a large sharp-edged rock when he heard noises coming from the
brush about forty yards to his left. He froze. His heart was pounding so loudly that he was afraid it was going to reveal his position. "Cather-cat!" he thought. The thrashing grew louder and he
changed his assessment. It was too loud and clumsy for a cat, more
of a scraping or shuffling sound. Pire raised himself ever so slightly
to see above the rim of the rock.

What he saw astonished him — Zerrit Apes! Ten, perhaps twenty of them were moving toward the large pile of rocks. Each had
something in their strong hairy arms. Something about the way
they moved seemed familiar to Pire; the way they carried their
loads, swung their shoulders and moved with such fluidity. At that
moment, the smell of the priot-vine basket flooded his memory,
and the strong, rhythmic movement of his captors came back to
him. "It wasn't Ka Warriors at all," he thought. "It was Zerrits ...
but why?"

Pire stretched to get a better look at the stone outcropping. In
the dim light he could see the Zerrits gathering around a large dark
spot on the face of a sheer cliff wall. He thought that if he could
get closer he might be able to find a way around, or even better,
through the rock fortress. Using the darkness as a cover, he crept
from his hiding place and moved about twenty yards over open
ground toward another large rock. "Works every time." Pire con-

gratulated himself, remembering his bold trek across an open snow field at the North Polar Station.

He could now see the entire scene. A hundred or more Zerrits were congregating in front of a large opening in the rock wall. One large Zerrit stood in front of the opening. Pire noticed that the Zerrit leader had a piece of cloth or matted vine around his neck as an adornment, perhaps a sign of status. He was amazed at the level of organization the apes were exhibiting.

The head Zerrit lifted a large wooden staff over his head and let out a yelp. The rest of the Zerrits yelped in turn and lifted their loads over their heads in unison. It was an incredible spectacle. Caught up in the moment, Pire lost track of his location. The apes suddenly fell silent. Pire realized that, without thinking, he had moved from behind his protective rock and was standing not fifty yards from the group. This time audacity was no help. He made a quick turn and headed back to the safety of the rock, but it was too late. The last thing he saw was the familiar cowl going back over his head as he was hoisted in the air by hundreds of groping, hairy hands.

In Diell's dream he is lying by a lake in the dead of summer, a fishing line drifting lazily in front of him. The line goes taught and he grabs for it. At first it scarcely budges but then it begins to surrender. Hand-over-hand, he retrieves it. The dark, cool water splashing on his face feels refreshing. Suddenly, his catch bursts through the surface of the water. It is Steera! Diell hauls her ashore and she falls into his arms with a look of love and admiration. He leans down to kiss her. A pesky buzzing insect begins flying around his head, darting between them. Diell is desperate to complete the kiss, but nothing is dissuading the annoying creature. It grows larger and bolder with each passing moment. Steera magically disappears from his arms and Diell is consumed with trying to swat the maddening insect. "Buzz … buzzzz … **buzzzzzzz**." The sound is maddening.

"Diell, wake up!" The sound was still growing. He saw Steera a few yards away, crouching behind a small bush. "Get down!" Diell instinctively lunged for cover. Overhead, a small reconnaissance aircraft was flying in large looping circles. They waited until the craft was almost out of sight before they crawled out of the thicket. "You're going to have to be more vigilant if we're going to get out of this in one piece," Steera admonished him.

"Well," he thought, "I'm back to being silly, young Diell. Who do you think they were?"

"My guess is Stomari," Steera replied. "If we assume that's who attacked the base camp."

"It had to be Stomari," Diell said. "Who else could have mounted such a well coordinated assault?"

"I suppose you're right." There was a hint of weariness in Steera's voice. She slumped back against the trunk of the tree. "These days I'm not sure of much of anything. I've been told that Stoma whom I have loved and respected all my life are not who I thought they were. I've watched my own kind, Faceer steeped in scientific discipline, turn from rational creatures into mindless, voiceless killers. I've been kidnapped, stuffed into aircraft, exposed to freezing cold and muggy heat, and separated from the one I love. Oh how I wish I were back at that little club in the Northern Islands crooning to Pire."

"Panta." Diell spoke detached from the moment as he stared skyward.

"What? You young greel, have you heard a word that I've said?"

"Oh, I'm sorry. I was just thinking about how good a cold panta would taste right now, you know, when you were talking about the club." Steera looked at Diell. He looked dirty and tired just as she was. Her selfishness made her feel small.

"You know, all things considered, I could go for a cold panta and a stalar stick right now as well." She gave Diell a wink. They both smiled. Steera took Diell in her arms and kissed him as a sister would kiss a mischievous little brother. It's wasn't the kiss from Diell's dream, but it would have to do for the moment.

CHAPTER 18

"How are you feeling today?" The voice soaked through the bandages and wounds and filled Druk-tasis' heart with a feeling of well-being that he had not experienced in a long time. The last few weeks had been a nightmare. The effects of the explosion at the Polar station had been bad, breaking his left arm and giving him numerous contusions, a concussion and some hearing loss, but the attention he had subsequently received had been almost too much to bear.

After he had been found at the site, buried under a pile of rubble, he had been whisked away to a Stomari medical facility in the Upper Midlands. There he was debriefed by the top Stomari security staff and treated for his wounds. Had this been the extent of it, he would have considered himself lucky; but an enthusiastic young officer at the newly expanded Ministry of Information got the idea that the Stoma needed a hero from the otherwise disastrous attack on the polar station. Druk-tasis was just what the ministry had ordered: "the son of the prominent Druk family, rescued in infancy from the clutches of the Faceer, valiantly returns to defend his people."

Druk had gone from family embarrassment to family hero almost overnight. Druk-Prime himself, along with Druk-tasis' mother and several of her relatives from the house of Klat, had been flown (by order of Takir Prime) to his bedside. There, a media circus ensued the likes of which had never been heard or seen on Osstar.

The news media relayed daily status reports on his condition over the radio frequencies. Being in its early development, the limited visual broadcasts that were produced flooded the airwaves with stories of Druk-tasis' early life as a captive of the Faceer, and his distraught family's search for him after he had been tragically lost on a trek through the Upper Midlands. His likeness appeared on government publications and newspapers by order of the Information Ministry. He was being called "the hero of the battle of the Polar Station."

For Druk, however, it was a tragedy. Seeing his past distorted and his beloved Faceer family slandered for the sake of Stomari propaganda was too much for him. As soon as the public frenzy had died down a bit, Druk concocted an excuse to leave the medical facility.

He made his way to the Layard Mountains, which rose from the plains of Istharth in the heart of the Upper Midlands, to the little Veertal village of Romass. There, he found the simple dwelling of Lirea and Nidire, the two beings he loved most in all the plant. He was received with open arms and many tears. No mention was made of the outlandish stories of his abduction by the Faceer. The horror of the ordeal of the last few weeks was subsiding under the loving care of these two, beautiful beings.

"How are you feeling, Tupo?" Druk smiled at hearing his Faceer name.

"Much better thank you, LiLi," Druk answered, using the name he had given Lirea as a child.

"You look sad my little one. Is there anything I can do?"

"No LiLi," Druk answered wistfully. "I was just thinking about three young Faceer friends of mine, and praying that they are all right."

"Nidire is going for a walk up the mountain, if you feel up to it he would love to have you join him."

"Yes, LiLi, I think that I might." Druk thought back to his youth when Nidire would stuff him into his pack and carry him on his back across the rills of beloved mountains. At the top of their climb, he would dump him out of the sack and challenge him to a race home. He knew now that Nidire was making him use his deformed foot to strengthen the muscles of his legs. But, at the time, it was nothing more than sheer fun.

Nidire poked his head around the corner. He seemed smaller and leaner than Druk remembered. Druk marveled at how strong

NeeDee, as he used to call him, must have been to carry a Stoma youth almost half his size hither-and-yon across the mountains.

"You'd better crawl into this sack, Tupo, if we're going to get back here before the next staddich." He was smiling as he opened the flap on his back pack.

"I don't think I fit into your pack anymore, NeeDee. Perhaps it's better if I walk."

"Suit yourself, but don't think that I've lost anything since last you saw me. I can still carry you and beat most of the Faceer males in the village up the mountain."

"Of that I have no doubt, revered father." Nidire drew in a long breath and smiled affectionately at Druk. It was a term of endearment once used by a Faceer for his Stoma master.

"Then let's go up a mountain." Nidire spun around and was half way up the path toward the summit of the Great Snowy Mountain before Druk could rise out of his chair. "Come on you greel calf, the Gods are waiting to talk to us." Druk quickly laced up his thick, corrective boot and bounded after Nidire. He always loved to hear what the Gods had to say, and they always talked to his father.

Steera and Diell continued to follow the narrowing stream upward. It was now no more than a muddy path. The jungle had long since closed in behind them, and the stream had become indistinguishable from the surrounding landscape. They paused to ponder their next move.

"All I can tell now is that we're still going uphill," Diell sighed. "We could be anywhere."

"We need to try and get some sort of fix on our position," Steera replied. "There must be a clearing or something around here where we can see the sky."

"The vegetation seems to be a bit less dense to our left and up about one hundred yards," Diell replied, "let's see if we can see anything."

The two pushed aside the dense priot vines and made their way off the path they had followed for so long. As Diell had predicted, the vegetation did begin to thin and soon they were standing in a fairly clear patch of ground. Steera took off the dirty Faceer Ka fatigue jacket she had been issued at the camp and sat down on a dusty-red rock. The stress of their trek was beginning to take its toll on her.

"Can you see anything?" she said.

Diell scanned the opening in the jungle canopy. "Kaakalls," he replied, "around fifty of them!" He was astonished at the size of these Osstarian scavenger birds. In the Northern Islands, they scarcely attained a wing span of over 4 feet, but even from this distance these appeared to be almost twice that size.

"What are they doing?"

"They're circling ... about five hundred yards farther up the mountain. It must be something big." The bigger the carrion prize below, the higher and tighter kaakalls circled.

"Think we should go take a look?"

"Well, the kind of animal it is could give us an idea of where we are."

"If it's a polar cather-cat, I'm giving up." Steera mustered the strength to smile.

Diell turned his attention back to Steera. He knew that her humor was masking a profound fatigue. "Perhaps we should rest here awhile; those birds aren't going anywhere."

"Thanks," Steera answered, "but we can't afford the luxury of rest right now. We've nothing to eat, and even the fittest of Faceer have to have nourishment once in a while. As disgusting as it may sound, that poor creature out there may do more than just give us information on our whereabouts."

Diell shuddered at the thought but knew that Steera was right. He hadn't taken substantial nourishment since he left the camp. "Let's keep moving, then."

Diell's original estimate of five hundred yards was a bit off. They had moved father up the mountain, but the Kaakalls didn't seem much closer.

"It's like chasing Layard," Steera said, referring to the large dark spot that circled Rebal. "They don't seem to be coming any closer."

"It could be that they have lost interest in what they're stalking, or ..."

"Or what?" Steera asked before he could finish the sentence.

"Or, whatever they are stalking isn't quite dead yet." Diell climbed onto an outcropping of rock and helped Steera up. The carrion birds were closer than before. From their vantage point they could see one or two of them drifting nearer the ground.

"I think that whatever it is, it's just beyond that ridge." Diell pointed to a long rocky ridge about twenty-five yards in front of them. "Stay here and I'll try and get a better look."

"I don't think so my young friend. If we go anywhere it's together. Besides, I don't want you getting first shot at all the tasty bits."

Steera's joke let Diell know that she was feeling better. He stuck his head just far enough above the rim of the ridge to see over it. "I can't see much. There's a clump of bushes just ten yards from here. It's drawing the birds' attention. I suppose I could ..."

"Listen!" Steera whispered. "Do you hear that?" A low moaning sound was coming from the center of the bushes.

"Yes," Diell replied.

"Do Kaakalls make a noise like that?"

"I don't think so." The sound grew louder. "It doesn't sound like an animal." Before he could say anything else, Steera crept over the ridge and made her way toward the bushes. Diell hurried after her. He caught up with Steera at the edge of the vegetation. To their mutual relief, the few Kaakalls that had landed scattered at their approach. The moaning, for the moment, had subsided.

Neither was too keen on venturing into the bushes. "Want to cast stones?"

"You've probably got three black stones in your tunic," Steera said, sarcastically. The moaning resumed. "It sounds almost Faceer-like." Diell stuck his head into the clump of vegetation. It was darker inside than he would have thought possible in the light of mid-Rebal. He could make out what appeared to be a boot. Before Steera could put her head in next to his, Diell had disappeared into the heart of the bushes.

Inside, his eyes quickly adjusted to the dim light and he confirmed that he had indeed seen a boot—and a Faceer boot at that. The boot was attached to a body that was lying curled-up in the semi-circle of a Faceer stasis position. Diell could see the powder blue/green color of a Faceer Ka tunic. He reached down to see if there was any life left in it. The figure twitched and let out a low moan. Diell jumped back with a jerk and smashed into Steera, who had decided to follow him. The impact caused both to lose their balance and pitch forward onto the prone form. Steera's face was pressed directly against the face of the unfortunate Faceer. She pulled her head back far enough to get a look at the face, and let out a yelp that caused Diell to leap to his feet.

"What is it?"

"'Who is it' would be more appropriate." Steera rolled the body over. His battered face caught enough light for Diell to make it out.

"Seelar!"

CHAPTER 19

Pire felt something pawing at him. He kept his eyes closed for fear of what he might see. The pawing stopped. He listened for any sound that might be recognizable, but heard nothing. Then he began to feel it, the low electrical signal given off by a Faceer, and one not too far away, either.

"Who's there?"

"Why don't you open your eyes and find out?" a familiar voice replied. Pire opened them slightly to let them adjust to the light—what little there was of it. He stared in the direction of the body signals he was receiving, and began to make out the form of a male Faceer. "Dark in here, isn't it?" The voice moved closer. Pire's heart rose at the sight of the face in front of him.

"Riatt! But how...?"

"I suppose I could ask you the same thing, my friend."

"I think I was kidnapped by Zerrit Apes."

"Kidnapped?" Riatt sounded slightly amused. "Why would they want to kidnap you?"

"I don't know. I don't know anything anymore." Pire was irritated. "I seem to keep getting stuffed into things and taken places against my will and I've about had enough of it. Now why don't you stop playing games and tell me what happened."

"I can tell you what I believe happened." Riatt handed Pire a small metal container. "Here, take this flask and drink." Without hesitation Pire took a large drink. A cool draught of keera water slid down his parched throat and helped bring him back to his senses. He noticed that he was in a large chamber with rock walls and dirt floors—a cave. In the dim light he could make out all manner of symbols painted on the walls and even on the ceiling. They weren't Faceer or Stoma in nature, but there was something familiar about them.

"It was the Stomari," Riatt continued.

"What?" Pire snapped out of his trance.

"Stomari," Riatt repeated. "The Stomari attacked the compound."

"I figured as much, but how did they find it? It had obviously been there for a long time and was well hidden."

"That is a mystery, but my guess is that they had help from inside."

"So, the Zerrits brought me here, how did you get here?"

"I walked."

"Very funny," Pire grumbled, "but there's not enough keera water to make me laugh."

"I've been exploring this jungle for a long time. One day, while I was supervising the collection of priot fruit, I wandered too far from my recruits. The next thing I know, I was being stuffed into a vine cage and whisked through the jungle. When I was finally released, I found myself lying in front of the opening to a cave, surrounded by hundreds of Zerrits. A large rock that was blocking the entrance slid open and the Zerrits ran like greel calves. I was dragged inside by something large and powerful. At first I thought it was simply a huge Zerrit, but then I get a look at it. It was like nothing I had ever seen, and yet, somehow familiar." Pire's head was becoming clearer thanks to the restoring effects of the keera water.

"I know what you mean. I saw something like that a few days ago when I was being brought here. I got just a glimpse of it. It was a face—strange and yet familiar."

"I must have lain in the cave for an hour or more," Riatt continued. "Finally a large Zerrit came and carried me into the main chamber where I met him for the first time."

"Him? Him who?"

"The being responsible—with my assistance—for your rescue."

"Rescue!"

"Yes."

"Who is this being? When can I meet him? Does he know where Steera and Diell are?"

"Calm down my friend. You'll meet with him when he's ready. For now, try to relax and finish your keera water. I've also left you food, and a pouch filled with keera water."

The word clicked in Pire's brain. "The pouch ... you switched the contents!"

"I told you that your questions will be answered. I've got to go and make ready for the meeting. Unfortunately, since he doesn't know you, you will have to stay here until summoned. Here, take this." Riatt tossed Pire a plain, brown tunic. "The Zerrits are used to me roaming around here in a Faceer Ka uniform, but two of us might make them nervous"

"But who's going to come and get me?"

"Several large Zerrits," Riatt smiled, "but don't worry, Zerrits are vegetarians." With that he turned and exited through a small, round hole in the chamber wall.

Pire lay against the hard rock wall drinking his keera water. He was too numb with exhaustion to worry much about Zerrits or strange creatures. He thought about Steera and silently prayed to the Gods of Leeth—the Gods of those in peril—to keep her safe. As he prayed in silence, his eyes scanned the walls and ceiling of the chamber. The symbols danced in front of him, shimmering in the harsh light of oil lamps. "Oil lamps," he thought. "Where in the fires of Rebal did the Zerrit's get oil lamps?" The symbols danced and played in front of him. Where had he seen them before? He lifted his flask to down the last of the keera water and stopped abruptly. The flask floated in front of his eyes, as if suspended in the damp air. "The flask, a cylinder ... it's a cylinder." The symbols on the wall stopped dancing. He had seen them before in the cold reaches of the North Polar Region. They were the symbols etched into the mysterious cylinder—the object that had taken him so far from home.

Somar-loors didn't wait for the pilot to get out of his flight helmet. He met the aircraft as soon as it touched down on the freshly repaired runway at what was now the Stomari's equatorial base camp. The surprised pilot nearly injured himself trying to get out of his flight gear while saluting his commanding officer.

"Well, Captain, what did you find?"

"I tracked a strong signal about 20 miles north/northeast." He hastily unfolded a map and pointed to a spot. "It was coming from here, at the base of these large rocks."

"You're certain of the location?"

"Yes sir. I flew a circular search pattern, making note of wind speed and the strength of the signal at different points of the circle. The strongest signals were definitely coming from that location."

General Somar studied the map. He wasn't happy with what he saw. "We're going to have to mount a ground operation. The jungle and the height of those rocks would make an airborne assault too risky."

"Sir," the captain interjected, "I also made some visual observations."

"Go on, what did you see?"

"Zerrits, sir."

"Yes Captain, we're well aware that there is a Zerrit colony in that area."

"But I saw hundreds, maybe more."

"You mean spread out over your entire search area?"

"No sir, they were only a few miles from the signal ... in the same General area, maybe closer to the rocks."

"Could you see what they were doing?"

"They seemed to be gathering something."

"Probably priot fruit, Captain. The Zerrits eat the fruit before it turns black and begins to ferment, after that all it's good for is turning our little Faceer friends into raving maniacs." Somar-loors snapped a salute to the captain who returned it immediately. "I wouldn't read too much into this, Captain. It may be a large colony, but Zerrits are Zerrits, and they're certainly no match for Stomari shock troops." The captain smiled in agreement and made his way toward the hangar looking confident. In his own heart, Somar-loors felt a sliver of doubt begin to creep in.

The keera water and the food had relaxed Pire to such an extent that his body began slipping into a deep sleep stasis. For Faceer deep stasis was more than just rest, it was a period in which the brain was free to process information, an ancient biological mechanism that had contributed to the Faceer's logical thought processes. It could be long and difficult, a swirling montage of forms and emotions. The events of the past few weeks made this one particularly arduous.

For many hours, his body twisted and turned uncontrollably. Eventually, his thought process began to slow, and the final stages of deep stasis took over: the extension of his spinal ridge and the relaxation of his muscles followed by a period of deep, restful sleep.

Pire was awakened by several rough slaps on the side of his head. He came up swinging at his attacker, mumbling an oath under his breath. Coming out of his haze, he looked up, expecting to see Riatt laughing and taunting him as his little sister used to do when he was coming out of a deep stasis. The form in front of him was too big for a Faceer. As the opaque lids that had protected his eyes during stasis began to retract, his vision began to clear. His tormentor was not Riatt, but rather a large Zerrit.

The beast was staring at Pire as intently as Pire was staring at him. He was wearing a woven headdress made from priot vines and interlaced with flowers of various other plants. His eyes were deep-set and reddish in color, but bright and soft, giving him a more intelligent look than one would expect. This was the Zerrit that he had seen leading the others.

The Zerrit, sensing that Pire was now fully awake, put both of his hairy arms under Pire's armpits and lifted him effortlessly to his feet. Pire was fully expecting him to sling him over his shoulder and carry him off, but instead he made a motion in the direction of the opening in the cave wall. Pire didn't need a further invitation. Wherever he was being taken, he was happy to be walking.

Pire moved through the opening and into another, larger chamber. The Zerrit maintained a respectable distance. Oil lamps were arranged around the circular room at intervals of 15 or 20 yards.

They gave off enough light to make it easier to move about, but it was still difficult to make out specifics. The flickering flames painted the walls and ceiling of the chamber in ever-changing patterns.

Pire sensed movement and Faceer energy from behind him. He tensed, but the long deep stasis had taken the edge off his fear. The vibrations proved to be familiar ones.

"Well, my friend, I hope you had a pleasant nap."

"The first I have had since leaving the Northern Islands," Pire replied extending his hand to Riatt. "How many rooms does this cavern have, anyway?"

"I'm not sure. Although I've been here many times, I don't think I've seen more than three or four." Strange forms were beginning to appear out of the darkness, aligned along the chamber walls. Pire realized that they were Zerrits and that they had been there all along. "Don't mind them," Riatt said, sensing Pire's alarm. "They guard the inner chamber." He made a 360 degree pivot, silently counting the Zerrits. "I'm not sure how they decide on shifts. I see them come and go at various intervals, but there's always the same number here."

"Guard it from what?"

"Anyone or anything that would try and enter without Nosh's permission."

"Nosh?" Pire said the name as if examining it as it flowed out of his mouth.

"The being we are going to see."

"When we were back at the camp, you acted as if you didn't know much about this Zerrit colony. Now you say you've been here many times. You claim that I was rescued and not abducted. You switched the contents of the pouch. We made a pact to trust each other, Riatt. I need to see a little of that trust now." Pire kept his hand on Riatt's shoulder while he looked him straight in the eye.

"I'm sorry, Pire." Riatt returned the gesture. "I wanted to make sure that you had gained sufficient strength before I told you more. Back at base camp ... well, let's just say that had our Ka friends any idea that I had made contact with Nosh, our little pact would have been finished before it was started."

"Just who or what is this, Nosh?"

"Ah, the famous Faceer curiosity." A voice resonated from directly in front of him. It seemed to fill the chamber. Pire could see the Zerrits scurrying around in the half-light, bunching up at the opening. The voice drew nearer. Pire stood looking up at the face of the creature he had seen only briefly from the inside of a dirty cowl.

He regarded this new creature with the analytical eye of a Faceer scientist. The head was large with a sharp nose and a pronounced brow-line and covered in thick, black hair. The mouth was Stoma-like, wide with thin lips. The neck flowed from the head into a pair of strong, thick shoulders. The arms were long and leanly muscular like a Faceer, yet the chest was broad. Waist and hips were sinewy, flowing into long, muscular legs definitely built for speed, both in and out of water. The biggest surprise was the feet. They were long and narrow, covered in a furry Faceer-like down.

"So, this is the little fellow that's caused such uproar." Pire stood speechless.

"Yes," Riatt answered for him. "This is the famous, Nubin Pire."

"Well, Nubin Pire, come closer and let me get a better look at you." As Pire approached he could see soft, blue/black Stoma eyes focusing on him. "Riatt tells me you are a peace-loving being. That's why I had you rescued; you see I am a peace-lover too." Pire was oblivious to Nosh's conversation, still too fascinated by his appearance to listen. He seemed to have been manufactured, as though he had been assembled from spare parts, some Faceer, some Stoma and some of unknown origin, but all put together beautifully. "It is unfortunate that peace seems to be an unpopular concept nowadays." Nosh studied Pire studying him. "Do you think that true, or not?"

"Oh yes, definitely," Pire stuttered, still too absorbed to really comprehend what was being said.

Nosh could see that his attempts at putting Pire at ease were getting nowhere, so he tried a more direct approach. "You're the one that opened the Polar cylinder, aren't you?"

Pire snapped out of his trance and started talking to no one in particular. "The symbols painted on all the walls ... they're from the cylinder. But how could you have seen them way down here?" Pire realized that he had been babbling. He answered Nosh's question. "Yes, I'm the one."

"And you saw its contents?"

"Yes."

"What did you make of them?" Nosh's tone was becoming lower and softer.

"Very advanced ... more Faceer-like than Stoma, but really, neither."

"Sort of like me?" Nosh was looking directly at him, smiling.

"Yes, but you're not like the creature in the book." Then it dawned on him. He wasn't referring to the creature in the book. The contents of the cylinder hadn't been discussed. He was referring to his own heritage. "Seemano," The word popped out of Pire's mouth before he could stop it.

"I prefer the term 'Seeyard,'" Nosh said, dispassionately. "Somehow 'half-breed abomination' is too limiting in its descriptive ability."

Pire looked at him again and it all fell into place, the Stoma neck and shoulders, the Faceer feet, and the strange blending of species in the torso and face. "I'm sorry," Pire said, embarrassed by his callous use of a derogatory term.

"No offense taken, young friend, it's a term that doesn't get much use in polite conversation."

"But I thought it was a myth. I mean, we have all heard the rumors but no one had ever seen one ... I mean, one of you." Pire was frustrated by his clumsy language.

"It's probably because that, as far as I know, I'm the only 'one of me.'" Nosh jokingly mimicked Pire's awkward phrase.

"Then you think that there's never been another?"

"Let me restate that. As far as I know, I'm the only one that exists. There most likely have been other Seeyard, but I imagine they didn't live very long. The mother most likely met with an 'accident' shortly after it was suspected that she might be carrying one. Accidents allow the Stoma to avoid sin."

"But how did you survive?"

"My mother, a Veertal, knew that she was carrying me long before anyone else did. She also knew what her Stoma master would
do if she were discovered. She fled to a small village on the edge
of the jungle and had me. Of course, in doing so her life was for-
feit. The trauma of a delivery of that complexity would be severe
enough in a well equipped hospital; it proved fatal in her circumstances."

"So how did you end up here?"

"The scrupulously religious Faceer of the village had a dilemma — how to deal with an abomination without committing a
great sin. Most of the villagers wanted to take me into the jungle
and leave me to die, but one of them had compassion. His name
was Faeed. He knew that Zerrit Apes would sometimes care for
orphaned infants of other species. He also knew that they wouldn't
have the built-in prejudice against a Seemano that the two so-called
intelligent species did. He left me in an area where Zerrits were
known to forage, and they brought me here. Later, after I had been
accepted into the Zerrit society, Faeed did a very odd and brave
thing — he came back to check on me. The Zerrits, sensing that we
were somehow kin, allowed him to stay with me. Thus began my
education.

Faeed taught me to speak and to read, and left me copies of
every book he could find in their impoverished little village. He
read me science and poetry and told me the great myths of both the
Stoma and Faceer. He was the wisest and kindest being I have ever
known."

"What happened to him?"

Nosh's tone grew dark. "The Faceer Ka came. They wanted
guides to take them to where the priot fruit grew, and had heard
tales of Faeed's frequent travels into the jungle. He knew that if the
Faceer Ka found me that they would kill me, so he refused. The
Faceer Ka took his non-compliance as treason. They tortured him
and ultimately killed him, but he never gave them any information
for fear of betraying my existence. That was the kind of being he
was, willing to stand for something in a world of selfishness and

self-interest, to give up his life to save that of an abomination."

The cave chamber fell silent. To Pire, Nosh no longer seemed fearsome or intimidating. The forces that had caused his pain were the same forces of hatred and violence that were taking hold all over Osstar. But Nosh's tale was unique, for neither side could claim him as either villain or victim. Nosh's antagonist was fear and hatred itself.

Nosh sat in silence for a moment, and then extended his hand to Pire. "But, enough of that, we have work to do and a world to save. Come with me, young Faceer, and we will talk of many things. I have wonders indeed to show you." Holding one of the oil lamps aloft, he led Riatt and Pire out of the chamber and deeper into the cavern.

Seelar's injuries were many but, for the most part, not life threatening. Steera looked at his badly battered form and found it difficult to be angry with him. Without the changes brought about by the daily use of katoc, he looked more as he had when they were involved in their younger days, smaller and not at all threatening.

Diell was less sympathetic. "I don't like this. We can't just sit here and expect these bushes to protect us from the Stoma. This is the individual they are all looking for." He gave the still unconscious Seelar a nudge with the toe of his boot. "How long will it be before a company of shock troops finds us? I say we move on now!"

Steera examined his legs and chest for wounds. "We can't just leave him here like this."

"And why not? Do you think if the situation were reversed that he'd be thinking about helping us?"

"That's just the point, Diell; it would make us just like him. That's what this whole struggle is about, isn't it? There are Stoma who want to kill us because we're Faceer. There are Faceer who want to kill Stoma because they're Stoma. Compassion can't be segregated by species any more than wealth or power."

Diell was taken aback by the forcefulness of Steera's appeal.

"My, you're becoming quite the philosopher. So what shall we do with him?"

"We stay here until he comes out of his stasis, and then we move on, taking him with us." Steera moved off to gather material for a bed.

It was a full day before Seelar began to come around. Diell had found a source of water nearby, and some ripe priot fruit. They had all eaten and were beginning to feel rested enough to push on.

"Well," Seelar began, "I must say that I am surprised and pleased with my new benefactors. I would have thought that you would have left me to the Stomari."

"The notion crossed our minds," Diell replied, sarcastically. Steera shot him a disapproving look.

"And you, my young soldier," Seelar said, turning to Diell, "I saw great progress in you back at the camp. You were becoming quite a good shot with a gas rifle. What happened? Did you succumb to the pacifist drivel of your companions?"

Steera took offense at Seelar's tone. "We've been slogging through this jungle for more days than we can count. That priot fruit we ate is the first food we've had in weeks, and it's hardly a meal for a Faceer. What's more, we haven't a clue as to where we are or where we are going. When we found you, the kaakalls were getting ready to turn you into dinner. I made the decision that we weren't going to leave you here to die, please try and do something to justify that decision."

"Ah, as beautiful as I remember. Never let it be said that the Faceer Ka don't know how to express gratitude. Perhaps I can justify your decision by giving you a direction in which to proceed."

"You know where we are?" Diell was suspicious.

"Of course, I've spent months in this jungle. Did you think I was just wandering around aimlessly? If I hadn't injured myself escaping the Stomari patrols, I'd be there now."

"Be where now?" Steera asked.

"A secret camp my compatriots constructed about five miles from here, a redoubt so to speak made for just such a contingency. It's stocked with food and keera water along with weapons and ammunition. If we get started, we can be there by Rebal-wane."

"Are you sure it's secure? The Stomari have been sending out reconnaissance aircraft. They may have spotted it."

"The Faceer Ka were clever enough to construct a base camp that eluded Stomari intelligence for years. I would think that we could keep a small rest camp concealed. Besides, what other choices do we have? You admittedly have no plan of action."

"I'm concerned about the kind of action you're thinking about."

"Steera, my pet, you misunderstand me. I simply want to get us to a place where we will be safe. After my Ka Warriors dispose of the clumsy Stomari troops back at the compound, they will begin to search for me. The redoubt will be the first place they will look. And you will be rewarded as heroes, as the brave Faceer who saved their leader from the Stomari."

"From the kaakalls," Diell mumbled.

"You would be treated like royalty," Seelar continued, staring at Steera, "and I know that I could find a high position for you in the movement."

"We don't want a position in your movement, Seelar. Your movement will be the ruin of our planet," Diell snarled.

"Your cynicism can be excused due to your weakened condition, but be careful not to push it too far." Seelar's tone turned darker. "The Stoma are already concerned about their dependence on us to keep their machines running. They're not stupid. They see where this dependence is heading—an equal partnership with the Faceer. This they will never allow to happen. We were fine as long as they felt superior to us, as long as we knew our place on their planet. But now we're becoming a threat, and with the discovery at the North Polar Station giving us a claim to Osstar, they are becoming desperate."

"So we must fight to survive." Steera responded almost in agreement.

Diell looked at Steera incredulously. She was falling under the spell of Seelar's rhetoric. "So, in order to take our rightful place on our planet, we must first tear it apart." Diell frowned at Steera as he made his comment.

"Enough talk!" Seelar rose to his feet. "We must make the camp by Rebal-wane. This discussion is ended."

"You're right. We must keep moving." Steera extended her hand to Diell to help him to his feet, but he refused it.

Seelar parted the bushes and scanned the sky and the surrounding area for any sign of Stomari. There was none. They began moving to the northeast, Seelar leading, Diell behind him, and Steera bringing up the rear. Storm clouds were building to the north. Steera had recovered some of her strength from the rest and the priot fruit, but the events of the last few weeks were having a cumulative effect and she began falling behind. Finally, Diell looked back and could no longer see her. He stopped and began moving back down the mountain.

"Keep moving!" Seelar barked.

"Steera has fallen behind. We'll have to wait for her."

"She'll catch up. We can't waste precious time. We've got to get to the camp soon."

"If it weren't for Steera you would still be lying in those bushes back there fighting off kaakalls. She's been through a lot lately, and I'm going back to see if she's all right. What are a few minutes going to mean?"

"It could mean the difference between a safe haven and a Stomari internment camp, Corporal," Seelar snapped. "It seems that our expensive military training was wasted on you. But don't worry; I know what will put you back on track. We'll discuss this when we get to the camp ... now move!" Diell felt his legs jerk forward involuntarily, but caught himself.

"Steera is the leader of this expedition. I go nowhere without her."

"Steera is weak. That's why she is no longer my chosen one. I'm going on without you." There was a growing tone of urgency in Seelar's voice.

"We'll all go together, or none will go." Steera's voice was strong even as she labored to catch her breath.

"He was trying to get me to leave you here, but I..."

"I heard, Diell." She turned to Seelar. "I was taken in by your persuasive voice once Seelar, but I'm learning quickly. From now on we do this together or we part ways. That's what true, patriotic Faceer are supposed to do, right? Stick together."

Seelar could find no answer for Steera. His mind was slowly succumbing to the ravages of katoc withdrawal. He swung around without a further word and began to forge up the mountain. Steera and Diell were amazed at this burst of energy from someone that had only a few hours earlier been near death. They scurried after him.

In due course, they reached a stone outcropping that separated the steeper portion of the mountain from the gentler slope that led to the crest. Diell studied the sky with a worried look. Great, grey storm clouds were rolling down from the high peaks, bearing down on them. The temperature was dropping. Diell could feel his dorsal ridge tucking into his spine.

He called ahead to Seelar, "How much farther?" There was no answer. Seelar was moving as if in a trance, ignoring brush and rock as if he were a greel and had been born to the mountain.

"Try and stay with him!" Steera had to shout to overcome the noise of the approaching storm. "He is Veertal, and well suited for this climate and altitude." Seelar's head disappeared behind a large boulder just as the storm hit. Great crashes of thunder and bolts of ice-blue lightening lit up the pale-pink sky. They made a dash for the protection of a huge rock. Steera put her arms out to brace herself, and noticed that a chunk of it appeared to be broken off. Diell had fallen in behind her, pressing against her back as waves of cold rain blew over the sheltering rock-face.

"Look at that!" Steera shouted over the din, pointing to the slab of broken rock. "It looks like it's been sliced out of the stone." Steera moved closer and gave the slab a slight kick with her sto-metal boot. It moved a bit. Diell put his shoulder on it and pushed as hard as he could. The slab fell away, revealing a passageway tunneled through the rock. The storm was reaching its peak. Steera dropped down and crawled into the passage with Diell close behind. The rain was pounding outside and the tunnel was being transformed by the deluge into a fast moving water pipeline.

"We have to move at once or the water is going to carry us with it," Steera urged. Leading the way — part crawling and part swimming — she began to move down the length of the passageway. The circumference of the tunnel was about one and one half times the size of the two desperate Faceer. Water was beginning to climb up the sides, increasing at an alarming rate. They were now swimming for their lives, no longer making any contact with the floor of the passageway. Just as the water reached the top of the tunnel, it opened and they were spit out by the swirling, bubbling maelstrom into a narrow ditch on the other side of the boulder.

Diell cleared the water from his throat and nose. "Let's make a vow never to do that again," he said, relieved to be alive. The two flopped down on the bank of the ditch and watched the water begin to recede.

They surveyed their new surroundings. The drainage way widened into a small valley enclosed on all sides by the mountain. The vegetation was lush. Several waterfalls poured clear, cold mountain water into pools that formed the perimeter of a well constructed camp. There was one main building constructed of vines and leaves and three smaller huts. The use of native plant materials in their construction provided a perfect camouflage, and they were sturdy enough since the tempest raging outside had made very little impact on the interior of the valley.

"Amazing," Diell remarked. "Seelar may be full of more wind than the caverns of Triall, but he wasn't exaggerating about this place. It's practically invisible from the outside, and so situated in the mountain that it escapes all the inclement weather."

"So, you like my little hideaway." Seelar's voice was calm and soothing.

"Well done, Seelar," There was a tone of genuine admiration in Steera's voice.

"You should be proud of it as well. It represents years of evolution and education, the best of Faceer technology."

"Yes, evolution from the Gods and education from the Stoma."

Seelar ignored Diell's snide comment. "If you go into the main building, you will find food and keera water in abundance."

"Aren't you going to join us?" Diell asked.

"I've already had all that I need," Seelar replied calmly. "I'm going to take a short walk around the camp ... to make sure everything is in order."

Steera and Diell entered a side opening to the main building and found a table full of food and drink, just as Seelar had described. They fell upon it like kaakalls on a carcass. After almost a half-hour of uninterrupted eating, they slumped back in their vine hammocks, perfectly sated.

"I wonder where Seelar went?" Diell asked, finally mustering the energy to speak.

"I'm too full to wonder." Steera held her hands around her distended stomach. "Look at this. What a disgusting state for a Veertal!"

"I'm glad we Somacee aren't so body-conscious," Diell retorted. "I wouldn't have been able to eat that entire bowl of whatever it was I was eating. Come to think of it, I couldn't tell you much about what I ate. Diell lifted his arm to wipe the last vestiges of his meal from his mouth, and felt a numbness start to spread from his shoulder to his elbow and out toward his fingers. He tried to lift his other arm to rub the numbness away. It failed to respond. He realized that his whole body was going numb. The last thing he remembered was turning his head to see Steera slumped over in her chair.

CHAPTER 20

The Faceer Ka soldiers came through the Strail pass two abreast, their powder blue tunics blending with the pastel greens of early spring. They sang as they marched. When they reached the center of the little village of Romass they dispersed. Three squads hurried to surround the hillside house of Lirea and Nidire. The villagers, for the most part, stayed hidden in their homes. They knew these Faceer, and what they were capable of doing. A few of the braver males ventured to within eye and ear-shot of their good friends' dwelling. They watched as Nidire was taken from the house and tied to a tree. Lirea was restrained. Soon, the commander of the troop came and began to question him.

"Where is he?" The commander growled.

"Where is who?" Nidire answered, trying to remain calm.

"You know who, the Stomari spy you are hiding."

"I assure you that there are no spies here."

"Don't lie to me, not everyone in this area is a traitor. He was seen with you on several occasions in the mountains."

"If you are referring to my adopted son, he has gone."

"Adopted son!" The commander said incredulously. "A high-level Stomari security officer is your adopted son? The next thing you will tell me is that the old Takir is really a Ka Warrior." A ripple of laughter spread through the ranks of the troopers, but the commander didn't change his stern demeanor. His glare turned sinister. "Perhaps we can refresh your memory." The commander nodded to the soldier who was standing directly behind Nidire, and he began to twist the rope that bound him to the tree. Lirea screamed. Nidire stiffened to suppress the look of pain crossing his face.

"I tell you he has gone. The Stomari came for him two days ago to recall him to active duty."

"Then you admit that he is Stomari?"

"I admit that he wears the uniform of the Stomari, but to my wife and me and to the residents of this village he is one of our children, returned to visit."

"Then this is a strange village indeed," the commander snarled, "and in need of some enlightenment." The soldier suddenly threw Nidire to the ground and placed his boot on his neck. "I will give you until the count of three to tell us where he is hiding. One ..."

"But, I tell you he isn't ..."

"Two ..." The soldier's boot was beginning to crush Nidire's neck to the extent that he was finding it difficult to breathe. Some of the soldiers in the ranks began shifting on their feet nervously from side to side. Surely, they thought, he wasn't intending to kill this old Faceer, just scare him.

"Three." At the sound of three, the soldier put his full weight on Nidire's neck. The sickening sound made even the strongest of the soldiers wince. Lirea screamed again, even louder, and broke away from the soldier who was holding her to run to Nidire's side—it was too late. The weight of the soldier's body had crushed Nidire's windpipe.

Lirea looked in disbelief at the now lifeless body of her beloved husband. A low waling noise rose from her aging throat and turned to an agonized scream. Spinning around with a deftness that defied her age, she attacked the commander, nearly throwing him to the ground. Three villagers started to move to her aid. The commander grabbed her by her thick black Veertal hair and held his dagger to her throat.

"Move no closer," he warned. "This is what happens to traitors and all those who oppose the Faceer Ka." The other Ka soldiers half-heartedly stepped in to protect their commander. The villagers backed off, believing that the commander wasn't going to kill Lirea. "Now, go back to the village and tell the others that harboring a Stomari assassin carries a penalty of death." The locals turned and hurried back toward the center of the village, looking over their shoulders at Lirea.

One of the soldiers spoke up. "Commander, I think we had better be moving out of here."

"We're going Sergeant. Tell the troops to reassemble at the bridge on the outskirts of the village." He turned his attention back to his captive. "And you, my little Veertal cather-cat, you've seen too much already. I wouldn't want you to inform on me to your Stomari kinfolk." Lirea bit down as hard as she could on the commander's arm. Her blood soon mingled with his as his blade slowly sliced across her neck.

At the bridge, the mood was grim. The commander stood in front of his dazed, confused troops and spoke, "I know that some of you were upset by what you saw back there, but I assure you that had those traitors lived, we would soon be fighting our way through Stomari shock troops like our gallant brothers at the Equatorial base. I know that these first engagements can be difficult for those of you new to battle, so you must look to your squad leaders to strengthen you for the tasks ahead. The battle is joined. Only the fittest will survive ... only those steeled to their duty. We have gone too far in our quest for justice to turn back now." The commander raised his blood-stained dagger to the sky and began to shout, "Faceer for Osstar, and Osstar for Faceer!" The chant was repeated over-and-over until the whole troop joined in. "Now," he said as the chanting died down, "let's finish the job and leave a message to all who defy us." He pointed the dagger in the direction of the village. "Burn it down!"

A few of the more eager soldiers lit torches and moved off toward the village, but the majority of the troops simply picked up their gear and moved back onto the road. As they marched past the bridge and turned onto the highway that led to the coast and waiting ships, rifle shots could be heard in the distance.

The commander kept the troops moving but he was troubled deep in his soul. How many of his troops, he wondered, would return from the village alive? How many would be eager to return at all?

The captain of the Stomari shock troops was perplexed. The signals coming from the radio transmitter were as strong as he had ever seen them, which meant that it must be very close, but he had suddenly run out of mountain. All that stood in front of him now was the steep sides of a small valley ending abruptly at the base of a huge boulder. The boulder was too large to roll away, and the surrounding terrain made it practically impossible to go around.

"We've scouted the entire area, Captain. The signals are extremely faint, but they fade out completely as soon as we move away from this rock."

"I've never seen a rock this size," the captain muttered, almost dejectedly. "The entire top of the mountain must have broken off sometime in the past." Indeed, a large circular indentation at the mountain's crest attested to the origin of the boulder. "Well, how ever it got here, it's been here a long time," the trooper observed, "so it's not a decoy set up by the enemy. The Faceer are clever, but not that clever."

"Have you tried scaling it?"

"Yes sir, but we haven't the necessary equipment to get many of troops to the other side. He anticipated the captain's next question. "We've also tried going around it, but the valley walls are too steep and the rocky soil too unstable."

"Radio signals don't lie, Corporal. Somehow, the Faceer we're after got on the other side of this rock, and if they can do it, we can do it. I'm not going back and tell General Somar that they simply melted into a rock wall."

"Maybe they went under it," the corporal was making what he thought was a joke.

"Yes, maybe they did! You know what burrowers our furry little pets can be. Good thinking, Corporal. Take your squad and search the base of the rock, look for any irregularities in the stone. My guess is that you'll find a tunnel somewhere." The captain watched as the trooper scurried off to gather his squad.

Although the covering rock had been dislodged, the placement of the tunnel opening was so cleaver that the corporal almost missed it. Had it not been for a tiny radio transmitter in a shiny, sto-metal boot, the captain would have had to go back to his commander with the tale of yet another dead end. But this time they hadn't escaped him. This time he knew that they were closing in on what might very well be the catch of his career.

Steera awoke with a terrible aching in her head. As she came back to her senses, she instinctively looked for Diell. He was still laying half-way under the table that had held their toxic feast. She was stretching out her arm to reach for him when the table abruptly moved.

"Always the big sister, aren't you?" Steera didn't have to look up to know who was speaking. "Well he's going to need a big sister now." Steera pulled herself up and slumped back into her chair. Seelar was sitting at the end of the table, a gas rifle lying on his lap. She noticed the pupils of his eyes. They had darkened along with the tone of his voice. "When the Ka Warriors get here you're both going to be taken back to camp and tried as traitors."

"How can you have come to this," she asked, still groggy. "There was a time when I would have gladly followed you anywhere, now you have to use drugs to force your will upon us. I should have listened to Diell and left you to rot back there in the bushes."

"But you didn't, did you? You let your sentimentality rule your logic, and I fear that may prove fatal."

"It was the katoc wasn't it?" Steera looked at Seelar with disgust. "That's why you were in such a hurry to get here. Without it you're a simpering little coward, like the one we found back in the bushes. You couldn't control us without your dose of priot courage."

Seelar's pupils were now jet-black. "I am the leader of the Faceer Ka! The master of the Ka Warriors! I control not only you, I control the fate of all Osstar, and I will not let weak-spirited, nonbelievers endanger my cause. The Stoma hadn't made any progress in finding us until you came. You stole the contents of the pouch so that I couldn't use it to establish my claim to Osstar. You foment rebellion and treachery within my own ranks. Now there is treason everywhere. It must stop—and it will stop!" Diell had come around and joined Steera at the table. Seelar pointed in Diell's direction. "You caused Corporal Diell to turn his back on the movement. But don't worry," he continued, "someday the monuments of the great Stoma masters that you and your Faceer lap-cats worship will be melted down to make statues of me."

Seelar lunged about the room, ranting and waving his gas rifle. As he raised it over his head in a triumphant gesture, it suddenly froze in mid-air. He gave it a strong tug to no avail. He tried to turn around and see what was hindering its movement, but he was frozen as well. He gave the rifle one last, strong tug. The rifle snapped down in front of him, pinning his arms to his side. His feet left the ground, and he felt his body being turned towards the entrance to the building. There, he beheld a sight that took away his fighting rage—a Stomari officer.

"Well, well, well ... so they're going to melt down our statues and erect one to you, eh?" Seelar was dumbfounded. He looked back at the table to see Diell and Steera also being held by Stomari troopers. There must have been fifteen or twenty of them in the building, with more entering.

"But, how ... where ...?" The words stuck in Seelar's throat.

"Can't believe that you've been captured by the big, stupid Stomari? Did you think that we were going to sit by and watch you furry little vermin take over our planet? This is the beginning of the end for your movement." The captain walked past a shocked Seelar directly to Steera. "Thank you for the assistance, little one," he said coyly.

"What do you mean? Let go of me!" Steera struggled to loosen the grip of the officer who was holding her.

"Why for leading us here. We might have never found this little hideout if it weren't for you. I will admit that it is cleverly hidden."

"Me?" The Stomari officer stroked Steera's dark, silky hair and then bent down in front of her.

"What are you doing ... let me go!" The captain unlaced her

boots, took them off and examined each one closely.

"Ahhh… here it is." He twisted the heel of the left boot and it popped open. His large fingers could barely pull the tiny transmitter out of the boot, but soon it was resting in his hand. "This is what we have been following since the Polar Station."

Steera recognized it. She had seen students at the academy use similar devices to track the movements of animals in the wild. She had never seen one this small. Things suddenly began to make sense to her, the attack on the Faceer Ka base, the spotter aircraft. She recalled how proud she was that Klut had cared enough for her to provide her with expensive boots. All she could think of now was Pire's admonition about the naive Veertal. Steera could see the look of disgust on Seelar's face. She hung her head to keep from having to look at Diell.

"Take them away, Lieutenant," the captain ordered. There was no urgency in his voice. He was looking forward to taking his prizes back to camp and presenting them to General Somar.

The lieutenant and two of his troopers pushed the three discouraged Faceer through the door. Diell looked at Steera and tears began to form in his eyes. He feared that this was the last time he would ever see her. Seelar moved along as if in a dream, still disbelieving that the Stomari could have captured the great leader of the Faceer Ka in his most secret of hiding places.

Steera could only think of Pire, and of how ashamed she was that she had been the instrument of the Stomari's greatest triumph. Only that, and just how much at this moment she hated the name of Klut.

CHAPTER 21

osh led Pire and Riatt deeper into the cave complex. The terrain sloped upward rather than down as Pire had expected. The passageway was dimly lit with oil lamps, and there were no inscriptions on the walls. They traveled single file, and silently. Every so often a shaft of light from the outside could be seen playing softly on the cavern walls.

After about twenty minutes of slow travel, they arrived at the entrance to another chamber. Inside, it was configured in the crude shape of a five-pointed star. At the tip of each point sat a Zerrit, squatting and motionless. In the center of the chamber was another five-pointed star, this one created by an arrangement of hundreds of rectangular stones. In the center of that star was a stone altar surrounded (except for a small path to the altar itself) by piles of vines, fruits and other objects. Sitting atop the altar stone was the object of all this adoration—a shiny, silver cylinder.

"Pardon the mess," Nosh said, breaking the long silence. "The Zerrits are passionate about their rituals." The walls of the chamber were covered with symbols from the cylinder. Pire noticed that it was considerably brighter in this chamber than any of the others. Oil lamps were placed high up the walls, but the light seemed softer, less yellow than that produced by the crude oil lamps. He could see that the cylinder itself was giving off light.

Nosh studied Pire's face. "Go ahead, you can look at it. They won't hurt you as long as I'm here." Nosh made a subtle hand motion to one of the Zerrit guards. Pire approached the cylinder and reached out to feel the smooth metal. The Zerrit's eyes followed his every move.

The symbols seemed exactly like those on the polar cylinder, even to the arrangement around the outside. The lid was still firmly in place. Pire wondered if Nosh had made any attempt to open it; certainly the Zerrits were incapable of it.

"No one is quite sure when they discovered it," Nosh said.

"They?"

"The Zerrits. It must have sat in these caverns for centuries, maybe eons. The rituals they developed are complex, obviously built up over a long period of time."

"How do you know that?"

"The Zerrits were performing these rituals when I was first brought here. This altar room is ancient."

"But the Zerrits seem to revere you almost the way they revere the cylinder. How do you explain that?"

"I see why Riatt has such an appreciation of your scientific abilities; you are indeed observant. It happened quite by accident. I used this altar room as my play area when I was just a child. I was drawn to the cylinder and loved to read the books Faeed would bring me by its soft light. One particular day, the Zerrits where holding one of their rituals. The position of Osstar was such that Zenos was almost directly overhead and Rebal was in full wane on the other side of the planet. The rays of Zenos broke through a hole in the top of the chamber and alit directly on the cylinder just as I was putting my hand on it to lift myself up. To all our amazement, the cylinder began to shake and make whirring noises as the rays of Zenos crossed it. The Zerrits immediately fell silent, and lay prostrate on their faces. They remained that way until I finally left the chamber. Ever since then, they have assumed that the cylinder and I are somehow connected."

"So, you are a relative of their god," Pire asked.

"Yes, I suppose to them I am, although that wasn't clear to me until I was much older. Faeed knew it immediately though and made a point of treating me with great deference from that time on. He reasoned that I would be better protected if revered as a god by the Zerrits."

"He was obviously right. Were the Zerrits surprised when the cylinder top opened?"

"It didn't open. I would have been disappointed in you, though, if you hadn't asked. At the time I was too young to understand what was happening, but three years later to the day it happened again to a lesser degree. This time I made the connection between the rays from Zenos and the actions of the cylinder. I began to suspect that the cylinder was hollow. I thought that if the rays fell at exactly the correct angle at exactly the proper spot on the cylinder that it might open. I was not confident enough of my position with the Zerrits to risk moving the cylinder to an area where Zenos would be more accessible. I was forced to make the necessary adjustments every three years on the day the light entered the chamber. It was an exercise in patience. On several occasions a storm obscured Zenos' light, and I made no progress, on others the effect was dramatic, but short lived. I have tried nine successive adjustments over the years. The last adjustment produced the greatest and most prolonged movement in the cylinder.

"When was the last adjustment?" Riatt asked, breaking his silence.

"Ah, Riatt ... always the impatient one," Nosh said. "I'm glad that you weren't in charge of this experiment or I fear the cylinder would be severely battered by now." Pire was impressed by the easy way Nosh admonished Riatt without the slightest hint of anger or condescension.

"I suppose that is why I have been denied access to this area until now," Riatt countered good-naturedly. "Now, how about answering the question, or do gods have to talk to mere mortals?"

Nosh brushed off Riatt's verbal jab. "The last adjustment was three years ago minus two days."

"So you're saying that in two days Zenos' rays will return to the chamber?" Pire was intrigued.

"Actually, one day and eighteen hours, unless Zenos has somehow changed its course in the sky."

"So that's why we saw the Zerrits gathering the fruits and vines; this will be their big celebration day."

"The biggest—and I hope it will be a celebration day for us as well. We have a few hours; I invite you both to dine with me in my chamber. The Zerrits will be making plenty of noise tonight, so rest will not come easily."

Pire, Riatt and Nosh exited the alter room the way that they had entered, and continued deeper into the cavern until they came to another chamber opening on the left side of the central passage-way. Two large Zerrits were positioned on either side of the entrance, but quickly stood aside as Nosh moved towards them. "My humble abode is yours," Nosh said and motioned for them to enter.

Nosh's living chamber was larger than the altar room, but with a slightly lower ceiling. Light was provided by oil lamps, but Pire noticed that there were several circular holes in various places around the room, about half way up the wall. Soft light was wafting like a pink mist through the two portals on the left side of the room. By the intensity and color, Pire concluded that it was the last, faint light from a waning Rebal. Given the configuration of the room, it was clear that it never received too much light from the outside, from either Rebal or Zenos.

It was also damp — very damp. As his eyes adjusted to the lower light level, Pire saw the reason for the dampness. At least one third of the room was comprised of a circular body of water, a pool more than 50 yards in diameter and several feet deep. At the edge of the pool was a dining table laid out in a manner that would accommo-date diners from either the pool side or the land side. On the table were food items of various descriptions, partly Faceer fare, partly Stoma fare and some that the Zerrits would prefer. In the center of the room were objects that Pire instantly recognized, the missing contents of the pouch — the items that Riatt had taken before Seelar had had a chance to see them.

Nosh motioned for his guests to take their places at the table. Pire and Riatt each sat on the landward, or Faceer side as it was called, leaving a space in-between for Nosh. Before they could get a conversation started, Nosh thrust his muscular frame into the pool, and swam up to join them on the water, or Stoma side.

"Don't look so surprised," he said jokingly, "this way of eating seems to come more naturally to me, although I am perfectly ca-pable of feeding from the Faceer side as well." Nosh poured Keera water for them all and began munching on Kodoos (small, shelled sea creatures that were a staple of the Stoma diet). Pire and Riatt watched as he dipped them into the water and then threw his head back gracefully to swallow them whole—a feat that would have left a Faceer gasping for air. After about ten mouthfuls, he spoke to Riatt. "Would you be so kind as to retrieve the pouch and bring it to the table?" Riatt complied, returned with the pouch and spilled its contents onto the table. "Is this all that you found at the polar station?"

"This is what we considered to be the important things. There were other objects: utensils, a metal-like cloth, and a light instrument that heated the metal of the cylinder without burning my skin." Nosh rolled the metal disc around in his hand.

"So you left the light instrument to give the Stomari something to mull over ... very cleaver."

"I'm having second thoughts about it now," Pire confessed. "It was so advanced that the Stoma must be thinking that it was Faceer in origin. But we did save the most important item."

"And which item would that be?" Nosh asked as if he already knew the answer.

"The book, of course, not even the Stomari can believe that this is anything but Faceer-like," Pire pointed to the book lying open on the table.

"You think it's Faceer, then?"

"Look at the feet. Don't you see the resemblance?"

"I see through different eyes than you, my friend, to me it is neither Faceer nor Stoma in nature."

"If not, then what could it be?" Riatt joined the discussion.

"I have my own theory on all of this. In their rush to establish an absolute claim to the planet, both sides may be ignoring an important possibility. The Stomari officer that helped you, Druk-tasis, realized what it was, and how important it is to the future of Osstar." Pire was surprised at the use of Druk's name. He couldn't recall having ever mentioned it. "I believe that none of these items originated on Osstar. I believe they came here from somewhere else."

"But from where?"

"Perhaps from another planet, a planet not unlike our own." Nosh's eyes swept back and forth over the disc. "That is why I disagree with you on what is the most important item you saved from the Stomari."

"But the book shows us the form of these beings, and could tell us much about who they were and what happened to them, provided we are able to decipher its symbols."

"If these beings did all of this by design, as I suspect they did, each cylinder would contain a puzzle and a clue. When a society became intellectually mature enough to discover that they were hollow, and how to open them, the puzzle could be solved and the mystery unraveled."

"Perhaps they were trying to share their advanced technology with us, and some unexpected tragedy struck?" Pire reasoned.

"Perhaps they were trying to send us a warning?" Nosh asked it in a matter-of-fact way, tossing down another Kodoo. "At any rate, it's a mystery. That is why I believe that the most important item you saved was not the book, but the disc. If I have interpreted the clues correctly, the disc will lead us to the last cylinder. Perhaps then we will have all the pieces to the puzzle. Hopefully, if the weather cooperates, we will know more tomorrow at Zenos rise."

"I pray to the Gods of Aldor, that it does," Riatt said. "I don't think that Osstar has three more years to wait."

"Nor do I, my friend. But for now we have time to think, and as long as Osstarians have time to think, there is hope." Riatt stared at Nosh. He watched a gentle smile begin to crease the corners of his mouth, and noted the subtle muscle contractions around his eyes. The smile grew very naturally out of his hybrid face, spreading across it as the first, soft rays of Zenos-light spread across the surface of the sea. "An abomination?" he thought. "How quickly we condemn the things we don't understand."

Nosh swam to the edge of the pool and exited with a graceful leap onto the floor of the chamber. He had had two additional beds prepared for Faceer. He motioned in their direction and started to leave with two Zerrits.

"I must preside over some of the festivities, and I'm afraid that you are not invited. I will have them come and get you tomorrow, when it is time. Until then, feel free to use whatever you desire in my chamber ... but I must ask you not to leave it." Pire and Riatt nodded in agreement and watched as Nosh exited the chamber.

After he had been gone a while, Pire took one of the oil lamps from its fixture on the wall and began to look around. He felt a bit like a spy, but Nosh's knew Faceer, he must have expected that they would go exploring. He came upon a large, wooden structure with two large doors. He opened them. Inside was a Faceer's idea of heaven. Books — hundreds of them — filled the shelves. Here were all the great Stoma philosophers, the ones who had set forth the principles of government and law that were still in effect. Here also were the great scientific writings of such Faceer legends as Leenar (the teacher of Tieel, the greatest mathematician of the era) and Tyyre, the father of modern biology. It was the collection of a true intellectual, but it wasn't only philosophy or science, there were copious amounts of poetry as well as medical and astronomical texts.

"How long would it take one to read all of that?" Riatt said startling Pire a bit as he spoke from over his shoulder.

"If he has read them all, then he has been very busy. I know of no Stoma, and only a few Faceer with this intense a thirst for knowledge."

"How old do you figure him to be?"

"That's a good question. He said that he'd been working on the cylinder since he was very young, and had made nine adjustments to its position since the first movement, so he must be about 35 to 38 years old."

"Amazing," Riatt said. "From his appearance, I would have guessed no more that 21 or 22 years."

Pire covered the harsh yellow flame with one hand and pushed the lamp farther into the wooden cabinet. In the center of the middle shelf was a small box carved from soft stone. It had a crystal top and sat on a base of soft, red cloth. Pire debated for a moment whether or not to open the box. Finally, his curiosity overcame his reluctance.

Inside, encased in a beautiful metal frame, was a photo of a lovely Faceer female. She was quite beautiful, smiling and with the dark flowing hair of the mountain Veertal draping her shoulder. The metal frame had been rubbed and polished until it had become worn in some places. It glistened like a fire on the face of Rebal when the lamp light washed over it.

Pire didn't have to guess as to the identity of the female — it was Nosh's mother. He could see a faint resemblance in the mouth and around the eyes. But it was familiar in other ways. The eyes staring back at him from the faded photo were those of his beloved Steera. Pire felt tears well up in his own eyes.

"Faeed must have smuggled in a picture of Nosh's mother," Pire said, regaining his composure.

"Do you think we should be doing this?" Riatt asked.

"We need to know more about our host," Pire answered, ennobling his snooping by labeling it research. Riatt looked over his shoulder and made no further protest. The light from the lamp illuminated several other metal and stone objects, finally falling on a large stone box with a wooden lid painted with strange black markings. Pire picked it up and opened it. What he saw inside sent an electrical wave done his spinal ridge that Riatt felt from almost a foot away. Pire slowly withdrew a piece of cloth from within it. It was a white cloth armband with a symbol embroidered on it. The symbol was a large red circle with a black center.

"Stomari!" Riatt blurted out. "You don't suppose ... I mean he couldn't ...."

Pire looked at him in disbelief. The words would not come. He took the cloth and replaced it, being careful to put the lid back on with the proper alignment of symbols. Both stood silently for a moment, trying to come up with a rational explanation for the armband.

"We can't jump to any conclusions," Pire said, nervously. "Perhaps a Zerrit found it and brought it to him, or maybe he found it on a Faceer Ka that had strayed too near the colony."

"In all the times that I visited him," Riatt said, "only once did I hear him mention the Stomari. It was always the Faceer Ka that worried him. Of course the Faceer Ka were close at hand. I don't recall any Stomari incursions ever penetrating this deeply into the jungle. But the nature of the attack on the compound, I wonder ...." Riatt didn't finish his sentence.

"Well, whatever the circumstance, it's certain that we have no where else to go, and I for one am more curious about the cylinder and the future of Osstar than I am about my own safety. My dear father always used to say 'faith was the only antidote for fear,' so I will honor him by keeping faith with Nosh." Riatt nodded in uneasy agreement. Both lay down on the beds provide for them and sought some rest, but rest would not come easily this night.

P ire's eyes opened to light filtering in through the openings on the opposite side of the chamber. By its reddish color and its intensity he could tell that it was Zenos light. Rebal had made its way to the opposite side of Osstar. He estimated that it would be directly overhead in four or five hours. He rose and made his way across the room to the table that still held an ample supply of food. He poured himself a draught of Keera water to help shake off the lingering effects of stasis, heard Riatt stirring across the room, and handed him a glass as he made his way to the table.

"How long were we out?"

"It looks like about nine or ten hours," Pire answered. "I've certainly caught up on my rest since the polar camp."

"Have you seen Nosh?"

"Not since you have. I think the Zerrits expect him to preside over the celebration.

"So what do we do now?"

"We wait," Pire replied. "There are hundreds of great books here. I suggest we relax and read until we are summoned."

Pire opened the chest again and removed an ancient volume of Tyyre's commentaries on the development of complex organisms. Riatt, to Pire's surprise, took out a book of Veertal poetry.

Pire tried to read, but his attention wandered. His gaze kept skipping back-and-forth between the book and the cave floor. The soft rays of Zenos light were casting half-moon shadows across the tiny craters that had been carved in the floor by eons of dripping moisture. The fluctuating light made the ground seem as if it were alive.

After about three hours, two Zerrits showed up and bade them follow. They were led to the altar chamber and seated in two small chairs to the side of the altar. Nosh was sitting in a large chair that had been placed beside the cylinder. The room, though packed with Zerrits, was completely silent. A large Zerrit was standing at ground level directly in front of the cylinder holding an armful of fruits and vines. Rays from Zenos were slicing through the hole in the ceiling of the chamber, nearing the bottom of the cylinder. Pire and Riatt could sense the intense level of anticipation, as the red shaft of light slowly began to climb the side of the cylinder. The Zerrits, as if on cue, broke into a low, throaty groaning noise. Nosh remained motionless. Momentarily, the light dimmed, but Nosh did not raise his gaze to the ceiling, or change his position one inch. The light abruptly brightened again as the cloud passed. The low moaning sound began to swell to a crescendo as the shaft of light reached the top of the cylinder. The Zerrits fell silent. A faint whirring noise diffused, whisper-like, throughout the chamber.

The sound vanished as abruptly as it had started. The light struck the cylinder at just the perfect spot, and the top slid open in one fluid motion. The Zerrits, kneeling on the floor, were hiding their faces in their hairy hands, overcome with the experience of having heard the voice of their God. In mass, they began to back out of the chamber.

Nosh turned his gaze in the direction of Pire and Riatt, signaling that he wanted them to remain where they were. As the last Zerrit exited the chamber, Nosh rose from his chair and walked toward the entrance. He stood for a short time, making sure that all the Zerrits had left the area. Satisfied that they had all gone, he hurried back to the altar and motioned for Pire and Riatt to join him. Together they approached the open top of the cylinder.

A strange reluctance gripped all three. "Expectations are disappointments in waiting," Pire said, quoting the words to an old song. He plucked up the courage to peer in. At the very top of the cylinder, was a metal disc that appeared to be identical to the one found in the Polar cylinder. Pire removed it carefully. The front of the disc was the same as the polar disc, but there were engravings on the back as well.

"Oh joy," Riatt said with mock enthusiasm, "a new puzzle from our friends." He took the disc from Pire's hands.

"Here, let me look at it. Remember that the great Faceer scientist needed the lowly soldier to help him decipher the first one." Riatt examined the disc. Instead of the familiar circles and intersecting lines of the first disc, the markings illustrated what appeared to be an object. He handed it back to Pire with an apologetic look.

"What's the matter, great cipher" Pire smiled at Riatt, "not as clear-cut as the first one?" Pire studied the shape of the apparatus carved with great skill on the smooth metal. Straight lines intersected the objects at various points, and under each line was a section of the symbols found on the outside of the disc. "Writings again," Pire mumbled. "I do wish that we could decipher the writings." Pire set the disc aside and again reached into the cylinder. This time he had to use both hands to retrieve four cone-shaped objects made of a soft, gray metallic substance. One of the cones was smaller than the others. It glowed with a fiery-bright orange light that seemed to hover in the air. The cones were surprisingly light for their size, but too large for Pire to hold them all. He kept the glowing one and tossed another to Nosh. Nosh caught it in mid flight. He raised it to eye level in order to get a better look.

"It's translucent," he said. He sat the cone in the center of his palm. As he ran his hand over the smooth, pointed end, a soft, clear light burst forth and filled the area around the altar. Pire sat the two other, larger cones on the altar, and followed Nosh's example, waving his hand over them. The entire chamber was suddenly awash in light

"It's amazing how the light fills the room, yet doesn't hurt my eyes," Riatt said.

"They're still perfectly cool to the touch," Pire added. "I wonder what the source of energy is, and I wonder why this cone has such a different kind of light?" He put the smaller cone on the altar with the rest of them. It was burning with an intense red/orange light.

"Whoever made these were thousand of years beyond us in technology," Nosh said admiringly. Pire moved two of the white light cones along with the orange cone to the far end of the altar, and used the remaining cone to provide illumination for further examination of the cylinder. He reached his hand deep into the interior and, after fumbling around for a second, came up with a second treasure—another book. This one was unlike the book found in the first cylinder. It was heavier, and had no illustration on the front, only symbols. Pire was disappointed.

"This seems to be a step backwards," he said dejectedly. "The first book had illustrations from which we could glean some information, this is just symbols." Pire reluctantly opened the book. The pages, made of the same flexible fabric as the first, felt a bit thicker. He ran his hand across the page. As his finger passed close to the first segment of symbols, something miraculous happened—the symbols lit up. They glowed with an orange light that was fainter, but otherwise identical to the light produced by the small cone. At the same time, a sound could be heard, seemingly coming from the page itself. Pire, Riatt and Nosh looked at each other in amazement. The sound was alien but unmistakable. It was a voice!

"This thing is trying to talk to us!" Pire exclaimed. He continued to move his fingers down the rows of symbols, just above the surface of the page and the voice changed as each segment of symbols glowed with the eerie orange light. When his finger lingered over a spot, the voice would repeat until Pire moved on. "Then these segments must represent words, words made up of letters just as in our language. This is a written text!"

"This may be the key we have been searching for," Riatt said with excitement, "a way to decipher the writing ... to find out what these beings are trying to tell us."

"But how can we know?" Pire said, frustrated. "Until we can associate the alien words with something that we understand, some physical object or some rule of language, we're no better off than we were. The first book had pictures connected to the words, but no way of discerning the sounds. This book has sounds associated with the words, but with no way of connecting them with the objects that they represent. These people were extremely clever, there must be a key somewhere, a way to connect symbols, sounds and images so that they can make sense to another species or another life form." Nosh's voice suddenly overtook that of the alien one coming from the book.

"Look! Look at the book!" Pire's finger had come to rest on one of the words on the page. A square had formed in the center of the opposite page. Inside it was the image of a small tree or bush ... clearly some type of living vegetation. The voice repeated the word "Orstral"

"Clever does not begin to describe these beings," Nosh said, reverently. Pire's finger continued down the page. On some of the word segments a square formed and an object appeared. The three immediately recognized birds and animals even though they were alien in form. Other objects were less clear, sometimes evoking another symbolic representation in the square rather than a picture. Pire theorized that they were parts of the sentence structure that couldn't be represented pictorially: conjunctions, verbs and the like. He knew that with study it should be possible to build a working vocabulary using the alien symbols and illustrations. It should be possible to translate the alien language into Osstarian.

Pire sat in silence, considering the enormity of this discovery. Nosh reached out and took the book from his hand. His long boney finger touched one of the words on a random page, and a large square immediately formed. In the square there appeared the image of a being encased in a white suit that covered his entire body. Cradled in his arm was a large globe-shaped head piece with what looked like a visor made of pure gallite. The being was smiling, or at least it appeared to Nosh to be a smile. His eyes were light blue in color rather than the yellow/gold and green of the Faceer, or the blue/black of the Stoma. His mouth contained a full set of white teeth, each one differentiated from the other ... more like the teeth of Stoma than the boney, enameled teeth plates of the Faceer, "Drignafall" the voice repeated. Pire and Riatt had joined Nosh, trying to look at the picture over his shoulder.

"It looks happy," Riatt said. "If that's what happy looks like to these beings."

"It does look happy," Pire concurred. "I think that may be a hopeful sign."

Nosh continued to study the alien face. "I suppose. But with all its accomplishments, its knowledge, where is it now?" Nosh picked up the remaining light cones, put them on top of the disc and then put the disc on top of the book. He handed the small cone to Pire who stuck it in his pocket. "We will go back to my chamber and study this further. We must close the cylinder so that the Zerrits can't see that it is hollow and think that part of their god is missing."

Pire slid the top of the cylinder back into its closed position, and followed his two friends out of the chamber. The corridor, harsh and foreboding on the trip in, took on a kind of stark beauty in the soft light of the alien cones. They reached Nosh's chamber. He sat the cones in three separate places around it in a manner that lit the entire area. For several hours they discussed the contents of the cylinder and the nature of the beings that had created it. Finally, Nosh rose.

"Please excuse me. I must go and be with the Zerrit leader for a while. I saw the look on his face as the cylinder opened and he will be in quite a state by now. As much as they revere me, they revere the cylinder even more. I will have to reassure him that all is well with both of their gods." Nosh left the room to Pire and Riatt.

Riatt had fashioned himself a small hammock from the priot vines that lay almost everywhere in the chamber, and took the metal disc with him for further study. Pire was wearying of the damp confines of the cave. He longed to watch the waning of Zenos and smell the night air at staddich.

Without thinking of the possible consequence, he took the book and one of the light cones and made his way out of Nosh's chamber and down the length of the long corridor. The trip was much easier now that he had the light from the cone to show him the twists and turns of the passageway. He passed a few Zerrits en route who looked more puzzled at the light than surprised at seeing a Faceer in their midst.

At last he reached the cave entrance. He exited, turned to his right and climbed up the rocky face of the mountain. Small fires from the ruined Faceer Ka camp were still visible in the distant jungle. Near the top of the peak, he sat down and opened the book. He turned to a page toward the back of the book and let his finger fall on one of the words. True to its makers' design, a square formed on the opposite page while a strong, melodic voice spoke what Pire heard as DIEES STOFFFOM GIANNIA. A young face appeared in the square. The being was different from the one that Nosh had conjured up ... the body lines gentler, the face softer. If it had been the image of a Faceer it would surely be a Veertal female.

The thought caused him to put down the book and rest his head on his knees. He looked out across the vast expanse of jungle and his heart ached. His mind wondered back to the laboratory at the institute, and to his cozy house in the hills. Out across the rocky crags, the gentle staddich breeze was turning every branch and vine into a waltzing phantom. In the distance, a jungle bird called to its mate. It was a sound that he had heard before with a slight variation in pitch. It sounded like Steera's voice. He wondered if he would ever see her or his home again.

CHAPTER 22

Thick, stubby fingers grasped the paper spewing forth from the top of the telestrator machine and ripped it free. Klut stood staring at the top of the page.

COMMUNIQUÉ:
OSSTARIAN DEFENSE FORCES — ALL SECTORS
TO: HIGH COMMAND
**** RESTRICTED ACCESS****
***************HIGHEST PRIORITY***************

(SUMMARY)

SOUTHERN ISLANDS:

Substantial disruption of industrial activity due to incidents of sabotage ... Estimated at least fifteen independent cells of Faceer Ka operating from highlands of Dosomiel ... Three divisions of Stomari troops actively engaged on Donait ... Estimate 30 to 40% reduction in industrial output, 60% reduction in munitions output.

NORTHERN ISLANDS:

85 to 90% control maintained ... Cooperation from local Faceer village councils ... Some pockets of resistance forming in far northern areas of Lazos.

UPPER MIDLANDS:

Heavy fighting Layard Mountain area ... Reports of Faceer Ka terror attacks against loyal Faceer ... Two to four units of Faceer Ka engaging forces south of Strail pass ... One Faceer Ka unit reported to have left island in ships originating in equatorial region ... Five Stomari divisions actively engaged with two Regular Stoma divisions in support ... Stoma security forces aided by local Faceer ... Report of significant defections from Faceer Ka troops ... Joint Faceer/Stoma governing council formed.

LOWER MIDLANDS:
Sporadic fighting ... Acts of sabotage against power grid ... Forty lost (27 Stoma, 13 Faceer) at Stoma research facility at Croll due to suicide bombing attack.

CIRCULAR CONTINENT
Three islands in Faceer Ka control ... Heavy fighting on the main Island of Mannot ... Faceer Ka control all of the mountain areas, and are making inroads in the central area ... Stoma regulars cut off and surrounded in Capital, Seerot ... All local Faceer councils cooperating with enemy .... Without Reinforcements, Estimate complete Faceer Ka control in 15 to 20 days.

EQUATORIAL REGION:
Main Faceer Ka camp destroyed by two divisions of Stomari shock troops ... Heavy fighting and casualties ... Three top-level Faceer Ka captured and taken to Central Command Headquarters in Upper Midlands ... Faceer Ka in retreat toward mountains ... Stomari in pursuit.

***************END COMMUNIQUÉ***************

Klut let the report slip from his hand into the rubbish chute that led directly to the incinerator. It was not what he had hoped to read. He had hoped by now that the insurrection would be well under control. It was obvious that he and his security advisors had underestimated the strength and organization of their adversaries. Still, there were some encouraging signs in the report. Wide-spread support of the Faceer Ka had materialized only on the Circular Continent, which had long been a hot-bed of Faceer independence. Elsewhere, the insurgency wasn't having the effect on the average Faceer that the rebels had hoped. In fact, there was some evidence to the contrary. The reported murder of an innocent Faceer couple in the Layard Mountains was producing a backlash in that area. Local Faceer councils were cooperating with Stoma security forces,

and more significantly, some thirty Faceer Ka soldiers had turned
themselves in to the local authorities, asking for political asylum.

Klut disliked the idea of cooperation with local Faceer councils.
He had not interfered when it was proposed, but he knew that it
was the first step toward the sharing of power on Osstar, a concept that went against the very soul of the Stomari movement. But,
it was a delicate game that he was playing and he knew it. First,
the insurrection had to be quelled. He and his Stomari associates
couldn't risk alienating any of the more moderate Stoma houses
until overall Stoma dominance had been solidified. He had to be
sure that when negotiations for peace came, the Stomari were in
position to be the negotiators for all the Stoma houses.

There was only one thing that could hinder his plan—the mysterious cylinder and its contents. They had to be secured at all costs.

T he fighting between Faceer Ka and Stoma troops had spread
      northward, as far as the Layard Mountains (only 100 miles
      southeast of Central Headquarters). There had been a dra-
matic increase in security at the central government complex in
Prass, but on this day the activity was even more intense. The main
corridor of the command building had been made off-limits to all
but authorized personnel. Identification was being checked and re-
checked, even for senior officers.

At mid-Rebal two armored vehicles pulled up and a solid line
of Stomari shock troops shielded the arrivals from view. Druk had
returned from his respite in the mountains, but had not yet been
reassigned to duty. In fact, his intention was to try and stall any re-
assignment. He was surprised when no effort was made by the top
Stomari staff to bring their new "hero" back into active duty. Perhaps word of his trip to Romass had gotten out. He had taken great
pains to see that his trail was covered, even going to the extent of
booking passage on a sea transport to the Northern Islands as a
diversion. Still, if not enthusiastic about a new assignment, Druk-
tasis was curious about the new arrivals at headquarters, and knew
whom he could ask to find out.

Making his way down a side corridor, he found the office of Tomar Leet, head of custodial services for the entire complex. Druk-tasis stuck his head around the door frame to Leet's office and looked in. The old Faceer was right where Druk expected him.

"Come in, Druk-tasis." The gentle old voice made it sound as if Leet was singing the words. "I suppose you want to know what's going on." Leet was sitting with his feet up on his too-large-for-a-Faceer desk, carving the image of a Bajan stallion from a small piece of podwood. Druk was struck by the detail of the carving.

"You don't waste words do you, my old friend."

"At my age, time is an enemy not an ally, it is wise not to waste it," He sat the finished image of the horse on his desk beside at least ten others.

"Well, since you've done away with the need for idle conversation, I will ask straight out if you know who was brought to the complex today."

"If I know!" Leet said incredulously. "Who else would know if not Tomar Leet?" Druk shook his head and smiled. "What I hear — and that's all it is mind you, hearsay — is that it was three of the most dangerous, vile and vicious Faceer that ever sat on a Stoma lap. They were bound in chains for fear that they would break free and lay waste to the entire compound." Leet was unable to keep from laughing at his own description. Druk joined him. He reached into his desk and produced a small pipe that had been hastily hidden. It was still lit. He resumed his puffing. A large volume of cream-colored smoke formed a cloud around his head and then drifted toward the ceiling.

"Any idea of where they were from?"

"Some say they were taken in the battle at the Faceer Ka's equatorial compound. Some say they are defectors from the massacre at Romass."

"Romass!" Druk-tasis felt his heart pound in his chest.

"Yes ... terrible thing," Leet continued, noting Druk-tasis' obvious agitation, "Faceer killing Faceer, what a state we've come to. In my day, we knew who we were and what our place was. It seems now that these young calves want to run everything, want to ..."

"Yes, yes," Druk interrupted, "but what of the massacre? What happened? Who was killed?"

"A lot of beings were killed ... Faceer Ka, local villagers. It was a right awful mess. I thought everyone had heard about it. The news broadcasts sure made a big deal of it. They tried to burn the whole village down with everyone in it."

"Who tried ... why?" A knot was growing in the pit of Druk's stomach.

"The Faceer Ka accused two of the locals of harboring Stomari. They admitted only that they had had a visit from their adopted son who just happened to be a Stomari security officer—a Stomari officer, can you imagine that?"

Leet continued to talk, but Druk-tasis wasn't hearing anything. He slumped into a Faceer-sized chair next to Leet's desk and struggled to maintain his composure. He didn't have to hear the rest of the story. His selfishness, his need to get away from the spotlight, had cost the lives of the two beings that he had loved most. He was devastated.

Through his tears, Druk could see Nidire's face as plainly as if he were standing in front of him. He thought of those happy days of his childhood, climbing the face of the Great Snowy Mountain with his father and best friend. Higher and higher they would go, and Nidire would ask, "Can you see the Gods yet?" Druk-tasis would gaze skyward. The clouds would billow and shift, forming the images of the spirits that live inside the mind of a child. Nidire would then ask, "How close must we come before they can see if we are Stoma or Faceer?"

Druk understood, perhaps for the first time, what he had been saying.

"Are you quite all right?" Leet's voice brought Druk back to the present.

"Yes. I must have been thinking about something else." There was nothing he could do for his lost Faceer family, but there were Faceer here, in this complex, that he might be able to save.

"Well, don't let my long story distract you."

"No ... please, I would like to know who they brought in."

"As I said, many think they are Faceer Ka defectors from the Romass massacre."

"And you ... what do you think?"

"I think they are captives from the equatorial compound – the leaders of the Faceer Ka."

"And what makes you think that?"

"There are three of them, and one is a Veertal female. I have overheard Klut himself talking of a Veertal female in very hushed tones."

"Do you know where they are being held?" Leet looked at Druk-tasis for a moment, not knowing whether it was safe for him to answer the question. "Don't worry, my old friend," Druk said, "I will hold our conversation confidential." Leet spoke in a whisper, almost apologetically.

"I'm sorry to hesitate. Things are becoming so complicated and confused that I sometimes forget who is friend and who is foe."

"We're all having that problem of late. But with all that we have shared in the past, if I'm not a friend, then you have no friends left." Druk used the term "sunar" for friend, evoking the mythical friendship between two ancient Stoma heroes. Leet smiled and put his hand on Druk's arm.

"Security wants everyone to think that they are being held in the central corridor, but they are in separate rooms in the lower level of the communications building."

"I assume that you have a plan," he said, knowing that Leet surely did.

"I'll concoct something," Leet replied and winked.

Druk-tasis stood for a moment in complete silence. "I will say many prayers for them, as I know you will."

Leet looked confused. Druk exited the office. Suddenly, like a bolt from Mount Sagar, it came to him. "Lirea and Nidire! Oh Gods of all the winds, what an idiot I've been." Leet hurriedly put his Bajan horses in the drawer to his desk and picked up the receiver to the radio-phone.

"This is Leet," he said to the party on the other end. "We must leave – now." He started to exit the room but paused for a moment.

Reopening the main drawer to his desk, he removed one of the carved horses and shoved it into his pocket. He wasn't sure when or if he'd be back.

CHAPTER 23

The communications building was linked to the main building by a short hallway on the lower level. Druk decided not to take the main stairway. He wanted to avoid the constant traffic that was the norm these days at headquarters, so he found his way to the rear stairwell that served as a maintenance employee entrance. His new found fame (compliments of the propaganda ministry) had made him a very recognizable figure around Central Headquarters, and he was greeted with deference by the few Stoma that he did encounter.

After a trek of a hundred yards or so, he came to the short hallway that led to the lower level of the communications building. There was no traffic, which puzzled him. He had expected a guard at the end of the hallway; instead the way was completely clear. About half-way down the corridor on the left side, he noticed three separate doors approximately ten yards apart, far enough apart that communication between those inside would be impossible. Druk now understood why the Stomari had selected this area. "The Faceer might be the masters of technology," he thought, "but the Stoma knew security." On the right side, directly across from the center door, another long corridor led toward the center of the building.

He wasn't quite sure what to do next. He couldn't tell which room held which captive. He tried to think of a way to contact those inside without drawing too much attention to his presence. Then he remembered something—Steera was Veertal. Although he couldn't remember her village of origin, he did remember that she was a mountain Veertal. A tune started lilting through his head. It was a song that he had learned as a child in Romass ... a Faceer children's song that was common among the Veertal of the Layard Mountains. Perhaps it was common among all Veertal. He moved to the closest door, and started humming the song as softly as he could. The response was immediate.

"Who is it?" a hushed female voice spoke from inside.

"A friend," Druk-tasis replied.

"You're Stoma. I haven't had too many Stoma friends of late."

"How many Stoma do you know that can hum the 'Bryatt-Ta?'"

"Impressive, but right now I'm not inclined to give my trust that easily, even if you are a decent singer ... for a Stoma." The sarcasm erased any further doubt from Druk-tasis' mind.

"Ah, that Veertal wit, I'm glad to see that your ordeal hasn't dampened your spirits too much, Steera."

"How do you know my name?"

"You're one of three Faceer scientists I encountered at the North Pole." There was a momentary pause.

"Druk-tasis!"

"We do seem to have a way of finding each other, don't we?"

"But how....where...?" Steera stopped in mid-sentence. It could be a ruse to get her to talk. The naïve Faceer scientist had been left behind at the equatorial camp. "If you are who you say you are, then you'll remember what I was wearing the last time you saw me."

"It is wise to be cautious in these times. If I recall, you had on a Kaba-fur parka."

"Very clever, but of course anyone who didn't want to freeze to death at the North Polar Region had on some sort of parka, and Kaba-fur is certainly the most prevalent. I need something more specific."

"Well, I do remember one other thing. It was boots — shiny, sto-metal boots." Steera was relieved.

"All my senses were telling me it was you, Druk-tasis; I hope that you can pardon my mistrust. How did you get here?"

"It's a long tale, and now is not the time for its telling. I'm not sure how long I have. The hallway is deserted, which seems very odd to me. Have you been interrogated yet? Who is with you?"

"Diell, myself and Seelar."

"Seelar!" That treacherous little lothar. He has more lives than an ice worm."

"We were captured at Seelar's secret camp in the equatorial region. It seems that a tiny radio transmitter had been implanted in the heel of my shiny new boots."

"Implanted ... by whom?"

"By the only one who could have done it ... my great benefactor, Klut-Prime."

"Then it's true. Klut-takit has been in on this from the beginning. It confirms that the air transport accident that killed the old Klut was arranged. I had suspected Takir, but not necessarily Klut. Tell me, did you learn anything at the equatorial camp?"

"We learned much," Steera replied. "We learned that the Faceer Ka were far more numerous and well organized than first thought. We learned that their ferocity was maintained by daily doses of ka-toc, and that they were continuing to recruit young Faceer to their cause. And we learned that there were Faceer, even some among the Faceer Ka, who were becoming disenchanted by the message of hatred and violence."

"But the cylinder and its contents ... what of it?"

"With the help of a sympathetic Faceer Ka named Riatt, we solved the riddle of the metal disc."

"The riddle?"

"Yes, the markings on the disc were more than just decoration; they were a map of the planet. There was a mark — a small circle — where we found the first cylinder in the North Polar Region."

"Amazing!" Druk muttered.

"That's not the truly amazing part," Steera was talking in a continuous stream of words, trying to hurry. "The truly amazing thing is that there were two more small circles on the disc, one in the Equatorial Region, and another in the South Polar Region."

"**Two** more cylinders!"

"It appears so. The second circle seemed to coincide with a large Zerrit Ape colony not far from the Faceer Ka compound where Pire, Diell and I were being held.

"What of Pire?"

The words stuck in Steera's throat for a moment. "I don't know.

He was being taken to a meeting of the Faceer Ka council when the attack came. I can only pray to the gods that he is safe."

Druk knew now what he must do. If Pire had escaped the raid he had an idea of where and with whom he might be.

"I pray for him as well," Druk said solemnly. "But I have faith that he is all right. Since you have told me what you know, I will tell you something that I hadn't yet shared with you. A little over a year ago, just before I was assigned to security for the Polar Station, I was taken in great secrecy to a small village on the southern coast of the Upper Midlands. There I met a most extraordinary being, a Seeyard. His name was Nosh, and he was raised in a colony of Zerrits in the highlands of the Equatorial Region.

The Zerrits in this colony worshipped an ancient object—a metal cylinder. Nosh told me that he believed the cylinder to be the product of an alien technology, at least alien to our recorded history. We spent three days talking of the cylinder, of the fate of the beings that might have created it, and about the future of our planet. He told me of the Faceer Ka encampment and of an officer named Riatt, whom he had taken into his confidence. It was at that meeting that we decided to form an alliance—a pact to prevent civil war on Osstar. I have kept in contact with Nosh since the discovery of the Polar cylinder through a friend at central headquarters, and my guess is that Pire and Riatt are with him now. It is time that I join them. If Klut is part of the Stomari conspiracy it assures that Takir is as well. With two of the most powerful Stoma houses on Osstar running the movement, it won't be long until the government itself is completely under Stomari control and with it the military. If the violence continues to escalate, Faceer and Stoma will be forced to take sides in a civil war, and that I fear would be the end for any hope of peace on Osstar. These cylinders, if they are what we think they are, may provide us with a way of slowing the process. We must take what we learn from them to the High Council while it still has a semblance of independence."

"An interesting concept," a deep voice echoed through the corridor, "but I doubt that you will be able to carry it out—traitor!" Druk-tasis didn't need to see the speaker to know his identity. He recognized the voice of Klut-takit. "How fortunate it is that we picked the same moment to visit with our favorite Veertal." Klut moved toward the guard who was restraining Druk-tasis, "Not so roughly, you're dealing with a Stomari hero. We can't have the hard work of our Propaganda Ministry go for nothing." He stood staring into Druk's face. "No, my friend, I won't make you a martyr to your misguided cause. I don't have the gift of vision that some of your Faceer friends have, but I see a nasty accident in your future. This time we will finish a job that should have been finished years ago. Take him away." The two guards pushed Druk-tasis down the interior corridor from where they had emerged. "Put his coat around him," Klut commanded, "no one must see his restraints."

"Druk!" Steera yelled after him, but the guards had already taken him away. "You'd better not harm him, or you'll have to answer to the High Council," she snarled at Klut.

"I am the High Council, my dear, or soon will be. But I'm surprised at such a tone from you, and after all the effort I put into rescuing you from those Faceer Ka criminals."

"You used me! You used me to betray my own people!"

"Your own people! Are you claiming those fanatics as your own? I knew that you would want to help your government find and neutralize these criminal elements, so I arranged a little Stoma technology to help us. I didn't inform you so that if the transmitter were discovered, you could honestly claim to have known nothing about it. You see, it was all to protect my little one."

"Save the charm for your Faceer retainers, Nye-Nye," Steera gnawed on the nick-name a moment before she spat it out. "I'm not the little Veertal that used to sit on your lap by the feeding pool. My eyes have been opened in the last few months. I know who you are now, and I know what you and your Stomari friends want to do with troublesome Faceer. "

"That's a shame, little one, because it means that you must share their fate. We raised you as our own and this is the thanks that we get. Do you remember when I used to take you with me on my Bajan? I would ride all the way down to the sea shore with you on my lap." Klut paused. A wave of nostalgia unexpectedly swept over him, stronger than he would ever have imagined possible. Steera felt it too. There was no denying that they had held each other in great affection in those simpler days. "What happened?" Klut's tone softened. He looked at Steera through the observation port in the door. He inserted the key and opened it. "How did it come to this?"

Steera stood looking into the face of the Stoma she had once loved above all Stoma. She could find no hatred in her heart for him. She saw only the generous master who had helped raise her. "I grew up."

Klut watched the yellows, greens and gold's dance across the pupils in Steera's eyes and wondered for a moment if he had embarked on too radical a course. Perhaps it might be possible to come to some sort of understanding with these dangerous but fascinating creatures. A loud banging interrupted his thoughts.

"Let me out!" a high pitched Faceer voice was yelling. "I demand a hearing in front of a council of law. I am a free citizen of Osstar!"

Klut's mood shifted. "Take that squealing little cave rat to the interrogation chamber." He turned back to Steera. His black eyes were hard and compassionless. "I will see to it that you are well treated," he said with no emotion. As he turned to leave, he looked back over his shoulder one last time at his former companion. "Be well," he said and hurried off to oversee the interrogation.

The staddich had passed and Zenos' rays were rapidly warming the morning air. Pire awoke to find his body rolled in a ball, stuffed under a small outcropping of rock. He had spent the night listening to the call of the jungle birds. He was still amazed at the depth of his fatigue from long weeks in strange places.

He stretched his stiff limbs and looked out across the fresh face of the mountain. There seemed to be a lot of activity far below him. Zerrits were gathering excitedly at the opening to the cave, flailing their arms and grunting in the direction of a small troop of their comrades who were making their way up the slope. Pire's protective inner lenses deployed against the increasing harshness of Zenos' light. Rebal, lurking on the Eastern horizon, would soon join it in the sky. He could see that the troop's progress was hampered by a burden they were carrying—a vine hammock. They had captured something. Pire scrambled down the steep side of the mountain trying to keep his balance. He thought how easy it would be for a seasoned mountaineer like Steera. As he arrived at the mouth of the cave, he could see the Zerrits beginning to gather around a large figure at the entrance. Pire made his way through the hairy throng and joined Riatt, who was standing with Nosh.

"What's happening?" He asked Riatt.

"I'm not sure. The Zerrits have found something."

"Or someone," Pire countered. "I've seen that carrying device from the inside."

The main body of the troop had reached the cave opening, and Nosh moved to meet them. They laid the vine hammock at Nosh's feet and moved back. Pire looked for any signs of movement in the hammock, but could see none. Nosh bent over and pulled the top of the hammock apart. As the two sides of the structure fell to the ground, Riatt let out a gasp.

"Storm Troopers!"

Pire eased forward to get a better look. Lying motionless in the center of the hammock was the body of a Stomari Storm Trooper. Nosh seemed to be feeling the body for signs of life. After a moment he motioned for two of the Zerrits to take it inside the cave. He started after them then turned to Pire and Riatt.

"You had better come with me; we need to discuss contingencies." There was a serious tone in Nosh's voice. Inside the cave, Nosh had the Zerrits place the body in a small alcove and he bade them leave. He motioned for Pire and Riatt to come closer as he effortlessly lifted the body and sat it against the wall of the cave. He made a more methodical examination of the unfortunate trooper. "Broken neck, third spinal partition." His tone was cold and clinical.

"How do you suppose it happened?"

"I'd say that he came too close to us for the Zerrits' comfort. The

Zerrits protect their gods pretty well."

"You mean you and the cylinder?"

"I mean the three of us and the cylinder," Nosh replied. "You were with me at the ceremony, which tells them that we are family. They look upon you as they did Faeed, as visiting gods, otherwise they would have never let you leave the cavern last evening. They can accept Faceer as my kin, but they are much more wary with Stoma."

"That's quite obvious," Riatt retorted as he studied the body of the dead trooper, "but what does this mean?"

"It could mean any of several things," Nosh answered. "It could mean that the Stomari are mopping up scattered pockets of Faceer Ka resistance, it could simply mean that the trooper went too far up the mountain in search of food or water, or ... " Riatt finished the sentence for Nosh.

"... It could mean that the Stomari are still searching for something. What do we do now?"

"I have always known that this day would come." Nosh leaned over and raised the dead trooper's arm. On his left sleeve was an armband, a large red circle with a black center. He slid it off the trooper's arm and held it in his hand, staring at it as if he were contemplating some action. Blood coursed through Pire's temples and the muscles in Riatt's jaw began to tighten. Pire felt a warning flash of energy from Riatt as Nosh turned the armband over in his hand. Nosh also sensed the fear coming from both Faceer, and a wry smile crossed his face. "Faceer," he said coolly. "You can always count on their curiosity. I sensed a bit of panic in you two when I took this off that unfortunate creature. Are you no longer sure of my allegiance?"

"No ... no," Pire answered nervously. "Why would we think anything like that?"

"Well, let me think," Nosh replied. "Two Faceer, left alone in a room full of books, gadgets and other treasures. You wouldn't by chance have gone through my personal things as well—now would you?"

"No ... I mean we ... well ..."

" ... And perhaps found an armband like this one?"

"We ... I mean, I ..."

" ... And assumed that it was mine?"

 "Yes," Pire said reluctantly. We were only trying to find out more about you."

"Understandable," Nosh replied to the surprise of both Faceer. "But can you see how easy it has become to believe the worst about each other ... especially about those who are different from us. Any doubt sown, even the smallest of doubts, can turn us against one another. If we are to save our beloved planet, we will have to stop fearing and begin trusting. But that is not only my belief, it is also the belief of the Stoma who gave me his Stomari armband as a pledge of loyalty a year ago—your friend, Druk-tasis." Pire and Riatt suddenly felt very foolish and very guilty. "Don't be too hard on yourselves." Nosh noted their embarrassment. "To learn to trust, one must also learn to forgive. I knew that it was Druk-tasis that helped you at the Polar station, and you were to have been brought to me by his allies had not the Faceer Ka provided other transportation."

"So much is happening so quickly. You have met with Druk-tasis?"

"Once, in a village on the coast of the Upper Midlands. The meeting was arranged by an old family friend who works at the Central Government Complex, and whose name we do not bandy about foolishly. It was he who also forwarded reports from Druk-tasis on your activities at the Polar station."

"Why does it seem that everyone knows what's going on in my life except me?" Pire sighed. "You said we would discuss contingencies, what do you think we should do?"

"Riatt brought me the artifacts from the Polar cylinder purloined from you while you were being prepared for interrogation at the Faceer Ka camp. I immediately recognized that two of the circles represented locations on Osstar where cylinders had been found. The third circle I deduced as the resting place of a third cylinder. The location seems very near a series of caverns or, in this case, ice caves that I have heard of in the Southern Polar Region. The caves are known to Faceer and Stoma mainly in legend, since only sporadic attempts have been made to map or explore the Southern Polar Region, but I have spoken with a Stoma who has been there."

"Aldor," Pire interrupted.

"Yes, I believe that the legends say that it is where the weather is made."

"You mean the caverns actually exist! I thought it was just a myth."

"Many myths have their basis in reality, my friend, as the cylinders are proving. Your logical Faceer brain has trouble with the conflict between Stoma legends and scientific facts. The mixing of the two cultures on our planet has created a super-culture that is partly shared and partly unique to each species."

Pire had never really thought much about what Nosh was saying, but he knew that it was true. The Faceer had appropriated a great deal of the Stoma's legends and most of their deities, and molded them to their more practical way of thinking. Nosh's understanding of the two cultures, given his long isolation, amazed him.

"So, I assume that I will need to try and find another Kaba-fur parka somewhere," Pire said wryly.

"You are wise, my friend, but I am a bit ahead of you. I began making arrangements for supplies and transportation immediately after I saw the disc. I have been in communication with my friend since that time. The arrival of our unfortunate friend here simply adds an element of urgency to my preparations. I will put the Zerrits on high alert for any more wandering Stomari. We must hurry our efforts to depart. If this is simply a lost soldier we may have time, but if he is an advance scout his presence will be immediately missed. We must assume the latter and try to depart as soon as possible. Your personal supplies will be placed in your chambers tonight, please try and have everything in order for a departure sometime tomorrow around mid-Rebal." Nosh left the alcove in haste, leaving the body of the Stomari trooper to the Zerrits. Pire and Riatt made their way back to their chamber to await the arrival of the supplies that would sustain them on the next leg of their increasingly arduous journey.

The young Faceer entered the building the same way she had for over two years, taking the maintenance workers entrance near the South wall. Her slender frame was covered by a jacket of soft cammile cloth. There were no smiles to co-workers as she walked, not even a nod to the Stoma guard in the communications building corridor. For the young Faceer cleaner everyone knew as Liira, this was to be her last day on Osstar.

Steera had heard no sound coming from the other rooms since they had taken Seelar away. She worried about Diell. The thickness of the walls of her holding cell prohibited her from trying to rouse him without alerting the entire floor, but she thought she sensed a presence on the other side of the wall.

She heard the sound of footsteps on the stone floor of the hallway and knew instantly that they were Stoma and not Faceer. The door to her holding cell flew open and three large Stomari troopers, one officer of the rank of major and two enlisted soldiers, stomped in.

"So, this is the favorite of the great Klut-Prime?" the officer snarled. "Then you won't mind giving us some information that will help your benefactor save the planet from the Faceer rebels."

"I don't think I know anything that would be of any value to you." Steera tried to calm herself.

"Oh, really! You let me be the judge of that. You were with the team of Faceer scientists that opened a certain cylindrical object found at the North Polar Station, were you not?"

"I was at the station, yes."

"Rumors abound that what was found by the Stoma officials may not have been all of the contents. Is that true?"

"Yes, that is true." The Stomari officer nearly leapt with excitement at Steera's admission. "It is true that those rumors abound, Steera continued." The officer resumed his cool demeanor.

"I was hoping that we could do this in a civilized manner," he continued, "but it seems that the time for civility with you traitors is at an end." The officer motioned to the two soldiers. They left the room for a moment and returned with a dazed Diell suspended limply between them like a piece of taanar meat on a drying pole. Steera's heart nearly broke when she saw him. They had put an object in his mouth and sealed it shut with strips of cloth. She realized why he had been silent in the next room. "My instructions from Klut were not to injure you in any way, but he didn't say anything about this one."

The officer grabbed Diell by his silky, tan Somacee top-hair and bent his head back so Steera could get a good look at him. Tears came to her eyes. "So, let me begin again. Were there objects missing from the cylinder when we opened it?" Steera hesitated. The guards each took one of Diell's hands and wrapped a piece of metal wire around the thumb. "... I'm waiting." Steera didn't know what to do. She remembered her pledge to Pire and Riatt, but was terrified of what might happen to Diell. She said nothing. The officer nodded to the soldiers and they began to tighten the wires. Diell grimaced in pain, but the gag stifled his cries. Steera could feel the waves of pain pouring from him.

"Stop!"

"First he will feel discomfort, which will then turn to excruciating pain. I believe that he is entering that phase as I speak. If I continue, the thumbs will eventually come off. We will continue unless you talk to us freely ... and mind you, we know when you are lying. His fate is in your hands."

"What do you want to know?" she said, dejectedly.

"I knew that you would come to your senses. What were the objects stolen from the cylinder?" Steera hesitated. Again she saw the tendons on the soldiers hands begin to tighten.

"A book." She tried to recall the words as they left her mouth.

"What sort of book?"

"I'm not sure."

"Come now, an esteemed graduate of the Dynat Academy with a degree in linguistics and you don't know what type of book?"

The officer had been well prepared by Klut.

"It was unlike anything I had ever seen," she answered, reluctantly. On the other side of the wall, Klut-takit turned up the level of the microphone that had been hidden in the holding cell and strained to hear.

"Was it Faceer or Stoma in origin?" The officer quickened the pace of the questioning to prevent Steera from qualifying her answers.

"It was neither." Klut twisted the dials of the amplifier so hard that they nearly broke off in his hand. Had he heard what he thought he had heard?

"How could it have been neither?"

"I don't know, but the illustrations were not like anything we had ever seen in any of the historical finds on Osstar."

"What else did you find ... and I warn you, leave nothing out or your friend will suffer."

"Not much else really, some vials of a grey powder, something that must have decayed over time in the cylinder."

"And that was all, a book and some dust in a bowl?" The officer put his hand on Diell's head, looked at him for a moment and then looked back at Steera. "Are you certain?"

"Yes."

"I think you're lying." He pulled Diell's head back to expose his neck. "But, that's what you hairy little burrowers excel at." He raised his officer's dagger to Diell's neck. Diell's eyes were filled with contempt. They were urging Steera not to say any more, but Steera could stand it no longer. At that moment, not even Osstar was as important to her brave young companion.

"A metal disc," she said.

"Ah yes, then it was as we had heard. I suppose that you're going to tell me it was used to serve Kodoos to party quests."

"We didn't know what it was at first." Steera had given up trying to be deceptive. "One of the Faceer Ka officers at the equatorial camp finally deciphered it."

"Well ...?" The officer let go of Diell's hair.

"It was a map."

"What kind of map!" Klut was silently urging the officer on from the other room. "What was the nature of the map?" The officer asked, almost on cue.

"As far as we could tell it was a map of Osstar, although it had some peculiarities." The officer, pleased with Steera's new cooperative attitude, ordered the soldiers to loosen Diell's gag and take off the wires. Diell sat rubbing his hands, staring at the two soldiers who had moved back toward the door.

"Were there any markings on the map that you recognized?"

"Not really," Steera answered. With Diell free, she again became reluctant to talk.

"I can easily tell my compatriots to replace the wires and gag if that's what you want." Steera looked at Diell. He was staring at her with the same intensity that he had used on the soldiers, but she knew that it was futile to resist. The officer had known a great deal about the cylinder before he had started the interrogation, but there was something he was trying to get from her, something he was trying to confirm, and Steera knew that he would stop at nothing to get it. "Now try hard. Can you remember anything about the markings that seemed familiar to you?"

"There was a small circle in the General area where they discovered the first cylinder, and there was another small circle in the equatorial region not far from the Faceer Ka camp."

"The Zerrit colony!" The officer's knowledge again surprised Steera. A Faceer Ka, perhaps Seelar, must have succumbed to the Stomari's interrogation. "So there is a second cylinder."

"I would be guessing at that. We were captured before we reached the colony."

"Liberated," the officer corrected her. "Then the colony was where you were headed."

"I don't know. We were taken to a jungle hideout by the other Faceer that you have in custody ... I mean the other Faceer that you 'liberated.'" The officer smiled.

"The one they call Seelar," he said. "I don't think you would want to be in his boots right now. He's being taken to the medical treatment room." The officer didn't explain any further, but it was clear that Seelar wasn't going there to be restored to health. "So," he continued, "there was a circle on this map at the location of the North Polar cylinder, and a circle at the Zerrit colony. Were there any other circles?" Steera could feel Diell's stare cutting into the side of her face, but she refused to look at him.

"Yes, there was one more."

"STEERA!"

One of the soldiers moved to restrain Diell. "Quiet, my young friend. Your companion knows that it is useless to try and deceive us. Now go on, Steera," the officer's voice was soothing as he used her name for the first time. "Where was the last circle located?"

"In the South Polar Region." Steera hung her head.

"And that's all you know?"

"That's all ... I swear it." Diell was no longer looking in Steera's direction; he was staring at the floor. Steera could sense his disappointment. She had done it to save him

"I believe you." He ordered Diell returned to his cell, locked the door to Steera's and then opened the door to the small anti-room opposite Steera's cell to report to Klut.

Klut, however, was not there. Moments earlier he had dropped the headset and made a dash down the corridor to the main communications room. He was going to make sure that the Stomari were the first to get to the South Polar Region and recover the cylinder. The arrangements had already been made; he had only to give his troops a destination. The recovery of the last cylinder and the proper disposition of its contents would be in the capable hands of General Somar-loors.

Pire and Riatt moved with haste. Both noticed that the cavern was particularly quiet. The oil lamps had been allowed to burn out, but they continued to pack, awash in the light of one of the miraculous cones provided by the people of the cylinder.

"Bloody quiet," Pire said, breaking the silence.

"Yes, I noticed." Riatt stuffed several packets of dried priot fruit into his pack.

"I think the Zerrits have gone." Pire's observation seemed to get Riatt's attention and he stopped packing long enough to peer around the chamber, cocking his head to listen for any sounds of the great apes.

"I'm not sure I like the idea of that."

"Maybe Nosh sent them out to look for a few Shock Troopers to invite to dinner."

Riatt smiled. "I don't think we will have to look for them. You had better continue packing. You'll curse yourself for everything you leave behind when the gales of Aldor hit you." Pire resumed his preparations with renewed energy

Suddenly, the silence of the cavern was shattered by the wails of Zerrits coming from every direction. The two Faceer grabbed their packs and headed for the chamber entrance. The cavern was exploding all around in great flashes of light and thunderous noise. Zerrits were running everywhere, a look of fear and confusion in their eyes. They had encountered the Stomari and the Faceer Ka before, but never within the sacred caverns themselves. Pire and Riatt ventured out into the corridor to see if they could get an idea of the direction of the attack. The chaos was intensifying. Pire looked to Riatt to give him some idea of what to do, but Riatt's training had already taken over.

"Take this," he said, shoving the light cone into Pire's hand. "Make your way to Nosh's chamber."

"You'll need this!" Pire implored. "Where do you think that you're going?"

"I'll meet you there in a minute ... I've got to go back for something. I have the smaller cone that you gave me."

"There's no time for that now," Pire pleaded. "It's the Stomari."

"I know that. That's why I have to go back. I forgot to pack something and I don't want them to get their hands on it."

"What could possibly be so important?" A round from a gas rifle found its mark in the chest of a Zerrit not fifty yards from them. He staggered forward, a look of amazement on his face, and dropped dead almost at their feet.

"The pouch ..." Riatt was calling back to Pire as he ran back down the rock corridor towards their chamber, "... now go! I'll be there as soon as I can." Riatt disappeared into the chaos.

Pire held the light cone aloft. It had an amazing ability to cut through not only the dark, but also the tremendous amount of dust and debris that had been churned up by the conflict. He had gone no more than two hundred yards when he saw the same type of light coming from one of the passageways.

"Come this way!" The voice was unmistakable.

"Nosh!" Pire cried out. "We've got to wait for Riatt."

"There's no time. The Zerrits are putting up a gallant fight, but they are no match for heavily armed troops." Pire attempted to protest, but Nosh simply lifted him up and threw him across his back with the other two packs he was carrying. He made his way swiftly down the tunnel to the interior of the cavern, the Zerrit leader along side. Behind him, Pire could see the flash of gas rifles and hear the baleful howls of the Zerrits mingle with the sound of projectiles as they ricocheted off the stone walls. His heart cried out for Riatt, but nothing was going to deter Nosh.

They traveled on for a solid ten minutes, deeper and deeper into the heart of the mountain. Pire had long since lost his exalted position among the packs on Nosh's broad back and was trotting to keep up with him, the Zerrit leader and several other Zerrits. The air in the cavern was still and humid as they descended along an ever-narrowing path.

Finally, the troop came to a halt and Pire was able to catch his breath. In the cone light, it looked for a moment as if they had come to the end of the cave. The cavern widened considerably, and what appeared to be a smooth, solid, black wall loomed in the distance. Nosh and two of the Zerrits moved forward. To his surprise, they didn't come to the end of the cave at all; they came instead to the edge of an underground lake. The vast expanse of water had soaked up even the light from the cone so that nothing could be seen at any distance. An infinite expanse of black water stretched out in front of them. On the barren shore of the lake, Pire could make out several large, solid shapes.

"Get yourself and your gear into this boat." Nosh's voice was

insistent, but calm. He flung his pack into the boat and began pushing it into the cold, black water. Pire paused. He thought about
Riatt. Perhaps he would be able to find his way here. Perhaps he
already knew of this place. There were two boats remaining on the
shore, a larger expedition having been planned before the Stomari
intervened. Pire grabbed one of the packs that Nosh had stowed
in the rear of the boat and flung it back on shore as he jumped in.
Nosh settled in the center of the craft and took the wheel. He said
nothing, acknowledging Pire's devotion to his comrade with a nod.

The boat was a 'Soota,' a design used by Stoma fishing villages
around the House of Breet. It was equipped with a powerful (but
ponderous) electric motor. They were used mainly as transports,
plying the calm waters of inlets and bays, and were well suited
for the glassy-smooth waters of this underground sea. Pire settled
into a small space at the rear of the boat, and watched as the Zerrit
leader nervously made his way to the front to hide under the bow
covering. Even though two boats remained on shore, the rest of
the Zerrits stood and watched as Nosh's boat floated effortlessly
out into the water. The silence of the cave's interior was broken by
a low, forlorn sound. The Zerrits were mourning the departure of
their leader, their god.

The craft had drifted some two hundred yards into the smooth
waters of the lake when Nosh threw the lever that activated the
engine. The motor was whisper quiet, and the acceleration was per-
ceptible only by the presence of a breeze on one's face. Nosh's full
attention was required for navigation on the glassy surface of the
water. Even the light from the cones extended only twenty or so
yards ahead.

Pire lay back in his cramped quarters and tried without much
success to stop thinking about Riatt. He reached into his pack and
drew out the one thing he knew would hold his attention, the talking book. He held the book in his lap and turned the pages with
one hand, letting his fingers fall onto the words where they may,
listening to the foreign sounds that accompanied the pictures. He
repeated aloud the Osstarian word that came closest to it. He began to relax and unknowingly let his other hand glide across the

smooth, cool waters of the underground sea. With a deceptively swift move, Nosh reached over and snatched up Pire's hand. Just as he did, a long silvery form flashed to the surface only inches from where Pire's hand had been.

"While you're studying alien plants and animals, see if they have anything like that in their book."

"I didn't even see it. What was it?"

"Razor fish," Nosh answered casually, returning his gaze to the water ahead, "and you don't usually see them until you pull a bloody stump, minus a few fingers, from the water." Pire stared at his hand, waiting for it to topple over but it didn't. "We're entering lands that are as alien to most Osstarians as the creatures in that book," Nosh's tone was serious. "We will need to be vigilant, and you will need to stay close to me." Pire tucked his arms in tight to his sides and resumed his study of the book. Even with all he had been through in the last few months he began to realize that the most arduous part of the journey lay ahead. It was not a comforting thought.

Riatt raised the small, orange light cone above his head and tried to make out the entrance to the chamber he had shared with Pire. The cone wasn't working very well. It was giving off only about half of the light it had produced in the altar room. He pulled it back down to examine it more closely, shaking it back-and-forth. Two Zerrits flew past, heading down the dark corridor. They paused briefly as if to beckon him to follow, but he had his mind set on retrieving the pouch. He thrust the cone back into his pocket, and made a dash for what he reckoned to be the opening to the chamber. Before he got half-way into the center of the corridor, he came face to face with a Stomari Shock Trooper.

The trooper raised his gas rifle. Riatt leaped behind a large chunk of rock that had been dislodged by a hand cannon's explosive shell. The bullet whizzed over his head and tore through one of the oil lamps that had managed to keep burning in the midst of the mayhem, spewing burning oil across the cavern wall. Several more Stomari troopers rushed to join the fray. Riatt realized that it would be impossible to make it to the chamber opening, so he reluctantly turned back the way he had come. The two Zerrits were still where he had left them, bidding him to come with them. This time he followed.

The Zerrits moved quickly down the dark stone corridor until they came to a bend in the tunnel. The obvious course was the larger tunnel that curved to the right; instead they turned off into a smaller tunnel. It was obscured from sight by a cave formation that hung from the ceiling like a great stone knife. As they moved down the small corridor, Riatt could hear the sounds of the Stomari troops grow louder and then begin to fade. They were taking their pursuit down the main corridor.

Riatt stopped to try and get his bearings. The Zerrits also slowed their pace and were moving with much greater caution. The small tunnel was definitely descending into the heart of the cavern. The silence that hung in the cool, damp air around them was even more pronounced after the cacophony of the battle in the corridors above. Riatt could sense uneasiness in the apes.

Rounding another bend in the tunnel, the passageway abruptly widened into a room. The darkness was intense. It was impossible now to see more than a few feet ahead. Riatt inched forward to try and gauge its extent, and ran into one of the Zerrits. He was standing frozen in the middle of the cavern. A low pitched hissing noise was coming from somewhere in the room, but it was difficult to tell exactly where because of the echoes.

Riatt pulled the small cone from his pocket. All it was producing was a faint orange glow. Then he heard it, the sound of scraping across the rock floor of the cavern. Something was moving in their direction. The Zerrits panicked. They exploded across the cavern floor, knocking Riatt to his knees. As he tried to right himself, his foot got caught in a crack in the cavern floor. He reached down to dislodge it and his hand touched not rock, but coarse hair.

A shock wave so severe that it caused a burning sensation in his ears shot up Riatt's spinal ridge. "A groag!" he thought. He had seen the creature that this limb belonged to in a traveling carnival when he was a child. It had frightened him then and the effect now was no less intense.

He jerked his foot free and headed in the direction of the Zerrits who were whooping and flailing their arms in alarm. The three dived forward, heedless of any possible obstructions in their path, and fell through a small opening in the rock wall into another tunnel. Behind them, Riatt could hear the low, hissing sounds growing louder as the frustrated creature searched frantically for its lost meal. Riatt prayed that it would be too large to fit through the small opening they had just entered. After a minute or two the noise subsided.

Riatt got back on his feet and studied the new passage. The Zerrits were still huddled together, moaning and stroking each other in obvious distress. Riatt put his hand on the larger Zerrit's head, giving it a pat as he would his pet saarcat. The Zerrit responded by putting Riatt's hand on his face and rubbing it. The second Zerrit took Riatt's other hand and began doing the same thing. The contact had an immediate, calming effect on the Zerrits. He stood up and helped them do likewise. Making a quick scan of the new tunnel, he decided that the only option was to continue into the heart of the mountain. The three unlikely traveling companions started down the tunnel to begin the search for their lost friends.

CHAPTER 24

The Stomari soldiers laughed and made fun of Druk-tasis' deformed foot, as they bound it to the other one with rope. Druk made no attempt to struggle, knowing that to do so would only cause the soldiers to tighten the already uncomfortable bonds.

"Looks like he's trying to grow a flipper," one soldier said with a laugh.

"Maybe we will see if he has learned to breathe under water again." All four of the soldiers broke into laughter. It was quickly cut off by the arrival of the Officer of the Guard.

"Enough!" he snapped. "This is Druk-tasis, the hero of the Polar Station massacre, and we will treat him with some respect." Their Stomari training and the effectiveness of the propaganda Ministry's campaign kept the irony of his statement from dawning on any of the soldiers. They returned to their tasks taking more care not to pull the ropes too tightly.

After being adequately secured, the Stomari troopers departed. Druk-tasis was left to ponder his fate, but he was as concerned about his Faceer friends as he was about himself. The bindings were uncomfortable, but not so snug as to cut off circulation, and for that he was grateful. After a brief time, the door to his holding room opened, and four Stomari Storm Troopers entered. They threw a cowl over him that went all the way to his knees. Without a word, they hustled him out of the room and down the corridor. Druk heard the clank of a key in a lock and felt the whoosh of outside air. He was led another ten yards or so, and then told to turn around. Two guards took either arm and moved him backwards until his backside caught the metal ridge of the rear door to a motor transport. They pushed his head down in order for it to clear the door opening, and unceremoniously dumped him into the back of the vehicle. With a great lurch, the transport pulled out.

For what he estimated as two or three hours, the transport rolled down relatively smooth roads. Druk had paid attention to the direction of the turns they had made leaving Central Headquarters, so he had an idea of where they were headed. If they had taken the main road out of the complex (which he believed they had) then he knew that they were heading south. The smooth surface of the roadway meant that they were most likely on the main north/south highway that led to the seacoast village of Prameel, a village that Druk-tasis had visited once before. It was more difficult for Druk to estimate speed, but if they had been making normal time he calculated that they would be about twenty or thirty minutes from Prameel by now.

Just as he was about to congratulate himself on his powers of observation, the motor transport made a violent swerve to the right followed by an even more violent one to the left. Druk could feel the wheels leave the surface of the roadway. He tumbled wildly inside the vehicle. The transport skidded wildly and hit something with great force. Druk suddenly found himself pressed against the front wall of the enclosed cab. The entire transport tilted on its nose for one long moment, and then tumbled over on its top.

Druk-tasis was dazed but still conscious. The cowl had worked its way up his torso, but was still covering his head. Outside, he could hear the sounds of a struggle. It lasted for a brief minute and then abruptly stopped. He braced himself, waiting for the rear door of the transport to be opened, wondering who he would be facing when it did, but nothing happened. He waited and listened, still nothing.

Druk-tasis was beginning to wonder if he had dreamed the entire event, but he couldn't deny that the transport was no longer on the road, or even upright. He started moving his body back-and-forth rubbing the cowl against the sides of the cab until it finally fell off. It was dark inside the transport's rear cab, but he could see a dim light coming through a hole in the rear door. Finding a displaced seat mount with a rough metallic edge, he began working to cut the bindings on his hands. It took only a few seconds to sever the ropes on his hands and untie his feet.

He sat silently in the dark of the cab. Rebal had disappeared from the horizon, and the staddich was setting in. The breeze coming in from the hole in the rear door was becoming noticeably cooler. Druk-tasis knew that if he were going to make an escape from his Stomari captors the dark of staddich would be the time to do it. He braced his back against the rear wall of the cab and kicked forward as forcefully as he could. The damaged door burst open. Without hesitation, Druk-tasis jumped from the vehicle, and scrambled into a thicket of faar trees that lined the banks of a ditch some fifty yards from the roadway. The staddich air was cool and crisp and helped to drive the remaining fog from Druk's head. As his eyes adjusted to the faint light he could see the transport lying on its top. Smoke was coming from it, the result of internal liquids pouring over the hot engine. He could see nothing else. No bodies or signs of a struggle.

Biting insects were now buzzing about him in multitudes. He approached the wreck, being sure to keep it between him and the roadway just in case the Stomari had dispatched a trailing vehicle. There was no trailing vehicle. There was no driver, and there were no guards. It was as if the wreck had just materialized on the roadside.

Druk-tasis leaned his back against the upside-down door of the vehicle. He almost wished that someone would come along to reaffirm that he was still among the living. The gnawing pain in his left shoulder soon became affirmation enough. He knew that he couldn't sit at the site of a wreck on a main roadway for very long without drawing some attention. He was going to have to move on. Looking up and down the roadway in desperation, he sought a more comfortable alternative to the ditch, but saw none. It was back to the biting minions until he had put some distance between himself and the accident scene.

The ditch was thick with faar trees. Their long, whip-like branches and slender leaves formed a canopy that stretched from one bank to the other, making movement difficult, but keeping him out of sight of the roadway. Seedge flies swarmed, so thick that one could feel the wind from their razor-like wings as they sliced through the humid air. Both the insects and the humidity told Druk-tasis that he was not far from the sea. The drainage ditches had been dug to accommodate the powerful tidal flows caused by Rebal's mighty pull on Osstar. The water from the sea had once covered the roadway to a depth of three feet several times in the course of a day until Faceer engineers designed and built the intricate ditch system to serve as aquatic pressure valves.

Druk moved steadily down the ditch, pausing now and again to peer over the bank. There had been no traffic at all. He thought of how Nidire would have hated slogging through the brackish water, "Stoma soup" he would have called it. The slope of the ditch was becoming more pronounced. Druk-tasis stuck his head up one last time to see if there was any activity. This time he did see something. Behind him, a large, white spot of light was sweeping across the wreck area, scanning the roadway. He instantly recognized it as the beam from an electric torch. The size of the beam was consistent with the standard torch carried by both regular Stoma troops, and Stomari Shock Troopers. The beam jumped from the area of the vehicle, and lit up the tops of the faar trees only a few yards away from his position. He immediately moved back into the center of the ditch, taking care not to make any noise. The light swept across the tangled mat of limbs and leaves that made up the canopy of the faar tree thicket. Druk-tasis stood in the center of the ditch and remained motionless.

Just as suddenly as it had appeared, the beam disappeared, swallowed by the darkness of the staddich. Druk-tasis cupped his hand around the small rim of flesh that defined his ear and tried to listen, but he could hear nothing. At that moment, he wished that he possessed the furry protrusions of his Faceer friends and not the inefficient ear holes of the Stoma.

After a few minutes of listening, he was convinced that whoever had been examining the wreck site had left. He again surveyed for an easier path, but could find none. The dark water stretching out in front of him with its mud, insects and who knew what manner of animal life, was the only clear path. "What a place for a mountaineer." He continued to mutter under his breath, as he slogged his way toward the sea.

Druk was beginning to doubt that there still was a sea border-
ing the Upper Midlands when the ditch began to widen and flatten.
There had been no further encounters with possible search teams.
He watched as the rim of Rebal began to peek over the eastern horizon. Soon, Zenos would be joining it in the Osstarian sky and
"high" day would come.

But, he had a problem—several of them actually. He was
dressed in the informal uniform of a Stomari officer, a fact not likely
to win many friends among any Faceer he might encounter. He
was also headed toward the sea. Even the strong swimming Stoma
would stop short of attempting the swim from the southern coast
of the Upper Midlands to the Equatorial Region; and even if he did
manage to make it to the Equatorial Region, he had absolutely no
idea of what to do when he got there.

It was the sound of the waves pounding on the beach and the
absence of insects that brought him back to the present. He had
been in such deep thought as he waded along, that he hadn't noticed that both he and the ditch had reached their destination. He
scanned the coastline for signs of life as daylight began to etch a
sharper boundary between the shore vegetation and the beach. The
soft light of Rebal could play tricks on the eyes, especially around
the sea.

Druk-tasis assumed that that was the case when he saw what
looked like the pointed bow of a Stoma sailing skiff sticking out
from under a clump of giant sea grass. He waited for the image to
transform itself into something else as it continued to get lighter,
but it only became more pronounced. Seeing no sign of life, he
made his way to the apparition. He kicked at it with his good foot.
To his surprise, it returned the hollow thud of solid wood. It was
indeed a Stoma sailing skiff, and not a small one. It had been covered with cloth dyed to blend invisibly with sea grass waving in
the wind. The camouflage was incredibly effective. Faceer design,
he thought. He wouldn't have noticed it if it hadn't been placed at
exactly the proper angle in relation to where the ditch emptied into
the sea. Druk-tasis wondered if that was mere coincidence, but he

didn't have much time to speculate. Rebal was rising higher in the sky. Behind it, the smaller, more intense light of Zenos was shining like a red torch on the eastern horizon.

Druk-tasis threw back the cloth covering on the skiff, praying to find an intact sail—he found much more. Inside, placed carefully on top of the sail, was a bundle wrapped in sail cloth and tied with cord. He tore open the package. The outer wrapping of sail cloth flew off to reveal a gray/green unisuit, the type worn by members of Stoma trading guilds. He hurriedly stripped off his officer's uniform and put on the unisuit, stashing the uniform inside the hull.

It proved none-too-soon. Two male Stoma, strolling on the beach, came into view. Druk-tasis busied himself around the boat, looking at rudders and steering cables, checking to see if she were seaworthy. The two Stoma approached the boat. Druk-tasis calmed himself.

"Need any help?" The younger of the two asked.

"No, thank you," Druk-tasis answered nonchalantly.

"Getting ready to take her out, then?" The other asked.

"That's right."

"On a trading trip?"

"Yes, to the Equatorial Region," Druk didn't know why he had volunteered that information, but it didn't seem to surprise either of the two.

"Well, I envy you. It's a beautiful day for sailing." The three stood in an awkward silence. Druk decided to break it.

"Perhaps you can help." Their faces lit up. "How about giving me a shove into the surf, it will make getting past the shore currents easier if I'm already at the helm." He jumped into the boat and the two put their muscular shoulders into the bow of the skiff. It slid rather easily on the wet sand, and was in the surf almost as soon as Druk-tasis took the helm. As he drew away from the shore, he waved to them, shouted a "thank you" and made his way into open water.

"Nice fellow," the younger Stoma remarked. "I have always wanted to try the life of a trader."

"I suppose he was a trader," the other one replied, "but something about his face looked familiar, although I can't quite place it, and did you notice that mark behind his earhole?" The two thought for a moment, shook their heads and continued their walk down the beach, discussing the virtues of a life on the open sea.

Druk-tasis sailed until he could no longer see the two Stoma, or indeed, the shore. The trader's unisuit had probably saved him from an uncomfortable situation. What else, he wondered, was in this remarkable bundle? He tied off the tiller as soon as he was under full sail and turned his attention back to the bundle. It was unusually heavy for its size.

Sitting it on the deck in front of him, he peeled back the cloth layers as one would peel the leaves of the lapis fruit. The first thing he came to was a Rebalistra, an antique, but effective navigation device still used to fix one's position on the open sea. Whoever had packed the bundle had assumed that Druk-tasis would be making an extended voyage.

He pulled back another layer of cloth and found a folded map. He opened it to see that it was a map of the coastal area of the Equatorial Region. By comparing the positions of known landmarks on the coast, he determined that it defined an area southwest of his current position. On the map was a hand-drawn circle with an arrow pointing to a particular spot on the coast. Druk-tasis saw something else on the map, something that caused his great brow ridge to curl. Around the point designated by the circle were larger circles with a symbol drawn in each. He recognized the symbol. It was the tycor, the symbol of the Faceer Ka.

Opening the next layer of cloth, things became a bit clearer. Stacked neatly in two rows were ten shiny, orange/yellow bars of pure gallite, the most valuable metal on Osstar, worth about 50,000 Kalar. If he were being sent among enemies, he reckoned that they were enemies with a price.

He sat for a moment admiring the beautiful bars of gallite and wondering who had been responsible for devising such an elaborate escape. Whoever it was, he had been both imaginative and methodical, sparing no expense and overlooking no detail. He picked up the last bit of cloth and started to throw it overboard. As his hand closed around it, he felt a lump in its center. As his large hands fumbled to separate one final layer of the cloth a wide smile filled his face. In the palm of his hand, painstakingly carved from pod wood, lay a small Bajan stallion. He examined it closely. A word had been carved on the right flank of the beast, "Tiimat." He was not familiar with the word, but he knew the artisan quite well.

Sitting back in the bow of the boat, he leaned his weight against the great wooden tiller. The sails were straining against the north wind as the skiff fought against the currents being spawned by Rebal's rise. He thought of his dear old friend at Central Headquarters not thirty miles from where he now sailed. He imagined him sitting with his furry feet atop an oversized desk. It was Tomar Leet who had taken him into his confidence early on. It was he who had taken him to meet the one they called Nosh, and it was Leet that had now engineered his salvation. The world was stranger than Druk had ever imagined. He sat the carving on the top of the wooden cabin cover with its head pointed in the direction of the Equatorial Coast. "Lead on noble stallion." He laughed out loud and set the skiff sailing south into the unknown.

CHAPTER 25

The familiar figure of the small Faceer woman was ignored by the guard as she passed the entrance to the hallway leading to the communications room. Liira had blocked every thought from her mind except the image of her dear brother, the brother who had raised her in their impoverished village in the Northern Islands. Prier Datar had been taken away a month ago and questioned by the Stomari. His body was later found floating in Ossgar, the stream in which they had played as children. The official certificate gave the cause of death as a fall and an accidental drowning but Liira and everyone else had known better. Datar had been a trouble-maker, an instigator, a thorn in the side of the authorities. Some had even called him an outlaw. But to Liira he was brother and father rolled into one and life would not be possible without him.

Datar had warned that the Stomari would someday come for him. When that day came, Liira knew she would never see him again. Datar had prepared himself for the inevitability of a confrontation with the hated Stomari. Liira had been preparing as well, preparing to raise her brother to martyrdom for the cause to which he had given his life.

She stood silently, calmly in the center of the hallway where they had removed Druk-tasis only minutes before. At first the lone Stomari guard ignored her. He had seen her a hundred times, carrying her mop and pail down the hall. But he noticed that today she had no cleaning equipment with her. She was just standing there, as if waiting for some silent order to be issued, some direction to be given. Finally, the guard starting moving toward her.

"Are you all right?" he asked

"I'm fine," she answered, not moving an inch.

The guard stood for a moment studying her face. Her eyes conveyed no emotion at all. He had seen the look on a Stomari Storm

Trooper's face who had returned from the bitter fighting around the Strail pass in the Layard Mountains. His eyes conveyed it clearly. Life and death had become one.

"Do you need some help?" the guard asked.

"Help?" she replied dreamily. "Yes, I think that we all need help right now." The voice sounded distant, lifeless and almost apologetic. She reached under her coat, pressed a small switch and the hallway erupted in flame.

Steera found herself on the floor of her cell staring at what moments ago had been the wall separating her from Diell's cell. Her ears were ringing. Through the swirling dust and smoke she could see twisted metal and crumbled stone. Diell was leaning against the far wall. It was a few moments before the enormity of what had happened began to set in. The silence that accompanied the frightening blast, and the light shining through the clouds of dust, gave the scene an eerie, other- worldly feel. Everything looked to be moving in slow motion. Steera began moving in the direction of Diell even before realizing that she was on her feet. Diell was looking at her as if she were an apparition, reaching out his hand without knowing he was doing it. Steera got him to his feet. The eerie silence gave way to the sounds of yelling. Everything in the lower level of the building had been rearranged by the blast. Steera's brain began to function again.

"What in name of Rebal happened?" Diell asked, finally able to make words come out of his mouth.

"An explosion ... a bomb, I think." The shouting coming from the outer hallway was increasing. Steera looked to her left and saw a gaping hole in the exterior wall. She grabbed Diell and together they stumbled through the rubble toward the light. In the cell farthest down the ruined hallway another figure was stirring. Beaten and bruised by his interrogators, Seelar was moving toward the same opening in the outer wall. They reached it almost simultaneously.

"Well, brother and sister," Seelar said almost triumphantly, "another blow struck against the tyrants. Will you join us now? I will have need of you when I recover the third cylinder." Steera looked at Diell in disbelief. "Yes, I overheard your conversation with my old boss Druk-tasis and I assure you that the Faceer Ka will retrieve the cylinder and its contents before the Stomari or any Faceer traitors have a chance to tamper with it. This is your last opportunity to aid your own kind. Come with me and your names will go down with mine in the annals of Faceer history. It will be glorious, and you will have redeemed yourself to your people." Diell was searching Seelar's eyes for tell-tale signs. He was too energetic for one who had been through a Stomari interrogation.

"Did some of our 'own kind' smuggle you the katoc?" Diell asked in disgust. "No thanks, great leader. You'll have to make history without us."

"Look at you!" Seelar growled and grabbed Diell's wounded hands. "They nearly tore your thumbs off, and you still think it preferable to live in a world ruled by the Stomari over one ruled by us?"

Diell rubbed his hands remembering the pain of the wires. "I see little difference. The world of the Stomari and the Faceer Ka are worlds ruled by fear and brutality. Steera and I are finished with all of it. We have only one goal now, to find our friends and then try and find some peaceful place as far away from you and your kind as we can."

"Go find a hole and crawl in it then, but you will find no peaceful place on this planet until the victory has been won. We will meet again my friends, and you will pay homage to me as your leader ... or you will die."

Seelar bolted through the opening in the wall and disappeared into the dust and chaos. Steera and Diell said nothing else to each other until they had also cleared the opening and were safely away from the area. They moved cautiously but quickly, reaching a sheltered wood well away from the compound. Out of harm's way, they threw themselves on the soft ground.

"You're an amazing young Faceer," Steera said, folding her outer tunic and placing it under Diell's head as a pillow, "After all we've been through, I thought you might have taken him up on it."

"After all we've been through. I'm surprised you would think that," Diell answered, his voice betraying his profound fatigue for the first time.

"So, you meant it?"

"Meant what?"

"About our goal." Diell paused in thought for a moment.

"I see no other course. The forces of chaos on Osstar are gaining momentum. If somehow Pire and Riatt are still alive our only hope is to find them and the other cylinder." Diell looked up at Steera. Her eyes were red with tears. He put his hand in hers. "I know that he is alive, somewhere." She bent down and kissed his damaged thumb.

"I'm glad you are with me. I wouldn't trade a hundred of the healthiest Mountain Veertal for you."

Diell smiled. Steera's hands and lyrical voice began to sooth his pain. "Then we are agreed."

"We are agreed," Steera replied.

"So what do we do now?"

"Why don't we go out into the road and flag down a passing Stomari motor transport?"

Diell laughed until coughing spasms forced him to stop. "Seriously, do you have any ideas?"

"As a matter of fact I do. There is a Veertal village a few days journey from here — Romass. I have a relative there. She is my mother's sister, Dree. We will be safe with her until we can plan our next move. Unfortunately, we have no time to rest. The Stomari will seal off this entire region until they find out what or who caused the blast."

Steera helped Diell to his feet. Arm-in-arm they made their way along the edge of the forest that paralleled the highway, making sure to stay well off the roadway. As Rebal began to wane and twinight came, a cool breeze began to blow. They would cross the highway and turn southeast, heading toward the mountains and friendly territory, friendly, of course, if there were now any friends to be found on Osstar.

Somar-loors wasn't going to direct this operation from base camp as he had the capture of the three Faceer renegades a few weeks earlier. His advanced troops had carefully scouted the terrain around the Zerrit cave. When they were ready to move in, he would be at their head.

Just after Zenos rise, General Somar led the first wave of his Shock Troopers against the caverns. A lethal volley of cannon fire scattered the Zerrit guard at the cave entrance, and the troopers poured in. Somar-loors stayed in the middle of the fray, and his soldiers took heart at his courage. The Zerrits were now in full flight before the concentrated fire of the Troopers' gas rifles. The struggle didn't last long. Somar-loors made his way into the main tunnel area and waited for the return of his second-in-command.

Colonel Breet-Somar-treeg shook the dust off his uniform and reported to his commander and distant cousin. "The Zerrits have been routed sir."

"And prisoners, do we have prisoners?" Treeg's expression gave Somar-loors the answer without a word being uttered.

"By the winds of Aldor!" General Somar bellowed. "Are these phantoms that we pursue?"

"We did find something that might interest you. It appears to be an altar room. And in the center of it is a metallic object. The Zerrits died by the hundreds defending it."

"Take me there."

Colonel Treeg led his General down the dark tunnel to the altar room. Around the large, star-shaped construction of rock in the center of the chamber lay the broken and blasted bodies of hundreds of Zerrit Apes. The bodies were piled atop each other, suggesting that as one fell, another quickly took up defense of the altar. Somar-loors directed the Troopers to clear them away. After a few minutes, he made his way to the altar.

At least twenty Zerrit bodies where strewn in a tangled heap in the center of the altar stone. Without waiting for help, General Somar started pulling bodies from the site. As he lifted the last dead Zerrit off the pile, a shiny silver cylindrical object slowly rolled from under the body and landed on the cavern floor with a loud, hollow clunk.

The troopers immediately halted their cleanup, and gathered around the cylinder. It shone even in the darkness of the altar room. Somar-loors leaned over and touched it—nothing happened. He put his muscular arms around one end, and lifted it upright. His hands slid over the smooth, cool exterior, feeling the indentations of the strange symbols. The feel was like the runners of the hunting sled he had treasured as a youngster in the high mountains. Was this what Klut had bought with so much Stoma blood? Was this the great weapon of the Faceer Ka?

He turned to colonel Treeg. "Send a squad to check out the rest of the cave. There must be other rooms. We might find a clue as to the whereabouts of the Faceer Ka that escaped us at the Equatorial Compound."

The squad had only been gone for about twenty minutes when one of the Troopers returned breathless to the altar room.

"Sir—we've found something!"

"Calm down, Trooper," the colonel commanded. General Somar gave the colonel a brief, stern look of disapproval.

"What did you find Trooper, Gleer-fazid." General Somar spoke in a soft tone, reading the Trooper's name off the emblem on his tunic.

"I think you will have to see it for yourself, sir." The Trooper's tone had changed. It was calmer, more confident, and tinged with pride.

"Lead the way then, Trooper Fazid." The three moved out into the main tunnel led by the beaming Trooper, and made their way some three-hundred yards to a large opening leading into another chamber. Somar-loors didn't have to bend at all to enter. In fact, the opening was a good two feet above the top on his helmet. He was astonished at what he saw. A half-mile inside a cavern in the heart of the equatorial jungle was what appeared to be a Stoma feeding pool.

Without waiting to be asked, Trooper Fazid brought him an electric torch. The amber light from the torch confirmed that indeed it was a feeding pool. As well as the pool, he could make out several chairs and a large Darma-shell table of antique Stoma design. At the far end of the chamber, opposite the feeding pool, was something even more amazing. Laid out in classic configuration was a Faceer sleeping-cove. The round, fur-stuffed mat in the center was surrounded in this case with rocks rather than the more traditional wood. Every aspect of the layout was true Faceer design except for its size; it was at least three times larger than any Faceer bed that Somar-loors had ever seen.

Another Trooper approached the group, holding something in his hand. "Sir, I've found something!"

"Give it to me Trooper Seer-affad." Colonel Treeg was careful to emulate his general. The trooper handed him a cloth pouch tied at the top with twine. "Have you looked inside?"

"Oh no, sir," the Trooper replied. "It would be against regulations."

"So it would," the colonel replied and turned to hand the pouch unopened to Somar-loors.

"Your professional conduct will be noted, Trooper Seer," General Somar added. "Now return to your unit, and report your actions to your unit commander." Somar-loors took the pouch, and moved to the end of the chamber opposite the opening, sitting it on the Darma-shell table. Colonel Treeg stayed behind to guard the chamber entrance.

General Somar pulled the pouch open and emptied its contents onto the table. He caught the glint of metal. He lifted the disc to get a better look. It was incredibly light for its size, and had been etched with such precision that you could not see a seam or an edge anywhere on it. The circles and symbols were completely foreign to him, but seemed to be placed in precise relation to one another. The reverse side of the disc was blank. He sat it on the table and resumed examining the pouch. He lifted out round glass dishes filled with a grey/green powder taking care not to open the top of the dish for fear that it might be a poison.

The last object in the pouch was rectangular in shape and didn't want to come out. Somar-loors tugged at it awkwardly with his thick fingers, finally tearing the pouch into two ragged pieces. The object fell onto the table and its thin metallic pages fell open.

Somar-loors stared at the image in front of him. Standing at the entrance to a cave, was a figure clothed in a brown tunic with a short, thick ax in his furry hand. The face was unlike any he had ever seen, but the creature had a familiar aspect. Its form was like that of a Faceer.

"This is the weapon that Klut fears." He motioned for Colonel Treeg to assist him. Treeg approached the table and General Somar handed him the book. "What do you make of this?" he asked.

Colonel Treeg fixed his gaze on the beast on the cover. "I've never seen anything like it."

General Somar took the book back, opened it to the picture he had just seen and handed it back to Colonel Treeg "And this?"

Colonel Treeg ran his finger across the page. "It's so thin and yet there's not a wrinkle in it."

"I mean the figure on the page. What would you call it?"

"An ugly Faceer?" General Somar didn't need to hear more.

"Go through this room and find something to hold these items. And Colonel…"

"Yes sir?"

"… forget what you've seen here."

Two squads of Shock Troopers accompanied General Somar-loors down the mountain to base camp. Every soldier wanted to be his escort. General Somar, they were saying, personally killed thirty apes and saved the lives of fifteen Troopers trapped in the caverns.

Inside his command tent, the greeting was a bit different. Before he could take off his helmet and unbuckle his ammunition belt, one of his aides rushed up with a radio microphone in his outstretched hand. Somar-loors could see from the look on the officer's face that the call was top priority.

"General … it's Central Headquarters!" General Somar took a deep breath and finished taking off his gear. He poured himself a cup of "straa" tonic (the invigorating drink made from the blood of a sea mammal was standard issue for combat situations) and picked up the microphone switching on the radio. A voice crackled over the speaker.

"General Somar-loors, headquarters calling General Somar-loors ..." He knew the voice. This wasn't some mid-level radio operator; it was Klut-Prime. He motioned for the others to leave the tent and answered the call.

"General Somar-loors here."

"I trust you know who is speaking," the voice said.

"I do, sir."

"Good, then you will also know that what we discuss will require highest security."

"I do, sir." General Somar put on the headset he had been holding in his hand and secured the curtain around the radio receiver.

"The reports are that your campaign is going well."

"Yes sir. We have just taken the high caverns and are in the process of mopping up the last of the resistance."

"Then the Faceer Ka put up a fight?"

"Not the Faceer Ka, sir ... the Zerrit Apes."

"What happened to the Faceer Ka?"

"We found no Faceer Ka, sir."

"Did you find any Faceer at all, General?"

"No sir ..." There was a long silence.

"Did you find evidence of anyone or anything else?"

"I'm not quite sure I follow your question sir."

There was another long pause. "General, what I'm about to tell you is top secret. Do you understand—top secret!"

"Understood."

"We have been interrogating the three Faceer that you recently sent us. We weren't getting very much information until we learned through a source that Druk-tasis had spent an inordinate amount of time with them when they were at the North Polar Station."

"Druk-tasis, the hero of the Polar massacre?"

"The same, yes." Klut was becoming irritated at the effectiveness of his own propaganda campaign. "There was more to that story than made the broadcasts. There were some at the North Polar station who thought that Druk-tasis was involved in an anti-Stomari resistance within our own ranks. When we found out that he was trying to see the Faceer captives at headquarters, we let him make contact. We overheard only part of his conversation with the female prisoner, but it was a very interesting part."

"How do you mean?"

"He made mention of a leader of the movement, a Seemano!"

"A Seemano, are you certain?"

"A Seemano, named Nosh," Klut repeated.

"That would explain it." Somar-loors was thinking out loud.

"Explain what?"

"The bed ... the giant Faceer bed."

"General, you're not making sense. We have very little time. The prisoners have confessed to having pilfered the original contents of the cylinder found at the North Polar Station."

"Original contents ... cylinder?" Somar-loors was beginning to realize that he had been left out of a lot of what had transpired in the last several months.

"The purpose of the Polar Research Station was to open a strange metallic cylinder that was discovered quite by accident by a drical mining operation. Three Faceer scientists were brought there to open it, and they succeeded. The cylinder contained an instrument of unknown origin and some other, more mundane objects, but it was rumored that the most important items had been taken before we could examine them. We now have two of these scientists in our custody, captured at the equatorial base. They have confessed that one item that was taken was a map showing the location of two additional cylinders. One of the locations is very close to the Zerrit caverns that you now occupy. Is any of this making sense?"

"Yes," General Somar answered. "I have seen the second cylinder. But I think I have seen something else."

"What?"

"I think I have the lost items from the first cylinder." The news was almost too good to be true for Klut.

"The map ... do you have the map!"

"What would it look like?"

"I'm not sure. It would have markings on it like any map."

General Somar remembered the disc. "I believe I do have it. It is a metallic disc with small circles marking different points on the sphere."

"It is a map of Osstar. Look at it as such and tell me where the circles are located."

"There is one at the top of the disc, one in the middle ..."

Klut interrupted before he could finish. "Can you see a circle at the bottom, where the South Polar Region would be?"

"Yes sir. If the scale is true, it's not too far from the coast." As he finished the last word, a harsh static suddenly filled the line. "Your Excellency, are you there?" The static gave way to silence. "Your Excellency!" General Somar twisted the main volume control and adjusted the antenna. "Equatorial base calling headquarters ... equatorial base calling headquarters..." After almost five minutes of silence, the voice of Klut-Prime came back on the line.

"Are you still there, General?" Klut sounded shaken.

"Yes, sir...what happened?"

"You must mount an immediate expedition to the South Polar Region, General. You are going to retrieve that last cylinder. We have reason to believe that there are others headed there even as we speak. You must make sure that you get there before they do. If you do not, you must make sure that they do not come back. You will, if necessary, destroy the cylinder and whoever possesses it rather than let it fall into enemy hands. Time is of the essence General."

"What is it, sir? What happened?"

"Someone has just detonated a bomb in the Central Headquarters building. I fear that the three Faceer have escaped."

"A plot to get to the third cylinder?"

"It is a certainty, but it may also be a stroke of good fortune for us. The transmitter, the one that led you to them, the one in the boot of the Veertal female ..."

"Yes, I recall."

"We implanted it in the one they call Seelar. Proceed to the southern coast. Provisions for you and twenty of your best troops will be waiting—including a direction antenna."

"Yes sir. I will leave with Zenos rise."

"General," Klut's voice took on an ominous tone, "you've seen the contents of the first cylinder; was there anything in it that might strengthen a Faceer claim to Osstar?"

General Somar-loors thought carefully before he answered. "I had best begin preparation for the South Polar Expedition with due haste." Klut understood the message.

"May the Gods of Aldor be with you."

The radio went silent for the second time and Somar-loors knew that Klut was rushing to make arrangements for supplies. General Somar had never been to the South Polar Region, but had heard tales of its howling winds and relentless snow. An odd scenario for the most important battle in the history of Osstar, he thought ... twenty Stomari troopers, a half-breed, an assortment of Faceer renegades, all in the coldest place on the planet. He rose to his feet and made his way back to his tent to write a last letter to his mother before he disappeared into the icy, white mists of the South Pole.

CHAPTER 26

The harsh squawking of a flight of coola birds high overhead was a fitting accompaniment to the growing sharpness of the mountain winds. Steera and Diell had been traveling southeast for several days, moving only in the twinight of Rebal-wane to avoid the Stomari patrols that had been scouring the countryside after the escape. Steera had visited her mother's sisters several times as a child. She was still familiar with the terrain surrounding the village of Romass, and knew that the main road into the village would be a perfect spot for a Stomari checkpoint. She decided to skirt the edge of the village to the north then circle back and enter the southern gate.

Faceer villages nearly always had two main entrance points, as did Faceer homes. In their early days, the Faceer constructed strong walls surrounding the village so that the only access was through one of the two gates. The need for the security of the walls had diminished over the years with the declining population of cathercats. As villages expanded beyond the walled area, little attempt was made to expand the walls to compensate. Many newer Faceer villages had an older, walled inner-village surrounded by newer construction. Romass was an ancient village. Its location, high in the Strail Pass of the Layard Mountains, had prohibited expansion of any magnitude and thus it remained a true, walled village.

To her surprise, Steera found no Stomari at the southern gate, but rather a group of sullen looking Faceer. Both she and Diell were wearing the standard brown tunics issued them upon arrival at Central Headquarters. One of the Faceer guards gave them a long, hard look. He whispered to the Faceer who was at the gate controls then wheeled around and quickly left.

"From where do you come?" The gate guard asked.

"Prass," Steera said.

"From Government Headquarters?" Steera was surprised by the tone of his voice. The Layard Mountain Veertal were on good terms Generally with the Stoma government, but his tone was tinged with anger and mistrust.

"Is something wrong?" Diell chimed in, trying to put the guard at ease.

"Something wrong! Where have you been the last few weeks?" Diell didn't know how to answer that question.

"On expedition to the Equatorial Region," Steera replied, rescuing him.

"Well if you had been anywhere in the civilized world you would have heard about the village of Romass—or what's left of it."

Steera immediately thought of her aunt Dree. "What happened? I have relatives here, are they all right?"

"What happened was a cruel and murderous act."

"Stoma?" Diell asked.

"An act of brutality from our own kind."

"Faceer?" Diell couldn't believe it.

"Faceer Ka," the guard answered. "Don't try and put that murderous brood in with the rest of us. They came through the pass looking for a Stomari officer, a Stoma who had been taken in as an act of compassion after his own family had abandoned him as unsound. When they didn't find him, they murdered the two Faceer who had raised him and tried to burn the village to the ground. We showed them what Veertal are like when you push them too far. So you can understand that we are more than a little edgy about strangers—particularly Faceer strangers."

A troop of three Faceer approached. The leader was the guard who had left earlier. "We need you to come with us," he said, looking at Steera and Diell.

"But I'm here to see my Aunt Dree. I know nothing about this awful event."

"You'll see her soon enough, I expect," the guard replied. He took his gas rifle and motioned in the direction of the village. Steera and Diell knew that the conversation was over.

They moved slowly through the silent village. The acrid smell of smoke hung in the air. There were scorch marks on most of the buildings, but little damage. The fire brigades had done their jobs well. As they came to the center of Romass they saw the still smoldering shell of what used to be the Village Council building. The Faceer Ka knew where to put the stabbing knife; the council building was the heart of the village. They moved to another, smaller building directly behind it. This one was intact, and teeming with activity.

"Wait here," the guard said. After a few minutes, he returned and bade them enter. The room was almost too small for all the activity it contained. Villagers were coming and going, filling the side rooms with supplies of all sorts. Diell recognized the items immediately.

"It looks like someone's going on another Polar expedition."

"Very observant, young fellow," the voice came from directly over his shoulder. Diell looked up to see an elderly Faceer with a pair of small, round glasses perched precariously on his nose ridge. "I wonder if you and your lovely companion would come with me." Steera and Diell accompanied the old Faceer up a short flight of stairs and into a small room at the back of the building. He seated himself behind a desk so large that there was barely room for anything else. He motioned for Steera and Diell to take a seat in two small chairs at the front of the desk.

"I am Faceer through and through, but I've always thought that the Stoma make the best office furniture. But, you didn't come here to discuss my office furniture." He peered inquisitively over his glasses. "So exactly why did you come here?"

"We were brought here," Steera answered. The old Faceer was fidgeting about, looking in his desk, and having difficulty doing several things at once.

"Well … yes, you were … I suppose that's right." There was a pause, as if Steera's answer had caught him by surprise. "What I mean is … where are you coming from?"

"What gives you the right to question our movements?" Diell responded, trying to put a tone of indignation in his voice. The elderly Faceer gave Diell a long look that began to make him feel uncomfortable.

"I think you have been told of the events in this village of late," he said, his tone matching Diell's in intensity. "We are questioning any and all strangers in Romass, Faceer as well as Stoma." A guard that had been standing just outside the door leaned in and whispered something to him. "So you come from Prass. I suppose that you heard about the explosion at the Government Complex?" Another guard entered the room and sat a large travel case beside the desk.

"It would seem that we are not the only ones who have just arrived," Steera observed.

"Nor are you the only ones who have just come from Prass, my perceptive young Veertal. Let's not waste any more precious time. My name is Tomar Leet. I have just come from the Government Complex in Prass, which, I might add, is still in great disarray after the blast. The Stomari want to blame the bombing on the Faceer Ka, but I'm not so sure. All that I know is that there were three very important Faceer prisoners at the Complex who escaped in the confusion. One was a Veertal female. She had two traveling companions: a Veertal male of the Daas clan, and a young Somacee male. Have you seen anyone who might fit that description?" Steera and Diell remained silent.

"The rumor is that they had all been at the North Polar research station when a certain 'cylinder' was found."

"How do you know about the cylinder?" Steera shot Diell a withering glare.

"How do you know about the cylinder?"

Steera was beginning to see that Leet was not the doddering old Faceer that he appeared to be. "I think you already know the answer to that question," she said. "I think that you already know the answer to a lot of questions."

A sly smile spread slowly across Leet's face. "You are as intelligent and as charming as I have been told, but even my informants couldn't do justice to your healthful beauty. Close the door." Diell reached over his shoulder and swung the heavy, wooden door shut with a solid 'thunk.' "You are Steera then, and you must be Diell." Leet pulled his glasses down farther on his nose and appraised the young Faceer.

Leet's inspection made Diell uneasy. "How do you know that?"

"You're too young and naïve to be Seelar," Leet said, "and besides, I know what Seelar looks like." He continued to study the two weary Faceer. "You've come a long way, and you have an even longer way to go. Rest assured that you are in a safe place." The soothing energy coming from the old Faceer caused the two to relax a bit. "I'm going to let you go and rest now. We will have much to discuss tomorrow. I have someone here that will take you to your quarters." Leet squeezed out from behind his oversized desk, cracked the door open and poked his head into the hallway. He returned with a Veertal female only slightly younger than he was.

"Auntie Dree!" Steera rushed to embrace her.

"Yes, my precious one."

"Oh, Auntie Dree, I've missed you so."

"And I you, little one. But come, we have much to prepare before your journey and you have much to tell me of your life since last we met ... I hear there is a male?" Steera smiled, and let the soothing, familiar voice wash over her. It was more reassuring than anything Leet could have said or done.

Steera and Diell followed Dree out of the small building, across the council building courtyard and down a narrow, winding lane to the comfortable dwelling Steera had often visited as a child. As she approached, a flood of memories enveloped her. Blush-colored zenolilies surrounded the carved wooden door and long stalks of deep-yellow gallite grass grew around the figure of a garden lothar that still occupied the same place it had in happier days. The round windows on the ground floor were open, and the smell drifting from inside brought a feeling of home and safety. She wondered if the swing was still hanging from the laange tree beyond the garden and if the brook still bubbled up from the ground beneath its roots and gurgled happily down the hill toward the river.

Dree opened the side door and let the odor of freshly brewed chee and pastries greet them. Diell and Steera immediately plopped down on a sofa stuffed with coola down. The soft fabric held them in a secure embrace. Auntie Dree returned with two steaming hot cups of chee. They cradled the warm cups into their hands and drank. The effect was invigorating and immediate.

"Thank you, Auntie," Steera said. "But answer me something. Did you know that I was coming?"

"I learned just yesterday that you were the female Veertal that they were seeking."

"How did you find out?"

"Tomar Leet," she replied.

"Who is this Tomar Leet, and how does he seem to know everything?" There was a tone of indignation in Diell's voice.

"That is a question few Faceer can answer with complete accuracy. Suffice it to say that if the peace-loving Faceer on this planet have a leader, it is Tomar Leet."

"But I had never heard of him until just now," Steera said.

"There are many things about Osstar that both Faceer and Stoma are just learning. You have been living in the Northern Islands surrounded by your young scientist friends, but out here things have been happening. Suffice it to say that Leet is very wise and very discreet."

"So discreet that no one knows who he is?" Steera was thinking out loud. "But he knew about the cylinder and about the expedition, and he knew about Diell and me. He had a contact at the North Polar Station." Steera looked at Diell. "Seelar?"

"Seelar," Aunt Dree snorted in disgust, "not that drug-slave."

"No, not Seelar," Diell replied, "it had to be Druk-tasis."

Steera noticed tears beginning to well up in Dree's eyes. "What's wrong, Auntie?"

"I was thinking of those poor gentle souls, Nidire and Lirea."

"Who are they?"

"They were the two that paid the ultimate price for kindness ... the two butchered by the Faceer Ka for harboring a Stomari."

"How did Faceer come to have a Stomari officer in their house?"

"He wasn't a Stomari officer," she said, bitterly. "He was one of us, a peace lover, who had been conscripted into the Stomari movement by his embarrassed birth parents. They were no more parents to him than they would be to a stray saarcat. He was raised by us. He loved us, and we loved little Tupo as much and perhaps more."

"Tupo?"

"Yes, we called him Tupo, like the little lost greel calf in the children's story. It was because he was lost when he came to us. You called him by his Stoma name."

"Druk-tasis," Steera exclaimed. "It was Druk-tasis they were harboring."

"Yes," Dree said sadly, "and I pray that he doesn't find out that they are gone. It will break his heart." Dree wiped her eyes and rose to refill their drinks. She returned with the cups again brimming and sat them on the table. After a long pause, Steera worked up the courage to ask another question.

"Auntie Dree, how many sisters were there in your family?" Steera could sense some uneasiness in Dree.

"Why three, dear ... your Aunt Dela, your mother and myself. Why do you ask?"

"It's just that as a child I overheard a conversation between my mother and Aunt Dela. They were talking about someone else, another family member who was unfamiliar to me. They called her Reya." Dree quickly scooped up the still half-filled cups and hustled toward the kitchen.

"I suppose you've had enough chee," she said over her shoulder. "I wouldn't want to make you ill from it." Dree stayed in the kitchen for several minutes. Steera decided not to follow her; the question had obviously upset her. After a few minutes, Dree returned and sat down next to Steera.

"I'm sorry, child," she said softly. "I reacted poorly. You're of age now. It was a fair question, and one that I will try and answer. Yes, there was a forth sister in our family and her name was Reya. As a youth, she was taken in by the house of Takir. Our father wanted the best for his children, and he thought that the advantages provided by the most powerful Stoma house on Osstar would be many. He was right. The son of the old Takir and Reya became fast friends. She enjoyed all the privileges of Stoma sponsorship and even sat at the Great Table during High Holy days. Some of our friends teased us and called us the seeyard family because of how she was treated by the old Takir-Prime and his son. As time passed, the rumors about Reya and the young Takir began to turn dark."

"What do you mean?" Steera asked.

Dree was twisting in her chair, becoming visably uncomfortable about continuing the story. "The rumor was that she and the young Takir had become lovers."

"Oh gods of Leeth," Steera exclaimed. "It wasn't true was it?"

Dree pressed on. "The rumors reached the old Takir, and Reya simply disappeared from the world. Some said she met with an accident, some said she ran away."

"What do you think happened to her?"

There was a long pause.

"I'm not sure," she said, not very convincingly.

"Perhaps she's still alive," Steera said. "Has anyone looked for her? She would be old now, but she could still be alive."

"I don't think so, little one."

"Why not?" Steera asked.

"There was another rumor ... a more serious one. It was said that she was with child. Perhaps she could still be alive, but the difficulty of that kind of birth, alone in the jungle, means that the chances are remote."

"But she could have had the child."

"We can only pray that it was still-born," Dree replied, "or that it quickly died in the jungle. But we are not entirely sure." Dree, Steera and Diell looked at each other for a moment. No one was willing to say what the other was thinking. Finally, Dree spoke. "We have heard of a creature living in the Equatorial jungle. It is said that Leet has even met him."

"Before we left the Government Complex, Druk-tasis told us of a Seeyard, a creature named Nosh. He is, by all accounts, a remarkable being," Steera said.

The look on Dree's face ended the conversation. "Well, these things can wait for the morning. It's time that we all got some rest," she said. "Steera, you can sleep in your old bed chamber, and you, my fine young male, can do your stasis dreaming right here on this sofa." Diell smiled at the compliment. He would miss Steera's company, but liked the idea that it was no longer considered proper for him to be left alone with females. "Just make sure that you don't go into too deep a stasis," she continued, "we're counting on you to rouse us if anything happens. No one in Romass has rested very deeply since the trouble."

Dree left some extra coola-down pillows for Diell, and then led Steera to the stasis chamber. "I didn't get a chance to ask you about the male," Dree said, gently. "I suppose that things are becoming so confused these days that you haven't had time to contact him." Steera's sadness showed both on her face and in the subtle energy she was emitting. Aunt Dree felt them as only a Veertal blood kin could. "I'm sorry little one. I hope that these horrible days will end soon, and we can get back to doing the things that we Faceer do best: 'thinking, living and loving.'"

Steera reached out her hand and placed it on Dree's mouth. It was a Faceer gesture of appreciation for the kind words. She had used the lyrics from a traditional Faceer wedding song: "I want to tell you about him when the time is right. Next to my mother, I love you more than anyone else in this world." Dree gave Steera a hug, turned to go to her own room and then hesitated for a moment.

"It was strange that you brought up the subject of Reya," she said.

"Why do you say that?" Steera asked.

"When I saw you for the first time today, it amazed me just how much you resemble her." Dree gave Steera another, longer hug then walked down the hall to her stasis chamber. Steera stood staring into the mirror next to her bed brushing her hair with her fingers and wondering about her lost Aunt.

A wall of red light from Rebal began to rip through the wispy dark of Steera's room announcing the end of the staddich and the coming of Zenos. A new day was beginning. As was her habit, she began her day with prayer. Today, as she had

in the recent past, she prayed for Pire's safety. Just as she had ended her prayer, a coola bird landed on the thick sill of the small,
round window to her stasis chamber. The wispy top-knot of feath-
ers reminded her of the tuft of downy hair on Pire's head. The bird
cocked its head to one side and stared at her for a moment. Its eyes
had a sly spark to them, the same mischievous gleam that shone
in Pire's eyes. It strutted back-and-forth on the sill for a moment,
knowing that it was the object of Steera's admiration, and then flew
off into the rising light of Zenos. At that moment, Steera knew that
her prayers had been answered, that Pire was alive, somewhere.
She leapt from her bed and dressed. She found Diell sitting at the
breakfast table stuffing freshly made tarnn cakes into his mouth.
Dree was standing in front of the oven preparing to put in another
batch.

"I've never seen a Faceer eat like that," she said, bringing a fresh
pot of chee to fill Diell's empty cup.

"Well, in his defense, we haven't had homemade Faceer food in
quite a while," Steera replied.

"Muuuf fooo gooooch," Diell mumbled. His mouth was over-
flowing with food as he reached for the fresh cup of chee.

"Hurry up and finish," Steera admonished, "we've got to get
moving." Diell had just gotten the last mouthful of tarnn cake swallowed when a knock was heard at the front entrance. Dree hurried
to answer it. At the door were two of the local Faceer militia; this
time they were unarmed.

"Please be so kind as to accompany us," one of them said. The
tone of his voice was softer and more pleasant than the one that had
greeted them only the day before. Steera gave Dree a hug.

"When I have the time, I'll come for a long visit," she said. "I
apologize for not having come more often."

"You're always welcome here, and you can bring the young
eating machine with you." Dree put her hand on Diell's top hair
and gave it a playful scratch. Diell smiled and gave Aunt Dree a
hug as well. "Your mother would be very proud of you." A tear
formed in Steera's eye and slowly wound its way down her nose
ridge. Dree reached out and wiped it with her hand. "Now go ... go

and save us all. She yelled after them as they descended the path to the village ... and find that young Faceer."

Activity outside the remains of the Village Council building was at a fever pitch when they arrived. They were immediately ushered inside and taken directly to Leet's office. Leet was standing in the doorway directing the loading of the supplies that had been gathered.

"Ah, my young friends, I trust you rested well."

"More than well," Steera replied.

Leet walked over to Diell and began brushing the crumbs off his tunic. "And it looks as if you dined adequately,"

"Adequate would be an understatement," Diell said.

"Yes, I've had Dree's tarnn cakes," Leet laughed. "If there are any better on Osstar, I would avoid them for fear of exploding. Now, we must get down to business. I won't elaborate for the sake of brevity. I was in contact with Druk-tasis from the beginning of the North Polar operation. I know of the cylinder and of its contents. It was I who planted the idea of using young Nubin Pire to open the cylinder through one of my assistants who is close to Klut-takit. I didn't, however, count on Klut using you to monitor the expedition." Steera dropped her gaze toward the floor in embarrassment. "Don't feel ashamed. If it hadn't been for that transmitter we would have not known where the Faceer Ka had taken you. They had foiled my plan for your escape from the Polar Station. When I heard that the Stomari were preparing an air assault on a certain location in the Equatorial Region, I surmised that they had discovered your whereabouts. I was then able to contact Nosh and arrange a rescue."

"A rescue, I don't recall a rescue." Diell said, with a hint of sarcasm.

"Well, I'll admit that that didn't work out as intended either. Your friend Seelar foiled my plans once again, just as he had at the Polar Station. At least I was able to extract Nubin Pire."

Steera's couldn't believe her ears. "Then he's alive!"

"Oh ... yes. I thought that I had told you that. Silly me, I am getting old. Sometimes I forget the details."

Steera put both her arms around Leet's slender neck and gave him a massive hug that knocked his spectacles awry. "I knew it! I knew that coola bird was telling me something."

"Bird? What bird?" Lett asked, still a bit disconcerted by Steera's assault.

"Never mind," Steera said. "When and where do we go next?"

"So impatient," Leet said, readjusting his spectacles. "You young people have too much energy for your own good. Now let me finish." He stood for a moment, straightening his tunic. "Now, where was I? Oh yes, the cylinder. Just before the explosion back at Central Headquarters ..."

"Did you have something to do with that as well?" Diell asked.

"Sparks no!" Leet replied. "That's not how I do things. I was trying to figure out a way to get you released when someone took care of the job for me. Now please, let me finish, we have to get moving. As I was saying, just before the explosion we had intercepted a radio communiqué between Klut-Prime and General Somar-loors. Somar-loors had discovered the contents of the cylinder at the Zerrit cave."

"How in Rebal did the contents get there?"

"I imagine that Lieutenant Riatt had brought them to Nosh," Leet answered nonchalantly.

"Riatt! Then he's alive as well?"

"We can hope that they are together and heading south. Now let me finish! Klut has learned about the metallic map." Steera kept her gaze up this time, but she knew how Klut had gotten knowledge of the map. "It seems that there is a third cylinder in the South Polar Region. We believe that this cylinder may hold the key to understanding where they came from and their purpose. We must get to that cylinder before the Stomari."

"The Stomari are going after it?"

"Klut ordered Somar-loors to leave straight-way for the village of Jaakar where he would be outfitted for an expedition. We began our preparation at the same time."

"And what of Riatt and Pire?" Steera asked.

"We lost contact with them as a result of Somar-loors' attack on the Zerrit colony, but Nosh had been prepared to leave the caverns at any time."

"And Druk-tasis?" Diell asked. "What of him?"

"You let me worry about Druk-tasis. You worry about getting to the third cylinder in one piece."

"Then he survived as well," Steera said, hopefully.

"Survived! Why of course. You don't think I'd let a few Stomari thugs from my own office complex do him in, do you? But don't worry about him; he has his own course to follow."

"All alive!" Steera said incredulously. "Then we must leave for the South Polar Region immediately!" Steera rushed to the window to view the loading preparations outside.

"The preparations are almost ready, but we must be certain that we are well prepared. This will be a treacherous trip indeed," Leet said in a serious tone.

"When do we leave?" Diell asked, excitedly.

Leet pulled his spectacles down and peered at the two young Faceer. "We aren't leaving. It is far too dangerous a trip for an old soul like me. But, I can see that nothing will keep you two from going, and that's good. You'll need that kind of spirit. And who better to interpret the contents of the third cylinder than you two?" One of the villagers interrupted Leet, whispering in his ear. He thought for a moment and then addressed Steera. "It seems that you will be leaving at Rebal-rise. The plan is for you to be accompanied by ten of our stoutest villagers." Leet moved toward a large map of Osstar mounted on the wall of his office and bade the two to follow. "You will be provided with a Faceer steamer at the coast," he said, pointing to the village of Prameel. His ancient, bony finger carved a twisting path down the rough paper chart. "You will steam west through the Straits of Morate in the Equatorial Region, past Andorna in the Lower Midlands, directly to Suprameel on the southern coast of Donait in the Southern Islands. There you will be further equipped for your polar journey."

"Are you sure we can't talk you into joining us?" Steera said, playfully.

"An old lothar like me would only slow you down. Besides,

I have to get back to my post at the Government Complex. I only came here to assess the damage and speed up the arrangements for the journey." He paused for a moment. Turning toward the side window he gazed out across the busy courtyard, a look of pain washing over his old face. "And to pay my respects to two brave Faceer who gave their lives for our future." He spent a moment in silent meditation. "Now go and prepare. In a way, I wish I were going with you," he said, wistfully. "But I know that you will succeed." Steera took Leet's hand and kissed it gently.

"We all owe you so much," she said, "and one day everyone will know it." Leet smiled at them as they turned and made their way past the boxes and crates littering the hallway and out into the courtyard of the Council building.

At Rebal-rise, twelve Faceer set out for the coastal village of Prameel and a rendezvous with their transport to the Southern Islands. Leet accompanied them as far as the Strail Pass, and then watched from the last observation point as they made their way down the southern slope of the Layard Mountains and out across the plains that led to the sea.

CHAPTER 27

Pire had not moved from his position in the Soota nor had he taken any nourishment, only accepting the occasional drink of keera water from Nosh. He had kept his attention focused on the book, pouring over the symbols, pictures and sounds. Occasionally the light entering the huge cavern that contained the underground lake became sufficient to show details of the walls or ceiling. Huge ice deposits lined both sides of the lake, stretching up to the ceiling in many places. Pire speculated that they were the remnants of a solid block that once filled the cavern. A frigid, biting breeze blew accompanied them as they moved across the lake but, inexplicably, the water remained warmer than the air.

As Pire's fingers crawled across the silky pages, the book began to give up its secrets. It was telling the story of a people not unlike the inhabitants of Osstar, more advanced in technology, but similar in culture. They had family units. They valued life and their environment. They worked, but also enjoyed forms of leisure. They had a finite life span that encompassed youth, middle and old age. They required clothing to shield them from the extremes of climate just as Osstarians, and they required nourishment at regular intervals to sustain life. They had art and literature from a diverse range of cultures. They appeared to reproduce sexually, but didn't include a large amount of scientific information on the mechanics of procreation, instead devoting a great deal of their art and literature to the sex act itself.

There were also differences. The people of the cylinder exhibited a wider range of skin tone and hair color and texture. There also appeared to be only one intelligent species on their planet. One thing, however, was abundantly clear about these strangely familiar beings; theirs was not a culture of peace and harmony. The book categorized page after page of military actions—some on a grand scale. In comparison to the people of the cylinder, the conflict between Stoma and Faceer was a mere spat. The idea that species homogeneity was a cure for violence was shattered by the wars these beings had endured. Or had they endured them? Pire hoped he would find the answer to that question somewhere in a cavern in the South Polar Region.

Nosh left the wheel of the ship and made his way back to Pire's self-constructed cloister. "Learning anything?"

"Much. These creatures, whoever they are or were, are more like us than I imagined possible."

"Us?"

"Osstarians." Pire said.

"Osstarians, is it?" Nosh smiled. "Then the book is already having an effect."

"Yes, I suppose it is."

"I'm going to need your help," Nosh said. "We'll soon be leaving the caverns and entering the Stageel River that flows into the sea to the south."

"Help with what?"

"It may get a little rough when we exit the caverns."

Pire didn't like the sound of it. "What does 'a little rough' mean?"

"The lake exits the caverns through a narrow passage about three hours from here and it gets a bit choppy. These craft are not designed for rapid currents."

Pire liked "a bit choppy" even less than "a little rough." "So what do you want me to do?"

"When the time comes, I want you to tend the wheel."

"And what exactly will you be doing while I'm tending the wheel?"

"I'm going to using one of these to keep the craft off the rocks." He pulled a long metal pole from its resting place on the inside of the boat and stood it upright next to him. It was half again as long as he was tall.

"This is adding up to more than just a bit choppy," Pire said wryly.

"Never fear, my young friend. If this is the hardest thing we must do between here and the South Polar Region, we will have been fortunate indeed. Besides, you are Somacee, a lover of wind and sail, not some land-locked, hill-climbing Veertal cowering under the bow sprint like our Zerrit friend." Pire smiled a weak smile and went back to the book.

After about two more hours of gliding across the glassy surface of the lake, Pire began to hear an unsettling sound. It sounded like a dull, deep-throated growl. Nosh was still at the wheel, holding the craft solid on course. The entire cavern was becoming lighter.

Pire could now make out details of the inside of the massive cave. The ceiling had large rounded pockmarks where, over the millennia, great chunks of it had broken off and fallen into the water. The walls were surprisingly smooth, evidence of the long-term co-action of molten rock and moving ice. The cavern had probably been formed early in the planet's geologic history by volcanic activity that had long since subsided. The period of intense cold that followed, the "Long Winter" of Stoma legend, had filled it with a solid core of ice. Hundreds of thousands of years of gradual warming, along with probable geothermal activity from the core of Osstar, had caused the ice to retreat. The melting ice had carved the walls of the cavern and created the huge lake within.

"Take the wheel!" The command came thundering across the deck. Pire jumped to his task. The dull growl was now a steady roar, and the sides of the cavern had closed in on the vessel. The placid lake had acquired a swift current, which was becoming stronger with every passing minute. Pire strained against the wheel to hold it steady. Nosh, pole in hand, was leaning over the side of the boat pushing against the large boulders that had suddenly appeared all around them. The Zerrit leader had wedged himself as far into the cabin as he could. "Steer to the right!" No sooner had the words left Nosh's mouth than a flood of harsh light blasted aside the gloom of the cavern and the craft was flung headlong down the steep waterway that would eventually form the river, Stageel.

Pire was steering on instinct alone. Nosh moved quickly, fluidly from side to side using the long pole to push the craft away from each treacherous rock. Pire tried to steer away from the biggest ones, but the ponderous Stoma boat, so well suited for smooth water, was proving a severe challenge in the racing current.

"I'm losing control!" he yelled at Nosh.

"You're doing fine. Try and keep it in the middle of the channel if you can." Nosh's voice was calm and determined. The Zerrit leader moved forward far enough to peer out of the cabin.

Suddenly, the bottom seemed to fall out of the swift channel. The boat dropped so quickly that Pire had to reach out and grab the light cone as it hovered in front of his face. As soon as he had it in his hand, the boat landed with a heavy thud. Pire and the Zerrit were knocked to the deck and the wheel twisted from Pire's hand. The vessel spun wildly. Foam from the churning water flew everywhere. Nosh was nowhere to be seen. The craft had become wedged against a large boulder in the center of the channel and the rushing water was pounding against it, threatening to break it in two.

"Nosh!" Pire called as loudly as he could over the roar of the water. There was no answer. With all of the strength that he could muster, he pulled himself up, hand-over-hand, using the spokes of the wheel. He put all of his weight on the left side of the wheel, desperately trying to get it to turn enough to allow the craft to free itself from the rock. Nothing happened. The wheel wouldn't budge. As he continued to strain, trying to find a place to plant his feet for better leverage, he noticed a silvery object in the foam next to the boat. It was the metal pole that Nosh had been using on the rocks.

Pire's heart sank. He was at the point of exhaustion. He was thinking of simply letting go and letting the gods settle his and Osstar's fate when he felt the wheel start to move. Looking around, he saw the Zerrit leader tugging on the wheel with all his strength. Pire joined him and the wheel turned about a quarter turn. A solid sheet of water boiled up over the deck. The craft squirted out from behind the boulder and shot several hundred feet down the rapids.

The craft found calmer water. The boat was still slowly spinning, but the current had decreased dramatically. Pire got it under control and eased it to the shoreline. The Zerrit leader was wet but unharmed. Pire patted the Zerrit's shoulder and they both flopped down near the wheel, Pire shaking the water from his ears.

"We're lucky to be alive, my fuzzy friend," he said to the Zerrit who was preening his fur to remove the despised moisture. Then he remembered. "Nosh," he cried out.

The Zerrit immediately leapt to his feet at the sound of Nosh's name. He scampered back and forth across the deck whimpering and whining. Pire climbed atop the cabin and scanned the water. He saw nothing. He jumped to the deck and went to the bow of the boat, which was now grounded on the sandy bank of the shore. As he hung his head over in order to be able to peer down the shoreline, a gray figure glided up, and a sleek form lifted itself out of the water and into the boat.

"Nosh!"

The Zerrit leader threw himself at Nosh's feet.

"Yes, are you two all right?" he said calmly.

"Are we all right? We thought that you had drowned!"

"Really?" Nosh laughed. "You forget that I'm half Stoma. When it comes to swimming, I think it's more than half. I've come to the lake to swim since I was a child, although I must admit that I had never before tried the rapids."

"So what happened to you? I remember trying to free the boat from the rock and seeing your pole float by. Then, your Zerrit friend helped me with the wheel and we managed to break free."

"Oh you did, did you? Well done."

"How did you escape the whirlpool?"

"I didn't escape it. I used it to turn the boat back into the current ..." Nosh stopped and thought a moment. "... with help, of course, from your maneuver with the wheel."

"Then it was you that saved the boat."

"It was us—and all of us, apparently." Nosh lifted the Zerrit leader upright and put his hand on his cheek. The leader accepted it gratefully, rubbing it across the soft, bare skin of his face. "Are all the supplies here?"

"I wasn't worrying much about the supplies when we were going through the 'choppy' water back there," Pire said sarcastically.

He stuck his head into the cabin and returned quickly. "They seem to be."

"Good, that will mean no delays when we arrive."

"Arrive? Just where are we headed anyway?"

"To Jaakar, a Faceer village on the Southern coast where this river empties into the sea. I have standing arrangements for supplies and a transport for a South Polar expedition."

"And then on to the Lower Midlands?" Pire asked.

"No," Nosh replied. "We have no time to waste. We're sailing directly for the Pole."

"In this thing!"

"Hardly," Nosh replied, somewhat annoyed at Pire's lack of faith. "Do you think that I failed to plan for this expedition? We'll be sailing in a Stoma-designed tragoone, a ship worthy of the journey. By heading directly to the Pole we stand a good chance of getting there before the Stomari."

Pire was very familiar with the large, sturdy Stoma sailing ships and felt reassured. "So, let's get started." He pushed the gear into reverse.

"Not so fast, my impetuous friend. We'll be doing all of our travel by night from here to the coast. The river becomes quite tame past these rocks and navigation in the twinight should pose no problem."

"... And we have the light cones if we need them for the staddich."

Nosh hung his head for a moment. Pire could see the look of disbelief on his face. "I think the jolt from the trip down the rapids has loosened something in your brain. For a Faceer, you're not thinking too soundly. A Faceer piloting a Soota down this river is a bit peculiar, but not out of the ordinary. A Faceer with a Seeyard as a first mate and a Zerrit as lookout would prompt a great deal of attention; and at night, the cones would make us look like a Zaarian pleasure barge." Nosh turned an image over in his mind ... their little Soota, bedecked in colored lights and full of rowdy, drunken Stoma businessmen. He chuckled out loud, and Pire joined him. The tension of their perilous trip down the rapids was dissipated by the sweet relief of shared laughter. Nosh draped his two sinewy arms over Pire and the Zerrit. "Tonight my friends, we start down-river to the coast."

T hings had not gone well for Seelar since his unexpected es-cape from Prass. He had traveled to the west thinking that no one would be looking in that direction. Unlike Steera and Di-ell, the Stomari had left him only his Faceer Ka uniform tunic. In the first Faceer village he had entered he was looked upon with scorn. The news of Romass had traveled across the Upper Midlands. He had found neither friends nor even anyone who would offer infor-mation on a way back to the Equatorial Region. His only recourse had been to turn southward and travel down the coastline.

Outside a small Faceer fishing village, Seelar finally found a friendly face. He encountered a young Faceer standing beside a small sailing skiff. He recognized Seelar's tunic. "Have you been at camp?" The youngster had obviously spent some time at one of the Faceer Ka sponsored youth camps

"Why yes," Seelar replied. "I learned much at camp about how to be a good Faceer."

"I liked camp," the youth responded. "My parents made me quit going."

"But, why?" There was sympathy and concern in Seelar's voice.

"They said it was run by a bunch of drug-slaves." Seelar winced, beginning to feel the discomfort of his own withdrawal. "But that's where I learned to sail," the youth said, proudly.

"And a fine boat you have," Seelar commented, running his hands along the smooth side of the fishing skiff. "I'll wager that you can sail her as well as any Stoma merchant."

"Better," the lad answered. "Would you like to take her out?"

Seelar smiled. "Oh, very much. Are you sure it's all right with your parents? After all, I could be one of those drug-slaves." The young Faceer's face darkened for a moment and his eyes narrowed, but soon they were beaming again as he recognized the jest.

"Get in, I'll sail you around that point over there," he said, raising his hand in the direction of a wooded point of land to the southeast. Seelar jumped into the skiff, grabbed the tiller and unfurled the main sail as the boy pushed the boat into the sea. The nimble craft skated across the water toward the point at surprising speed.

"This is a fast boat," Seelar commented. "I'll wager you could sail a long way in this."

"I once sailed to Durrass," the youth bragged.

"Durrass! Do you mean the village in the Equatorial Region?

"Yes."

Seelar doubted the youth's claim, but surmised that the skiff could make it across the North Equatorial Sea if properly piloted. As they neared the point, Seelar gave the appearance of struggling with the tiller.

"What's wrong?" the youth asked.

"It's the tiller. I think something has fouled it. Could you jump in and see if you can clear whatever it is? You are a good swimmer, aren't you?"

"The best," the lad said bravely, trying to impress his new friend. Without another thought, he slipped over the side into the shallow water some one hundred yards from the point. Seelar needed no further prompting. He pushed the tiller to the right and headed the skiff due south into the sea. "Hey!" the lad cried.

"You should be able to swim in from there," Seelar responded. "Consider yourself lucky. You have just made a major contribution to the future of your species. Be proud."

"But what about my parents," the lad yelled back, "how can I explain the boat?"

"Tell them that drug-slaves took it." Seelar smiled and leaned back against the tiller. What was one small Faceer's dilemma in comparison to the future of an entire planet? The Faceer Ka would be reformed around a new and vital mission—to recover the third cylinder.

The wind picked up and the small craft sped out toward the open sea and then turned southeastward toward the Equatorial coast. With luck and the wind, Seelar would be there in a few days. A few days would give him time to come up with a plan to make it to the South Polar Region. He reached into his pocket and took out a package that had been smuggled to him in his cell at the Government Complex. He unrolled it and dipped his finger into the dark, sticky substance clinging to the center of the paper. Putting the finger to his lips, he let the invigorating feeling course through his body. "Ahh… katoc," he thought. "Without it we would be nothing more than pets on a leash."

Somar-loors' company was exhausted by the time they finally caught sight of the Faceer village of Jaakar. They had been traveling for three days without letup in the equatorial heat. The village, situated at the mouth of the Stageel River, did a lot of trading with Stoma merchants, so the sight of twenty or so Stomari Shock Troopers drew only brief attention from the residents. General Somar held the company at the edge of the village to dispel any fear that their presence might engender. His troops began to set up their cotaans.

About twenty minutes after they had arrived, Fazid appeared at the front of the cotaan with an embarrassed Faceer in tow.

"Pardon sir, this fellow says he has business with you."

"Show him in, Trooper Fazid." Gleer-fazid directed the Faceer to the General and took a position beside him. Colonel Treeg was about to tell the trooper to return to his post when General Somar spoke. "We can't let the company sit idly, Trooper. I would like for you to form a small unit and see that everyone has his equipment in top order. We're going to be making an arduous journey and their very existence depends on it."

"Yes sir." Fazid snapped a salute and spun around smartly to discharge his new responsibility.

"And you, my friend," Somar-loors used the superior to inferior form of the word, "I think that we have some business to transact." The Faceer bowed his head in agreement.

"My name is Rowand Leesh. I have been contracted through mutual friends to provide transport for you and your party to the Southern Islands." Colonel Treeg twisted in his chair at the syrupy-sweet voice of the Faceer merchant.

"When do we leave?" General Somar asked.

The merchant dropped his head, wadding and unwadding a piece of paper in his hands. "Well, I will try and get everything together as soon as I can ... but I don't think the price I was quoted will be adequate to ..."

Boom! The sound of General Somar's massive fist meeting the table top startled colonel Treeg, and had a devastating effect on Leesh. "We will leave at Mid-Rebal." General Somar's voice was calm but stern. "You will have the boats ready and the provisions on board, or you will receive nothing. And, if everything that was requested is not there, you will receive what you deserve." The frightened Faceer merchant made no further attempt to bargain; the message was clear. He simply bowed his head and exited the cotaan.

"How do we know he will do what you instructed?" Colonel Treeg asked after he had left.

"Did you see his eyes? I've seen that look before on the face of a defeated enemy. He'll grumble and complain, but he'll do as he is told. We'll have no trouble from him. I'm going out to see that the troops are preparing for the journey, and to support Trooper Fazid ... that is how future officers are made. At Mid-Rebal we leave for the Southern Islands." Colonel Treeg watched General Somar with admiration as he strapped on his side-arm, grabbed his helmet and exited the cotaan.

Had there been enough light in the dark cavern to produce them, Riatt would have cast three shadows, his own, and those of the two Zerrits who were now practically attached to him. When he moved, they moved. When he stopped, they stopped.

He held the small light cone aloft trying to squeeze a modicum more of the dull, orange light from it but it was to no avail. It now emitted only the faintest of glows. The path had flattened and widened, so it was difficult to get any kind of notion as to their direction.

He reached down and picked up a stone, flinging it across the narrow cave corridor in frustration. It struck the opposite wall with a dull 'thwack.' He tossed another. The Zerrits looked around them for stones of their own. Soon all three were heaving stones in all directions. The noise of the stones hitting the walls of the cave echoed through the passageway. One of the apes, lost in enthusiasm, let fly with a mighty heave directly in front of him. The cave walls resonated with a different and very distinctive sound—a splash!

Riatt dropped his remaining stones and immediately followed the sound. To his left, the darkness was softening a bit. He moved in the direction of the light until he felt the cold sensation of water. He looked down to see the tufts of hair on his feet waving to-and-fro, swaying with the gentle waves like the silky strands of sea grass attached to the rocks at water's edge.

To his left, the interior of the cavern was growing lighter. He returned to his two friends and took one of them by the hairy hand, noting how alike in form and structure it was to a Faceer hand. Pointing in the direction he wished to take, he started off. The Zerrits hesitated. Riatt stopped briefly, motioned to his companions and moved forward again. The fear of being left behind overcame their fear of water, and the Zerrits followed.

They walked for almost two hours. The light level in the cavern had increased dramatically and occasionally small shafts of Zenos light would break through a fissure in the high ceiling. He could see that they had been traversing the shoreline of a vast underground lake. The Zerrits were calmer now that they could see what lay ahead of them. They approached a narrow passage where a massive outcropping of rock had pushed its way almost to the lake's edge. At its narrowest point, the rock wall left only about two feet of space between it and the water. Riatt squeezed the Zerrits into single file and they navigated the narrow path to the other side. There, the floor of the cavern opened into a broad, sandy beach.

Riatt could see a dark form resting on the sand. He picked up his pace. The amorphous form began to take the shape of a familiar object—a boat! He broke into a run and the Zerrits matched his pace. He reached the boat nearly out of breath.

It was a Soota, a craft he knew from his childhood. A few yards away he saw a large lump on the beach. He pointed to one of the Zerrits to retrieve it, but the Zerrit would have none of it. He walked over and picked up a large pack, which was stuffed with clothing and provisions. Ten yards farther down the beach, he could see a jagged path in the sand most likely made by the launching of another boat. "Nosh and Pire," he thought. "They want me to follow."

Riatt picked up the pack and threw it into the Soota. He put his shoulder to the bow and began to push. The rough texture of the laange-wood tore at his tunic. The Zerrits stood frozen, caught between their need to stay with Riatt and their fear of the water. Finally, the smaller (and consistently braver) of the two joined Riatt and pushed. The second, faced with abandonment, joined in half-heartedly. Gaining momentum, the craft slide down the beach and into the water. The Zerrits scrambled onto the deck.

Once into the open waters of the lake, Riatt took the controls while his two cohorts hid behind the wheel housing. He turned the engine switch to the "on" position and listened with relief as the electric motor started to whirr. "Steer in the direction of the light," he thought, and turned the wheel to the left. The craft glided across the water so smoothly that the Zerrits began to relax.

When he was fairly certain that he was safely in the middle of the lake, Riatt thought about what he planned to do next. It seemed certain that Pire and Nosh had taken the other boat, so the lake must provide a way out of the cavern. He knew of a Faceer village on the coast that stood at the mouth of a great river, perhaps this underground lake was the source of that river. He would take the Soota down the river and reunite with Pire and Nosh at the village. "And, if it all goes well, I shall have cerrlo salad with my tarnn cakes," he laughed at the confident simplicity of his plan.

The gentle humming of the motor led Riatt to stretch out and relax, keeping only his bony knee on the wheel to prevent any deviation from course. He studied his companions. It interested him that he had not noticed the differences between the two earlier. Besides the size difference, the expressions on their faces, the markings on

their ears and under their eyes gave each a distinctive personality.
The words of an old Faceer poem came to him:

"How much more do things we prize

 When the light travels first through our heart

 And then to our eyes."

For a moment, Riatt envisioned the two dressed in Faceer clothing. Whom did they look like? The Zerrits seemed amused at Riatt's attention. Suddenly, Riatt spoke out loud. "Andar and Driell,"
he threw his head back in a laugh, startling the timid Zerrit. They
reminded him of two of his Faceer Ka corporals back at the Equatorial Camp. Andar thought too much about everything and Driell
(always the first to volunteer) rarely stopped to think about anything.

Riatt pointed in the direction of the larger Zerrit, "Andar," he
said, and then to the other, "Driell." The Zerrits looked at Riatt and
then at each other. Finally, Andar pointed to Riatt and waited. After
a moment, Riatt realized what he was doing. "Riatt," he said. All
three seemed quite pleased. Riatt continued going back and forth
naming the two until he was certain that they understood. Their
quickness in picking up the concept amazed him. Had they been
underestimating their intelligence?

His interaction with his new friends had made Riatt inatten-
tive to his main task. With a sudden lurch, the Soota ran aground.
He assessed the situation, and concluded that it would be an easy
task to push it back into the deeper water provided that he could
get someone to take the wheel. After thinking for a moment, he
pointed at Driell and called his name. The Zerrit perked up his ears.
Riatt then bade him come to the stern of the boat, and he complied.
He showed him the wheel and how to turn it, thinking all the while
that this would be too difficult a notion for even the cleverest of
Zerrits. He was amazed when Driell turned the wheel exactly as he
had been instructed.

Riatt switched off the motor and jumped over the side into the
shallow water. Pushing with his legs, he waved at Driell to turn the
wheel to the right. Driell turned the wheel with such efficiency that
the boat shot back out into the lake with Riatt clinging precariously

to the bow line. He now had no free hands with which to gesture. He feared that he might spend the rest of the voyage skimming along the surface next to the boat, but he was soon drawn from the cold, black wetness by a hairy and very muscular arm — Andar!

Back in the vessel, Riatt took the wheel from Driell and patted him on the head. He reached into the pack. Lying half-open on top were several tarnn cakes that had been hastily wrapped in water-resistant paper. He gave two of the cakes to Driell who immediately handed one to Andar. Andar's sharing of his meal had been automatic. He took one for himself. The three compatriots settled down in the Soota to eat and relax.

Several hours passed. Driell remained seated on the cowling covering the bow section of the boat, watching the black water slip by, while Andar napped. Riatt was fighting fatigue. He could see Driell's head periodically turn at an angle and then back, as if he were hearing something. Soon, Andar awoke and joined Driell. Both seemed to be sensing something ahead. Finally, Riatt heard it as well, a low, hissing sound that was growing with each passing minute. The Zerrits were becoming panicky. Ahead, the light was pouring in from a great opening in the cavern wall. A frothy mist swirled around a narrow area of the lake, and the hiss became a roar.

Riatt didn't have time to shout a warning to Driell and Andar. He pushed his shoulder against the wheel and hung on as the craft shot out of the cavern and down the narrow rapids. Driell screamed a high pitched scream, a sound that Riatt had never heard from a Zerrit. He tried to grab on to whatever he could to stay in the boat. Andar, quiet even in this horrendous circumstance, threw himself under the bow cowling. The boat shuddered and spun like a top as it ground against the rocks that littered the rapids. Driell was being flung from one side of the boat to the other.

All at once, the craft slammed against a huge boulder. The power of the water tried to force the Soota up and over the rock. The violent jolt threw Driell over the side. In desperation, he clung to the bowline. Andar, seeing his predicament, plucked up all his courage and leaned over the boat, grabbing the line and Driell in one hand. Riatt was in a quandary. If he let go of the wheel to go to the aid of his comrades, the boat would surely be lost. He watched helplessly as Andar was pulled over the side and both he and Driell disappeared from sight. The sound that now filled his ears was that of a boat breaking up. The wheel spun freely in his hand, and he was flung into the foaming maelstrom.

Riatt remembered seeing the pack float by him and reaching out for it calmly, as if in slow motion. There was no sound in his recollection. It had all been like a lazy dream. The pack proved to be his salvation. He drifted to shore and gathered himself, and then climbed onto a rock that was resting just out of the waterline. He scoured the river for any signs of his two friends. He called their names over and over again, hoping that perhaps they had survived and had just lost their way.

After about half an hour, he knew that they were not coming back. He sat down on a rock in deep despair. Hiding his head in his lap, he cried uncontrollably. He cried for his lost friends ... all of his lost friends, and for himself and the lonely road that he knew lay ahead. After a while, the pain began to subside and he drug himself to his feet. Washed up on the shore, not three feet from where he had landed, Riatt found the wheel of the doomed Soota. He lifted it onto dry ground and stood it upright. Bracing it with rocks on either side, he made a humble monument to his lost companions.

Zenos was now shining full-out, and Rebal was chasing it across the eastern sky, gaining on it as every minute passed. Riatt knew that he had to move on. He would follow the river to the seacoast; it must be what Nosh and Pire were doing. He could see a road that followed the river just a few yards from the shore. This was still, for the most part, Faceer country, at least until he got to the coast. He could travel the road without drawing much attention.

Turning to start his journey, he noticed a clump of small flowers blooming by the trunk of a laange tree. He picked two, making sure that one was slightly larger than the other, and set them adrift in the now-gentle current of the river. "Whatever notion you have of heaven," he thought, "may your soul's journey together in death as they did in life." He bowed his head on last time, then turned and headed toward the road. The quest was now to find his other lost friends.

CHAPTER 28

The wind had been kind to Druk-tasis as he sailed west-south-west along the Northern coast of the Equatorial Region. The smooth sailing he had enjoyed since he had left the Upper Midlands had given him time to study the map left him by his benefactor, Tomar Leet. He hadn't noticed it at first, but the map showed a tiny blue line leading to the circled area. Druk-tasis read this as a small stream or canal. The map also contained a reference to the position of Rebal and Zenos at Rebal-wane, in relation to the stream.

Using the Rebalistra as a guide, he felt that he was coming close to the point on the shoreline indicated on the map. He didn't like the idea, however, of going in at Rebal-wane or even an hour or two after Rebal-wane. He had on a common traders' unisuit, but this was most likely dangerous territory for any Stoma, regardless of how he was dressed.

Druk decided to try and identify the entrance point and then wait until the staddich to make his way in. He drifted parallel to the shore, hunching down in the skiff and lifting his head just enough above the tiller to see out across the coastline. After about an hour of drifting he was unable to locate the entrance to the stream. He was beginning to lose faith in his plan when he noticed that the sound of the waves breaking on the beach had been interrupted. Turning the tiller to bring the skiff nearer the shore, he listened intently. The sound was not there. A few minutes later, and a few yards farther down the coast, the sound returned. He was certain that he had found the mouth of a small stream or canal. Druk turned the tiller hard over, and the skiff scraped to a stop on the pebble beach. He pulled the sail cover over the open area of the skiff and waited for Rebal to follow Zenos below the horizon.

The staddich brought with it a cool sea-breeze blowing in to-

wards the land. Druk-tasis had only to tighten the line to the running sail and the skiff glided down the shoreline. As he paralleled
the shore, Druk could see the mouth of the stream just where it was
supposed to be. His Stoma reckoning and the tried-and-true Rebalistra had brought him to precisely where he wanted to be.

By the markings on the map, he was in the heart of the unincorporated territory, a patchwork of areas beyond the reach of the
government at Prass, organized under the control of a boss or "warlord." The stream narrowed as he moved farther inland. Overhead,
faar trees were beginning to weave their branches together, blotting
out the faint sparks of the stars above him. It was deadly quiet. The
only sound was that of the insects, in particular seedge flies. They
were chirping out their mating calls, back-and-forth from bank-to-
bank, with one long fleeeeeeep and two short chirps. It created an
eerie accompaniment to the soft splash of water against the side of
the boat.

Abruptly, the chirping stopped. Druk scrunched down in the
skiff unable to see anything on either bank of the stream. Two metal
claws suddenly flew out from either shore, catching the craft and
stopping it dead in the water. Druk-tasis decided to lay still as the
boat was reeled into the left bank.

"Come out!" a voice commanded. "Come out and give us the
word." Druk rose to his feet amid a muffled buzz of voices. The
bank was lined with Faceer. They were all dressed in a uniform of
sorts, but not like any uniform he had seen. As he stepped onto the
shore he was met by a malevolent looking and fully armed Faceer.
"Give us the word, or die!" he said, drawing a short stabbing sword.
From the dark tone of his voice, it was clear that he meant it. Druk
searched his memory for a "word." Surely Leet wouldn't send him
all this way and not be aware of some password. His mind raced.
He tried to stall for time.

"I have journeyed far and have come from ..." His hands fumbled nervously in his pockets.

"The word!" the Faceer snarled. Druk's hand closed around
something in his pocket. He withdrew it. There in his palm was the
podwood Bajan horse.

"Of course!" he thought. "Tiimat." The word fairly flew out of his mouth.

The Faceer leader frowned in disappointment. He sheathed his sword. "We have been expecting you. Get your things and come with me." Druk-tasis grabbed the heavy sailcloth bundle and followed the Faceer leader down a path to a large clearing in the equatorial jungle.

What he saw when he arrived in the clearing amazed him. Here was a collection of buildings and market areas as large as a Stoma trading village. Hundreds of figures were milling about; some of the Faceer were dressed in Faceer Ka uniforms, some wore the strange uniform of the Faceer who had "greeted" him at the mooring, and some wore no uniform at all, just the simple tunic of the Faceer tradesperson. Even more amazing to Druk was the presence of Stoma. They were dressed as was he, in the grey/green unisuit of Stoma traders. One of them gave him a passing glance, but continued his business as if it were not an unusual occurrence.

His escort led Druk-tasis through the front opening to the most ornate of the compound's buildings. Inside it was bustling with activity. Along each wall was a line of tables covered with goods of every description. Behind most of the tables were Faceer of one uniform or the other, but more than a few were being run by Stoma. Druk was led past the tables and into a room directly across from the opening to the indoor marketplace. A Faceer was seated at a large Darma-shell desk with his back to Druk. The escort indicated that he should stay, and promptly disappeared into the crowd. After a few minutes, the Faceer turned around and studied him.

"You know our ancient tongue, then?" He asked, not really seeking an answer.

Druk had to think for a moment to discern his meaning, and then it came to him. "Yes, I was instructed before I started out on my journey. I have come from ..." Druk-tasis was interrupted before he could go any farther.

"I know from whence you come. You seek provisions for a journey south. Negotiations have already been concluded. It is a business trip, then?" Druk-tasis didn't know how much this Faceer knew, or to what extent he could be trusted, but his instincts told him to guard his information.

"Yes, a business trip."

"To the Southern Islands?" The Faceer studied Druk's face for any signs of tension.

"Perhaps," Druk replied casually, "but of course you would know, since negotiations have already been concluded." The Faceer leaned back in his chair and smiled.

"Then you have the negotiated fee."

"Yes." Druk hesitated for a moment "Five bars of pure gallite." The number simply slipped out of his mouth.

"Five bars!" The Faceer momentarily rose from his chair, but quickly regained his composure and sat back in his chair. "Well, you really are a trader. You had me worried. Don't think I hadn't noticed that mark behind your ear-hole." Druk-tasis' hand shot up the left side of his head. He thought himself an idiot for forgetting that the Propaganda Ministry had painted a temporary Stomari symbol behind his ear. "You don't have to feel self-conscious," the Faceer continued, "some of my best customers are Stomari." He laughed out loud, and Druk-tasis nervously joined him.

"Well, business is business." Druk said with a smile.

"So it is." The Faceer stood and extended a hand to Druk-tasis who shook it in Faceer fashion, side to side. "My name is Tyage. My family has controlled this sector for six generations. We have done it by being good at business, and by keeping petty prejudices from getting in the way of a good deal. Look around you. You'll see Faceer and Stoma at every trade table. You will see Faceer Ka uniforms mingling with the unisuits of the Stoma traders. We have only one political belief here—the belief in profit. It even extends to the Stomari, if they are concerned with profit and not politics. I had my doubts about you at first. You look like a thinker. Thinkers are bad for business. But when you tried to cheat me, I knew that you could be trusted, even in these troubled times."

"And just how did I try to cheat you?" Druk asked innocently.

"Oh, but you are a slick one. How much did you say you brought me?"

"Five bars of pure gallite."

"That was not the negotiated price."

"And just what was the negotiated price?"

"Twelve bars," Tyage replied without raising an inner lid.

"Who's trying to cheat who?" Druk replied. "The price was eight bars and not a quarter-bar more."

"Eleven bars."

"I only have eight bars with me," Druk replied, "and I have no way to get any more."

Tyage drummed his fingers on the smooth table top, but his eyes never left Druk-tasis. "Nine bars ... final offer."

"Accepted." Druk thrust his hand out in the traditional palms up position to close the deal.

"You strike a hard bargain my Stomari friend, but a good one. I'll wager that you even left a bit of profit for yourself?" Tyage pushed a small button on the underside of his desk, and an assistant arrived. "Take this trader to Neeras in stall seven." He stood, laying his hand backside up in Druk-tasis' hand. "Your provisions and transport will be ready in a few days. You will make payment to Neeras. May you have a profitable journey."

"Thank you," Druk answered. He withdrew his hand slowly from under Tyage's and let him see that it was still empty ... the traders' way of closing a deal. Druk-tasis followed the assistant out of the room and, weaving in and out of the busy market place, made his way toward stall seven.

Tyage followed Druk's progress through the crowd. When he was out of view, he pushed the button again. This time another Faceer appeared—one dressed in the uniform of Tyage's security forces.

"I want him followed and watched," he said. "He's no Stoma trader, and I doubt that he's Stomari either. He's a thinker ... thinkers are bad for business."

"Then we are to detain him?" The officer asked.

"Not until I tell you. He has some powerful connections up North that are sponsoring him. He must be on a very important mission because they have purchased some very expensive and highly secret equipment for his vessel, equipment that I could sell for a tidy profit. Continue with the preparations for his journey, but drag it out a bit. He may eventually sail south, but it's going to cost him more than nine bars of gallite." The security officer bowed and left the room. For a moment Tyage thought that he saw Druk's head at one of the stalls along the wall opposite his office. He sat back in his chair and smiled. "A very profitable day, indeed."

Riatt had been traveling the river road for a full day. He had seen a few Faceer tradespersons and a lot of grazing keesa, regarding him with suspicion and flicking their stubby tails nervously. The river was widening with each mile he traveled, and river traffic had picked up considerably. He felt confident that he would be able to get some information on the location of his two friends at the village. Rounding a bend in the road, he came upon a Faceer trader with a problem. His tricart had lost its front wheel and he was struggling to lift it enough to get the wheel back on.

"Can I be of assistance?"

The trader looked up from his work and studied Riatt. "If you can help lift, it would be appreciated," he said nervously. His present situation overruled any misgivings he might have about his helper. Riatt put his muscular shoulder to the front of the tri-cart and it lifted off the ground.

"Get the wheel on it," he said. "I can hold it long enough."

The Faceer trader quickly retrieved the wheel and slid its hub in between the two forks that stuck out in front of the vehicle. "All right," he said, and Riatt let the weight of the tri-cart settle back onto the newly replaced wheel.

"It seems to be holding," Riatt said, waiting for his friend to identify himself.

"Yes, you've been of great help, thank you." The trader started to get back into the cart to leave. Riatt sensed discomfort in his demeanor.

"Are you headed to the village?" Riatt asked, before the trader could pull away. Reluctantly the trader turned off the electric mo-

tor to the cart. Faceer must show courtesy to other Faceer, especially when they have done them a favor.

"I am."

"Would you mind if I rode along?"

The trader hesitated. "Are you sure it is wise?"

"What do you mean?"

"To go to Jaakar?"

"Yes, if that is the name of the village. Is there something
wrong?"

"Look, I'm just a simple trader. I don't want to get mixed up in
political things and I don't want to get into trouble."

"What sort of trouble are you speaking of?" Riatt tried to remain
friendly. "I'm just visiting the village to look for some friends."

"Your uniform," the trader said, "it may not be safe for you
there." Riatt had completely forgotten that he was still wearing a
Faceer Ka tunic. "Don't get me wrong," the trader continued, "I'm
a supporter of the cause. I've seen what the Stomari have been up to
the last few years and I don't like it one bit." The trader's tone was
nervous and insincere. More like someone who supports any cause
that would keep him out of trouble.

"So you don't think it safe for me to go into the village like
this?"

"Oh no! A contingent of Stomari shock troops arrived a few
days ago with some big-shot Stoma General."

Riatt was troubled. If Stomari Shock Troopers were in Jaakar,
it was not likely that Pire and Nosh would be also. "Where would
it be safe for a Faceer Ka to go?" The trader thought for a moment.

"Tyage territory."

"And where would that be?" The trader again hesitated.

"To the West ... on the coast, it's an unincorporated area. I've
done business there. They don't ask questions if you have the cash
... but of course it was nothing illegal."

"What wasn't?"

"My business there, it was all above board and legal." The trader was becoming desperate to leave.

"Thank you, my friend. You too have been most helpful, but I wonder if I might impose one more request on you?"

He forced a weak smile. "Certainly, friend, how can I aid you further?"

"A fresh tunic would be nice," Riatt said. "This one is soiled and torn." The trader looked in one of his many sacks and pulled out a formal black tunic, the sort that waiters at inns and cafés wear.

"This may be a bit small."

"Is this all you have, friend? It's a little formal for my needs." Riatt held the tunic to his chest to measure its size.

"Sorry," the trader replied. "It's an order I'm filling for an inn in Jaakar. But you're lucky; I normally don't deal in clothing at all."

He restarted the tri-cart motor and engaged the clutch. The vehicle lurched down the road toward the village. Riatt was left standing in the road trying to decide whether it would be worse to look like a Faceer Ka officer or a doorkeeper at a local entertainment spot. Finally he stuffed the formal tunic under his belt. For the time being, better to be a Faceer Ka.

Riatt's miscalculation had cost him precious hours. He had to head west and he had to do so in a hurry. Nosh and Pire probably avoided the Stomari Shock Troopers and were in the unincorporated area themselves. There was a crossroad just ahead that connected with a major east/west highway. He would take it as far as he could. As Riatt turned west he could see Rebal waning on the horizon. The hope of ever seeing his friends again was waning with it.

General Somar-loors wasn't watching as the last of the provisions were being loaded onto the two medium-sized sailing ships that were to transport him and his contingent to the Southern Islands. Of greater interest to him was the loading of a large tragoone moored just a few hundred yards down the dock.

"Get me Rowand Leesh," he snapped at a near-by trooper. The trooper sought out Fazid who retrieved Leesh quickly and brought him to the General.

"I trust that everything is going according to schedule," Leesh said, trying to hide his anxiety.

General Somar ignored Leesh's question. "Who does that tragoone belong to, and where is it headed?"

"The House of Breet ... it is a supply ship carrying provisions to their security troops at Suprass."

The House of Breet, located in the Lower Midlands, was the third most powerful of the Great Houses on Osstar, behind only the Houses of Takir and Klut. It had also been one of the most troublesome for the Stomari and a thorn in the side of Takir-Prime. Somar-loors stood for a moment, pondering the idea of boarding the ship. He didn't want to precipitate a conflict within the High Council at this crucial juncture. It was dangerous, so close to the main residence of Breet-Prime, to use his radio and get authorization from Klut. Still, he didn't trust Leesh.

"What is its cargo?"

"As I said, sir, supplies for their security forces." Leesh was doing his best to remain calm. General Somar motioned to Colonel Treeg to join him.

"These are your relatives, do you believe this story?"

"The House of Breet could still have security forces in the Southern Islands. I served at Suprass before joining the High Council security force. As to whether this is a Breet supply ship I do not know for sure. The House of Breet does own a fleet of tragoones and activity has picked up in the region as of late."

Somar-loors turned back to Leesh. "Perhaps we should inspect the cargo of this 'supply' ship." Rowand Leesh's mind raced.

"Great sir," Leesh answered in his sweetest voice, "the tragoone is loaded and if it doesn't sail immediately it will miss the tide. It will then be delayed some seven hours before a favorable tide returns. I suppose that would be all right if ordered by General Somar-loors, but I would have to prevail upon you to explain it to Breet-Prime's representative.

Somar-loors thought for a moment, "Very well." He dismissed Leesh with a wave of his hand. Leesh was more than happy to comply. "Get the troops loaded," he said to Colonel Treeg. "We mustn't miss the tide either."

As his two sailing sloops cleared the harbor at Jaakar and head-ed southeast, General Somar kept a keen eye on the tragoone. He saw her sails unfurl and heard the hum of the pilot motors that would take her out of the harbor, but he saw no movement. The tide was a strong one, brought about by the confluence of Zenos on the western horizon, and Rebal waning to the west, and the ships were moving swiftly toward the open sea, yet there were still no large sails on the horizon. The tragoone had missed the tide after all. Had it been bad luck, or treachery? General Somar was sure of one thing, it was too late for him to change course now.

A s he guided his fishing skiff into the harbor at Durrass, recreating the feat of the unfortunate lad whose boat he had commandeered, Seelar was greeted only by suspi-cious stares. He had hoped that his tattered Faceer Ka tunic would prompt a compassionate response from these most loyal of Faceer Ka supporters, but most on the dock moved to avoid him. He tied the skiff to a mooring post and went into the village. As he walked the streets, he looked for uniforms but saw none. Either the Faceer Ka had been driven out of this area, or they were ashamed to wear the uniform in public. Seelar's heart sank. Even the katoc he had taken just an hour earlier couldn't bolster him. Tired and discour-aged he looked for the first place he could find that would get him off the unfriendly streets.

Just around the corner from a transport station, he found what he was looking for—a small tavern. He entered and took a seat at the long laange-wood bar, letting his eyes adjust to the darkness. The smoke from stalar sticks formed a peppery scented cloud over his head, mingling with the smell of panta, musty tunics and sweat. This was a dock-side joint for the local workers, not a high class drinking club.

From an antique music player, the soft vibrations of a sonnage singer filled the bleak room. The sound was soothing, but the play-er couldn't replicate the subtle electrical impulses given off by live performers. Seelar's eyes began to focus on two dark forms at the back of the room. They were definitely focusing on him. One of them motioned for him to join them. As his vision cleared in the hazy surroundings, he realized that the two were wearing Faceer Ka tunics.

"Sit down, friend," one of the Ka said, slurring the words. "It's always good to see a Ka who isn't afraid to wear the uniform in public ... although yours looks a little the worse for wear. Been in a scrap recently?"

"What is your unit?" Seelar asked in a commander's voice, ignoring his comments.

"Well, now, that's not very friendly of you. We need to stick together in this difficult time," the second soldier said.

"You two are obviously intoxicated. I should report you to your commander."

"And just where would you go to do that?" The first soldier replied. "We haven't seen a commander since the Stomari scattered our base camp to the seven winds."

Seelar softened his tone. The soldiers were demoralized. The attack by the Stomari had dealt the movement more crippling a blow than he had realized. "So where do you report for duty?"

The two looked at each other and laughed a drunken laugh. "Right here! As far as we can tell, we're the only two Faceer Ka in the area."

"What happened to the others?" Seelar asked.

"They just meelllllted away," the soldier said. He wiggled his fingers in the air, simulating rain, and sang the word "melted" to the tone of the recording on the music player.

"All of them?"

"All except for some of the Ka Warriors ... I think. It started when the troops came back from Romass. The minute that they had gotten off the ship, the rumors of the massacre started to spread, and the mood of the locals turned ugly." Seelar looked puzzled. The soldier continued. "Faceer who had supported and helped us suddenly turned their backs on us. Most of the Ka soldiers that returned from Romass simply put down their weapons and went home. Those of us that remained were treated as outcasts. Still, we were able to hold some troops together until the final blow."

Seelar was trying to make sense of the story. Apparently much had happened since his escape. "The final blow?" he asked.

"Most lost heart when we heard that our leader had been taken prisoner by the Stomari."

The waitress came by with a tray of full mugs. "Panta?" she asked.

Before the two soldiers could accept, Seelar waved her off. "Hey! Who do you think you are?"

"I am Seelar." It took a moment for his words to soak through the panta.

"But you're captured!" the soldier said.

"A Stomari lie. I escaped my capturers, and I have come with a new mission for you. Are you ready to serve again?"

The two straightened their tunics and sat up in their seats. They were suddenly transformed. "We are, sir," they said in unison. "We've been rotting away here. We are proud of our uniforms. It was the faint of heart that abandoned the cause."

"Good," Seelar replied, trying to build their enthusiasm. "The Cause is far from finished and it has need of such Faceer as you. But we will need more. The Stomari are feeling overconfident after their shallow successes and wish to complete our destruction, but I have a plan. It will take the bravest of us to the South Polar Region. There, we will retrieve an object that will solidify our claim to Osstar and rekindle the movement." The two soldiers looked at each other. Their bravado diminished as Seelar's words sunk in. The thought of the South Polar Region was testing their dedication. "I need for you to go out and gather up one hundred of our best Faceer Ka troopers. Bring them to the docks at Zenos-wane. I will instruct you from there."

The soldiers stood instinctively and saluted. Neither knew where they would find these troopers, but an order was an order, and at least they had one to try and carry out. Seelar straightened his tunic, brushing off as much dirt and dust as he could, and moved to a table in full view of the rest of the patrons. The waitress came by again. This time he waved her over to his table.

Bruce Williams

"Can I get you something?"

"Yes, a glass of keera water." He heard a few muffled laughs but paid them no mind. When the waitress returned, she sat the glass in front of him and watched as he pulled a folded paper out of his pocket. Scooping a bit of the dark, tarry substance onto his finger, he looked her directly in the eye and deftly lifted it to his mouth in plain site of the patrons who were all watching him by now. This time he heard no laughing. He drained the glass in one gulp and sat back to let the katoc take effect. "At Zenos-wane, I will again be the leader of the Faceer Ka."

Zenos-wane had come and gone with no sign of the two soldiers. Most of the patrons who had watched his show of Ka bravado had long since left, and the only ones remaining were so full of panta that they were for the most part asleep at their tables. Just as he was about to give up hope, one of the soldiers stuck his head in the door of the tavern. From the look on his face he was hoping that his leader had gone. Seelar leaped to his feet and met the soldier at the door, dragging him in to assure that he couldn't slip back out.

"Well? Are they assembled?"

"Uh ... yes, sir." the soldier was hesitant.

"And how many are there, one hundred?"

"Uh ... no, sir ... three."

"Three hundred! Well done trooper! Have you assembled them on the dock so that I may address them?" The soldier spoke again, looking at his boots rather than Seelar.

"No, sir. Not three hundred — three." Seelar still didn't comprehend.

"You mean that there isn't room for all three hundred on the dock?"

"Not three hundred, sir. Counting Sanar and myself there are five Faceer Ka. We were only able to find three other troopers — but one of them is a Ka Warrior." The trooper was proud that a Ka Warrior was among the company, Seelar was not. He sat back in the chair and rubbed his head, regarding the soldier's rumpled tunic and the slight look of a hangover on his face. If he were going to deliver Osstar to the Faceer he would have to do it with the force of his own will and five Faceer Ka soldiers.

"What is your name, Trooper?"

"Pylo, sir," the Trooper answered.

"You've done your duty trooper," he said, and put his arm around the soldier as he escorted him out the door. Outside he found Sanar and the other three Troopers. They snapped to attention and saluted. Seelar went down the line, putting his hand on each one's shoulder and thanking them for their loyalty. He saluted the Ka Warrior with the crossed arm salute used only by their ranks. "You Faceer are going to be provided a rare privilege—the privilege of fighting and perhaps dying for a worthy cause. In the future, there will be many a Ka soldier who will wish he had done his duty this day, and had come with us." The soldiers looked at each other nervously.

"Come with us where, sir?" Sanar asked.

"I don't have the time or the resources to mount a major expedition, but I have had time to think, and whenever a Faceer has time to think there is hope. We are going back to the camp."

"The Equatorial Camp!" Pylo blurted out.

"Yes, it is where they will least expect us to go," Seelar replied coolly. "And if I'm not badly mistaken, they will have done what the property-loving Stoma always do ... leave their equipment intact." Seelar turned and ordered the motley band to move out. He knew he had a chance to get to the South Polar Region before any of the others if his luck and his katoc held out.

Rowand Leesh fairly flew down the narrow village street to the small dwelling near the river. Not waiting even to knock, he flung himself against the podwood door, stumbled over the doorstep and fell head-over-heels onto the floor. Pire immediately helped him to his feet.

"My goodness, what an entry!" Pire said. Leesh brushed his tunic furiously with both hands.

"I have news. Is he here?" Leesh said excitedly.

"Is who here?" Pire asked, trying to calm the excitable Faceer.

"You know...Him...Him!"

Nosh had to bend at the waist in order to pass from the dining area to the reception area of the tiny Faceer dwelling. "I assume that I am the 'Him' of whom you speak," he said, leaning down to look directly into Leesh's eyes. Rowand Leesh stopped talking and stood transfixed by Nosh's stare. After a long moment, he composed himself enough to speak.

"Uh ... yes ... I have news." Leesh couldn't break eye contact with the strange, yet fascinating creature. He started backing towards the sofa situated under the front window, never taking his eyes off Nosh. "Mmmmay I sittt down?"

"I am a Seeyard, not a cather-cat, Brother Leesh." Nosh used the informal or familiar case Faceer word for brother, indicating an actual blood relation, and added a slight, soothing electrical emission. It produced immediate results in Leesh's demeanor. "Now, what news do you bring?"

Leesh was now distracted by a strange smell. He sat waving his nostrils back and forth with a look of studied concern on his face. "What's that I smell? It smells like a wet jaroo."

Nosh knew exactly what he smelled. He pressed Leesh to stick to the subject. "I trust that your other senses are as keen as your nose," Nosh replied. "So tell us the news."

"The news ... oh, yes, I remember. The Stomari General and his troops departed a few hours ago, at the quarter-tide."

"In what type of craft?" Nosh asked.

"Two small sailing vessels of the Dynard class," Leesh replied.

"Good," Nosh said. "Not suitable for a long journey. They won't be able to go very far in those ... the Southern Islands at best."

"It wasn't for lack of trying on their part," Leesh said. "The general took a strong interest in your tragoone. I had to convince him that it was a supply ship belonging to the House of Breet, or he would have boarded it and found your supplies. I'm afraid that I wasn't totally convincing. I told him it was headed for Suprass and that if we delayed long enough for him to inspect the cargo that the ship would miss the tide, but I'm sure that he knows by now that she didn't sail with the quarter-tide." Nosh put his hand on Rowand Leesh's shoulder.

"Don't blame yourself, my friend. If not for your foresight in posting sentries on the river, we might well be in the Stomari ship's hold right now. You have risked a great deal hiding us here and we owe you much. Now, we must waste no time in departing. With luck and the wind, we can be in the South Polar Region in two weeks."

"I would caution against departing too soon," Leesh said. "General Somar-loors is no fool. He may be lying in wait for you."

"Somar-loors," Nosh repeated the name. "So he is the one who attacked us at the caverns ... I should have guessed."

"You know this Somar-loors?" Pire asked.

"By reputation," Nosh replied.

"A typical Stomari bully?"

"Quite the contrary," Nosh said. "He is known as a great leader and brilliant strategist. He will prove a challenge to our will and our cunning."

"All the more reason to use caution as Rowand Leesh advises."

"I'm not a bad strategist myself." Nosh spoke without emotion. "The General's ships are too small to carry the equipment needed for a Polar expedition. He will need to be further outfitted somewhere in the Southern Islands. My guess is that he will head for Suprass. Once there, he will be able to both re-supply and check out Leesh's story. We, on the other hand, are heading in the opposite direction, along the Narial Strait and down the Inner Passage between the Southern Islands of Donait and Dosomiel."

"But that would take us through the Sea of Storms!" Pire said.

"I'm aware of that. It will be perilous, but it will cut several hundred miles off the passage by way of the Sea of Aldor and give us the best chance of finding the ice caverns without having to confront a group of armed Stomari." Nosh could see the look of concern on Pire's face. "Perhaps it will be as exciting as the ride we took down the rapids of the Stageel River." He smiled and gave Pire's hair a thorough mussing.

"Well, you're steering this time." Both broke into a laughter.

"You're very brave for a scientist," Nosh joked. "Now, let's get our gear together so that we can leave with the early-tide. Pire, I'll trust you to get everything to the docks. I've got to go to the cellar and explain to our other friend why he's not going along."

"The Zerrit," Pire remarked. "I'd almost forgotten that he was still with us."

"Zerrits ... Zerrits ... here in my cellar!" Leesh was beside himself. "I knew I smelled something amiss."

"I assure you that he has done no harm to your dwelling," Nosh said. "Anyway, he is as much a part of this expedition as Pire or I."

"But they're dangerous, smelly beasts!"

"Perhaps I'll bring him up and you can tell him that for yourself," Nosh replied, annoyed at Leesh's prejudice toward his old friend.

"No ... no ... that's fine," Leesh moved quickly for the door. "I must get back to the dock to make sure all your provisions are ready." There was a long pause and Leesh stuck his head back inside the door. "Uh ... if he's not going with you, exactly where is he going?"

"I will make arrangements for him to be taken back to the jungle, unless of course you can find work for him here. He might make a good government official." Leesh snorted and closed the door, drowning out the laughter from within.

Pire picked up the gear that had been stowed in a spare sleep-stasis room during their seclusion, and stepped warily into the street, following Leesh to the docks and the waiting tragoone. Nosh stood for a moment, silent in thought, and then opened the door to the cellar. He knew that it would be difficult to make the Zerrit leader understand, but he also knew that the trip ahead would be arduous even for those well prepared. If water and Zerrits didn't mix, Nosh knew that ice and Zerrits was an even worse fit.

The Ka Warrior sat munching on a slightly under-ripe priot fruit, his expressionless eyes following his leader's every move. He was feeling much better since Seelar had shared the last of the katoc with him before leaving. Seelar had spirited his small band through town without seeing so much as one local security officer, and had moved back into the jungle. The Ka Warrior felt at home as the humidity rose. The vegetation changed from the wispy faar trees and giant laange common to the coastal areas to thick mats of fern and the umbrella-like leaves of the jungle, galba trees.

Sanar, Pylo and the two other troopers were less comfortable. The jungle was a reminder of the chaos of the attack by the Stomari, and the thought of returning to the scene was not a pleasant one. Seelar was not concerned about the state of mind of his "Ka army." The jungle was the home of the priot fruit and the birthplace of ka-toc; soon enough, the troops would be in fighting shape.

Two days of almost continual marching brought the small band to the outskirts of the ruined camp. The smell of burnt cloth and explosive powder still lingered in the air, mingling with the sweet scent of priot flowers. Seelar cautioned his troops to stay low, and eased himself up onto a small boulder that overlooked the compound from the northwest. He raised his head ever-so-slowly and peered out into the twinight, toward the camp. The group expected to see Seelar's head explode from a round from a Stomari gas rifle, but after a minute or two he eased back down to join them.

"Sanar," he snapped, "Give me your distance glasses." Seelar took the glasses from Sanar's pouch and climbed back up onto the rock. After another five minutes of observation, he climbed down with a cynical smile on his face. "It's just as I told you. They are completely unaware of our presence. And, even better, what I need the most is right where I left it. Rebal is waning; we'll move out during the staddich when most of the Stomari will be asleep ... communing with their ancestors. By the time they realize what has happened, we'll be on our way to the South Polar Region."

The staddich was nearly two hours old when Seelar gave the order to move out. The six remaining members of the Faceer Ka army crept down a slight embankment and toward the ruins of their former compound. To the surprise of all, they met no resistance. In fact, the compound seemed deserted. Finally, about two hundred yards from the dormitory building where Sanar and Pylo had been billeted, they saw a figure with a gas rifle. The company froze. Seelar motioned for them to move around the building to the left. The large courtyard that formed the boundary of the three main dormitories was alive with Stomari troops. Pylo's heart sank at the sight, but Seelar seemed pleased.

"Good. They are, as expected, all in one place. How predictable they are," he said, with disgust in his voice. "In a few minutes we're going to be out of here and on our way to the pole, but first we are going to let the Stomari provision us for the journey. We must split up and move individually so that we don't draw attention. Think to yourself that you are just taking a stroll around your old camp. The less self-conscious you feel, the less chance you have of being noticed. Make your way to the storage shed. The first one there may have to deal with a guard, but I doubt it. If you do, don't hesitate to kill him. Remember it is the future of all Faceer that is at stake."

They moved out, one at a time, heading in slightly different directions but each with the same destination. Sanar was the first to reach the shed. He stood at the junction of the side wall and the front wall, fearing to look around the corner. Another of the party approached. He plucked up his courage and peeked around it — no guard! Wanting to impress the others with his courage, he strolled around the corner and pushed open the door to the shed. The sleeping Stomari soldier inside didn't budge. Sanar, his spinal ridge about to tear a gash in his tunic, was frozen. The other trooper strolled in. This time the Stomari soldier did budge. He sat up rubbing his eyes, staring at the two small figures in the doorway. That was the last thing he saw in his short life on Osstar. The Ka trooper wiped the blade of his stabbing sword on the Stomari soldier's tunic and put it back in the sheath.

"Thanks, Trooper," Sanar said, coolly. "I was about to do that when you startled me." The trooper showed no emotion, simply smiled and dragged the body of the Stomari soldier across the rough wooden floor, leaning it against the wall of the shed. The rest of the party entered. No one had been detected.

"Look around, and take what provisions you can find," Seelar ordered. "There are several parkas in the back. They aren't Kaba-fur, but they'll have to do. It will be cold as you have never encountered in your lives."

They began going through the scattered boxes and crates, looking for anything that might be of value to them on their journey. Seelar, who had disappeared for about fifteen minutes, reappeared wearing an overlarge parka and sporting a pair of rugged, trekking boots. "I suggest you find a pair of these boots if you can. Don't worry if they don't fit so well, you can stuff them with cloth. They will protect your feet better than the ones you're wearing."

After several minutes of rummaging around, the party completed its task and stood awaiting Seelar's orders. The sight was almost comical. Standing in the center of the shed, dressed in oversized parkas and ill-fitting boots, stood the future of Faceer society — a Ka warrior and four Faceer Ka troopers, looking as if they were going to a costume ball. Seelar hid his bemused look deep within his parka. He called them to attention

"In the hangar not far from here sits, I will wager, a long-range air transport. It is the same transport I used to bring certain Faceer scientists here from the North Polar Region. It will be the transport that will take us to the caverns of the South Polar Region where we will rescue an artifact that will solidify our claim to this planet. It will hold us all if we take no more than we absolutely need. Pylo, you are the largest of us, I want you to put on the Stomari soldier's uniform. You will lead us at gunpoint out of this shed and to the hangar. If you are approached by any Stomari officers, don't let them get close enough to see you. Use your best Stoma voice and say that we were found in the remains of the infirmary, and that we are being taken to quarantine because of the fear that we may have Straid Fever. That will discourage any curious Stomari guards from further investigation."

Pylo changed into the uniform of the dead Stomari. Soon the parka-clad, trek-booted remnants of the Faceer Ka army were making their way in the darkness of the staddich, out across the compound toward a transport that they hoped would be waiting.

The ruse worked perfectly. Along the way, a Stomari sentry called out to Pylo, inquiring as to his destination. When he answered, "Straid Fever" with near perfect Stoma inflection and tone, the sentry quickly waved then on. They reached the hangar and entered. There, sitting exactly where it had been when he left it months ago was the transport.

"Quickly, into the aircraft," Seelar ordered. The troopers scrambled into the craft and found what room they could in the cramped cargo area. Seelar climbed into the cockpit and switched on the engine. The interior lights blazed to life, and the console lit up. "Pylo, open the hangar doors." Pylo jumped down from his spot in the bay, flung open the metal doors to the hangar and quickly returned to his cramped quarters. Seelar pushed the button to start the first engine. It roared to life. Knowing that the sound would alert the Stomari, he switched on the second engine and pushed the throttle forward. The craft lurched and began to move toward the hanger door, slowly gaining speed.

Once outside he could see figures running toward the hangar. The ground was uneven, but there was no time to consider safety. He pushed the throttle full forward and the large craft rumbled down the path to the runway. As the transport gained speed, a glowing round from a gas rifle shot by the cockpit window. Seelar noticed a large, dark object in the middle of the runway. The Stomari had not been completely negligent in their occupation of the camp. They had shut off the approach to the runway with an armored vehicle. Seelar surmised that they had done this at the end of the runway to prevent unauthorized craft from taking off; perhaps they left the other end free for air transports to land.

He pushed down hard on the braking mechanism, and revved the left engine while fully extending the right flap. The craft spun around and, regaining its momentum, made for the opposite end of the runway heading directly for the Stomari troops that had been following it. The soldiers were surprised by the sight of the large transport now bearing down on them. The line of soldiers broke to either side of the runway. Many dived head-long into the ditch that drained it.

The gap in the line gave the transport just enough room to lift off. Seelar pulled back on the controls and the transport leaped into the air amid the sharp cracking of hundreds of gas rifles. It gained altitude. Seelar made one last pass over his ruined camp then turned south, heading towards the pole.

Sitting smugly in the pilot's seat, Seelar gloated. He had pulled it off. *The Faceer Ka will live to fight another day*, he thought. His eyes scanned the wiggling arrows and indicators of the instrument panel. All the gauges were showing normal parameters ... all except one. The fuel gauge was registering only three-quarters full. There were no refueling stations between his current position and the South Pole. Three-quarters of a tank may not be enough. He reached into his shoulder sack and took out one of the precious white packages he had managed to stow away. He tore open the package and dipped the end of his smallest finger into the dark, gooey katoc.

CHAPTER 29

The departure from Prameel had been uneventful for the contingent of Faceer from Romass. The steamer that Leet had promised was waiting and fully loaded. The party barely had the time to take a bit of nourishment before boarding and heading west for the Morate Strait.

Diell was sitting on the deck reading from a book he had borrowed from Aunt Dree when the steam-horn sounded, signaling that they were headed into the Strait. He looked up to see the shores of the Equatorial Region in the distance flanking the sides of the narrow opening to the strait. The activity level on deck increased dramatically. Smoke from the boiler stacks turned a darker shade of blue/gray and the ship lurched and shuddered as its speed increased.

Diell stopped one of the sailors as he made his way toward the stern. "What's happening?"

"We're heading into the Strait." The sailor replied as if Diell should understand.

"Why are we picking up speed?"

The sailor looked at Diell with a puzzled look on his face. "Because we're heading into the strait," he said again.

"Is the current that strong?"

"It's not the current…" The sailor hesitated. "You've never been here before, have you?"

"No," Diell replied, "what's the problem?"

"Unincorporated territory," the sailor answered.

"What does that mean?"

"It means pirates."

"Pirates!"

"Well, they would say 'entrepreneurs.' Depending on how big and well defended your ship is, they either try and charge a toll for passage or take your cargo and sink your ship."

"And how big a ship are we?"

"... Big enough and fast enough to outrun these lothars."

Steera was leaning over the railing when Diell approached. "Isn't it exciting ... pirates!" No sooner had she gotten the word out than a call rang out from above.

"Ship ... twenty points off the anchorage beam!"

Diell tried to remember his sailing jargon, but the rush of sailors moving to the right-front of the boat made it unnecessary. There, under full sail and moving rapidly, was a medium sized skiff of Stoma design. The steamer was still picking up speed and the skiff was barely gaining on it. The captain of the steamer pushed the craft to the anchorage side and the sailors on deck let out a whoop as the steamer positioned itself perfectly to "steal the wind" of the sailing ship. The skiff quickly receded amidst taunts from the sailors and was finally seen turning back to its clandestine port to await the next ship. Steera and Diell relaxed. The sailors returned to their tasks, but soon a second call rang out.

"Ship ... ten points to the swoonson tiller!" Again the sailors rushed the railing, this time to the left side and to the stern of the ship. What they now saw gave them cause for concern. It was not a pirate ship, but rather a Stoma tragoone, and it was moving swiftly to intercept the steamer.

"What do you make of it?" Steera asked Diell.

"Looks like a Stoma patrol ship. The markings aren't familiar, one of the lesser houses I assume, but it will be armed to the hilt."

An officer approached them. "We need you to gather the others from your party and come with us at once." The ten other villagers from Romass were summoned and accompanied the officer to a small cabin below deck.

"What is it?" a villager asked.

"It's nothing to worry about," the officer answered, "just a Stoma patrol ship form the House of Trios. We knew that this was a possibility. The reports of Faceer Ka activity in this area have them on alert. I have additional uniforms for all the passengers. You will need to put them on and stay below decks until the tragoone leaves.

If you are questioned by any of the Stoma security troops, say that you are sailors from the Braccar trading consortium being taken to assignment on a new ship. As villagers silently rehearsed their alibis, a sailor entered and went around the small room passing out uniforms. When he came to Steera, he froze. "What's wrong, sailor?" the officer asked.

"Beg your pardon sir, but I don't think she's going to pass for one of us."

The officer stared at her for a moment. "No, I don't suppose she will. You'll have to hide in the hold until we tell you it's safe." Steera nodded in agreement.

The Stoma tragoone pulled alongside the steamer as the captain slowed her engines. The steamer prepared to be boarded. It might have been possible (with the Mid-Rebal tide causing the currents to shift) to outrun the tragoone, but to try and do so would have alerted every Stoma patrol along their route. The wiser course was to act as if nothing were out of the ordinary.

Three Stoma Security Troopers armed with gas rifles stood at attention as an officer of the great ship walked the narrow, rolling wooden ramp between the two craft with the deftness of a Zaarian acrobat. As soon as he had stepped onto the deck of the steamer, the guards joined him. The streamer's captain met him on deck and, as was the custom, offered him the comfort of his cabin. The Stoma officer declined.

"I need to inspect your vessel," he said, forgoing any official courtesy.

"Is there something wrong?"

The Stoma officer's eyes scanned the deck of the steamer. "If there is, I will know it." He replied without looking at the captain and then motioned for the Troopers to fan out. "Check below decks and report anything suspicious."

"If there is anything I can do to assist you please let me know," the captain maintained his composure. "The crew is a bit ruffled at the moment; we were just pursued by pirates. It's always an adventure going through the Strait." The Stoma officer made no reaction to the captain's attempt at casual conversation. His attention was elsewhere.

Two troopers lifted the cowling to the main hold and were surprised to discover Diell and the other Romass villagers squatting inside, dressed as merchant sailors. They were immediately ordered on deck. The Stoma officer walked over to inspect the line of sailors now formed across the anchorage side of the deck.

"Well," he said. "We don't often see a sailing crew of this size on a steamer." He walked up and down the line of villagers with a skeptical look on his face.

"They're not our crew," the captain replied. "We are transporting them to assignment on a sailing vessel in the Southern Islands."

The Stoma officer stood directly in front of one of the villagers and bent down to peer into his eyes. "Really," he said, "and just what is your assignment on the ship?" His face was inches from the nervous villager, a Veertal trapper and hunter from Romass who had never set foot on a sailing vessel. He knew that he would be unable to answer even the simplest of sailing questions should the officer ask. The villager thought quickly, as only a Faceer can think when they are pressed to do it.

"Cook's mate, sir," he answered coolly. The other villagers hid their amusement. The officer snorted and rose back to full height. He started to move down the line and question another villager, when he was interrupted by a trooper escorting another surprise from the hold. The officer sneered as he studied the female Faceer. "And I suppose that this is the chamber maid for this sumptuous vessel." Steera said nothing.

"A small luxury," the captain answered. "The sailors need diversion from their daily grind, so we are also transporting an entertainer for one of the clubs on Donait." The Stoma officer's eyes covered every inch of Steera's body.

"I see where you could be very entertaining, little one." The Stoma guards chuckled as the officer turned to them with a sly grin on his face. Diell felt his hand tighten around the small stabbing sword that was part of his new uniform. "Just exactly what do you do that would induce someone to pay for such a long, expensive journey?"

"She's a singer," Diell interrupted. The officer snapped his head around to see which one of the villagers had dared to speak out.

Steera quickly intervened. "I am Dya-Klut Steera; perhaps you have heard the name." The reaction was not what she had expected. The officer remained inquisitive.

"So, a plaything from the great House of Klut. Since I can't have your friend there show us his cooking ability, let's hear you sing." Steera hummed silently to herself and then let the volume build. Soon, the soft, lilting hum of a Sonnage filled the air. Sailors from every part of the steamer strained to listen. Even the Stoma guards began to fall under the spell of the song. Steera sang for a few more minutes and then abruptly stopped. She looked directly at the officer, who was beginning to lose his harsh demeanor.

"That song was the personal favorite of the Great Klut, and also of his successor, the new Klut-Prime. He is only letting me go to Donait Island for a brief stay and, I presume, would be greatly upset if I were delayed too long." There was a long, pause. Steera had stolen the wind from the officer's sails.

The officer recovered his voice. "The House of Trios is and has always been a close ally of the House of Klut," he said. "We regret any misunderstanding, and will delay you no further. You must understand that these are disturbing times, and we must all be vigilant for evil doers. I wish you a safe journey." The officer gave a slight bow to Steera and made his way back across the plank to his ship. As soon as the tragoone was safely out of range, the crew of the steamer crowded around and let out a great cheer for Steera. The captain escorted her into his cabin where she remained in comfort for the rest of the journey to Suprameel, emerging in the evenings to sing for the crew and their guests.

As he was being led down the jagged path to the dock, Druktasis hadn't noticed the two, green-clad Faceer shadowing him. Tied up in the slips were ships of various sizes. Only a few were sturdy enough to make a trip in the open sea. Druk noticed the pace of the young Faceer who was serving as his guide slowing and then quickening again without reason. It was making him a bit uneasy as they neared the dock.

They reached the entrance to the dock and the young Faceer stepped aside, letting Druk enter the wooden walkway first. As he turned to see where the youth had gone, he was suddenly confronted by two male Faceer dressed in the green uniform of the Tyage security forces.

"Not so fast," one of them sneered. "Where do you think you're going?"

"I believe that that sailing vessel over there is the one consigned to me." Druk pointed to a Stoma designed commercial sailer moored to the end of the dock.

"Oh, you do, do you? Well, we think that you're trying to steal one of our boss's boats." The larger of the two raised a small stabbing sword and waved it menacingly in Druk-tasis' face. Druk played for time.

"Now look here, I paid a lot of gallite for this ship and I'm going to take it." Druk's display of bravado had little effect.

"Do you have any papers?"

"Papers?"

"To prove your claim. If you have no papers, then we will have to arrest you."

"Tyage and I shook hands on the deal. Where I am from, that's enough."

"Well, you must not come from around here. Here we trust only paperwork." The smaller Faceer lifted his tunic to expose the handle of a single-shot pistol. Druk backed up, but the other Faceer quickly moved around him to cut off his retreat. He held the stabbing sword as if he were ready to use it. Druk was resigned to follow them when a new voice entered the conversation.

"I'll take him from here." A muscular Faceer in a dusty, light-blue Faceer Ka officer's uniform stood at the entrance to the dock.

"And just who would you be?" the larger of the two asked.

"That is none of your business, unless of course you are not working for Tyage."

"You're Faceer Ka," the other soldier said.

"Very observant, but we're all Faceer Ka at heart ... aren't we?" The two stood looking at each other, not knowing how to answer.

"What are you going to do with him?" one soldier asked.

"We are looking for something he is hiding," the officer replied. He spoke through Druk as he examined him, as if he weren't there. "We think that it may already be on the boat that he chartered ... which one is it?"

"He had it right, it's the commercial sailer." The Ka officer motioned to Druk-tasis to lead the way to the boat.

The two security soldiers hesitated then hustled to join them. "Hey, don't you want us to come with you? It may be dangerous."

The officer thought for a moment. "I think I can handle one gammy-legged Stoma, but you're welcome to come if you want." Druk-tasis stumbled forward onto the deck of the ship as the officer shoved him from behind. "Get up there you gimp-legged freak," he snarled. "You two watch him. I'm going below to check out the cargo hold." The officer disappeared into the hold and the two soldiers dutifully raised their weapons to keep Druk-tasis at bay. After a few minutes, he returned, looking frustrated. "Nothing!" he said. "Tyage is going to be very upset if we don't find it." The mention of their boss got the soldiers' attention.

"Find what?" one asked.

The Ka officer appeared to be deep in thought and didn't answer. "I know! It's tied to the keel."

"What is?" There was a sense of desperation in the soldier's voice.

"If we find it, there will be a reward in it for all of us!"

The possibility of a reward did the trick. The Tyage soldiers completely forget their original mission. "What ... what do we need to do?" they spoke, simultaneously.

"Go back to the entrance to the dock. I will take the ship from its mooring and turn it into the channel. You must then try and examine the upper portion of the keel and see if there is a large object attached to it."

The two nearly fell over each other trying to be the first to comply with the officer's orders. Druk-tasis stood by, unheeded in the clamor. Lines were cast off as the soldiers positioned themselves as instructed. The Ka officer deftly maneuvered the ship out of its slip and into the main channel of the stream. The two security soldiers stood watching as it sailed down the channel and toward the open sea, picking up speed.

"Hey ... HEY...!" The soldiers waved their arms and shouted, but the ship simply kept moving out of the channel. Soon, it was just a dot on the horizon. They looked at one another in confusion. They tried to think of what they were going to say to their boss. Finally, in a moment of unspoken agreement, they discarded their green uniforms, got into one of the smaller boats tied to the dock and followed the source of their embarrassment out to the open sea.

The Ka officer secured the wheel of the ship to keep it on a southerly course, and turned to face his bemused captive. They regarded each other for several minutes until finally Druk-tasis broke the silence.

"Where am I being taken?"

"It seems that we are both being taken wherever the winds will lead us."

Druk recognized the quote from a Faceer poem. "A poet as well as a warrior," he said, "impressive the way you handled those two back at the dock."

"And I am impressed by a Stomari who knows Veertal poetry."

Druk remembered the tattoo behind his earhole. "I am not truly Stomari as I think you know, and my guess is that you are not entirely Faceer Ka."

"You are very wise, Druk-tasis, as I have been told." The officer said.

"You know my name."

"I have heard it mentioned by a friend of mine."

"A Faceer friend or a Stoma friend?"

"Yes to both," the officer replied. There was a pause. Druk-tasis made the connection.

"Nosh!"

"Correct ... Lieutenant Riatt at your service," he said, bowing low in the old Faceer to Stoma fashion.

"You are Riatt, the companion of Nosh!" Druk-tasis could hardly believe his luck. "But how did you come to find me?"

"It is not so difficult to track a Stoma in a den of Faceer thieves. I have had encounters with Tyage before, he's devious but predictable. But let's secure the helm and see if there are any provisions below; then we shall talk of many things."

Tomar Leet had acquired the finest in food and drink for the intended passenger, but he hadn't bargained on a Faceer companion. There was hot chee in quantity, a large role of durog (the fish paste loved by all Stoma), and various small shellfish and dried meats. Riatt was overjoyed to discover an oil-paper package filled with tarnn cakes, a favorite of both species.

Their shared perils made instant companions of the two. They sat on the deck eating and sharing tales of their adventures until well past Rebal-wane. Riatt spoke of his initiation into the Faceer Ka and his ultimate disillusionment, and his adventure in the equatorial caves. He showed Druk-tasis the orange light cone, now clouded and dark. Druk-tasis told of his childhood among the Faceer and his later assimilation into proper Stoma society ending with his unhappy duty with the Stomari. They talked of Pire and Steera, Leet and Tyage, and they spoke of their admiration of Nosh. They talked until the sky darkened with the staddich, and the tiny sparks of light above them flickered like distant candles.

"So, my new friend, where do we go from here?" Druk-tasis said, after the end of their long meal and even longer conversation.

"If this ship was procured by Tomar Leet," Riatt replied, "there will be instructions aboard her somewhere. He leaves nothing to chance." He stuck his head under the covering to the wheelhouse. Inside he noticed a large, complicated instrument attached to the panel that activated the lights and other electrical equipment on the craft. The power switch placed prominently on the front panel was set to the "Off" position. Faceer curiosity dictated the next move. He pushed the instrument's power switch to the "On" position, and it whirred to life. The sound of electric engines and gears filled the wheelhouse and spread across the deck. The wheel began to turn by itself, and the mainsail came about with a whoosh as the craft began to pick up speed. Riatt jumped back, startled by all the activity.

"Instructions you say!" Druk-tasis laughed. "It seems that our aged friend has no confidence in the sailing abilities of a Stoma. This seems to be some sort of automatic pilot. I have seen them on flying craft, but never on a sailing vessel."

"Indeed," Riatt replied. "This explains why Tyage was willing to risk offending Leet to procure your ship." Druk-tasis picked up a small pad of paper that was lying next to the auto-pilot. On it were written two words: "Orial" and "Breet."

"This must be our destination," he said, handing the pad to Riatt. "I have long suspected that the House of Breet opposes the Stomari. I have trusted Leet with my very life so far, I see no reason to doubt him now." Riatt turned the pages of the pad, but there was nothing further written. The two went back out on deck to take in the cool staddich air and digest their repast. The humming of the motors making continuous adjustments to the tiller and sails eased Riatt into a mild sleep-stasis and Druk into a full blown Tiirra. Two days later, with favorable winds, the ship came within sight of a large harbor. Leet's phantom pilot had guided them safely to Orial.

CHAPTER 30

Twenty-two snorting, pawing Bajan stallions stood tied to the dock as a line of Stomari troopers unloaded the hold of the two sailing ships just arrived from the Equatorial Region. Somar-loors had sailed the calmer passage around the Island of Couson in the Lower Midlands to the Stoma city of Suprass on the Southern Island of Dosomiel. He pulled an officer's jacket over his tunic to ward off the decidedly cooler winds of the Southern Islands and made his way across the walkway of the dock to a waiting motor transport, stopping occasionally to speak to a trooper. As he approached the vehicle, a Stomari officer in full dress uniform snapped to attention and opened the door. The insignia on his tunic was of the House of Loors, the main Stoma House on the Island of Dosomiel (the other being the House of Gleer), and the family of his mother, Kaalat. His father's lineage, the House of Somar, was the principal Stoma house on the Southern Island of Sunor. They did much trading with Dosomiel and their females were often wed to the Loors males as well as to males from the House of Gleer.

Somar-loors was not looking forward to his next meeting. He disliked the cloying and conniving Loors-Prime intensely. He was known to mistreat his subordinates, both Stoma and Faceer, which made him a coward in the general's eyes. And if there was one thing that the general could not abide it was cowardess.

The vehicle swayed to a stop in front of the opulent home of Loors. A bevy of retainers raced to open the main gate and escorted the general, who was accompanied by Colonel Treeg, to the reception area. A small feeding pool had been adorned with all manner of food and drink, and in the midst of it (already in the pool and munching on Kodoos) was Loors-Prime. General Somar-loors handed his jacket to one of the retainers and stood looking around the room. Colonel Breet-treeg didn't bother to take off his jacket, having been with the general long enough to read his moods.

"So, General, or should I call you, cousin, won't you refresh yourself? I know that your journey has been an arduous one." Loors waited for some movement from General Somar, but there was none.

"I'm afraid I don't have much time for leisure, Excellency. I have an even more arduous journey ahead of me."

"Yes, and that reminds me. Why won't the high council fill me in on the details of your mission? I was instructed to supply a tragoone with provisions for twenty-two soldiers. They wouldn't even say where the expedition was headed, although I suspect it will be very cold from the amount of cold weather gear that has been requested. They act as if I'm the enemy," Loors whined. "I've supported Takir, Klut, and the rest of the Stomari from the beginning, and they treat me like some Zaarian trader ... as if I'm not to be trusted. I'm the one who has had to endure the sabotage and attacks from the Faceer Ka creel worms, and with no help from Central Headquarters I might add. My production has been cut in half. You can't even get decent lapis juice because of the disruptions. All this and they treat me, a loyal Stomari, as if I were from the House of Breet. Colonel Breet-treeg's hand went pale as it squeezed the hilt of his officers' sword.

General Somar felt the sting of the insult on Colonel Treeg and pushed the conversation ahead. "I assure you, sir, that I have been kept in the dark on many matters as well, but you must realize that the nature of this mission is so sensitive that only a few at the very top levels of the High Council know of it. I'm sure that they refrained from giving you the details so that if it fails, you will be able to deny knowledge of it ... a precaution you see."

"Yes, I see the wisdom of it." Loors waved his hand in a wide arc, encompassing the feast that was laid out around the pool. "But I've had all of this prepared as a welcome to the great general who destroyed the filthy little broogs at the Equatorial camp. If you don't eat it, whatever shall I do with all of it?"

"Give it to your servants?" Colonel Treeg volunteered.

"My good colonel, you obviously don't have servants of your

own. If I were to lavish feasts like this on my servants, before long they would be expecting luxurious treatment all the time. Your General will tell you that the surest way to ruin good troops is to coddle them. Am I right, General?" Somar refused the bait, keeping his attention on the expedition.

"So, sir, have you supplied the provisions that were requested?"

"Of course."

"Then we will leave for the coast at Rebal-wane." Somar-loors motioned to Colonel Treeg to follow him and they made for the gate.

"But General, I was hoping we could talk about the fighting ... about the provisions you have made for my security."

"No time. We must be on our way or we will lose the mid-tide."

"But my party ... the food! Somar-loors summoned one of his troopers who had been standing guard at the gate, and whispered in his earhole. The trooper turned immediately and headed back toward the dock.

"You are a loyal Stomari, aren't you?" the general asked.

"Yes, of course," Loors answered, now forced to shout from his position in the feeding pool.

"Then I have the perfect way for you to show that loyalty and to provide for your security at the same time." General Somar slid into the passenger compartment of the transport vehicle before Loors could question him further. Colonel Treeg joined him. "You handled yourself well back there," he said to the colonel. "If I could, I would exchange relatives with you."

"What did you tell that trooper just now?" Colonel Treeg asked discretely. A smile came over Somar-loors' face.

"I solved both of his Excellency's concerns. In about ten minutes there will be twenty hungry, thirsty Stomari security troopers lounging around Loors' feeding pool ... and I'll wager there won't be a Kodoo left on Dosomiel come Rebal-wane." As the transport sped away, laughter could be heard echoing against the cold, stone walls of the great House of Loors and down the streets of Suprass.

Riatt and Druk-tasis watched as a large war sloop, flying the colors of the House of Breet, made its way alongside their craft. The ship's security officer and a pilot made their way on to the sailer and greeted Druk-tasis with a crisp salute.

"Welcome to Orial. It is an honor to have you, sir. I have been instructed to see that you are piloted safely to port." The officer saluted again and he and the pilot disappeared into the wheelhouse.

"Well, I'm impressed," Riatt said, mockingly.

"Don't be," Druk-tasis replied. "I imagine that what you are seeing is the legacy of my recent stint as the 'hero of the Polar Station massacre.'" Riatt looked confused. "I'll explain it to you sometime, when all this is over."

The ship pitched back as the motor to the automatic pilot shut down, and they watched as she was manually steered down the narrowing inlet to a small dock at the mouth of the Andular River. Waiting on the dock was a contingent of Stoma from the House of Breet, dressed in the brilliant red uniforms of the House Guard. The commander of the contingent approached Riatt and Druk and bowed. "Please, follow me," he said.

Riatt and Druk-tasis were led to a waiting vehicle and transported through the heart of the city. The wide avenues were crowded, but the feel of the city was almost leisurely. The graceful lines of the buildings along the way were patterned from the elegant, sweeping forms of Stoma art from the pre-inclusion period, and blended with their surroundings so well that it was difficult to tell where one ended and another began. Druk-tasis felt a sense of pride in this Stoma city and in the Great House of Breet and its noble traditions. Riatt was in awe of the broad scale of the city's streets and buildings. As they moved along, he watched well-dressed Stoma bending down to pick up every stray piece of debris off the sidewalks, as if it were part of their normal activities. Outside their shops trades folk worked, sweeping the storm water culverts until they shone like burnished gallite in the pale, pink light of Zenos.

The vehicle moved out of the city and continued down a wide highway, heading toward several magnificent structures that sat on chalk-white bluffs overlooking the sea.

"Donnalier," the driver said, pointing to the stone columns that framed the entrance to the mansion's access road.

"It's named for the flame-red Donna Lilies that grow in the shallows of the harbor," Druk-tasis said, pointing out a patch of the blood-red lilies in the distance. The transport made its way up the winding road to the main building where Druk and Riatt were escorted into a large, open-air courtyard that provided a panoramic view of the entire complex. Riatt could see that the beautiful name was well deserved.

The residence of Breet-Prime and his household was built on descending levels. The main building, high atop the bluff, was huge, containing the apartments of Breet-Prime and his wife and the highest ranking members of his family. Each living area was adorned with flowers and plants of every description. In fact, there was so much vegetation that it was possible to walk among the apartments and not catch so much as a glimpse of anyone inside.

From the main residence building, cobbled pathways led down the bluff to progressively smaller structures, each serving a specific function. The family gathering room gave way to a recreation area complete with fresh-water pool and waterfall, which then led down to sea level, and a magnificent feeding pool filled with the brackish Osstarian sea water so central to Stoma cuisine. Riatt had never seen anything so beautifully constructed.

"We have so much to give to one another," Druk-tasis said, stepping up to join Riatt at the wall that guarded the overlook.

"We do indeed," Riatt replied, "...we do indeed."

A high-level Faceer retainer interrupted their admiration of the Great House. Bowing low to both Riatt and Druk-tasis he spoke. His form of address was perfectly scripted and appropriate for either a Stoma or a Faceer audience.

"His Excellency awaits you in his sitting room."

Druk and Riatt made their way through the lush vegetation and entered the main living chambers of Breet-Prime. The head of the House of Breet was sitting across a large dharma shell settee, facing the doorway. A thick, skieen-cloth curtain separated the sitting room from a small alcove cut adjacent to the front window. Stoma often had small devotional areas set aside in each chamber of their house. Riatt and Druk-tasis bowed low and waited for Breet to speak before returning to their standing position. Breet acknowledged the act of respect.

"I thank you both for the show of respect for the traditions of the House of Breet. You come well recommended, but I admit that I was expecting only one of you."

"May I introduce my traveling companion, and the citizen that saved me from the treacheries of Tyage ... Riatt."

"Come closer, young friend, and let me get a look at you. I have heard your name spoken before by my friend, Tomar Leet. Are you the associate of the one they call Nosh?"

"I am, sir," Riatt replied.

"Then you are welcome here, and welcome to sit in on our discussion. We have much to talk about." Riatt bowed once more and took his place on a Faceer-sized seat next to a table filled with Stoma delicacies. "My retainer will bring some fare more palatable to Faceer." Breet motioned to the young Faceer who had brought Riatt and Druk-tasis to the sitting room. He returned a moment later with a tray full of snacks for Riatt. "Tyage was it?" Breet asked, turning to Druk-tasis. "How did you come to be in the company of that scoundrel?" Druk explained his escape from the Government Complex, and his timely meeting with Riatt, all the while sipping lapis juice and munching on Lodoos. "It seems that the gods are smiling upon you, Druk-tasis. It is fortunate that the lieutenant showed up when he did." Riatt realized that he was still wearing his Faceer Ka officers' uniform. His hand unconsciously moved to cover the insignia. Breet reached out and placed his own hand on Riatt's shoulder. "Perhaps we're all a bit ashamed of our past, my friend. There have been more than a few Stomari uniforms in this House ... why even your esteemed friend here wears their mark, but it doesn't mean that we can't learn from our mistakes. The future of Osstar will either be one of harmony between us, or constant war and misery. The choice is ours to make." Riatt relaxed and let his hand fall to his side.

"You are an ally of Leet?" Riatt said, ending the momentary

silence.

"Ally would seem to imply a war," Breet replied. "So far we have experienced scattered violence from a few radical groups, but full-scale war has not erupted. Let's say that we share certain values, and have certain concerns about some of our citizens." A loud "snort" came from behind the curtain. Breet acted as if he had heard nothing.

"Concerns about Faceer citizens or Stoma citizens?" Druk-tasis stared at the curtain as he spoke.

"Both."

"And would your concerns go as far as the High Council?" Another snort was heard, this time it was loud enough to make Breet shift in his seat and reach out for a snack to try and divert attention from it.

"I have recently been made aware of certain actions taken on the High Council's behalf that were done without consulting the entire membership. I am concerned that some individuals on the Council have an agenda ..." Suddenly the alcove curtain flung open and a striking female Stoma dressed in a sheer, flowing gown glided across the room as smoothly and gracefully as an ice skiff across a frozen lake. Riatt was transfixed by the elegance and fluidity of her movement.

"Oh for the sake of Trague, will you get to the point?" The three sat silent.

Breet finally spoke, his tone conveying a slight annoyance and a deep pride, "May I present my wife, Tarsa. She has never been reluctant to express herself."

"You males spend so much time in not saying what you're trying to say that it is a wonder anything gets accomplished on this planet. We all know of whom we speak—Takir and Klut."

Druk-tasis hadn't heard a word. He sat lost in Tarsa's image. Never had he seen a female so attractive and with so magnetic a personality. She filled the room from the minute she revealed herself. Riatt felt it as well, and he rarely found Stoma females interesting. The few to which he had been exposed were, true to Stoma traditions, reserved and completely subservient to their spouses, the opposite of the assertive Faceer females.

Druk-tasis came back to his senses. "You speak the truth, Madam. It was Klut himself who ordered my execution."

"Execution!" Breet was incredulous.

"You see," Tarsa scolded. "I told you that you were being naive. I have never trusted him and I certainly don't trust our esteemed leader of the High Council."

"Tarsa!" Breet reprimanded her. "You mustn't speak of Takir in that manner."

"Have you forgotten, my dearest, that my given name is Tarsa-Takir-seer? I knew Takir-Prime when he was a youth, shooting defenseless coola birds with his gas pistol for sport. I didn't like him then, and I like him even less now. He and Klut are out to turn the High Council into nothing more than a vehicle for their personal ambitions. Takir has allied with that fat miscreant Loors and is moving to gain control of industrial production in the Southern Islands. With the power of the Stomari and the wealth of the Southern Islands at his disposal it will be little time before our planet has another warlord — and this time it will be a warlord that will control all of Osstar."

There was a long pause. Finally, Breet spoke, "My wife is as intelligent as she is beautiful. I have been trying to deny the obvious for too long. Just yesterday I received a report from sources friendly to our cause that troubled me greatly. It seems that Klut has dispatched general Somar-loors to the southern-most region of the planet on a mission. The mission was shrouded in secrecy, but I suspect it may have a connection to something that happened several months ago in the North Polar Region. Shortly after the death of the old Klut and the others in that unfortunate accident, information between the heads of the various departments of Government and the members of the High Council slowed to a trickle. It became clear that some of the Houses were receiving instructions from the Council while others were being left out of the discussions." Breet reached over and gently wiped a crumb of tarnn cake from Tarsa's mouth. "There was something found up there that the Stomari will go to any lengths to possess — or destroy." Breet turned his full attention to Druk-tasis. "I know that you were there. If we are to fight this common battle, I need to know what it was that they found, and how it fits into our current situation."

Druk-tasis leaned back in his chair and reached for a handful of lodoos. "It is a long and quite remarkable story," he said. "I suggest that you and your lovely spouse make yourselves comfortable." Tarsa smiled at Druk-tasis' unhesitant invitation for her to remain. "What I leave out I trust my Faceer friend will fill in."

For the next several hours Druk-tasis and Riatt took turns telling the story of the discovery of the cylinder and its aftermath. Breet would interrupt occasionally to ask specific questions, but it was Tarsa who kept the conversation flowing, asking question after question regarding Nosh, the Faceer Ka and the Ka Warriors, and the strange contents of the cylinder. The conversation ended with the food and the company exhausted.

Breet next pronouncement took both Druk-tasis and Riatt by surprise. "We leave at Rebal-rise for Croll. There we will board a tragoone for the South Polar Region."

"We?" Druk-tasis asked.

"Yes, I am going with you," Breet said. Tarsa put her hand lovingly on Breet's broad shoulder. "Yes, dear one," he said, meeting her gaze. "You know that I must. It is the time for action. The time for all that male talk you dislike so much is ended. If there has been a schism in the High Council, then I must discern the path that I must take. Tomar Leet has informed me that another delegation, one from Romass, has already departed Prameel in the Upper Midlands. We will attempt to provide support. They will be no match for General Somar-loors if he finds them before we do. But enough talk, I have arranged resting quarters for you in my apartments. Get what rest you can, my friends. Tomorrow we begin an arduous journey."

The retainer returned and led Druk-tasis and Riatt on a dreamlike walk through the gardens of Donnalier to a sleep-stasis chamber overlooking the sea.

"I trust this will suffice?"

"Yes, Riatt answered. " It is more than adequate, thank you."

The retainer made no move to leave. Riatt watched him from the corner of his eye as he fashioned a Faceer bed in the center of the chamber.

Finally, the retainer broke the uneasy silence. "Pardon sir, but would you know the number of the party that will be leaving tomorrow. I must make travel arrangements, and I am a bit confused as to how many will be going."

"I'm not certain," Riatt said without thinking. "I expect that it will be me, Druk-tasis, your master and several security troops."

"Yes," the retainer replied, "that would make sense. Excuse me for bothering you." He bowed and exited the room.

Riatt lay down on his snug bed and curled into a ball, burying his spinal ridge in the soft Kaba-fur surrounding the edge of the structure. His thought of how his life had changed in the last few years. Here he was, a trusted officer of the Faceer Ka, at the grand abode of one of the members of the Stoma High Council, and accompanied by a Stomari security officer. He laughed out loud. The gentle songs of the sea birds on the cliff below soon began to lull him into a soft sleep-stasis. He stretched his arms over his head and felt a soft, cool breeze envelop them. He laughed again. "If we survive this," he thought, "what a tale it will make."

The next morning, Zenos and Rebal rose as one through the morning mist, an alignment that occurred only once every few months. The Stoma called it the Luceriat, and used the occasion as cause for eating a particularly large breakfast. Riatt made his way unaccompanied to the front of the great house and found Druk-tasis and Breet just finishing their repast.

"We felt no need to call you," Breet said, "knowing the miniscule amount of nourishment you Faceer seem to need."

"You are, of course, correct, Excellency," Riatt replied. "If we Faceer ate like you Stoma, we would need another planet to provide the food." Breet laughed a hardy laugh and bade Riatt to join them.

After breakfast, Tarsa walked the three of them down the long entrance road to a column of motor vehicles that stood smoking and clattering at the main gate. She rubbed each cheek against Breet's mouth in the Stoma version of a kiss, reached into a large beaded pouch she was carrying and pulled out a long, intricately woven scarf made from the fur of the Hircus, a small creature that inhabited the higher elevations of the mountains in the Northern Islands. She wrapped it around the slender indentation that served as the Stoma neck and kissed him again.

"This will be a guard against the polar cold," she said. Her eyes spoke more vividly than her words.

"The thought of this beautiful face waiting at home will be warmth enough for me," Breet replied, returning the kiss. Druk-tasis and Riatt made way for Breet to enter the vehicle and then joined him, Riatt in the middle and Druk-tasis on the right-hand side. The gas engine roared and the vehicle, situated three back from the lead transport, joined a column of seven others. The trip from Orial to Croll, on the eastern shore of the Island of Couson, would take just under two days by Druk-tasis' reckoning. The column moved out, turning south along the main highway from Orial until it made the junction with the east/west road that covered the length of the Island, ending at the sea in the city of Croll. Druk-tasis noticed that squads of security troops were stationed at regular intervals along the highway.

Breet stared dispassionately out the window of the vehicle. "We've had a bit of a problem with our power grid," he announced to no one in particular. "At first we thought it due to aging transmission lines, but the pattern and frequency of the outages soon pointed to sabotage."

"Faceer Ka?" Druk asked without thinking of his companion.

"Yes, we believe so. We think that they were also responsible for the bombings at the research station in Croll."

"Research station!" Riatt caught himself. "Pardon, Excellency. I am not proud of the indiscriminate violence of my people, but we do not see your research stations in the same light as do you." An uneasiness was growing in the vehicle.

"No need to ask pardon from me, Lieutenant. I was as taken

in as most of the other members of the High Council when your good, Dr. Lateer began requesting more and more funds for these so-called research stations. I know now that he was only following orders from the head of the Ministry of Research. I am not proud of our actions in this matter either. I mourn for the lost lives at the station, Faceer as well as Stoma." Breet's words were spoken from the heart. The uneasiness subsided.

The column of transport vehicles continued east, stopping only for refueling, repairs and short breaks when they were needed. Riatt passed the time by computing the distance traveled in relation to the intervals between the security stations. The countryside was changing from the flat marshlands around the coast to rolling hills and ravines.

Upon crossing three such ravines, a sense of apprehension overtook Riatt. Something was the matter, but he couldn't quite name it. Suddenly, it hit him — the security station! The last one had not been where it was supposed to be. In fact he now realized that there had been no security encampments in the last several miles. Druk-tasis saw the worried look on Riatt's face.

"What is it, Riatt? You look as if you're becoming ill."

"Could we slow the column?" There was urgency in Riatt's voice.

"Yes, all of our vehicles are equipped with a radio," Breet answered. "Are you ill?"

Riatt struggled to think of a way to explain his sudden fear. Breet leaned forward and tapped on the glass window that separated the driver's compartment from the rear passenger area. The vehicles were descending a steep hill. As they rounded a turn in the road, a long narrow bridge came into view. The lead vehicle was just entering the bridge.

"Excellency!" Riatt blurted out with a great deal more urgency, "... the security troops ... where are they?" Breet took no time to answer. He grabbed the microphone from the hands of the radio operator and shouted into it.

"All vehicles **STOP**! Reassemble at the command vehicle!" Both of the transports in front of the command vehicle were now on the bridge. The second transport started to back up. **"GET OFF THAT BRIDGE!"** Breet shouted so loudly that it was doubtful he needed a radio to be heard.

The command came too late. The two front supports of the bridge lifted into the air and, with a mighty thump, the entire front half of the bridge collapsed, taking the two helpless transports with it into the ravine below. The occupants of the other five vehicles watched as a cloud of thick blue/yellow smoke climbed along the narrow walls of the ravine and snaked its way skyward, rising into the morning air as if in slow motion. Several of the security troopers in the other vehicles rushed to the edge of the chasm, but it was clear that there could be no survivors. The ravine was several hundred feet deep and lined with jagged rocks on all sides. Breet leaned back in his seat and let out a mournful sigh.

"How could they have known? I have kept this journey a close secret, and only made final plans within the last few days." Breet got back on the radio and ordered the remaining vehicles of the column to form up. When all were present, he exited his vehicle and walked to the edge of the chasm as the smoke continued to rise. He stared into it for a long time, mumbling what sounded like a prayer, and then turned to address his troops.

"Loyal soldiers, you all know the risks of service to your House and to Osstar. We have paid the price of that service today. A great task lies before us. How we meet the challenge could well determine the future of our species and our Planet. We mourn the loss of our brothers, but we do so by continuing the mission that they began. This is not a struggle between Faceer and Stoma; it is a battle for the soul of Osstar, and for the future. We will take this trip together for the good of all of our friends and families. Return to your vehicles. We will circle back and take a crossing to the north. They will be expecting us to take the southern route to avoid the Mororall Mountains. This time we will not be so cooperative." Breet climbed back into his vehicle and ordered the driver to take the lead.

Riatt struggled with how to say what he had to say. "Excellency, how well do you know the retainer that served Druk-tasis and me while we were at Donnalier?"

"Who do you mean?" Breet replied.

"A tall, rather thin young Somacee with a decided streak of silver in his top hair."

"Yes, I do remember such an employee, although I have never spoken to him myself. He had only been with us a short while ... less than a year."

"Do you remember who sent him to you?" Riatt continued.

"Yes, as a matter of fact I do. He was the nephew of one of my wife's old retainers ... from Amiel, I think, in the Upper Midlands. Do you suspect that he was Faceer Ka?"

"Amiel is the main residence of the House of Takir, is it not?" Breet sat for a moment staring a hard stare out his window. Riatt could see that his words had found a home. "Before we left, he made certain inquiries about the expedition that made me a bit uneasy."

"What sort of inquiries?"

"He said that he was in charge of logistics for the trip, but had forgotten the number of troops that would be going." Breet needed to hear no more. He reached for the radio transmitter and contacted his security chief at Donnalier.

"Captain Breet-kosar, I want you to take my wife's new retainer into custody and hold him there until I return. If she asks any questions, tell her that I will explain when I am able to talk freely."

"I'm afraid that won't be possible, sir," Kosar answered.

"What do you mean, Captain?"

"The retainer is dead. He was found an hour ago, floating in the water beneath the sea-gate to the feeding pool. He must have fallen in."

"Captain, I want you to examine the body before you send it back to his family."

"Yes sir. But what exactly will I be looking for?"

"Signs of a cause of death other than drowning," Druk-tasis broke in. Breet nodded in agreement.

"Let me know the results, Captain—Breet out." Breet sunk into a deep silence as the transport made its way into the Mororall Mountains. His left hand fidgeted with one of the buttons on his tunic until it was almost detached.

"I'm certain she knew nothing of this, your Excellency." Druktasis spoke softly and cautiously. "My guess is that Takir and Klut have spies in all of the Great Houses, keeping an eye out for disloyalty. Over the years, many Faceer have disappeared after routine questioning at some of our Stomari facilities. I have always suspected that they were still alive and being used as hostages in order to force other Faceer to provide them information."

Breet kept his gaze on the mountains as he spoke "What have we become? Is security now so dear that we give up all that makes us Stoma to attain it? Do we become barbarians in the name of civilization? I for one will die before I see our civilization fall to these evil forces." The rest of the journey to Croll was made in silence.

CHAPTER 31

At one point, just off the northeast tip of the island of Donait, Diell thought that he could make out the rectangular sails of a ship, floating just above the horizon. He cupped both hands around his eyes, but the image melted into the fog and mists of the inner passage. Their steamer was pulling into the harbor at Suprameel. The clouds, mingling with a faint hint of snow at the top of Mount Saan, draped across the tops of the coastal mountains like soft, white comforters on a snug Faceer bed. The large port bustled with activity.

The captain approached Diell and Steera, who had joined him on deck. "When we disembark, stay close together. I imagine we'll garner some attention when we get to our docking area."

"Should we keep the sailor outfits on?" Diell asked.

"Yes, as far as anyone here is concerned you're still a crew in search of a ship. Hopefully, we'll be loaded and off again before anyone can get too suspicious."

"Just what kind of cargo are we taking on?"

"I'm not completely sure," the captain answered, "but from the configuration of my hold, it's live cargo. The twenty cubicles in the aft section were designed for holding animals."

"Narros," Steera said.

"What are you talking about?" Diell asked.

"Leet knows what we will be up against in order to make it to the caverns. Narros were made for ice and snow. They're strong, and they can live for extended periods without much food. I'll lay a wager that there are sleds as well."

"We'll know soon enough," the captain said as the steamer made its turn and eased in alongside the long wooden dock. As they crossed the walkway onto the dock, the sound of high-pitched yelping filled the air. Young Faceer and even some Stoma youth were crowding around the pens that held the Narros, holding out bits of food and trying to pet them. The Faceer dock workers had their hands full, shooing the youngsters away from one pen only to have them form up again at another. In spite of their pet-like appearance, Narros were wild animals and not easily domesticated. They had a "pack" mentality and would accept a "sledder" (an expert Faceer sled driver) as their pack leader, but were loyal only to him. They were immensely useful as beasts of burden in the rough, cold reaches of the Polar Regions, and adequate as guardians on the large Stoma estates of the Southern and Northern Islands, but only females could be kept as pets and only one female at that.

Steera had been correct. Behind the pens, laid out with full rigging, were four polar sleds especially made for use with Narros. The sleds were long and slender with a raised ridge down the center of each runner to cut down resistance when traveling across ice or packed snow. The runners flared to a wide, wing-like shape on both ends to provide support in deeper snow. The rear of the runners extended beyond the cargo area to allow for the driver to stand and control the direction of the sled. Two long, wooden poles ran the length of the sled on either side, each with a taanar hide strap down its length. The hide straps would be attached to the lead Narro's outside leg on either side, and used to direct the animals. A slight pull on the strap, and the lead Narro would instinctively struggle against it and steer the sled in the opposite direction. The straps were crossed in the middle of the guide poles to avoid confusion by the driver, so that the driver could pull left to turn left, and right to turn right.

"Pretty impressive," Steera said, her admiration for Leet growing with each new miracle he produced.

"We need to get loaded and get out of here," Diell said.

The captain agreed. "These beasties are drawing too much attention. The sooner we are at sea again, the better."

He hurried off to supervise the loading of the provisions. Steera and Diell walked down the wooden wharf to stretch their legs a bit. Both knew that traveling too far from the steamer would not be wise; the commotion created by the Narros had drawn the attention of Stoma security.

As Diell scanned the far end of the dock, he thought he could make out a small unit of uniformed Stoma security troops making its way through the crowds. The troopers were upon them before they knew it.

"Are you a crew member of that steamer?" The trooper asked. Diell tried to stay calm.

"Yes sir," he answered. Two of the other troopers were looking at Steera with great interest.

"Kind of young for the sailor's life, aren't you?" There was a tone of suspicion in his voice.

"It's my first voyage," Diell answered.

"And her first voyage too?" the trooper continued, looking at Steera.

"I'm not sure. I don't know her very well."

"Well if I were a young Faceer, you can bet that I would want to get to know her very well indeed." The other troopers broke out in laughter. Diell forced a smile. The trooper turned his attention to Steera.

"Pretty far south for a Veertal, aren't you?"

"I go where my employer sends me." Steera used her most sultry voice.

"And just who is this lucky employer?"

"Klut-Prime," Steera answered, looking the trooper straight in the eye to make an impact. The trooper didn't flinch.

"Well, we're from the House of Gleer, and you're in our territory now. And as a matter of fact, we've been instructed to be on the lookout for a band of Faceer lead by a Veertal female that fits your description."

The encounter was turning very wrong. Diell's hand searched for his sword. He looked back over his shoulder to see if any others of the steamer crew were watching the proceedings, but could see no one. The area where the supplies had been stored was clear, and he assumed that they had been loaded. "I think you need to come with us."

Steera laid on all the charm that she could. "Now, Trooper

Gleer-Seer-rainor (Steera read from the name badge on his tunic), how could an innocent little Faceer like me be of any interest? I'm just an entertainer, heading to Broll to bring a little joy to your own people."

"It's <u>Gleer</u>-rainor. I make no claim to kinship with the Seer weaklings on Mannot, even though my mother was one of their kin. And you won't need polar sleds and Narros in Broll." The trooper was unmoved by Steera's affectations. "We've been watching you since you arrived."

"She can't talk about the mission," Diell butted in. Steera gave Diell a puzzled look.

"So, now it's a mission." The trooper turned to one of the other soldiers: "Take them to central security. I'll get on the radio phone to headquarters."

The trooper wouldn't take the bait. Diell's heart sunk. To have come so far just to be taken into custody seemed too cruel a fate. Steera looked at him with apprehension. She too was out of ideas. Just as the soldier was taking them both in hand, a voice broke in.

"What do you think you are doing?" To Steera and Diell's amazement a large Stoma, wearing the uniform of an officer in the Stoma regular forces confronted the trooper.

"Who are you?" the Trooper inquired, looking at the insignia on his tunic.

"I am major Loors-Klut-patar. Where are you taking these Faceer?"

"You have no jurisdiction here, Major. Suprameel is clearly in the Gleer area of influence on Donait." (Since the Island of Donait did not contain the residence of any of the major houses, it had been divided for political and economic reasons into areas of influence by the Houses of Gleer, Loors and Somar).

"I am here by order of the High Council of which your master is a member. I am to facilitate an expedition that is of the highest importance. It is my duty to see that it is not delayed. These Faceer are a part of that expedition."

"A young sailor and an entertainer?" The trooper laughed, sarcastically. "My orders come from my commander in Dosomiel."

"They are concealing their real identities as they have been instructed to do ... and I doubt that your commander's orders come directly from Gleer-Prime. I have a letter from Klut-Prime as to the importance of this mission." Major Patar handed the trooper a folded paper with a seal on it. The trooper recognized the official seal of the House of Klut. "I must warn you that I am carrying this message directly to Gleer-Prime. If you break the seal, he is going to want to know why it was broken ... and by whom."

The trooper struggled with his dilemma. His gaze shot back and forth between the official looking document in his hand and the officer in front of him. Finally, he turned to the trooper who had taken Diell and Steera into custody. "Give them to him," he said, reluctantly.

"I'll escort them to their ship," Loors-patar motioned for Diell and Steera to follow him. The three made their way quickly back down the wharf to the steamer just as the sailors were casting off the mooring ropes.

"And whom do we have to thank for this?" Steera asked.

"You don't need to know that, friends," the Stoma answered.

"But the document ... how did you get Klut to sign it?" Diell asked. Major Patar slid his stubby finger under the seal and popped it open. Inside, the page was blank.

"It is easier to forge a seal than a signature," Patar smiled.

"Then if that trooper had opened it, we'd all be in custody right now."

"Or worse," he replied. "It looks like the gods are smiling on you."

"And have sent us a few protectors in the bargain," Steera said, smiling and putting her hand in that of her new benefactor. The three stood for a moment in awkward silence not knowing how to say good-bye, seeming like old friends even though they had just met. The steamer's whistle let out a loud blast and the engines came to life as it began to pull away from the dock. Steera and Diell leaped onto the deck and waved a hurried farewell. Steera knew that it had taken great courage for major Patar to step in when he had.

Their friend stood watching on the wharf as the steamer moved down the harbor toward the open sea. Steera watched his figure growing smaller. She no longer felt alone. For the first time, she felt herself a part of something bigger, something that encompassed the whole of Osstar. The steamer turned east out of the harbor and then headed south. Below decks, all that could be heard was the high-pitched yelping of the Narros.

The Bajan stallions had made short work of the trip from Suprass to the port city of Broll on the southwest coast of Dosomiel. They had supplied the element that Somar-loors had wanted most—speed. Not having to follow the main highway, they were able to cut many miles off the trip. The party had arrived in time to see the last of their supplies being loaded onto a thick-hulled cargo freighter of the type that regularly plowed the icy waters of the sea of storms. All twenty of the troopers had made it back to the camp in time to embark on the overland trip to Broll, in spite of some foggy heads and full stomachs after the big party at Loors-Prime's residence. Somar-loors and Colonel Treeg had called Seer-affad to their cotaan shortly after arriving at Broll and made him describe the party in detail, taking great pleasure at each misadventure.

At mid-Rebal preparations had been completed, and General Somar ordered the troops to board the freighter. Fazid (recently promoted to corporal by General Somar himself) arrived at the cotaan to report on the status of the troops.

"All is in readiness, sir," he said, snapping a salute.

"Thank you, Corporal. How are the troopers' spirits?"

"Very high sir, I think the party given by his Excellency Loors-Prime did a lot to lift them."

"Good. And from what I've heard from your friend Affad, I'm sure his Excellency has much to remind him of his sacrifices for the cause." Fazid turned to leave as one of his troopers was being brought inside the cotaan by the security officer on duty.

"This trooper says he needs to speak with Colonel Treeg ... says it's urgent." Colonel Treeg motioned for Fazid to stay. The trooper, in awe of being in the presence of his commanding officer, was momentarily speechless.

"Be at ease trooper. What do you have to report?"

"Pardon sir, but I was given the responsibility by Corporal Fazid to operate the directional radio receiver. He told me to report any signal that I might receive, no matter how weak."

"And you've received a signal!" Colonel Treeg rose from his seat.

"Yes sir."

"When did you receive this signal, trooper?" Fazid caught himself too late.

"About twenty minutes ago. At first I thought that something was wrong with the receiver. The signal was weak and only lasted a few minutes, but I decided to report it just the same."

General Somar gave the corporal a quick glance and took up the questioning in a calmer tone. "And why did you think that the receiver had malfunctioned?"

"It was the signal sir. I had been told that we were looking for the signal from one of the Faceer Ka that had escaped from the battle at the Equatorial base, so that's what baffled me."

"The intensity of the signal surprised you?"

"No sir, it was the direction. The signal was coming from above."

"Are you certain?" Colonel Treeg asked looking the trooper directly in the eye.

"Yes sir. The signal was overhead to the west. It was strong for about five minutes, and then it faded away."

"Thank you, trooper. You were correct in reporting this, but be advised to keep this information confidential. I can count on you, can't I?"

"Absolutely sir," the trooper replied, straightening up to full height. Corporal Fazid escorted the trooper from the cotaan.

"What do you make of it, Colonel?"

"I'm not sure, sir. It could be a false signal."

"Or it could be a true signal," General Somar said darkly. "If it's true then our elusive Faceer Ka leader has either sprouted wings, or has gotten his hairy little paws on an air transport." General Somar stood and strapped his gas pistol to his waist. "We have even more need for haste. We must get to the ship and get underway at once. Leave anything that hasn't been loaded. We will have to make do without it." Colonel Treeg barked an order to the security officer who was still standing at attention and he began to gather all the maps and papers that were on the table in the center of the cotaan.

"Leave any nonessential items, and report to the dock ... and see that my and General Somar's personal trunks are loaded immediately." Somar-loors was already out of eyesight by the time colonel Treeg left the cotaan. The General had put everything out of his mind except reaching the coast of the South Polar Region. From this point on, it was a race, pure and simple.

Nosh's long, brawny armed draped over the shoulder of the Zerrit leader as he watched the mists swirling in front of the great ship grow thicker. The wind was picking up, and it looked as if the Sea of Storms was preparing to live up to its name. The Zerrit sat hunched over, taking some solace from the companionship of his leader but obviously distressed by his circumstances. Though he had tried mightily, Nosh could not get the Zerrit to leave his side. Rather than delay the expedition, he had had no choice but to bring him along.

The vessel's crew had an easier time accepting the presence of a Zerrit in their midst than a Seeyard. For the first few days Nosh had stayed in his cabin, going over sketchy maps of the South Polar Region. Eventually, though, he had had to come on deck to take some fresh air.

Initially, the sailors stayed well away from him, but slowly their celebrated Faceer curiosity began to get the better of them. Finally, one mid-Rebal, while Nosh was standing on the foredeck, one of the sailors plucked up the courage to speak.

"Just what are you, anyway?" he said, not the least bit embarrassed by his bold question.

"What do you think I am, friend?" Nosh used Faceer to Faceer terms. The sailor studied him. Other sailors began to gather round.

"Half and half ... and half," the sailor finally answered. There was an uneasy silence.

Nosh peered down on the sailor. "Half and half and half," he repeated. "I don't think I have ever heard it put more concisely than that." He let out a huge laugh that started in the low, Stoma register and ended in the high-pitched Faceer whinny. A grin broke out on the sailor's face and he looked around to see the others grinning as well.

"Half and half and half," he said again, and the others joined in the laughter.

Nosh sat down on the ships railing, lowering himself to eye level. "I suppose you'd like to hear my story," he said.

The sailors stopped whatever they were doing and sat on the deck of the rolling ship. They listened with rapped attention as the strange creature recounted the story of his life. He spoke of Faeed and his days with the Zerrits, and then steered the tale to the situation on Osstar and the struggle in which they were now engaged. Nosh spoke in the Faceer vernacular, looking each sailor in the eye. At the end of his oration, he made a simple plea.

"My dear, fellow Osstarians," he said. "We are in a most difficult struggle. It is a battle against our own fear and prejudice. I stand before you labeled an abomination by many, but I ask you to hold your judgment of me. I ask you to heed my words and not my appearance. We are on a mission to retake our planet from those who would bring division and death. You have all become a part of that mission, and a most vital part. How we fare in the next few weeks will decide the fate of all our citizens. Strive to do your best in the difficult days ahead. I ask it for your families and for all peaceful inhabitants of Osstar."

Not a word was spoken. The sailors dispersed to their individual tasks. Nosh watched as the sailors made fast the lines and secured the hold. There seemed to be a new energy in their work. He faced the railing and stood looking out across the threatening sea.

"Looks as if we are going to get our storm," Pire said, taking a place next to Nosh.

"It's been coming for a long time," Nosh replied, not taking his eyes off the wind and waves.

"I think the crew will be up to the challenge."

"They are good souls," Nosh said. "It's heartening to know that good souls still exist on Osstar. We will need them all." They sat together silently, watching the sailors trimming the sails and tying down anything loose on the deck of the great ship. The storm ahead was intensifying and they were sailing straight for it.

Seelar used his glove to scrape the ice from the covering of the fuel gauge; it showed a little less than half a tank remaining. Using only a compass, visual landmarks, and his considerable skill as a pilot, he had managed to traverse the Equatorial Region and skirt the western portion of Dosomiel, avoiding the skies over the Stoma city of Broll. His five passengers had not made a sound since their dramatic escape from the equatorial camp, but Seelar knew that the cold and the cramped quarters were beginning to take a toll.

"There's keera water in those flasks and I have katoc enough for a few days." No one spoke. The keera water was passed from hand to hand, and the Ka warrior took a small dose of katoc. The party settled back down into a tangled ball, trying to conserve what little heat their lowered Faceer metabolisms were now producing. Visibility was now down to almost zero. As soon as the transport had cleared the southwestern coast of Dosomiel and entered the Sea of Storms, the weather had turned from bad to horrendous.

The Sea of Storms was situated in a convergence zone of several strong sea currents. Warm water came down through the outer passage between Sunar and Donait, and around Dosomiel through the Sea of Aldor and collided with the icy currents off the South Polar coast forming strong downdrafts and swirling cloud banks. Waves of low pressure regularly crossed the southern coast of Dosomiel, so the massive storms were more or less continuous.

Seelar was now employing a piece of metal as a scraper to clear the side window. He decided to try and get higher, perhaps above the storm. The engines labored as the transport strained to gain altitude. The slushy precipitation quickly turned to pellets of ice. The stick felt like a ton of gallite in Seelar's hand, and it took every ounce of his strength to move it. He was beginning to think that it had been a mistake to ascend when the clouds thinned dramatically. The warmth from the radiation of Zenos began to melt the ice that had been building on the wings of the transport. Seelar didn't relax his grip on the stick; he knew that the clear, warm skies would be short lived. The fuel gauge had unfrozen but moisture condensing inside the covering had fogged it, making it difficult to read. The gauge still read more than half-full. Seelar was beginning to suspect its accuracy, but it made no difference. He would fly above the storms as long as he could. The air transport itself would make the final decision as to where and when to land. It was headed towards the South Polar Regions, hopefully in the area of the Caverns of Aldor. What ever happened now was in the hands of the gods.

Security was at a fever pitch in Croll as the expedition arrived. Word had been received of the attempt upon the column, although no one knew of the presence of Breet-Prime in the company. The bombing at Prass had prompted a tripling of security forces at all Government facilities, and the complete shutdown of a few. Not generally known was the fact that Breet had ordered the detention of all Stomari security staff at all facilities located in the Lower Midlands.

The armored vehicle carrying Breet, Druk-tasis and Riatt barely hesitated at the checkpoint at the entrance to the city. It made its way speedily to the administration building of the research complex. Breet exited with his overcoat pulled up over his head. Once inside, he stood revealed to several surprised officers of his own guard.

"Excellency!" the senior officer spoke at last. "We had no knowledge of your presence on this mission."

"As it was intended, Major," Breet answered coolly. "I am told that you have a high ranking Stomari officer here. Bring him to me." The officer turned and exited the room, returning quickly with a Stomari officer of the rank of colonel. "What is your name, Colonel?"

"I was ordered not to give such information ..." The colonel's remark was interrupted by the sound of a massive hand smashing onto the top of the Darma-shell desk in front of him. The sound reverberated throughout the room and down the narrow hallway. The officer nearly jumped out of his uniform, but maintained a composed look on his face.

"I am Breet-Prime, head of the House of Breet and a member of the High Council. You will answer my questions quickly and accurately or by the seven winds, I will have your hide on a cotaan pole." Every soldier in the room felt his legs go weak. "What is your House?"

"Takir, Excellency." The tone of defiance was gone from the major's voice.

"And what exactly was your mission here at the facility?"

"Security, sir."

"And why would the House of Takir have to send security to a facility under the control of the House of Breet?"

"I'm not sure, sir. I was just following my orders."

"Orders," Breet snorted, "The refuge of every scoundrel in the history of Osstar. I think you knew full well why you were sent here, Colonel. It was because your mission was more than just innocent research, and because Takir believed that I couldn't be trusted."

"I was not briefed on anything like that, Excellency. I swear it."

"You may not have been briefed on specifics, but you knew your mission, and it wasn't research. I am now on a mission as well. If successful, it will put an end to this Stomari charade once and for all. Take him into custody."

Two soldiers of the House of Breet moved to comply. As they did, three security guards, who had been standing in the doorway, reached for their gas pistols. Breet looked directly at them. "Will it be Stoma against Stoma?" The guards backed down and the colonel was led away. Breet-Prime pulled one of his officers aside. "We may have gotten all the Stomari confined, but we will have to methodically root out sympathizers. This is no time for sentimentality. It will, unfortunately, be necessary to get some of the innocent with the guilty, but you must make sure that you can totally trust those that are left in your command." The officer nodded his understanding.

"Harsh, but necessary," Druk-tasis spoke with approval.

"Contrary to my dear friend Takir-Prime's opinion of me, I can be decisive when necessary. I would like to stay and deal with this entire situation, but our transports are waiting and the Southern winter is not." The company exited the room and returned to their vehicle. As it sped through the city back to the harbor, Druk-tasis noted the empty streets and locked shops. Fear was beginning to gain a foothold on Osstar.

T he smoke from the steamer's boiler was becoming indistinguishable from the thick mist surrounding it. Sails designed to aid the vessel in calm seas and strong breezes were now employed as stability against the gales, and to aid in maneuvering. The waves were becoming increasingly rough as the ship broke free of the confines of the inner passage and rolled into the northern region of the Sea of Storms.

Steera and Diell stayed topside despite the frigid winds. The undulating deck was preferable to the dark unknown of the cabins below. As the old Stoma saying went, "Imagination makes a fear that the eyes can't hold" The unnatural silence from the Narros' pens far below decks confirmed it.

The first call came at the beginning of the second day. "Crystal Ship ... twenty points off the Swoonson beam!" Steera watched as two of the stronger sailors grabbed large metal poles and headed to the front of the steamer on the left side. They waited and watched, struggling against the increasingly violent rise and fall of the deck. The hiss of the wind cutting through the ropes was the only sound that could be heard. Every sailor was frozen at his post, his eyes straining to get a glimpse of the icy giant that was plowing its way through the waves. The great steamer now seemed a tiny, fragile life raft at the mercy of the raging sea. Then it appeared, bursting out of the rock-gray wall of clouds, a mountain of floating ice headed almost directly at them.

"Tighten the slip sail!" the call came. "Let go the mainsail! Steer to anchorage!" The ship lunged to the right, and Diell lost his balance. Frantic, he reached for Steera's hand but missed. He began sliding across the icy deck. Steera watched in horror as Diell slid helplessly toward the railing. A sailor, tying off the slip sail, saw Diell's predicament and cast the end of the rope toward him. Diell was able to grab it with one of his gloved hands, but the ice on the rope made it too slippery for the taanar-hide covering of the glove. He felt it slithering through his hand and did the only thing he could think of at the moment—he raised the rope to his exposed face and bit down as hard as he could. The boney teeth plates in his mouth held the rope firmly until he could be hauled in by the sailor, like a fish on a bait-line.

Diell had bitten down so strongly on the line that it took him a moment to loosen his jaws and remove it from his mouth. The crystal ship had moved by, barely missing the steamer. Everyone relaxed. The call rang out again.

"Crystal ship ... thirteen points to anchorage beam!" As if on cue, the steamer rolled to the right and the sailors rolled with it. This time the crystal ship was in full view, only about one hundred yards from the bow, and moving directly towards them. The wind had suddenly died. The mainsail was hanging limply, sheathed in ice, and slapping against the mast. The pilot didn't hesitate. He thrust the throttle forward and a great cloud of black smoke belched from the stack. The steamer again lurched—this time forward—directly towards the approaching crystal ship. The two were on a collision course. Steera wondered if the pilot had cracked under the pressure, but the steamer stayed its course. As the ice giant moved to within twenty-five yards of the seemingly doomed steamer, a blast of wind ripped through the mainsail and tore it to shreds. The sea rolled, and the crystal ship started to veer to the left. Just as it did, the pilot pushed the tiller hard to anchorage and the steamer veered right. The icy mountain churned past the steamer so closely that chunks of ice pelted the deck like an enormous hail storm. The sailors cheered and waved their hircus fur caps in the direction of the crystal ship as if to direct it on its way. Steera and Diell slumped onto a pile of ice encrusted rope.

Diell cocked his head to one side. "What's that?" he said, turning back to Steera. "Do you hear that?" Steera pulled the hood of her parka back, exposing her fur-rimmed ear to the elements. Over the sounds of the cheers, and the hissing of the reinvigorated wind through the ropes, she heard another sound ... a high pitched whine.

"What is it?" she looked at Diell.

"I don't know? It sounds like it's coming from above." Steera cupped her hands around the opening to her hood and scanned the stone-gray sky. For a brief moment, she thought that she saw a metallic glint in a tiny break in the overcast. It disappeared. A new cry came from the lookout.

"Land ho ... land thirty points to anchorage bow!" The crew hurried to their posts. Steera grabbed one of them by the arm.

"Are we there?"

"That depends on where there is," he replied.

"The South Polar Region." Steera continued.

"If we are not then all I have learned as a sailor has been wasted. But the challenge is not so much getting here," he said, "the problem will be finding a safe harbor before these frozen tragoones turn us to floatwood." He continued to his post, and began hauling what was left of the mainsail onto the deck.

They steamed for the better part of the day, still surrounded by a great, gray bank of clouds. Finally, the winds began to relent and the cloud bank lifted from the top of the waves. Ahead, the two shores of a large inlet could be seen through the falling snow. The pilot steered a course down the center of the inlet while the lookout searched for a protected place to drop anchor. The rest of the party from Romass was now on deck, grateful to be freed from the confines of their little cabins. The Narros began to make noise again. The great hull of the steamer rode up over the thickening ice of the inlet. The ice sheet groaned and gave way with a loud crack and the ship dipped down again into the newly freed water, moving forward slowly to repeat the process. The pilot was turning to swoonson, and the engines began to slow. Diell could see tall cliffs of ice looming in the distance, some of them hanging precariously over the water.

The silence was ghostly as the craft drifted between the giant cliffs. The pilot cut the engines and let the ship glide into the inlet. The only sound was the cracking and groaning of the ice. The steamer seemed a tiny stick floating down center of a great canyon of blue/white glass. The vessel turned harder to swoonson and the engines roared back to life as the pilot made an attempt to get the ship as close as he could to a flat landing area. When they had gone as far as the ice would allow, the pilot shouted out the order to drop anchor.

"We're here," Steera said. Diell said nothing.

The sailors had to unload the supplies and get back into deeper water as quickly as possible. The groaning of the ice walls was due to melting brought on by the coming spring. It meant that new crystal ships would soon be born. They worked with disciplined intensity, first unloading the food and sleds then carefully leading the Narros out of the holding pens and onto the landing area. Each Narro, except for the four lead Narros, had been blindfolded to aid in the short walk down the slippery ramp — lead Narros would never accept a blindfold. After all supplies and animals were unloaded, the ship's pilot called the entire party together.

"We have become friends and fellow travelers on our journey," he said to Steera and Diell. "I can tell you now that from the beginning of our journey we have had four non-sailors among us. I was the only one who knew, and did not reveal it to protect the other sailors should we be captured. You will be counting on these beasts to get you to your destination," he said pointing to the Narros snarling and playing on the ice below. "You will be in good hands. Four of the crew may lack something as sailors, but they are the finest 'sledders' on Osstar. I have prepared lots for the ten of you." He looked in the direction of the villagers. "The four that draw the black stones will stay with us," he smiled, "we'll make you sailors by the time you return to Romass."

There were no arguments. The villagers drew their lots and accepted their fate, happy to have made it so far from home still in one piece. The four sledders took their place with the expedition party and made their way down the ramp to hook up the Narros to the sleds. The sailors drew in the ramp, raised anchor and began steaming back out of the inlet. As the steamer drew away, it unfurled a large Osstarian flag where the small standard of the Braccar alliance had flown. It was a sign of hope. The expedition stood at the farthest edge of Osstar, but they were not alone.

CHAPTER 32

Seelar scraped the ice once again from the instrument panel and tapped his nearly frozen fingers against the fuel gauge. It was still reading almost half full. He now knew for certain that it was broken. It was the only thing he did know for certain. He didn't know exactly where he was or where he was headed. The clouds he had managed to rise above were once again filling the sky in front of him, and the intensity of the ice and snow pelting his craft was increasing. Thanks to dolling out the last of the katoc, the company in the cargo area had remained quiet, disturbing him only occasionally with a moan or a short cry when the transport was buffeted by the winds. He had hoped to maintain a southerly course but could not get a visual fix on his position.

He pulled back on the stick and heard the engines groan as the craft struggled to gain altitude. The stick began to thrash in his hand and slid from between his numbed fingers. The engine sputtered, the groan turning to a high pitched whine and then fell silent as the transport began to slip back into the soupy clouds. The members of the last contingent of the Ka army were tossed around like sacks of grain. Seelar tried desperately to restart the engine, but his worst fear was confirmed — the craft was out of fuel.

His pilot's training took over. He feathered the engines and tried to edge the nose of the transport up. The descent was becoming controlled, but still he could not see anything in front of him. After another few minutes of descending, he thought he saw a thinning of the clouds to his right. He steered the transport in that direction and found a break in the clouds.

He was much lower than he had calculated. The vast, white plain of the South Polar Region stretched out to the east and west, but ahead, the view was obstructed by an intense blizzard. The blowing snow assaulting the windshield and the sharp whistling sound of the wind rushing through the frozen propellers had a hypnotizing effect. It seemed that the aircraft was hanging, frozen in the frigid air with the snow blowing past it.

A shadow appeared directly in front of him. Before he could react and pull the nose of the transport up, he felt the undercarriage meeting snow and ice and heard the grinding of metal on rock. That was the last thing he and Pylo remembered hearing until they awoke several hours later. It was the last sound the rest of the party ever heard on Osstar.

Wrapped tightly inside his parka, Pire watched the slate-gray clouds spiraling inside the snowy mist like the first drops of cold lapis juice swirling in a cup of chee. Icy polar winds whipped around him. It was impossible to estimate how far they were from land. The sailors were feverishly working to keep ice from fouling the lines to the mainsail. Nosh had seen to it that the Zerrit leader was safe below decks; he had put him in his own quarters. He joined Pire and watched as the churning bank of clouds moved closer to the ship.

The first blast from the storm hit them head-on. The mighty ship popped up and down in the swells as if it were a toy. The pilot called out his commands and the crew responded. They hauled on the ropes controlling the various sails, handling them with a precision that comes with years of practice. The ship stayed on course.

The second blast was unexpected; as it had appeared that the clouds were breaking. It tore through the mainsail like a stabbing sword through skieen-cloth. All hands worked quickly to cut the sail free so it would not foul the other lines. Without the mainsail, the ship lost much of its forward momentum. The next blast turned it almost completely around, and the tragoone began taking on water. Pire ran across the rolling deck and grabbed for whatever support he could find to stay upright.

"Nosh!" he cried, "are we going down?" The wind-driven sleet and snow made it difficult for Pire to hear the reply, but he could see that Nosh was helping the crew get the last part of the mainsail overboard. Pire felt a bit ashamed at his outburst, and rushed to help. The ship was maintaining its course even though it was being tossed about like a coola feather in a stiff breeze.

"Fine sailors." Nosh shouted over the wail of the wind as he returned to where Pire had taken refuge next to the opening to the hold. "I've read much about sailing, but have never had the opportunity to actually do it. Trust Tomar Leet to pick the best sailors on Osstar."

The winds subsided a bit and gave the crew time to adjust the other sails to compensate for the loss of the mainsail. The snow, at the moment, was falling straight down. Nosh was about to say something to Pire without having to shout when the hatch slid open and a wide-eyed Zerrit Ape put both of his hairy arms around his leg. Nosh stroked the Zerrit. "Poor fellow, I'd almost forgotten about you in the excitement. It must have been very exciting below decks." Pire managed a nervous laugh. The Zerrit relaxed a little, staring up at the strange white powder floating down from the sky. "He's never seen snow." He held out a finger and caught a flake, letting the Zerrit get a closer look.

"He's had a lot of firsts lately," Pire added, putting his own hand on the Zerrit's head. The Zerrit's eyes widened as he gazed out across the grey/white expanse of the sea. His mouth fell open.

"Zayahheeee, zayahheeee," he was gesturing, excitedly.

"There, there," Nosh said, trying to stroke the Zerrit's head. He would have none of it. "He is upset." Before Nosh could get him back below decks, a cry rang out.

"Crystal ships ... crystal ships to Swoonson and Anchorage beams!"

In front of them, bearing down from both sides of the ship, were two mountains of ice. Given their current course and speed they would meet at the ships' present location. To make matters worse, a solid bank of dark-gray clouds was forming, threatening to envelope the vessel. Visibility was dropping dramatically.

Nosh remembered his treasure. He reached into his pocket and brought out a cone. A flood of pure, white light ripped through the clouds and mist. The shadowy silhouettes of the crew danced across the rigging and sailcloth. A few sailors cried aloud, fearing some manner of silent explosion had occurred, that the ship had caught fire. Nosh moved to the beam and held the cone aloft. Ahead, one of the crystal ships had collided with the other, tearing a great chunk of ice from its flank. The collision had changed the course of both. Nosh saw an opening.

"Steer to Swoonson beam!" he cried to the wheelhouse. The pilot immediately cut the great ship to the left. The shift was violent. A sailor lost his grip on the railing and plunged into the frothing, icy waters. His mate reached for him, but couldn't grip his flailing arm. Nosh tossed the light cone to Pire and grabbed a metal pole. Moving to the railing, he thrust it into the chop. The pole came back empty. The two massive mountains of ice flowed silently and gracefully past, but the crew was transfixed by the plight of their brother sailor. Again the pole reached the swirling water, and again it came back empty. The crew became resigned to the loss of their friend, but Nosh would not give up. Stretching his long frame as far over the railing as he could, he thrust one last time. This time he felt something solid. Two freezing hands latched onto the pole with all their remaining strength. With a mighty heave, a frightened, frozen Faceer flopped up on the deck as if a fish plucked from the icy depths. He lay motionless. Several of his mates moved to help him into the wheelhouse. The rest went back to their stations, giving a respectful nod to Nosh as they passed.

The light from the cone, now resting in Pire's hand, was revealing an open sea in front of them—at least for the time being. The sea began to smooth a little, and the winds died down. It was as if the whole planet had let out a sigh of relief for the rescued sailor. Soon, a new call came from the lookout.

"Land! Land ten points to Swoonson beam!"

The tragoone glided into the calmer waters of a natural harbor cut by the fracturing of ice sheets along the cliffs of the coastline. Nosh joined Pire and the two studied the bleak yet beautiful landscape of the South Polar Region. A constant stream of frozen mist flowed across the plateau of ice that covered the polar land mass. As it reached the sea, it cascaded over the edge of the ice shelf in a vast, phantom waterfall of fog, disappearing before reaching the waves far below. In the clear, white light of the cone, it looked more beautiful and much more forbidding than the North Pole.

The tragoone gave a slight heave and came to rest on a finger of solid land jutting out beneath the sheet ice. A long wooden plank was lowered on the swoonson side and crews of sailors began to unload the hold of the ship. Soon, a pile of parkas, tins of food and packages of medical supplies were lying in a heap on the snow. Pire was still wondering about transport. How were they to navigate the ice and snow to the caverns? Surely Leet wouldn't have them walk all the way.

He had started to pose the question to Nosh when an unfamiliar machine poked its front end out of the hold, followed by five panting, grunting sailors. Its nose raised high into the air and then abruptly fell forward, sliding all the way down the plank and finally skidding to a halt fifty yards from the rest of the supplies.

"Electric sleds," Nosh said matter-of-factly. Pire watched as two more of the giant sleds were deposited on the snowy plain.

"Why three?" Pire asked. "One would be all that you and I will need. One of the sailors overseeing the unloading of the hold interrupted them.

"Pardon, sir, but you get more than a boat ride and three sleds in this bargain. Six of us are going on with you ... wherever it is that you're going in this forsaken place."

Nosh looked surprised. "You don't know what you're saying. This will be a dangerous, perhaps life threatening journey."

"Never-the-less, we're going. You can't make speeches like the one that you made on the deck and expect us to just drop you off and wish you luck. Besides, we have our orders too."

"Orders?"

"Yes. Our deal with Tomar Leet included an escort to wherever it is that you are going. We are now a part of this quest—Leet's instructions." Nosh thought of Leet, his feet propped up on some oversized piece of Stoma furniture, puffing on a battered old pipe, and smiled. He had done all of this is less than a week's time. What a marvel he was.

The crew finished unloading the great ship and testing the motors on the sleds. The supplies had been packed aboard when one of the crew led a reluctant Zerrit slowly down the plank. As soon as his hairy feet touched the solid ice, the expression on his face changed from fear to astonishment. He had never before felt the ground this cold. Nosh came to his aid, lifting him onto his shoulders and carrying him to the lead sled. Pire followed Nosh. Sliding into the front, he put himself between Nosh and the Zerrit leader. The rest of the company suited up in their parkas and took their places in the other two sleds. Dark clouds were boiling in the distance.

Nosh took the steering mechanism in his hands and turned the starter switch. The electric motors on the sleds whirred to life and he pushed the stick forward. It gave a slight jerk and began to move ahead. The two other sleds followed, slicing through the calm air of the protected harbor and out into the growing storm.

With each passing minute, the intensity of the storm was increasing. Ice was covering the thick coats of the Narros. Inside the sleds, stuffed with equipment, it was a snug fit. Steera and Diell sat crunched together, rolling into each other with each twist and turn.

The sledders were expert and the group was making steady, if slow progress. The main problem was navigation. No stars were visible anywhere overhead. The blinding storm was so powerful that even Rebal was out of view most of the time. From the research she was able to do before she left Prameel, Steera reckoned the caverns — if indeed they even existed — to be to the southwest of where they had landed. She had given the heading to the sledders and could only hope that they were going in the right direction.

Everyone had heard tales of the fierce storms in the South Polar Region, but nothing could have prepared them for what they were experiencing. The snow was falling at such a rate that it was necessary to clear it away from one's goggles every half-minute or so. The Narros were showing no signs of being effected by the cold, but it was obvious that they were struggling against the wind and ice. The surface beneath them was becoming uneven and the sleds had to make directional adjustments every few yards to avoid ice ridges and crevices.

Diell cleared the snow from his goggles. The sky ahead, as improbable as it may seem, was actually getting darker — occasionally even the crack of thunder could be heard. The sledder made another course adjustment. He was now heading directly towards the dark patch of sky. Diell thought he saw a flicker of bright orange just below the cloud. The sledder yelled to the lead Narro, and pulled back hard on the brakes. He tried to yell back to the other sledders, but his cries were muffled by the thick walls of snow descending all around them. Before he could get his sled moving, the three trailing sleds were upon him. The lead Narros snarled at each other. In the distance, black smoke was billowing up from a heap of twisted metal. Diell recognized parts of an air transport.

"What is it?" Steera shouted to the sledder, trying to overcome the effects of the blowing snow and ice.

"It looks like a wrecked aircraft," he shouted back. "Shall I approach it?"

"No," Steera answered. "I'm going to have a look."

"Not by yourself you're not," Diell climbed out of the sled to join her. Steera knew that it would do no good to argue with him, and in truth, she was not too sure about venturing that far from the sleds in this weather.

"You're right," she yelled back. "Look in the sled and see if you can find some rope." Diell searched the cargo compartment on his side of the sled and found a length of strong rope coiled inside. He hauled it out and showed Steera. "Good. Tie one end of it to the front of the sled and the other around me. Follow me about half way out and then let the rope out slowly as I move forward." Diell started to protest, but Steera cut him off. "Don't let the rope go slack or I'll box those furry ears of yours." Before he could think of a reply, Steera was making her way toward the wreckage.

Diell let the rope out slowly as he was instructed, and in just a few steps, Steera was completely out of visual range. The rope continued to be drawn out for a few more minutes, and then it stopped. Every few minutes it would twitch and jerk and then it stopped altogether. Diell guessed that Steera was returning. He began to pull on the rope. Finally, Steera came back into view. The other members of the party had separated the quarreling Narros and had gathered at the lead sled to stare in awe at the sight of a fire in the midst of a blizzard. Steera made it to the sled and stood for a moment.

"Does any one of you have medical training?" A hand went up from the rear of the group. "What's your name?"

"Deelus."

"Well, Deelus, get some supplies together. We're going back."

"Steera," Diell pleaded, "what is it?"

"No time to explain, and if I had time I'm not sure that I could. Tie another rope around Deelus." Two other members of the party tied a rope around Deelus' waist and he and Steera made their way back into the storm. The group waited. After about twenty minutes, Diell and the villager holding Deelus' rope felt two strong tugs. They began pulling. Soon, both could tell that they were doing more than just guiding Steera and Deelus back. Two more villages joined them. Out of the swirling snow two familiar figures came into view. Behind them, tied to the ends of the ropes, they were dragging two dark objects covered in ice and snow.

Diell motioned to two of the villagers nearest the sled. "Give them a hand."

The two rushed out to help Steera and Deelus pull the figures to the sled. Three other villages stretched a sturdy, sto-metal cloth between two sleds and set up a makeshift shelter for the injured. The two were dragged inside. Deelus pulled apart the frozen hood of one of the parkas. It revealed the face of a young Faceer, badly banged up and suffering from hypothermia. His spinal ridge was retracted so far that it made a strange protrusion in the middle of his chest all the way up to his neck.

"Any idea as to who he might be?" Diell asked.

Steera stooped over to get a closer look. "He's wearing a Stomari uniform under the parka."

"Stomari! What in the name of Leeth?" Steera moved to the other figure and pried the hood of his parka open. Her expression froze as she stared into the open hood. "What is it, Steera?" She could not answer. She looked up at Diell and tore back the parka's hood to expose the entire head of the unconscious figure. It was Seelar!

CHAPTER 33

The slushy muck of snow and sweat that covered the Bajan Stallions' insulating blankets made them more of a burden than a help to the tired beasts. General Somar-loors had hoped that the harrowing sea journey from Broll would spell the end of the bad weather, but that had been a forlorn hope. In the twenty hours since they had landed at the South Polar Region, eight soldiers had fallen out, along with their suffering stallions, and the storm was only getting worse.

Necessity had caused general Somar to do something he had never done. It had caused him to go into a potentially dangerous situation under-equipped and without a proper knowledge of the terrain or the climate. He knew that the price of his indiscretion would be counted in lives. Still, one thing was in his favor. Fazid had taken over the operation of the directional radio and was receiving a clear but faint signal to the southwest. They still had an idea of where they were going.

Colonel Treeg cupped his gloved hands over his eyes and tried to see through the blinding snow. He had sent two troopers ahead to find a safe passage. Large chasms were developing as the thin ice that covered them broke under the weight of the Bajans and the heavy supply sleds.

Treeg put his distance glasses to his eyes and slid the snow filters onto the eyepieces. He could see nothing. Suddenly, he heard the high pitched whinny of a stallion in distress. He swung his glasses in the direction of the sound just in time to see the rear end of a stallion break through the ice. The frantic beast was pawing the air with its front hoofs trying to find some solid surface. In a matter of moments both the stallion and its rider were gone. The blizzard quickly swallowed the sound of it as efficiently as the chasm had swallowed the two. It was as if they had never existed, as if some giant creature had sucked them into his icy lair. Treeg knew that the entire party was in serious trouble.

Colonel Treeg made his way back to the last known position of the main body. He found general Somar-loors, corporal Fazid and trooper Affad along with six other troopers huddling next to their frightened Bajans. The wind was howling so hard that it was impossible to hear anything more than a few feet away. General Somar was yelling at the top of his voice with the others straining to hear.

"How many are there of us now?"

"I think we are all that remains sir," Fazid shouted back.

"This area is riddled with chasms. We are going to have to proceed with great caution. The caverns will give us shelter. The sooner we get to them, the better." The soldiers took heart at the sound of confidence in General Somar's voice, but General Somar was anything but confident. He took a long look at the faces of his troopers. They stared back at him, impassively. For a moment he felt as if he were somewhere else. He saw himself as an old Stoma looking at a roster of those lost in the great South Polar Expedition, their hollow eyes leering like phantoms from a worn photograph. These soldiers would not make it on their strength alone.

"Form up in a single line. Tie a rope from your Bajan to the sled in front of you. We'll move together."

Without awaiting further orders, Colonel Treeg called to Affad and instructed him to join him at the rear of the column. General Somar needed to lead and he needed to be at the rear to keep them moving. As the winds continued to howl, the column moved out. General Somar had on every layer of clothing that the supplies provided, yet he was extremely cold. He tried to make conversation with Fazid but his jaw was becoming so numb that even speech was difficult. Fazid was hardly moving at all, staying scrunched down in the sled, his head cradled in his arms. The General knew the look of a trooper who has given up.

After only a few minutes, the sled gave a mighty jolt and pitched backwards a few yards. "Can you see anything behind us, Trooper?" General Somar shouted directly at the spot on Fazid's parka where his ear hole would be located. Fazid stirred slowly and turned without comment to look behind their sled. The rope to the next sled was limply dragging across the snow. He rose with great difficulty and tugged at the line. It gave easily. In a few moments he had retrieved the entire length of the rope. At the end of it were three frayed strands and nothing more. He looked at general Somar-loors with emotionless eyes. General Somar put his arm around the demoralized trooper and spoke to him as softly as the raging weather would allow. "Trooper Fazid, we are in a most precarious spot. The weather was far harsher than we anticipated, and while the Bajans served us well to this point, they are proving to be of little use in this forsaken place. It is a difficult situation that we face. Our companions may already be dead. But we cannot give up. This storm can't last forever. We will stop here, use our sled as a shelter and wait it out as best we can."

General Somar got out of the sled and fought through the icy gale to the exhausted stallion. He unhooked the harnesses and led the bewildered creature back to the sled. Trooper Fazid struggled to unload a large taanar hide, finally laying it out on the ice. Attaching two pieces of cotaan pole to the sides of the sled, General Somar stretched the hide far enough to cover Fazid, himself and at least a portion of the now prone Bajan. Once inside the makeshift shelter, he broke open a firestick and tried to direct the acrid smoke it produced toward the opening.

"Well," he said in a resolute tone, "if the storm doesn't get us, the smoke probably will."

A faint smile crossed Fazid's face. "An interesting place for a water-loving creature to meet his end, wouldn't you say?" he said softly.

"An interesting place indeed," Somar answered, "but we're not done-in quite yet. We still have a mission to complete, and I haven't failed to complete one in my career." Fazid curled up against the motionless Bajan and pulled his parka around his face. General Somar lay still, listening to the winds wailing like tormented animals and wondering if morning ever broke in this desolate place.

Two stubby, Stoma fingers adjusted the fuel mixture to the sled's internal combustion engine as it burped and stuttered in the icy winds. In all, three "hot fuel" sleds had been unloaded from the tragoone—room enough for Breet-Prime, Riatt and Druk-tasis and six security troopers from the House of Breet. The direction finder (an instrument that used the magnetic properties of Osstar's poles in relation to Rebal's magnetic field to give approximate positions) was pointing south-southwest. Breet Prime wasn't sure how accurate the readings were, but he was sure of one thing—they were not alone. In the harbor where they had made land sat an ice covered tragoone bearing the insignia of the House of Loors. It looked as if it had been there for twenty years or so, but Breet knew that it had probably only landed a day or two before them. The fierce storm had long since obliterated any trace of the number, or direction of travel of the party the great ship had carried.

"We'll take the direction finder," Breet yelled to his troopers above the wail of the winds. "Make sure we stay together; this region is riddled with chasms and crevices." Each sled had been modified for artic uses, and had a flashing red lantern attached to the rear. Breet pushed the lead sled forward, its combustion engine belching blue/black smoke. The other two sleds followed closely, each struggling to keep visual contact with the sled in front. Riatt and Druk-tasis snuggled down as best they could in the passenger area.

"It's not until situations like this that you realize the size difference of our two species," Druk-tasis said, almost apologetically, as he tried to make room for Riatt. Riatt smiled from deep within his Kaba-fur lined parka.

"Well, Tupo," he replied wryly, "I don't recall any stories about your adventures in the Caverns of Aldor. Perhaps you could tell me one?"

"Oh, would that I was that lonely little greel-calf right now," he chuckled, "and back in my warm pen in the Midlands. I would never jump the fence again."

The two settled down, getting as comfortable as the cramped, noisy sleds would allow. They bumped along slowly, each sled stopping when the flashing light of the trailing sled faded from sight. Suddenly Riatt and Druk felt their sled wobble to a stop. They poked their heads out the passenger section. The wind had died down and the storm seemed less ferocious. Breet-Prime had already gotten out of the driver's compartment and was walking cautiously ahead. Riatt could make out a small mound about 75 feet in front of the sled. It looked like snow, and yet something about it seemed to be wrong. At the far end of the mound, Riatt could just make out a dark mass. It was fluttering in the winds like the sea grasses along the walkways at Donnalier.

"It looks like grass."

Druk-tasis had retrieved a pair of distance glasses from the cargo compartment, and was clipping on the snow filters. "Here, you look," he said, handing them to Riatt. Riatt pulled his hood farther apart and put the glasses to his eyes. As he focused, the figure of Breet-Prime came into his field of vision. He was leaning over the mound. Riatt refocused on the dark area. It was indeed blowing with the polar winds, but it was too course to be grass. It looked more like animal hair of some kind. "What can you see?"

"It looks as if some sort of animal has been covered in snow. Breet is returning; we'll know more in a moment."

Breet walked past his sled directly back to the two others and bade them to join him. "I now know the identity of the party on board the tragoone we found when we landed. In the snow just ahead is a dead Bajan stallion. Just in front of him, under a makeshift shelter constructed from a sled, are the bodies of three Stoma troopers. They carry the mark of the Stomari and insignia from the Houses of Klut, Takir and Somar."

"What does it mean?" Riatt asked.

"I believe that we have found the expedition that had been reported to me. It is General Somar-loors' party. It is difficult to say how large a contingent it is, but if they are depending on Bajans to get them to the caverns we may yet be in time to make a difference." He waved at the other sleds and shouted, "Back to your sleds troopers, we can waste no more fuel here. We must try and make up for lost time." The snow was decreasing and the winds had gone from a gale to a stiff breeze. In the far distance Druk-tasis could make out yet another mound of snow. General Somar-loors, it seemed, had marked his trail well ... tragically well.

"Why does all this sound so familiar?" Diell said as he listened to Steera's argument.

"Well, we can't just leave him here."

"And again," Diell noted, "the exact words I believe you used in the jungle the last time we came across our friend here." But Diell knew she was right. The situation was different now. To leave Seelar and his companion in the midst of this blizzard would be the same as murder. There would be no way that they could hope to survive. Steera had already made the decision.

"Make room for them in the cargo compartments of my sled," she shouted to the two closest villagers. "We don't have time to see to their wounds. If we don't find shelter from this storm soon, their wounds won't matter much." The four sleds moved out again to the southwest. The Narros seemed to be pulling harder, heading in a definite direction. The storm showed no signs of letting up.

"Is it me, or do these beasts seem to be pulling with greater determination?" Diell asked Steera, pulling the hood of his parka apart far enough to be heard in the stuffy confines of the sled.

"I sense that as well," Steera answered. The wind had reached a crescendo, when an anguished howl arose from behind them. Diell lifted himself to try and see out of the sled. What he saw sent a chill down his already frozen spinal ridge.

The rear of one of the sleds was sticking straight up in the air. The front end of the trailing sled had slid under it and the Narros were howling at the top of their powerful voices as they tried to claw their way back to solid ice. Diell prayed that he would see the shapes of villagers clambering out of the two stricken vehicles, but he saw only the vain struggles of the Narros as the two sleds and their entire cargo of villagers disappeared beneath the ice. The other two sleds were helpless. The snow was still coming down in torrents. Any attempt to turn around would have only resulted in the loss of the rest of the expedition.

Steera screamed at the sledder to turn back, but the experienced driver knew that they were past the point of no return. He knew something else. He knew that the Narros were sensing shelter. That was why they had thrown their usual caution to the wind and were pulling with such enthusiasm. They had not even stopped to acknowledge the cries of their compatriots. The beasts were on a mission, and the sledder knew that he was only along for the ride.

The two remaining sleds picked up speed as the winds started to diminish, and for the first time in many hours the snow started to abate as well. In the distance Steera thought she could see the slope of the land changing. The sled was definitely starting to climb. Diell could feel the guide ropes on the Narros tighten, as the sled became more of a burden. The Narros intensified their efforts. They were definitely heading up-slope. The sleds were now side by side as the Narros made a contest of reaching the summit, finally reaching a passage between two massive walls of ice. As if by magic, an opening in the icy mountain revealed itself.

There was no stopping the Narros; they headed for the opening without regard for safety or any other consideration. They were tired, cold and hungry, and for them this was the end of the line. The sleds bumped to a stop inside the mouth of a vast ice cave. Steera, Diell and the remaining villagers roused themselves from their compartments, shaking off the effects of their wild ride. They slowly gathered together and starred in awe at the enormity of their new surroundings.

"So, this is where the weather is made," one of them muttered.

"The Caverns of Aldor," Steera said with a reverence in her voice. "We've made it to the end of the world."

The "hot fuel" sleds were proving to be far superior to the unfortunate Bajans in the artic wastes. Druk-tasis and company had encountered two more snow-covered mounds filled with frozen Stomari troopers and stallions. They were navigating giant apertures in the icy ground that appeared to be only recently opened. Whether these were tombs for more Stomari troopers was unknown, but if anyone or anything had fallen into them it was certain that they would never come out again.

Breet-Prime had gone against the advice of his two companions, and continued with them in the lead sled. He was in charge and he was not going to lessen his own danger by putting others at greater risk. The snow had almost stopped. The winds were still swirling from all directions, but not as fiercely. Breet, constantly scanning the horizon with his distance glasses, caught sight of another lump in the snow. He pushed the control stick slightly to the right and made for the mound.

The snow was beginning to pick up. The new mound appeared much fresher than were the others. The top of it had a square appearance. Upon closer examination, it turned out to be a canopy of taanar hide stretched over two sections of wooden poles. The blowing snow had given it the appearance of a baark, a type of hunting shelter still used by the Faceer in the northern regions.

Druk-tasis and Riatt got out of their sled and joined Breet at the structure. Breet ordered two troopers to dig the snow away from the opening. After a few minutes of shoveling one of the troopers called out "There are two Stoma in here! I think that they're alive!"

"Bring them out, gently." Breet-Prime turned to two nearby troopers. "Make a place for them by the heaters." Breet, Riatt and Druk watched as the troopers lifted the unconscious bodies from the shelter and placed them in newly cleared compartments within the lead sled.

"There's a Bajan in here as well," a trooper called. "I think that it's dead."

"Cover it with the hide and mark the area with an ice pole ... we may need that Bajan before it's over." Riatt knew that Breet was right. They were not yet half-way through their journey. Getting here was one thing, getting back would be something else altogether.

The sleds stood idling as the snow continued to increase. The two Stoma had been incubating in the warming compartments for over an hour. Breet was becoming concerned about the amount of fuel that they were consuming without making progress towards the caverns.

"Sir, I think they're coming around."

A large, hooded Stoma head emerged from the sled followed by a slightly smaller one. Slowly, as if they had been frozen for decades, they straightened their long frames and stepped out onto the ice.

"Identify yourself!" Breet commanded.

"I am Corporal Gleer-fazid, First Stomari Shock Battalion," the smaller Stoma replied.

"And you?" Breet directed his question to the larger Stoma. The General slowly peeled back the frozen hood of his parka and revealed himself to the astonished party.

"I am General Somar-loors, Your Excellency."

After moving far enough into the cave to escape the now worsening weather, Steera called the remaining villagers and sledders together. She asked for their silence and then offered a prayer for those lost in the chasm. Two sleds had survived. Along with Steera, Diell, and their sledder, there were two villagers and another sledder, the still semi-conscious body of the Faceer Ka trooper and, of course, Seelar.

"Better another sled with villagers had made it than these two," Diell said, making no effort to disguise his contempt. He poked at the unresponsive Faceer Ka with his stiff, gloved hand.

"We have no wish to anger the gods," Steera scolded. "If our appearance just in time to save Seelar once again isn't the product of some divine fate then I don't know what you would call it."

"Blind luck is what I would call it ... and bad luck at that."

"I can't say that I would dispute that," a voice emerged from the center of the sled, "... the blind luck that is. Where am I?"

"The Caverns of Aldor," Steera replied, "although we don't exactly have photographic plates to confirm that."

"Let me see." Seelar arose from his cramped quarters and climbed out of the sled.

"Stay where you are!" Diell growled. One of the sledders produced a gas pistol from under his parka and pointed it directly at Seelar's head.

"Now, now, let's not do anything in haste," Seelar said coolly. Pylo was also beginning to stir.

"Do you know something about these caverns?" Steera motioned the sledder to put away his weapon.

"I have heard a few stories. One was from a Faceer Ka who had ancestors who made the journey here."

"What a pile of Kaakall droppings," Diell sneered. "He's just trying to gain our confidence again like he did back in the jungle."

"Would you believe me if I told you that it was Laymar Daage, the son of the great Faceer explorer, Tyne Daage?"

"Tyne Daage has been dead for fifty years ... and I have never heard of any expeditions of his to the South Polar Region," Steera said.

"Of course you haven't. They were financed by Takir-raase who happened to be Takir-Prime at the time. It seems that there had been rumors of large deposits of gallite down here. Takir contracted with Daage, but of course had to keep it a secret. He didn't want the other Great Houses on Osstar to know what he was up to."

"And of course they found nothing," Diell scoffed.

"It's not certain what they found, but it's fairly certain that it was enough to cost Tyne Daage his life. Not long after his return, a supply wagon broke free of its moorings and ran poor Daage down in the street ...an unfortunate Stoma accident.

"Tyne Daage died in a climbing accident," Diell spat.

"So they say," Seelar replied coolly, "so they say."

"So, this Laymar Daage, what did he know of the Caverns?"

"He said that his father mentioned them only once. It was just before he died. He said that they had made progress into the caverns, but that they were complex and full of diverging tunnels. They marked the tunnels that led into the heart of the caverns, but stopped before reaching the center."

"Marked them how?" Diell was still skeptical.

"They carved a tycor into the rock at each correct cave entrance."

"What a coincidence," Diell said, "the sign of the Faceer Ka."

Seelar was now completely out of the sled and standing with his back to the Cavern entrance. Pylo had also straightened up and exited the sled; the long trousers of the Stomari uniform he had purloined at the equatorial base were dragging the frozen ground.

"If I'm not mistaken," Seelar continued, "there will be three main cave entrances about a thousand yards from here. If we look for the tycor, we will be on our way."

"You're not going anywhere," Diell barked.

"Always so hostile, young one. Would that you could channel some of that hostility into our movement. What possible harm could it do to take my 'Stomari' companion and me with you? We could be of use to you if you encountered problems."

"What problem could we encounter that would be a bigger one than you?" Diell shot back.

Steera had had enough of the bickering. "He's not telling us everything. He knows something else. He's going to keep it hidden so that we are forced to take him along."

"So beautiful and so smart," Seelar grinned. "You would have made an excellent Faceer Ka ... a worthy partner for the ruler of Osstar."

"Was there something else?" Steera asked. "You said that they stopped before reaching the heart of the cavern, why?"

"Just before he ended his tale, Laymar said his father became very agitated and mumbled something about 'the guardians.'"

Diell snorted so loudly that the Narro closest to him reacted.

"We'll leave the Narros here with the sleds. Leave food and water enough to last them a good while." Steera turned to Seelar. "We're going to test your first theory. If indeed there are three cave entrances ahead, and if there is a tycor etched on one of them, then you and your friend will be permitted to accompany us. But mark me well, if you make any attempt to deceive us in any way, I will not hesitate to hand you over to one of my friends from Romass.

They have a score to settle with the Faceer Ka. Do I make myself clear?"

"I am at your service," Seelar replied.

"Then lead the way," Steera answered. "I want to keep you in front of me until we reach our destination."

"Oh, I intend to stay in front ... I'm a born leader."

The half-mile to the cavern's first divergence turned out to be closer to two miles. Seelar and Pylo led the way. Two villagers (armed with gas pistols) followed closely with Steera and Diell behind them. Leet had equipped the expedition with high intensity electric torches. The light they produced revealed an immense cave system with massive rock formations. The divergent chambers had been channels for the molten rock that had flowed millions of years ago. Long since cooled, it had left behind a labyrinth of remarkably smooth tunnels and passages in the heart of the South Polar Mountains.

The party came upon a low-hanging rock ledge that, once they had ducked under, opened into a massive chamber. At the far end of the chamber were three distinct openings, just as Seelar had described them.

"I suppose you will see my worth now," Seelar gloated.

"We'll see if the markings are there, then we'll decide," Diell said. Steera, and one of the villagers with a torch, moved forward to examine the opening on the right. After a few minutes of searching, they moved to the center tunnel then without comment to the entrance on the left. They returned with worried looks on their faces.

"Well, it looks as if your friend wasn't totally truthful," she said to Seelar.

"It can't be," Seelar protested. "Let me look."

Steera nodded to the torchbearer and he reluctantly handed the torch to Seelar. He and Steera moved to the opening on the right. Diell moved to join them, taking one of the gas pistols with him.

The right hand opening was smaller than the other two. Seelar moved the torch up and down both sides of the circular opening. The light revealed a colored vein of dark material running the length of the left side of the entrance, but nothing else. They moved to the larger, middle opening, and again Seelar examined it thoroughly. A few large rocks, probably dislodged by seismic activity, littered the front of the entrance. Seelar moved to the third opening with a concerned look on his face. It was the largest of the three, but was farther up the wall of the cavern and looked the least likely to be the tunnel that led farther into the mountain. He was about to turn back to the first opening to reexamine it, when he put his boot into some soft dirt on the right side of the entrance. Reaching down to brush it off, he noticed that the area was covered in fine powder.

"Hand me something I can use to brush this away," he said to Diell. Diell didn't respond. Steera gave him her glove. Seelar quickly brushed the fine material away from the rock of the cave wall. There, crudely chiseled into the cool stone, was the image of a tycor.

"It's true!" Seelar said, sounding surprised.

Steera instructed the torchbearer to call to the others and they started into the tunnel. Suddenly, she stopped. She went back the tunnel entrance and laid her glove on the rock floor, folding the fingers back so that one was pointing in the direction they were heading, and returned to lead the party into the passageway.

Small rocks and crystallized deposits covered the floor of the tunnel, but for the most part the going was smooth and easy. About a thousand yards in, it took a slow turn to the right and began a gradual decline. The light from the electric torches cast shadows on the tunnel walls. Phantom figures ducked and dodged in and out of the rock formations. Diell noticed Steera looking around uncomfortably. "These must be the guardians Tyne Daage was talking about," he said, trying to comfort her, "the monsters that inhabit the mind and only come out in dark and unfamiliar places."

The party had walked for nearly half-an-hour when the passageway expanded and became a chamber even larger than the first. The huge room had eight separate openings surrounding it. Several of the villagers flopped down on the damp floor in exhaustion.

"We'll rest here a while," Steera said. "These caves have been here for millions of years, and they will wait a little longer for us." The company sat in a circle. One of the sledders took out a small oil stove and lit it. The others moved closer, sharing the warmth of the stove, letting their fatigue lull them into a sleep-stasis.

"Is there anything for a being to eat in those packs?" Seelar asked one of the villagers. The villager looked to Steera for her approval before handing Seelar and Pylo a small piece of koost (a form of dried hircus meat common to the diet of Faceer from the Northern Islands). Diell took a piece, sniffed around on it for a moment and forced himself to take a bite.

"Phfff," he said. "I hated this stuff when I was home, and I still hate it."

"Better eat while you can," Steera admonished him. Diell retrieved a bottle of keera water from his pack and sat back down by the stove. In a matter of minutes he drifted off into a deep sleep-stasis, dreaming of Auntie Dree's cozy kitchen and hot tarnn cakes.

Seelar feigned sleep until he was sure that the entire party, including his ever watchful villager, was in stasis. He quietly leaned over to nudge Pylo, making a gesture that told him to remain quiet. Pointing in the direction of the cave openings, he grabbed an electric torch and bade Pylo follow. The two slipped silently away from the sleeping party and made their way to the far end of the chamber. Seelar stood for a moment, surveying the arrangement of the eight openings. Finally he whispered to Pylo to return to camp and find some implement with a sharp edge. Pylo returned with a staiil, a type of hammer used for caving and mountaineering. For the next half-hour Seelar scoured the cave entrances for the sign of the tycor. Finally, at the next to last opening, he found it.

"Here it is," he whispered to Pylo. "Now we will make life interesting for them." Pylo watched as Seelar returned to the first opening and, using the staiil, carved a crude tycor on the left hand side of the opening. He then went down the line, carving tycors in different places on the opening to each of the other tunnels, being careful to rub dirt back into the carving to give it the appearance of age.

When he had finished, he turned back to Pylo. "Now go back and put as many supplies as we can carry into a pack. The Faceer Ka will finish this expedition and retrieve the object." Pylo complied, and after a few minutes returned.

"Are you ready to make history?" Seelar asked. Pylo hadn't thought much about history of late. He was thinking about Sanar and his own family back in the Equatorial Region. He nodded in agreement and put the pack on his back. Within minutes he and Seelar had disappeared into the inner regions of the cavern, leaving behind a bedraggled group of Faceer with a big problem.

CHAPTER 34

The deep, grinding sound coming from the electric motors on the three sleds indicated that they were laboring in the cold and snow. Electric motors had been used for many years on Osstar, but only recently had been reduced in size to be of any practical use on smaller transport vehicles. They had never been tested in such extreme conditions. The cold weather was putting a tremendous strain on the gears and other mechanical parts of the motors. The Breet troopers were having to stop at increasingly short intervals to recharge the batteries with the manual generators.

Pire sat crouched inside the sled studying the book. As cozy as the confines were, it was still too cool for a Faceer, and the groaning of a disgruntled Zerrit made matters worse. He had hoped, given a warm place to study and a day or two, that he would be able to make significant progress on the translation of the book. But, at the moment, a warm place was something he could only conjure in his dreams. The clouds, boiling with snow, had rolled back in and were sitting on the ground. The ice had become increasingly uneven, and several large fissures had opened as they crossed them. It was impossible to see more than a few feet ahead.

Nosh tried not to appear worried, but from his vantage point as the sled driver, he knew that they were in a perilous situation. He took a second light cone out of his pack and called to Pire. "I need you up here." Pire extracted himself from his hiding place next to the Zerrit leader and pushed himself out. Snow blew up under the Kaba-fur surrounding Pire's face as Nosh handed him the cone.

Pire scooted forward, waived his hand over the cone, and held it aloft. The combination of light from the two cones caused a fourfold increase in luminance. Ahead they could now clearly see the ground rising. A large ice-cliff lay in front of them, only about a thousand yards away. Nosh turned his cone back toward the other sleds, and waived it backwards and forwards to catch the attention of the drivers. He shouted for them to stay close and then resumed his progress.

It took the better part of an hour for the three sleds to make the thousand yards to the base of the cliff. The snow was coming in torrents, so intensely that even the powerful light from the cones was evaporating in the swirling, white maelstrom.

"Can you see an entrance?" Pire cried to Nosh over the howl of the wind.

"No, it just looks like a wall of ice."

"It has to be around here somewhere, or old Leet was wrong, and I can't believe he would get us all the way here just to have us die from exposure."

"We'll follow it to the right," Nosh shouted. "I believe I see an indentation up there." Nosh pushed the sled's controls and moved westward along the face of the cliff. The two other sleds followed. Pire tried to lift his cone high enough for it to provide some light for them. About five hundred yards along, a break in the wall occurred. Nosh steered his sled into the breech and discovered that it was in actuality a gapping hole in the cliff face.

"I think we've found it!" Nosh cried loud enough for the others to hear.

"Bless the gods," Pire mumbled under his breath. The three sleds moved into the opening and out of the raging storm. They stopped abruptly and Nosh leapt from the sled, making straight for a large rock in front of it.

"What is it?" Pire called after him.

"Come and see for yourself." Pire struggled to pull himself from his cramped position. His legs were numb from inactivity. He made his way clumsily to the rock. Nosh was crouching by it, running his hands over the ice-covered stone of the cave entrance. In the ice near the rock were the tracks of several large animals with long, narrow indentations. "Sled runners," he mumbled.

"What do you make of it?" Pire asked as he reached him.

"I've never seen them, but I have read of them ... Narros, the best sled animals on the planet."

"Do you think that these tracks have been here for long?"

"In this sheltered area it's hard to tell, but my guess is that we are not the first to reach the caverns."

"Do you think it is Stomari?"

"The Stoma like their Bajans too well. No, I see the hand-print of someone we know. This party was well equipped."

"Tomar Leet," Pire said.

"Very possibly."

"Then they are allies, or even someone that we know. It may even be ..." Pire couldn't finish the sentence.

"Perhaps, my friend, perhaps. We will know soon enough, the trail leads off in that direction." Nosh pointed ahead and to the right. "Are you up for it?"

Pire brushed the snow from his parka. "We didn't come to the end of the world to stop now," he answered. "Let's go."

The two jumped back into the sled and beckoned the others to join them. Together the three sleds set out across the slushy ice, following a trail of paw prints and runner marks into the heart of Aldor.

Breet didn't like letting the sleds idle, but he had to know more about General Somar-loors' mission.

"What is your business here?" he asked, using a strong, superior-to-inferior, inflection. General Somar hesitated. He had heard Klut's remarks as to Breet's sympathies, and the presence of a Faceer in his party reinforced his apprehensions. Still, lying was something for which he had little stomach.

"I am on a special mission authorized by the head of the High Council—Takir Prime."

"And what is the nature of that mission?"

"I am to retrieve certain items which are the property of the High Council." Somar-loors was answering slowly, taking time to turn each word in his mind before letting it come out of his mouth.

"I am a member of the High Council. Why am I not aware of this mission, or this lost property?"

"I'm sure, Excellency, that you would have been fully apprised by Takir at the next council meeting ... provided of course that my mission was successful. As you can see, it was in some difficulty."

"You're lucky we found you. A few more hours in this cold and Takir would have had to look for another topic at the next Council meeting. Suffice it to say, General, that we are more than likely on the same mission, and I can assure you that you are not here under the auspices of the High Council." General Somar did not argue the point. He was, in fact, here on orders from Klut-Prime. He wasn't sure if Takir-Prime was even aware of it. "At any rate, you are now a part of my expedition, and I expect your cooperation. Are there any more of your troopers around?"

General Somar bowed his head for a moment. The extent of the calamity was just soaking in. He gazed out across the endless, blowing snow and answered in a soft voice. "No sir, as far as I know there are no others. Twenty Stomari troopers and a like number of Bajans lay under the snow and ice — out there." General Somar lifted his hand slowly and pointed out into the swirling snow storm. Breet could see the pain in the General's eyes. He knew what Somar-loors was feeling. He was a leader who had failed those he had led.

"General Somar, there has been a great deal of scheming within our own kind in the last few years. Some of our leaders have taken it upon themselves to try and engineer the future for all of us, without our knowledge or consent. Your troopers have paid the price of that deception. We will need the help of Stoma such as you if we are to avert catastrophe on a scale that our world has never before witnessed. I know that you are Stomari and that you may distrust those who are not, but I ask that you keep an open mind as we try and complete this mission. Perhaps, when you hear the entire tale, you will see why some of us resist."

"I know your reputation for integrity, Excellency. I will consider well your words." Both nodded, their chins ending upward in the Stoma sign of respect.

"Now, we must resume our quest," Breet continued. "If we don't find the shelter of the caverns within the next few hours, all our sacrifices will have been for nothing. If only I had some way of telling in which direction we should head. This blasted snow looks like it comes from every direction at once."

Fazid, who was standing behind his General, approached Breet. "I may have something that can help." He glanced at General Somar. Slowly, from under his parka, he produced a rectangular box with a cup-shaped cone on the front end.

"The direction finder!" General Somar blurted out.

"Yes sir," Fazid answered. He blew away the flakes of snow that had landed on the indicator panel and gave it a shake. In the top left-hand corner of the grid that made up the faceplate a small red light was flashing. "We still have a signal," he said.

"What does this mean?" Breet asked.

"Somewhere out there is a Faceer Ka with a radio transmitter that is still transmitting," General Somar answered. "He may be dead and under ten feet of snow and ice ... or, he may have reached the safety of the caverns. It's a small hope, but the only one that we have."

Breet asked no more questions. He ordered his drivers back to their sleds and, asked Druk-tasis and Riatt to split up in the other two sleds to made room for General Somar and Fazid in his. The directional signal was coming from the southeast. Breet headed in that direction as the other two sleds followed closely behind. The snow was coming down fiercely and the fuel indicator in Breet's sled was showing less than a quarter of a tank remaining. He assumed that the situation was the same for the other two sleds. Whomever or whatever they were following, they had to find it soon.

Nosh and Pire had been following the Narro tracks for a few thousand yards when the sheltered gap in the cliffs began to expand and the opening to a huge cavern revealed itself. "Aldor," Pire said with awe. "It must be!"

Nosh stopped the sled and waited for the others to catch up. "Follow me closely," he instructed the two other drivers, "the floor of the cavern is not completely frozen; there are some areas of bare rock that could damage the sleds." They moved forward slowly in single file. The low pitched whirr of the motors made soft echoes rumble through the cave, as if they were surrounded by an army of ghosts on electric sleds. The Zerrit leader buried himself deeper into the cargo compartment.

Pire's ears were picking up another sound. "Do you hear that," he said, pulling on Nosh's parka to get his attention.

"Hear what? You must excuse me; I don't differentiate sounds as acutely as you do. Stoma ears you see." He flicked the small round, fleshy arc around his ear.

"A lower-pitched sound ... coming from just ahead." Nosh pulled the hood of his parka back and listened more intently. He did hear something. He signaled for the sleds to stop. Then they all heard it—a low growling noise coming from dead ahead. The Zerrit leader arose from his self-imposed exile and began aggressively sniffing the air.

"I think I see something moving," Nosh said. "Come with me." Nosh took out the other light cone he had replaced in his pocket and handed it to Pire. They held them aloft together and saw the source of the sound. Approximately two hundred yards in front of them, was a pack of Narros, busily quarreling among themselves over something.

"Don't alert them!"

Nosh was as animated as Pire had ever seen him. "They seem to be tethered," he said.

"We need to make very sure before we approach them!" Pire moved forward to get a better look, and caught the Narros' attention. In unison they turned toward him, snarling and yelping. "Don't provoke them! Make sure they are restrained!" Nosh was pleading with Pire.

"They're restrained, or they would have been on me by now." Pire held his light cone higher. He could see that the beasts had been tied to two sleds. They were fighting over an opened sack of food that had been placed between them. He moved cautiously back to his own sled. I think that they are more concerned with the food than with us," he said, trying to reassure Nosh. "At least we have solved the riddle of the tracks. We know now that they were made recently."

"From the condition of the animals, it seems recent indeed," Nosh replied, somewhat calmer. "We'll move around them and see what the terrain is like. If the party who left these beasts had to proceed on foot, we may have to as well."

The sleds soon left the Narros behind, the sound of their yelping fading as they moved farther into the cavern. Water was oozing from the ceiling and falling in giant drops onto the floor of the cave. Icy slush was giving way to rock and mud.

Nosh stopped his sled and switched off the electric motor. "We've gone as far as we can with the sleds; we'll have to continue on foot." He threw back the covering to the cargo compartment and extended his hand to the Zerrit leader. The others crawled out of their sleds and stretched to revive cramped limbs. "Take what supplies you can carry. We don't know how far or for how long we shall have to travel." The members of the party started stuffing their packs with food, heat stoves and other essentials.

"Don't waste any space on water," Pire counseled. "From the looks of this mud, we will have plenty of it along the way."

Each of the sailors stuck a gas pistol into his parka, and three of them took gas rifles out of their sleds and slung them over their shoulders. The party of nine moved out with Pire leading the way, and the Zerrit leader sticking close to Nosh. They moved determinedly through the slush, following the tracks of those who had only recently gone before.

"Who do you think they are?" Pire asked.

Nosh studied the tracks, "Definitely Faceer. But who, and how many, is impossible to tell."

About a mile-and-a-half into the main cavern, the smooth ceiling of the volcanic chamber began to narrow.

"This isn't a dead-end is it?" Pire asked.

"I don't believe so," Nosh answered. "It looks like there may be something on the other side of this rock ledge." Nosh had to contort his large frame in order to duck under the outcropping, but when he did so the light cone revealed a new chamber even larger than the one they had just traversed. From his position Pire could see the light from the cone illuminating a solid rock cliff at the far end of the cavern hall.

"It looks like the room comes to an end up there," he said, pointing in the direction of the cliff. The party made its way to the end of the chamber and discovered the three openings in the face of the cliff.

"Well, here's a puzzle," Nosh said. "The tracks are so confused around the cliff face that it's impossible to tell which entrance they took." Just then a voice rang out from the fringes of the cone-light: "Here! Look at this!" One of the sailors had discovered something.

"What is it?" Pire shouted.

"You had better come and look for yourself!"

The sailor was standing in front of the opening to the far left of the cavern. At his feet lay a glove, the extended finger pointing to the opening.

"Whoever they are," Nosh said, "they know others will be following."

"I think that is a hopeful sign. If they are Faceer, as it appears that they are, then they may be an expedition sent by Tomar Leet." Pire said.

"Perhaps, but they may also be an expedition of Faceer Ka, Seelar and the remnants of his followers."

The mention of Seelar and the Faceer Ka made Pire think of Steera and Diell. "I will pray to the gods of Leeth that we are on the trail of our lost friends," Pire said and turned to one of the sailors. "Gather everyone together. We are going into the cave."

Pire led the way with Nosh, his light cone and the Zerrit bringing up the rear. It was becoming noticeably warmer. The walls of the passageway were slick with moisture. Pire was moving cautiously, not knowing if behind the next bend in the tunnel he would come under fire from a troop of Ka Warriors. After thirty minutes of slow progress, Pire thought he could see an end to the tunnel. He held his hand up, signaling the others to stop and motioned for Nosh to join him. "Can you hear it?" he whispered.

Nosh bent his head forward in the direction of the sound. "Yes

... just barely."

"Is it what I think it is?"

"What do you think it is? You have the advantage on me."

"It sounds like ... like snoring. Snoring, of all things!" Nosh again strained to hear.

"Better snoring than growling," he said.

"What should we do?" Pire whispered.

"Take the light cone and one of the sailors with a rifle. If you find the source, don't try and confront it yourself, return and we will all go together." Pire motioned to the nearest sailor with a rifle and they quickly disappeared into the darkness. They returned in about ten minutes. Pire was breathing heavily.

"You are not going to believe what I have just seen," he said, swallowing in order to speak. "A company of Faceer is sprawled out around an oil stove, in deep sleep-stasis."

"How many would you say?"

"I counted six."

"Could you make out anything to identify them ... insignia, or special clothing of any kind?"

"I didn't want to risk getting too close, but I don't think they are Faceer Ka."

"And why not?"

"The camp is too disorganized. This wasn't a soldiers' bivouac. There was no sentry posted."

"I agree," Nosh said. "If it were a military group they would have had better security."

"Perhaps it's a trap," the sailor chimed in. Pire and Nosh felt foolish that they had not thought of it.

"Perhaps," Nosh said. "We had better plan as if it is. We'll put four of the sailors up front. The Zerrit and I will stay at the rear. If they are friendly, I don't want them coming out of a deep sleep-stasis with me being the first thing that they see." Nosh smiled and winked at Pire.

The company moved forward. After a few hundred yards they came to the end of the tunnel, and the beginning of a new chamber. The group bunched up at the entrance to the chamber and tried to get a look at the party inside. Pire moved into the chamber and the four sailors spread out, two to a side. They could now see the party more clearly. Pire's eyes fixed on a small Faceer wrapped in a large parka, his back leaning against a rock by the stove. Something about him seemed familiar.

Knowing nothing else to do, he picked up a small piece of stone from the cave floor and tossed it into the middle of the sleeping group. Nothing happened. He tossed another, larger stone, and the Faceer he was watching stirred a bit. Within a moment, he was sitting upright and pulling the hood back from his face. Pire was dumbstruck. His heart was pounding so powerfully that he thought it might tear through his chest. Before he could make another move, the Faceer had jumped up and was shouting in his direction.

"Who is it? Who goes there?"

"By the seven rings of Dathos!" Pire exclaimed. "Diell!"

Diell didn't move. The sound of the voice coming from out of the strange light was familiar to him. "Who goes there?" he said again. "How do you know my name?"

By this time the other members of the party were aroused. One of the sledders reached for a gas pistol. A sailor quickly stepped out of the light and leveled his rifle at him. He drew back his hand in a slow and deliberate manner. The rest of the group froze in their positions as the three other sailors made their presence known. Diell, however, would not back down. "Put down your weapons and no one will get injured," he said, using the best command voice that he could muster.

"My, but you've gotten bold. The jungle must have done you good." Pire was purposely staying behind the light so that Diell could not make him out, but he had not reckoned on another member of the party. Steera recognized the voice. Disregarding the sailors and their rifles, she made a headlong dash to Pire. Pulling back her hood, she stood in front of him. Pire's eyes filled with tears. He dropped the cone and smothered Steera in his arms. Diell didn't know what to do or say.

"Diell ... it's Pire! Pire has found us! I knew you'd come," she cried hanging on his neck until she almost brought him to the ground. "The Coola Bird foretold it!"

"Coola Bird?" Pire was laughing and crying at the same time. Diell had joined the embrace.

"Where have you been?" he asked. "We thought you had died in the attack, but Druk-tasis told us that you may have been rescued by some being that lived in the heart of the jungle." Diell could see that he was not getting much of Pire's attention. Finally Pire turned to him.

"We will have time to discuss our adventures soon enough. I would like to introduce you to someone." Nosh recognized his cue. Emerging from out of the shadows with the Zerrit leader trying to hide behind him, he stood in the light of the cone and pulled back his Parka hood. A collective gasp went up from Steera's party.

"This is Nosh," Pire said. "This is the being that saved my life and has led us here." Steera tried not to stare, but the sight of a real Seeyard captivated her. Her fascination was reciprocated by Nosh, but for another reason. He stood gaping at her, as if seeing a ghost. All the Faceer present, regardless of clan or group, could feel the enormous emotional currents coming from him. Nosh moved toward Steera as if in a trance. He reached her and put out his hand to touch her cheek. Steera started to feel a bit uneasy. Suddenly he came to his senses and quickly withdrew his hand.

"Pardon me," he said, trying to regain his composure, "it's ... it's just that you remind me of someone ... someone from long ago." Steera was puzzled but not afraid. Pire remembered the picture in Nosh's belongings back at the Equatorial caverns.

"I remind you of someone?" Steera repeated. "Who?"

"I never met her, although I loved her very much. I have only tales of her from an old friend and her image on a faded photograph ... but you ... you look so ..." Nosh's voice trailed off as he stared at Steera's face. "She was my mother."

Steera remembered her discussion with Aunt Dree at Romass, about the other sister ... the one that had been involved with a Stoma. "What was her name?" she asked.

"Reya," Nosh replied. Steera said nothing, but moved to Nosh and put her arms around his muscular shoulders. Nosh wrapped his arms around Steera. Great tears rolled down his face. She let his emotions mingle with her own memories of her mother, and cried with him. They communed without a word being spoken. After a long embrace, Nosh composed himself and broke the contact. "I will have much to discuss with you, sweet lady, when there is time. But now, there are greater tasks at hand." He surveyed the stone cliff face and the eight openings. "Do you know which opening leads to the interior?"

"We don't, but we have someone with us who does," Diell answered. He turned to look for Seelar among the party, but couldn't see him. A sickening feeling came over him. He started a frantic search, looking behind every rock and every possible hiding place but it was to no avail, neither Seelar nor Pylo was anywhere to be found. "That broog! That thankless, treacherous broog! He's done it again."

"Who's done what? Pire asked.

"Seelar," Steera answered.

"Seelar! Seelar's here!"

"He was up until we went into sleep-stasis," Diell replied. "We found him in a wrecked air transport, half dead in the snow. And this isn't the first time we've saved his life only to have him return the favor with treachery."

"How did he know the way to the interior?"

"He told us a story about the explorer, Tyne Daage. He said that he had come here before and marked the way. I didn't believe him, but when we found the mark of the tycor on the first opening, we had no other choice but to follow it."

"But where is Seelar now?" Pire asked.

"My guess is somewhere farther into the interior of the cavern."

"Then we must follow him with all haste," Nosh said. The Romass party looked to Steera for approval. She nodded her head resolutely. "Take these light cones and check for the sign of the tycor on each of the eight openings — time is of the essence."

The party members followed their instructions. Soon, calls rang out from the cliff face.

"Here ... it is here."

"No, here," came another call.

"I've found it," yet another voice chimed in.

"They can't all have found it," Steera said. "Something's amiss."

Nosh reached for the third light cone of the four that he liberated from the cylinder. He put it in his hand and held it out to Steera. "Wave your hand over the top," he said. Steera complied and to her and Diell's amazement a soft but powerful light flooded the area.

"Where in Zenos' orb did you get this?" Diell exclaimed.

"The second cylinder," Steera said, excitedly, "you've opened it!"

"Yes, in the Equatorial Caverns."

"What else ... what else was in it?"

"We'll have time for all that after we have secured the third cylinder. There must be a single route into the interior. Each of you check out an opening," he said, tossing a light cone to Diell. They spread out and double checked the crew's claims.

"There's a tycor here!" Diell yelled.

"...and here, as well," Pire shouted.

"...and one here too," Steera said.

The three reassembled in the center of the chamber. "Your companion, Seelar, is more treacherous than I imagined," Nosh snorted.

"What do we do now?" Diell asked.

"I'm not sure."

"We could split up the party ... each take a tunnel," Pire suggested.

Steera would have none of the idea. "Nubin Pire! We have just been reunited after months of separation. I will eat Kaakall meat before I part with you again."

"That won't be necessary," Nosh reassured her. "There are only fourteen of us, not counting the Zerrit. It's too dangerous. If we split up only one or two of us will find the interior, and they would have Seelar and his friend to contend with."

"...and perhaps something else," Diell added.

"What do you mean by that?" Nosh asked.

"Oh, just a vague warning from Tyne Daage's son," Steera said.

"He said that his father warned of guardians in the interior. I think he was just trying to scare us."

"None-the-less, we will have to be cautious. We don't want to fail because of some foolish oversight. My troop is hungry, and I am as well. Let us rest and think this over. If Seelar returns, it must be by this path; he will not slip by us if we stay here and stay vigilant. Perhaps, after a rest and a meal, a course of action will be reveled to us."

The party settled down. Warmed by the oil stoves and the illumination of the cones, they opened their food reserves for a well deserved meal. Nosh walked over and sat down next to Diell.

"Are you hungry?"

"Not for koost if that's what you have," he grumbled.

Nosh laughed. "Well, I have some Stoma provisions. It's what I mostly like to eat, and things that were available to me in the jungle, but I was able to come up with the ingredients for one of my favorite delicacies." Nosh reached into his pack and pulled out a large piece of wrapping paper. He opened it as Diell strained to get a look inside.

"Tarnn cakes!"

"Yes, it is my friend ... Faeed's own recipe. When I was very young he used to bring me tarnn cakes." Nosh hadn't finished his sentence before Diell had one of the sweet cakes stuffed into his mouth.

"Let me try one of those before they are all inside Diell." Steera laughed and took one of the cakes offered by Nosh. "Why, they're delicious. They taste almost as good as the ones Aunt Dree makes."

"Better, I think." Diell mumbled as he ate.

"It must be hereditary," Steera said. She wished that she could have taken back her words.

Nosh turned his head to one side, looking every bit like an inquisitive Faceer. "What do you mean?" Steera remained quiet and Nosh let the statement go. The rest and repast was having a relaxing effect on all.

Pire had spread out his parka on the damp floor of the cave next to Nosh. Studying his face as he ate the tarnn cakes, he mustered the courage to speak. "I've been meaning to ask you something." Nosh continued to eat in silence, anticipating Pire's question. "Back at the entrance to the first cavern you were positively petrified by those Narros, why the strong aversion."

"Oh, nothing really," Nosh answered, sounding uncomfortable, "just a childhood memory."

"That was a pretty strong response for a distant memory."

"It was a traumatic memory. I was just a child."

"Out with it. What happened?"

Nosh realized that Pire was going to persist. "I had a pet viaal, a creature not unlike those beasts at the cavern entrance, perhaps a bit smaller. The Zerrits found it abandoned by its mother in the jungle. I felt great empathy for it, it being rejected by its own kind, but alas it was not a pleasant experience for me."

"So what happened?"

"I was trying to feed it one day ... the first time that I had tried without Faeed's help."

"And ...?"

"And it bit me." Pire waited for the tale to continue, but it didn't.

"It bit you ... that's it?" Pire laughed.

"It hurt!" Nosh was irritated at Pire's lack of sympathy. Diell and Steera began to laugh along with Pire. The sound of laughter floated through the hollow tunnel until finally Nosh joined in.

The merriment began to ease the tensions of the groups ordeal. Pire reached into his pack and drew out the talking book. "This is what has been commanding most of my attention in the last month." He opened it and inched closer to Steera. "If you had been with me, this would be translated by now. But I have made some significant progress." Pire's finger ran over the words and the strange alien voice floated from the pages.

Steera was astounded. "It speaks!"

"That's not all." He let his finger rest on one of the words and Steera watched as the picture formed on the opposite page.

"We can learn their language!"

"Yes, I've already learned a lot. The book is activated by your voice as well as by your touch. It seems to learn along with you, showing more complex forms and diagramming sentence structure as you go. It's mainly the structure of the language, the nouns, verbs and clauses, that I don't quite understand, but I believe that we will find the key to it all in the third cylinder."

"Why do you say that?" Diell asked.

"Because of this," Pire replied and pulled the metal disc from his pack.

"It looks like the disc we recovered from the first cylinder," Diell said.

"It is, except for the reverse side."

"Let me see," Steera said, taking it from Pire's hands.

"It's the map of Osstar on this side." She turned the disc over and examined it. "What's this? It looks like a technical drawing."

"Ah, my beautiful scientist," Pire said admiringly. "That's precisely what I believe it to be ... the design of some sort of sophisticated machine, perhaps a translator. If we can retrieve it and learn how to get it working, it could explain the entire mystery.

"Then we must move out as soon as possible."

"But first, we must decide how we are going ..." Nosh stopped in mid-sentence. Something was wrong. A smell, a vibration, something had set off an alarm in his head. He rose slowly and held a light cone aloft. In the distance, standing perfectly still he could make out three large figures. Two of the sledders had noticed also and were trying to creep out to the side of their encampment to flank the intruders. Before they could get very far, a booming voice shattered the blackness of the cavern.

"Stay where you are!" The faceless voice moved closer. The party could now make out three armed Stoma against the conelight. They had their gas rifles pointed directly at Pire and Diell. Pire reached for Steera. Nosh was nowhere to be seen. No one moved, but Diell could not stay silent.

"Who are you? State your business." The troopers said nothing. Pire noticed that they wore the uniforms of security forces from the House of Breet. A long silent stalemate was finally broken when another Stoma moved up from behind.

"Who is the leader of this expedition?" A powerful Stoma command voice echoed through the cavern. Pire looked around for Nosh. He wondered if he should speak in his absence, but before he could, a voice intervened.

"I am." It was Nosh.

"What is your mission?"

"I believe that you have me at a bit of a disadvantage," Nosh said calmly. "I don't know your name."

"I am Breet-Trios, head of the House of Breet and member of the High Council. Who am I addressing?" Nosh stepped from the shadows into the soft light. One of the troopers dropped his rifle and it discharged in a deafening boom, sending a shower of sparks as the bullet met the cliff face. The armed members of Nosh's party reacted by reaching for their weapons. The Stoma troopers raised theirs. "Stand at ease!" Breet's voice rang out above the dim. "Let him speak."

"I am Nosh, leader of this expedition."

"I hope you will excuse my staring. I have never actually seen a Seeman ... I mean a Seeyard before, but I have heard of you."

"Heard of me?" Nosh said, surprised by the admission.

"It seems that you are quite well known for a mythical creature." A new voice had come from the darkness.

"And have gotten quite far away from home I might add." Another voice had joined the chorus. This voice Pire did recognize and he hurried to greet its owner. Riatt and Pire embraced as Druk-tasis moved out of the shadows and approached Nosh with his arms outstretched. Steera and Diell rushed to join in.

The reunion was long and warm. The Breet troopers put their rifles away, pleased that they were obviously among friends, and fraternized with the sailors, sledders and villagers that made up the rest of the party. Food was passed around from their combined supplies. After almost an hour of commiserating, Breet called Nosh, Pire, Druk-tasis, Steera, Diell, and Riatt together for a conference.

"We have two others in our party," Breet told them. "They are being held at the back of the cavern. I believe that they have been sent by Takir and Klut to retrieve the cylinder. One is a Stomari shock trooper; the other is General Somar-loors."

"Yes," Nosh said. "We almost tangled with the good General back at Jaakar. I am certain he is here on orders from Klut-Prime."

"So what do we do with him?" Diell asked. "We can't take him with us."

"Perhaps we shouldn't," Breet said, "but I have talked with him, and have a feeling about General Somar. I do not see in him the usual fanaticism of the hard-core Stomari. What I do see is a sense of honor and of duty. If he believes that he has been misled by Klut and Takir, I judge that he could change his position."

"At this point it doesn't really matter," Pire broke in. "We have lost the trail to the interior. Our captured Faceer Ka leader has slipped away and destroyed the markings that we were using to find the passageways. As for now, we are stuck right where we are."

"We may be able to help with that particular problem," Druktasis said. "The Stomari did us one service when they had Seelar back at headquarters. They implanted a radio transmitter under his spinal ridge. The trooper with General Somar-loors has the direction finder. That is how we found you. We will need General Somar's cooperation if we are going in there." Breet pointed to the cliff face and the eight openings.

General Somar-loors and Fazid were brought to the meeting by two of Breet's security troopers.

"We will need the direction finder if we are to make any further progress into the mountain," Breet began.

Somar-loors was listening, but his gaze was fixed on Nosh. "The bed," he said as if thinking out loud. "You're the Seemano!"

"Seeyard, if you don't mind, General. I assume that you refer to my accommodations back at the Equatorial Caverns. A lot of brave Zerrits died that day General ... a great waste of life."

"Many brave soldiers died that day, and many more lie frozen in the snow outside this forsaken labyrinth. I am beginning to wonder what all of it is for."

"We have been asking that question for quite some time," Breet said. "There has been a lot of death and destruction in the last few years. It seems that only a privileged few know the answer to your question. I know that you are a soldier, and a Stoma of high reputation. I value my honor as well. I do not ask you to betray your honor, but simply to hold your conclusions until we find what we have come so far, and at such a cost, to retrieve."

Somar-loors pondered Breet's words. He had taken a liking to Breet at first meeting, finding him to be a Stoma of reason and not at all the reactionary traitor that Klut had described. "For a long time, Your Excellency, I have followed leaders that I believed in. I admired the strength of their convictions even if I did not always understand the source of those convictions. I am beginning to think that my loyalties have been misguided. The Stoma philosophers say that one cannot achieve true wisdom without continuing to examine the base upon which that wisdom rests. Being the ranking Stoma member of this party, I will submit to your authority. How may I and my Trooper help?"

"Thank you, General," Breet answered. "I will not betray the trust that you have so graciously placed in me. The direction finder, if you please." Fazid took the radio receiver from under his parka and switched it on. The red light sat directly in the middle of the grid.

"What does it mean?" Breet asked.

"It means that we are not detecting a signal," General Somar answered.

"Splendid," Pire said, dejectedly. "Seelar must have discovered the transmitter and destroyed it."

"I doubt that. It's more likely that the stone and the mineral deposits in this cavern are creating interference. Take the receiver and scan each opening," General Somar instructed Fazid. "If he is not too far in, the red light on the receiver should glow brighter in the tunnel he has taken."

"I pray that you are correct," Breet said. "If not, our only course of action will be to split up."

Fazid, joined by one of the villagers from Romass and one of Breet's Troopers, made his way to the far end of the cavern and began scanning the first opening. The rest of the party waited and watched. Finally, the call came from Fazid.

"Here ... I think I have found it!"

General Somar and Breet-Prime rushed to the opening. The red light of the receiver was definitely stronger, and was pulsating slightly.

"What does the blinking mean?" Breet asked.

"It means that it is receiving a signal, but can't lock onto a direction. In our case it doesn't matter; Seelar can only go where the passageway leads." Breet called the party together. Nosh remained silent, hoping that Breet would naturally take charge of the group.

"In order to complete our mission," he began, "we must proceed into the mountain. It will be dangerous. We must not be separated. We will need a leader that has experience in these matters. Nosh has spent much of his life in the heart of a mountain. I therefore turn control of my Troopers over him." Nosh was surprised. He looked in General Somar's direction to try and gauge his reaction.

"I agree with Breet." This is now an expedition of both Faceer and Stoma. I can think of no one better suited to lead both." Nosh nodded in respect to both Breet and Somar-loors but the look of concern on his faced was difficult to hide.

"I suggest that we leave a contingent behind in case any other parties arrive," Nosh said. "This is becoming a popular destination on Osstar." The joke eased the tension of the moment a bit and gave him a shot of confidence. "The expedition will be comprised of Diell, Riatt, Pire, Druk-tasis, General Somar-loors and His Excellency and, of course, Steera. We will take trooper Fazid and the directional finder, one Security Trooper from Breet's command, one villager from Romass and one sailor from our tragoone. The rest will remain here."

The remaining party (including one anxious Zerrit) began construction of an encampment. No one knew how long the trip to the interior might take. One of the sledders was designated to return and make sure that the Narros were adequately provisioned. The twelve that were selected to go began checking their equipment and lightening their packs as much as possible.

"Don't burden yourselves with water," Nosh advised. "I believe that we will encounter sufficient on our journey. I also think that the temperature has stabilized so what we are wearing should be warm enough, staying dry may prove a greater challenge than staying warm." Nosh put the group in single file, taking the lead with Somar-loors bringing up the rear. He distributed the light cones at four intervals, creating a soft halo around the entire party. Nosh called for a moment of silent prayer and then motioned for the group to move out. The party left behind at the encampment watched as one-by-one they disappeared into the passageway.

The farther the expedition traveled into the passageway the larger it became. The light from Nosh's cone revealed small streams of water flowing from the side walls of the chamber. It was becoming wetter and even a bit warmer as they made their way down the length of the great room.

"Fan out," Nosh ordered the others. "There may be crevices or pits formed by this water. Keep your light cones high and mind your steps." Steera, Pire and Diell were in the middle of the group, sharing a light cone, Riatt and Druk-tasis were just behind them.

"Look at this!" a voice rang out. Steera and Pire hurried over to see what the villager had found.

"Deelus, isn't it?" Steera asked, recognizing the voice.

"Yes."

Steera strained to see in the dimmer light on the fringes of the cone. "What is it?"

"Dreelites," he replied.

"Let me see that." Diell had joined them. He took one of the thin, leathery pieces of fungus and bit off a chunk. The pasty liquid it oozed coated the hair on his hands, staining them an ashen white. "Hummm ... not bad. These would do well in a taanar stew." Nosh had joined the group and was examining the dreelite.

"There could be an entire ecosystem down here. Where there are dreelites, there are probably things that eat dreelites. Another voice rang out from the far left side of the chamber. It was Somar-loors.

"There is water over here, and quite a lot of it." Stretching out in front of him was the smooth surface of an underground pool, two to three hundred yards in diameter. He stopped at the edge and put his hand into it. He called out across the room to the others, "It's incredibly warm to the touch; it must be fed by thermal springs."

Nosh looked toward Druk-tasis and muttered beneath his breath, "Could you tell the General to mark the edges of the pool, and move around it."

"My friend, you are either the leader of this expedition or you are not," Druk replied.

Nosh shouted his instruction to General Somar. The General complied and the party continued to traverse the vast chamber. Another thousand yards and the room began to shrink again. The light from the cones took on a pale yellowish hue as the ceiling of the great hall moved down to meet them. Huge veins of gallite streaked the sides of the chamber, running from the crest of the ceiling down the cavern walls to the floor. Waves of yellow/orange flame danced across the walls and ceiling of the cavern, created by the light from the cones.

"Seelar's friend didn't tell all that he knew," Pire said.

The party started to move on when Nosh called them to a halt. "Do you hear it?" He turned to Diell. "You're the one with the biggest ears, can you make it out?"

"It sounds like scratching ... or perhaps something or someone stumbling in the dark." Nosh made his way back to the pool and held his cone aloft. Away from the light of the others its intensity strengthened, blazing forth with a piercing white light. At the far edge of the pool he could make out a crouching form.

"Come out from there, whoever you are!" he called out. In a moment, a cringing creature made its way around the rim of the pool and sat cowering at Nosh's feet. "Stand up, old friend," he said and placed his hand lovingly on the head of the Zerrit. "Somehow I knew that you'd find a way to join me. Well, I must say that I am glad that you did. Our lives have been intertwined since my youth and somehow I think that they will continue to be so as long as I am on this planet of ours." The Zerrit leader fell in behind Nosh as he rejoined the group. "We have another member of the expedition, friends." The others gathered around to rub the Zerrit's head in greeting.

"What is his name?" Diell asked innocently.

Nosh stood for a long moment. "You know, I'm ashamed to say that he hasn't one. I have always known him as the leader of his tribe. When I lived among them at the Equator, he treated me as one of his own."

"Then we must give him one. We can't have a member of this group referred to simply as 'the Zerrit.'"

"You're the linguist, Steera. What is the ancient Faceer word for 'friend?'" Riatt asked.

"Tiimat," Steera answered without hesitation.

"The word from my pod wood Bajan," Druk-tasis said. Steera gave him an inquisitive look. Druk smiled. "I'll tell you the entire tale someday."

"Then Tiimat it is," Nosh said, and pointed at the Zerrit.

"Tiimat," he said, "Tiimat." The ape pondered it for a moment. Then, something happened that astounded every member of the party. From deep within the Zerrit's throat, a sound began to form. It was unlike any they had heard coming from him.

"Keeemasss," it said in a guttural hiss.

Nosh looked even more surprised than did the others. "I had no idea! You've been holding out on me," he said shaking his finger at the Zerrit in jest. The ape cowered at his feet, thinking that he had done something wrong. "No, no friend," Nosh said helping him to his feet. "Tiimat." He said it again to the ape and smiled.

"Keeemasss." The ape began to dance around the group repeating his new name over and over.

"All right ... Keemass," Nosh relented.

Every member of the party got the opportunity to repeat his name. Soon, they were all imitating the ape's dance and singing his new name.

The celebration died down as the reality of the party's situation again set in. They couldn't afford to let Seelar's trail get too cold, or they might not be able to find the cylinder. Without a word spoken, they gathered themselves and began moving. The chamber was definitely narrowing when they came to another cliff face. This one was only about half as high as the previous one, with three widely spaced openings.

Nosh called the group together. "Diell, take Deelus and a sailor and check for tycors. Seelar may have been in too much of a hurry to deceive us." Diell and the other two hurried off, each carrying a light cone. Nosh turned to Fazid. "Can you give us a direction if they can't find a marked tunnel?" Fazid jiggled the switch to the receiver and the red light began to glow. The light spun in slow uneven circles around the grid. Fazid shook the device a few times and gave it a sharp slap on its side, but the red light continued on its erratic path.

"Sorry," Deelus said as the three returned from their mission, "tycors on all three passageways."

"It was a slim chance," Nosh replied. "What does this signal mean?"

"There must be interference," General Somar answered. "It's picking up a host of signals, probably bouncing back off the walls. I suspect that the gallite might be the cause."

"So what does it mean?" Pire jumped in.

"It means that we have no way of telling which passageway our elusive little friend has taken." The news was not welcome to the weary group. They shook off their packs and sat down on them, staring at the grey walls of the cliff glowing with the yellow/orange gallite.

"Let's take a break," Nosh said, trying to keep a confident tone in his voice. "Start a fire," he said to Breet's trooper. The trooper and the sailor from Jaakar pulled several sticks of faar-wood from their packs. With its high oil content it could create a roaring fire at just the touch of a flame. Within a matter of minutes, the faar-wood was hissing and crackling, lighting up the cavern with a light harsher than that produced by the cones. The company settled down, uneasily.

"We will have to split up this time for sure," Steera said dejectedly.

"Only as a last resort," Nosh answered.

"What other choice do we have?" Druk-tasis asked. "We can't just sit here and wait for Seelar to come back out."

Nosh had his head in his hands, his long arms resting on his knees. He was at a loss as to what to do.

Breet summoned one of his troopers. "Take another from the party and search each passageway for footprints or other signs of activity, but don't venture in too far; we don't know what kind of twists and turns these tunnels take." The rest of the party gathered closer to the fire and waited. In about an hour the two returned with the bad news ... no tracks, nor signs of any kind. It was as if the cave had swallowed Seelar and his companion. There was nothing to do but wait and think.

Several of the group fell into a light sleep-stasis. Riatt was leaning against his pack, staring at the ceiling of the chamber with Diell sitting opposite him. He had pulled off his parka and was using it as a pillow. The fire was beginning to ebb a bit and the shadows were diminishing. An ember made a loud "pop" and skittered across the floor of the cavern, landing near Riatt's leg. The spark seemed to grow and even strengthen. Diell stared intently at it for a moment, thinking it just a trick played by the shadows. The glow now looked to be coming from inside Riatt's clothing. Diell jumped to his feet and ran over to him.

"Riatt ... your pants ... they're on fire!" Riatt jumped up and began swatting at his trouser leg.

"Where?"

"There," Diell pointed to his right pocket. Nosh and the others gathered round Riatt. Something in his pocket was glowing like an ember from the faar-wood fire. Riatt reached inside cautiously and grasped something in his hand. It was cool and smooth to the touch. He withdrew his hand and opened it slowly. The area was bathed in a ghostly orange light.

"The fifth cone," Nosh exclaimed, "I had forgotten all about it!"

"As had I," Riatt said. "It had stopped working shortly after I was separated from you."

"And now it is working again," Nosh said. "I wonder why?"

"Do you remember how brightly it shone when we first took it from the cylinder?" Pire spoke up. "Perhaps the cone's light was somehow tied to it."

"... or to any of the cylinders," Nosh continued.

Pire completed Nosh's thought. "The closer it is to a cylinder, the brighter it shines. Oh, thank the gods of Leeth!" Pire exclaimed. "We have our direction finder again, perhaps a better one than we had before!"

Nosh took the cone from Riatt's hand and moved swiftly to the farthest opening on the cliff wall. The cone shone steadily. He moved to the middle opening and again the light from the cone stayed constant. At the third passageway, the light flared a bit and turned a deeper orange. "This is it," he said.

The party needed no further instruction. They gathered up their packs and formed up at the entrance to the passageway. Diell was already so far inside the tunnel that Steera had to retrieve him.

"Come on, let's go!" He said impatiently. "I can't wait to see the look on that scoundrel's face when we catch up to him."

"Patience, young one," Nosh cautioned, "we have the luxury of patience now that we know that we can find the cylinder no matter where Seelar hides it. The caverns are still fraught with peril. I don't want to lose a single member of the party if I can avoid it."

Diell reluctantly rejoined the group and they moved out with Nosh leading the way, and the orange glow of the small cone breaking the darkness ahead of them.

CHAPTER 35

General Trios-Takir-deenar's hands moved nervously up and down the ceremonial stabbing sword hanging from the belt of his formal uniform. He had been summoned to a meeting with Takir-Prime, which was rarely a good thing.

The door to the inner office swung open and a surly young Stoma greeted him. After the bombing, there had been a wholesale sacking of Faceer workers, so most of the Faceer retainers in Prass had been replaced with Stoma. The retainer led General Trios in and bade him sit down. Within a few minutes, a rear door opened. Takir-Prime entered and seated himself at an ornate Darma-shell desk.

"Well, General, I hope all is well with your family. I haven't had the chance to get down to the Lower Midlands lately to visit my dear cousins."

"They are well, thank you Excellency." There was an awkward silence. Takir fiddled with something in his desk drawer while general Trios squirmed in his seat.

"I'm not so sure about these new retainers," Takir said, breaking the quiet. "These young Stoma bucks aren't very well suited for this type of work. I can't seem to find a thing in my office anymore."

"What happened to your previous retainer?" Trios asked.

"Faceer," Takir answered cryptically, "...couldn't be trusted."

"Are they all like that now?" General Trios was genuinely interested in Takir's response.

"Enough of them are. We've pretty well cleaned them out here at headquarters. About the only one left is that old janitor. He's more concerned with the size of his furniture than with rebellion." General Trios managed a week smile. "But, getting to why I called you here; I have been checking your record. I find that you have been very effective in controlling the Faceer Ka situation in your area. I also know that you and your family have been loyal party members since the beginning of our organization."

Trios' fear turned quickly to exuberance. "We have, Excellency. We are always ready to serve the cause."

"Good ... because I have need of you. Did you hear anything about an incident at our North Polar Station?"

"I heard the rumors that the Faceer Ka had stolen something from us — something potentially dangerous."

"The rumors were correct. We have reason to believe that the stolen items were taken to the south."

"The Southern Islands?"

"No, farther south."

"There is nothing farther south, just the South Polar Region."

"Exactly," Takir said. General Trios' elation faded. "You would not be alone. I have already dispatched General Somar-loors and a detachment of Stomari Shock Troopers."

"What was his destination?"

"We believe that a party of Faceer, and a few misguided Stoma, are in route to the Caverns of Aldor. We believe that they are seeking something that belongs to us. It is imperative that we keep them from getting it."

"Aldor!"

Takir could read the look on the general's face. "I assure you it is real, and we must get there quickly to reinforce General Somar."

"I can have my brigade ready next week," General Trios said confidently.

"Your brigade is already here and is being equipped as we speak, General. You will leave on the Zenos-tide tomorrow."

"I will join my Troopers straight away."

"Thank you, General. Your mission is of the utmost urgency. I would not trust it to just any line officer. We must support General Somar at all costs." General Trios-deenar snapped off a salute and left the room. Takir continued his expedition through his desk. "Wretched shame about those Faceer," he grumbled aloud, "I can't find a blasted thing."

Nosh's party had come upon three more cliffs with multiple passageways and each time the cone had pointed the way. The members of the expedition were beginning to shed articles of clothing. The temperature was growing warmer the farther into the mountain they ventured, and larger bodies of water were appearing. They often found themselves wading rather than walking. In the center of a large chamber glowing with gallite and other mineral deposits, Nosh called the group to a halt.

"What is it?" Pire asked, joining Nosh at the front of the column.

"Take a look," he said holding aloft one of the larger cones. In front of them stretched a vast lake. The cone-light couldn't discern an end to it.

"What do we do?"

"Get Breet and come with me. I'm going to take the orange cone and walk down the shoreline to see if I can get a reaction."

The rest of the party broke ranks and found places to rest. Diell, Druk-tasis and Steera made a semi-circle with their packs and sat down on them to avoid the damp floor of the cavern. Diell looked as if he was distracted by something.

"There it is again," he said in a hushed tone.

"There what is again?" Steera replied. "You're hearing things. I think Seelar's nonsense about guardians has your mind telling your ears what to hear."

"I swear I hear it ... a scratching sound."

"Our senses can play tricks on us down here," Druk added. "The more intelligent one is always the one more prone to flights of fantasy."

Diell shrugged off the compliment and pointed to Keemass. "Then what about him?" The ape was standing upright, his head tilted to one side, sniffing the air. "He's been doing that off-and-on since we came through the passageway."

After about an hour-and-a-half Nosh's party returned. The lake was even larger than they had suspected and the light from the small cone had actually grown fainter the farther they had gotten from the camp.

"We'll proceed in this direction," Nosh said pointing to the path in the opposite direction.

"How will we get across the lake?" Deelus asked. "Old master Leet though of a lot of things for us to bring on this little jaunt, but no one could have imagined that we would need a boat down here."

"No one indeed," Nosh said. "We will follow the cone. Either it will show us a way, or we will fail in our mission. I see no signs of our friend Seelar, so it would seem that he, at least, has found a way over or around this barrier."

Diell was watching Keemass. He was making a low whining noise and sniffing the floor of the cavern. He heard the sound again and took Nosh aside. "You know how you rely on my extra-sensitive sense of hearing?"

"We couldn't do without it," Nosh replied.

"Well, I've been hearing things, and I think that the Zerrit, I mean Keemass, is hearing it too."

"Does it sound like scratching noises?"

Diell looked shocked. "You've heard it as well!"

"Since we came through the last passageway."

"What do you think it is?"

"I'm not sure, but I imagine that we will find out soon enough if we proceed into the heart of the mountain. I need you to do me a favor."

"Anything," Diell replied.

"Watch Keemass for me, I think he's getting jumpy."

Diell smiled and immediately went over to the ape and rubbed his face with the side of his hand. "You're with me, my fuzzy friend," he said, and put his arm around Keemass's muscular shoulder.

The group formed up once again and moved out, led by the glow from the small cone. As Nosh had suspected, the glow increased ever-so-slightly in intensity as they made their way down the shoreline. About a mile along the shore the white cone illuminated a large rock formation rising from the floor of the cavern. It formed a knifelike ridge that stretched out into the lake as far as could be seen. The closer they came to the ridge, the farther out into the lake it appeared to reach.

"Are you thinking what I'm thinking?" Pire said to Nosh.

"Yes, it's possible that the rocks form a ridge that stretches the breadth of the lake—a natural bridge. We'll set up camp here for a while."

The group dropped their packs at the base of the rocky ridge. They passed around koost and keera water, and Nosh shared the last of his tarnn cakes with the villagers. Breet produced several tins of Kodoos, and he and Fazid gathered at the edge of the water, eating Stoma-style. Nosh, Somar-loors and Druk-tasis soon joined them. Pire took the book and the disc from his pack and settled down with Steera. The others exchanged jokes, laughing to ward off the damp and darkness of the cavern. The sound of mingled voices and low laughter floated across the wide waters of the underground sea.

Only Diell and Keemass failed to join in the communion. They were sitting at the fringe of the group, near the base of the rock that formed the bridge. They were not laughing or even smiling— they were listening. Far out on the bridge, smothered in the dark of Aldor's great cavern, they could hear it ... scratching and clicking. The sounds were becoming clearer. And, there was something else. It drifted from the far side of the lake, at first barely audible even to Keemass. Soon, however, Diell began to make it out as well. It sounded like a cry.

CHAPTER 36

General Trios had lost over half of his brigade of 100 troopers. Just two hours out of the landing area, ten of his hot sleds had broken through the ice at one time with all hands lost. Four sleds had broken down, their occupants forced to stay where they were until they could effect repairs and catch up with the main party. Four other sleds had lagged behind in a fierce storm, and were either lost or stranded.

Trios wished he could stop and try to gather them up, but he had never seen weather quite like what they were now experiencing. He knew that to stop was to die, so he drove his remaining force onward. The navigational aides that Takir had provided were useless in the blinding snow and Zeno-less sky. Even Rebal was obscured from sight most of the time. His only help was a trooper named Nomes-tassid who had trained with special snow troops at the Southern Pole. He knew approximately where the caverns were rumored to be. With Tassid in his sled, General Trios and his armada of twenty remaining sleds thundered onward through the blizzard and prayed with the fervor of the desperate that they were heading in the right direction.

Even confined inside his boot, Pire's furry toes spread out instinctively to grasp the smooth, damp rock. The bridge across the vast underground lake was proving difficult to traverse. The sides were smooth and rounded, and there was only a narrow, flat pathway on the very top of the ridge where one could walk safely. Occasionally, someone would dislodge a bit of the loose rock and it would fall silently, ending in an almost inaudible splash far below. The size of the lake was impressive, but the size of the chamber that enclosed it was staggering—and, of course, there was the sound.

At first, only Diell and the sailor heard it. It was intermittent, rising and falling with no apparent pattern, but becoming more distinctive the farther into the darkness that they went. No one mentioned it, but it was certain to Diell that everyone was hearing it.

Nosh led on. The increasing intensity of the orange cone's light attested that they were heading in the right direction. He came at last to an area on the bridge that widened enough to allow for a gathering. He stopped and waited for the others to join him.

"Is everyone all right?"

Somar-loors was the last to join the group. "All accounted for."

Nosh studied the eyes of each member of the party. He was struggling with how to broach the subject. It was Deelus who finally broke the uneasy silence.

"Sounds like something has its foot caught in a triing," he said with a serious look. He was referring to a crude trap that the Stoma used to catch small game.

Breet's Trooper, Loors-toopal, gazed around nervously. "What do you suppose it is?"

"It's a warning," the sailor blurted out.

"I think it's one of the guardians that our young friend was talking about," Deelus said.

"It doesn't sound supernatural to me," Nosh said calmly. "It sounds like a cry."

"It does sound like a cry," Steera agreed.

"A cry from where ... from whom?" Breet asked.

"I thought I recognized the voice," Diell said. "It's him, I'm sure of it."

"Seelar again," Steera said without giving Diell time to say any more.

"We'll keep moving ... but with caution," Nosh said. "Perhaps Seelar has fallen and is stuck like a hircus in one of Deelus' triings." The party laughed. The though of a "flesh and blood" enemy eased their fears a bit. Shouldering their packs, they moved on.

Within an hour, the path started to slant perceptibly downhill. Travel became easier, but more hazardous. The weight of their packs increased their downward momentum and they had to struggle not to pick up more speed than would be safe on the slippery rock. Nosh had become a speed break as well as the chief navigator for the group. Soon, the bridge began to widen and the negative grade became more pronounced.

"I think we're approaching the end," Nosh announced. The white light from one of the large cones showed the land widening out in front of him. The crying noise hadn't been heard since their rest stop in the middle of the bridge, but the other sounds, the scratching and clicking noises, had returned with increased intensity. When the last member of the party had made it safely across the bridge, the party reassembled. "I'm not sure how much farther we have to go, but I have a feeling that we are nearing our destination. I want Faaige and Fazid to scout ahead. We want to know just where we are before we proceed."

As Nosh spoke, the sound of a mournful wail pierced the stillness. The party froze. It was without doubt a Faceer voice. "Go quickly," Nosh said to the two. "Keep to the rocks and don't expose yourselves. If we can help Seelar and his companion we will, but we're not going to risk the entire company for him."

"It may be a trap," Diell spoke up.

"Always thinking, my young friend," Nosh said and put his arm on Diell's shoulder. "He's right. Try and see what you can see, but don't risk being detected. Report back to me in one hour at the most."

The two acknowledged Nosh's instructions and moved out into the darkness with one of the cones placed under a piece of sailcloth to tone down its light if just a bit. The rest of the company took off their packs and sat down. No fire was started, and talking was kept to a minimum. General Somar took a position as sentry some distance from the main party and Breet did likewise on the other side. The assembly waited and listened. The cries continued, obviously much closer now. In the dark quiet of the cavern, the eerie sounds ricocheted with every angle of the exposed rock. Necks could be seen jerking and twisting in all directions. They sat, trying to fend off fear until two panting scouts came into view.

"We saw them!" Faaige said, gasping for breath.

"Yes, we saw them!" Fazid repeated.

"Settle down," Nosh admonished. "What did you see?"

"Them," Fazid said again, regaining his composure. "Two Faceer ... one had on a Stomari uniform. They're the ones that have been doing the howling."

"And why are they howling? Are they in trouble?"

"I'd say so," Faaige said. "They're in some sort of pen constructed in the rocks."

"Who put them there? Were they being guarded?"

"That's just it," Fiaage said, "the pen didn't really look that sturdy. It looked as if they could have broken out if they had wanted, but they didn't seem too eager to do it. They were just cowering at the back of the pen, wailing loud enough to raise a sunken tragoone."

"And you saw no one, nothing else?" Breet entered the interrogation.

"We didn't see anything, but I'm sure that there was something there," Fazid said.

"What makes you say that?"

"Just a feeling," Fazid said. Faaige nodded in agreement.

"How good a look did you get?" Steera asked.

"An excellent look," Fazid said, "and we didn't have to rely on the cone-light. The whole place was lit up like a Zaarian pleasure barge."

"Lit with what ... fires ... torches?"

"Just lit up. I didn't see any fires or anything; it was lit with a bright, orange light."

"Like this?" Nosh pulled the small cone from his pack. It was glowing brighter now than the larger white cones, filling the chamber with its light.

"That's it!" Faaige said excitedly. All around the group, the sounds of scratching could be heard. Nosh was now able to identify it. It was the sound of feet scraping across the rock floor of the cavern, feet with claws on them. Something was definitely out there.

"My friends," Nosh said solemnly, "I believe that our goal is within reach. Take the gas rifles from your packs. Form up in rows of three and follow me." Nosh started in the direction indicated by the two scouts. He got no farther than a few yards when he caught a movement in the corner of his eye. A white blur flashed in front of him ... then another. Nosh raised the now powerful orange cone. In front of him and arrayed to either side were apes — dozens of them. They were smaller than Zerrits and pure white in color. From the snarls on their faces and their exposed fangs, they were none-too-happy to see them.

"Guardians" Steera said in a hushed voice. "I knew there was something to Seelar's story."

Nosh continued forward. The guardians retreated at the sight of the orange light, but it was obvious that they were not going to let them go much farther. One of the apes moved forward in an aggressive manner. Breet's trooper raised his gas rifle and shook it in the direction of the ape. The ape kept coming. Suddenly, he stopped. His facial changed expression dramatically. Nosh looked around at the other apes and saw the same expression spreading through their ranks. The leader took one more hesitant step forward then put his face on the rocks in a cowering position. The other apes followed suit.

Nosh noticed a form standing next to him that had not been there before. It was Keemass. They moved forward, Keemass leading the way. The congregation of white apes parted. The guardians reformed after letting the group through and approached Keemass. They gathered around him. One approached cautiously and touched his furry hand. Soon, others became bolder and several moved to touch and smell him. Keemass grunted and acknowledged their attention. Soon the entire group gathered around Keemass, chattering and touching him.

"Help us!" The cry was coming from the pen that lay against the wall of the cavern. Nosh motioned to Diell to take Faaige and free the prisoners. Diell and Faaige made their way across the wide expanse of cave floor, keeping one eye on the gathering of guardians in the distance. They reached a cowering Seelar hugging a rock spire at the back of his cage. Pylo was standing calmly at the gate.

"Come out of there you howling greel calf."

"Oh bless you ... thank you." Seelar groveled. "Please don't let them get me."

"Don't thank me, you lothar. If it were up to me I'd have you spitted and served to these apes as lunch." Diell unlatched the gate and motioned to Pylo to exit. Seelar was still holding onto his rock, frozen with fear. "I suppose you'll put more faith in your own stories from now on. It seems that your friend Laymar Daage knew what he was talking about."

"I never dreamed that he was telling the truth," Seelar confessed, whimpering with fear. "They came at us from everywhere."

"Yes, life without katoc can be a frightening experience ... now move!" Diell grabbed Seelar's tunic and flung him through the gate. With Faaige holding the gas rifle on the two captives, the four made their way back to the main group.

Nosh spoke directly to Pylo "You have been as much of a victim of your leader's deceit as have we. Behave yourself, and you can become one of our party." He turned to stare into the depths of Seelar's eyes, now restored to their natural hue. Seelar winced at the sight of the Seeyard, a creature he had heard of often but never seen. "And you," he said. "If we have any more trouble from you, we will leave you to the apes." Seelar made his way in silence to the rear of the group. "I trust Keemass to keep the guardians occupied. The glow coming from the rear of the chamber can only be from the third cylinder. It is time for us to fulfill our mission."

The cone in Nosh's hand glowed brighter and brighter as they neared a large semi-circular rock formation that lay against the face of a cliff. There were no openings or passageways in the cliff face. It was the end of the cavern. Standing in the center of the semi-circle, against the cliff face, sat a silver cylinder, glowing bright orange.

Pire and Druk-tasis moved to get a closer look. This cylinder was marked in the same manner as the other two, but was noticeably larger. As Nosh brought the small cone closer, a low whirring noise could be heard. In an instant, the top of the cylinder slid open. The entire company fell silent. The guardian apes gathered closer to the object that their kind had watched over for who knew how many millennia. Nosh called for General Somar and Breet-Prime to join him at the cylinder. Almost reluctantly, they peered into the opening. Inside, they could see a large metallic object covered by a crystal dome. Two handles rose from the base of the object and stuck out slightly above the dome.

Nosh took one handle in his hand and Breet took the other. Together they lifted it gently from the cylinder. As soon as it had cleared the opening of the cylinder, the orange glow faded and was replaced by a soft white light similar to that of the large cones. Nosh took the smaller cone from his pocket where he had put it, and its light had also shifted to white. They sat the shiny, silver device delicately on the floor of the cavern and stepped back to ponder it.

"What do you make of it?" Breet asked.

"It looks like something you would keep keesa cheese in," Deelus said, completely serious. The others laughed. "...Well, it does!"

"I don't think that the beings who made this were trying to show us a means of food preservation," Nosh said.

"I think that I know what it is." Pire moved closer to the object and took the metal disc from the second cylinder out of his pack. "The markings on this disc coincide with those on the cylinder, and with the markings inside the cover of the talking book. This is the master translator."

"Do you think you can get it to work?"

"I've been studying this disc for quite some time now, and I've learned enough of their language that I should be able to activate it. The inscriptions on the disc definitely refer to something called an 'archograph,' whatever that may be."

"Well by all means, proceed," Nosh said.

Pire studied the base of the device, running his fingers around its circumference. At the rear edge of the smooth metal object, his finger passed over a small indentation. The machine started to glow. It began at a small spot in the center of the dome, and then extending outward until the entire globe was pulsing with light. Pire's finger continued around the back of the machine. An alien voice suddenly seemed to float in the air around them. It had to be coming from the object, but it didn't appear to emanate from any particular point on the device. It sounded as if it were coming from outside and above it.

"TRIIANS SAD DOMMIFF DOON STRATOOR," it said. Pire could make out a few of the words he had learned from the talking book. 'Doon' was the word for book and 'stratoor' referred, he thought, to something round or disc shaped. He took the talking book from his pack to verify the language and noticed that a blue/white light surrounded it as well.

He opened the book. The light was coming from the back cover. There, a small coin-shaped object was visible just beneath the covering to the metallic backing. It was shining with an intense blue/white light. "The chip goes in the machine, but where," Diell thought. He started moving the chip around the base of the machine. Along the right side, a slot opened and the chip was drawn from Pire's hands into the machine as if it were being ingested.

"It swallowed it!" Deelus exclaimed.

The machine began to pulsate and glow with varied intensities. Within the dome itself, pictures began to form from nowhere, flashing in rapid succession.

"It looks as if it's reading the chip ... as if it's learning!" Steera exclaimed.

Pire opened the talking book and watched in astonishment as individual words on the pages began to glow, first green, then red, then blue/white in rhythm with the pulses of the machine.

"The book and the machine are communicating!" Diell said.

Pire realized what was happening. "All along I assumed that I was learning from it. Now I understand. It was learning as much, or more from me." The alien voice again drifted from the machine, but this time what it said caused the entire party to gasp in unison.

" ... NEED MORE INFORMATION." The voice, alien though it was, spoke in perfect Osstarian. The pictures inside the dome became a series of graphs and grids. Steera recognized it from her studies at the Dynard Academy.

"It's looking for language structure," she said. "It's trying to become fluent."

"Can you help it?" Nosh asked.

"With Pire's help, I believe that I can. With their technology they surmised that it would be easier to learn our language than for us to try and decipher theirs. I think I know what we can do."

For the next hour, Pire and Steera sat in front of the glowing dome of the alien machine talking to it and referencing the book when possible. The machine was proving an incredibly fast learner, taking in the subtleties and nuances of the language before Steera had answered ten questions.

Then, just as suddenly as it had activated, the dome went dark.

"What do you suppose it's doing?" Diell asked, after a long period of silence from the group.

"Ruminating," Deelus said, completely certain of his assessment.

"Ruminating?" Druk-tasis laughed. "Do you mean digesting ... like a greel?"

"More like a taanar," Deelus replied without taking his eyes off the machine.

"He may be right," Nosh said. "It may be trying to put all that it's learned in order."

"Well, I wish it would get on with it," Faaige complained. "My tail-end is getting cold."

The machine teased them a few times by flashing to life and then again going dark. Then it started. A series of vibrations could be felt through the rock floor. The clear dome filled with a smoky substance, colored first pink, then blue and finally, an astonishingly clear silver-white. A figure appeared inside the dome, dressed in a long, flowing, white robe tied with a length of a material that shimmered and glowed with all the hues of the spectrum. It was configured, as were they, with two arms, two legs and a body set in proportion to a rounded head, covered in perfect symmetry by curly dark hair. Its skin was a smooth, tan color with just a hint of yellow hue. It appeared to the group to be a male. It stood in the center of the dome and looked as if it was regarding them one-by-one.

"It must be a projected image," Pire said, captivated by the specter, "like a visual transmission."

"Perhaps," Nosh answered, "but it may be something more than a mere projection. It may be waiting for us to introduce ourselves." He said it half-jokingly.

"Yes, perhaps I am." The voice, masculine and speaking perfect Osstarian, had come from the creature in the crystal dome. Several members of the party moved back from the machine in fear. "Don't be alarmed," it said. "I've been waiting a long time for this meeting." The group was silent.

Finally Nosh spoke. "Who are you?"

"A fair question, and not unexpected. My name is Simon Vargus. I am First Consul of the Maritime Confederation, the last such confederation on the planet." There was a pause, as if the being was rethinking his answer. "Perhaps I am confusing you," he said. "I should have said that I was Simon Vargus. I must remember that a very long time has passed since this virtual program was created."

"Then you are not alive?" Pire declared.

"That is difficult to answer. We have learned not to take too narrow a view of what life is and is not. It is a fact that I am communicating with you at this time and in this place. The corporeal being that was Simon Vargus has been transformed into the image you now see ... so in those terms, I am very much alive. But I am becoming tedious. I had that problem in my other form as well. May I begin again?"

"Certainly," Nosh replied, finding the being's admission of fallibility comforting.

"As I was saying, the image you are seeing is that of Simon Vargus. And since you are seeing me, it tells me that you have progressed enough to solve our little puzzle. We are very pleased."

"We?" Steera interjected. Simon Vargus made a graceful turn in Steera's direction and spoke directly to her.

"You might say that my people are your forbearers: your great, great grandparents a million times removed ... so to speak."

"You are our ..." The being interrupted before Somar-loors could finish his sentence.

"Please, I think this would be easier if you would let me explain. As you have ascertained, the cylinders that you have found have been lying beneath the surface of this, your home world, for millions of years. We placed them here. When we did it, your world was little more than a tiny, frozen ball of rock. But we knew, locked in the structure of your rocks, and deep below the surface of your world, that the building blocks of life existed. And that in time, with the growing warmth of the red star that you call Zenos, your world would begin to harbor life. We wanted to encourage that. I come from a planet in the same star system as your planet, although we refer to your world as a moon. There were nine major inner planets orbiting this star, although now, if our calculations were correct, only six would remain. The star that now warms your world once warmed ours. It was much smaller, and burned yellow/white. Our scientists knew that in a billion years or so as we reckoned that it would begin to exhaust its fuel and start to expand. It meant death for our planet but life for yours.

Our Confederation surveyed the known universe, starting with the surrounding planets and their moons, and calculated which bodies could provide an environment for life to develop when they reached a temperature suitable to sustain liquid water. It was to be our last great experiment ... the last task of a dying culture. We decided on several that were promising, including this world. I, of course, cannot be sure precisely which of those worlds I am now on, but given the information Pire and Steera have provided me, I believe it to be a satellite of a large gas giant planet in our system." The image in the dome made another fluid turn toward Pire and continued, "You found the objects we included in the cylinder?"

"Yes," Pire answered, still reacting to the use of his name by the alien creature.

"And I suppose that you thought that the books or the light tools or this communicator were the greatest treasures in them?" Vargus answered his own question. "Yes, that would be like us, drawn to the brightest, most ornate objects. Well, you were wrong. The real treasure was in the glass dishes."

"The gray powder?" Druk-tasis said disbelievingly.

"That gray powder is what gave rise to you and all the life on your planet. It is a mixture of simple forms of plant life and certain bacterium that thrive without oxygen. They were timed to activate in a precise sequence. Triggered by the warmth of your oceans, they began to transform your world from a lifeless ball with a caustic atmosphere to a world of oxygen-creating plants, and eventually, oxygen-breathing sea creatures, ultimately evolving into the life forms that inhabit your world today." Vargus walked around inside the crystal dome and studied the faces staring into it, "...And from what I can see, it did its job most prodigiously."

"But we don't look like you," Breet said.

"To the contrary, given the complexities of evolution and the differences in our environments, you look remarkably like me, especially the smaller, hairier ones among you."

"So why did you go to all this trouble," Pire asked, "... the cylinders, the clues, the books? If you had just wanted to encourage the development of life why did you need all that?"

"... Encourage the development of intelligent life." The creature corrected Pire. "We knew from our own experience that the development of intelligence was a delicate process. If you had discovered our message too soon, it might have done more harm than good. That is why we hid the cylinders as we did. The first cylinder was discovered because of an emerging civilization's need for certain mineral resources. Drical, as you call it, is lightweight, strong, and used in hundreds of industrial applications. The deposits most easily accessible to a developing industrial society, a society of inter-reliant beings, were buried in the North Polar Region of your world. Curiosity, spawned by a common education system, would drive the rest of your quest. The clues were too enticing for an intelligent species to pass up. You have passed the test. We hope that we have come in time to be of assistance to your further development."

"Two intelligent species," Somar-loors spoke up. "And just what do you mean by 'assistance'? What makes you conclude that we need assistance—and that you can give it to us?"

Simon Vargus smiled and seemed to search for the proper words. "Pride," he said, finally coming out of his meditation and looking directly at General Somar, "a trait we once exalted as noble.

It can lead to great accomplishments ... or to great tragedies." So-mar-loors shifted his position uncomfortably. Simon Vargus again scanned the assembly. "I see uniforms among you, and weapons. I would conjecture that all is not peace and harmony on your world. From the talking book, you probably know that our culture knew its share of war and conflict. For tens of thousands of years we took the easy path to our desires, taking from each other by force that which we reckoned we needed. It sapped our resources and created a hatred that sustained the conflicts in one form or another until the Great Cataclysm brought us to the brink of annihilation."

Diell broke in, "Great Cataclysm—a war?"

Simon Vargus managed a wry smile. "I wish that the explanation were that simple, my friend. No, we had our 'great war' and survived it. We vowed never again to use violence to obtain our ends. It ushered in a golden age of growth and development. Our scientists created incredible new technologies. We conquered disease and want. We started to explore the solar system and soon the stars. We colonized worlds that were like ours, and spread our culture across a substantial part of this galaxy. But, in the end, we failed in our task. The colonies would thrive for a time and then fall into division and conflict; it seemed to be an illness that we carried with us. Freed from want in the physical sense, our minds had turned from our spiritual roots and sought pleasures on other levels of consciousness, more compelling and insidious than mere corporal desires. In spite of all of our technological advancements—or perhaps because of them—our civilization and the ones we had created on other worlds began to wither and die. It was a plague that even our best technology could not stem."

"A plague," Steera said, "...a disease?"

"Yes, but it was not one of the body, that would have been easy to cure. It was a sickness of the spirit. We retreated into our own minds. We no longer cared to interact, to exchange ideas or views with each other. We became estranged from our own kind. Eventually, we split into small groups of like-minded individuals. We called them Confederations. Ours was the last Confederation involved in space exploration. Near the end, we were simply sending out cylinders to random destinations. I think that we really didn't want to know what or who was out there anymore. Instead of a bringer of life and civilization, our cylinders became warnings — a sad distress signal from a once-great culture.

"But the plague?" Steera pressed the point.

"The source of this disease — the thing that brought our great civilization down — was within us. It was the slavery of self, the one affliction that all our knowledge and technology could not cure." Simon Vargus paused for a moment and then continued. "My world is now only a memory, captured in the form of the being you see in front of you. I pray that this last attempt to reach out to others will be the legacy my people leave to the universe. I pray that some of the good that once resided in us and in our culture can be passed on."

Simon Vargus stood in the center of the dome with his head bowed and his arms pulled into his chest. He looked to be in prayer. Those assembled could feel the pain of his silence, of his utter isolation, this phantom trapped inside a silver cage. He stood before them a beautiful shadow cast by a world now long forgotten.

After a lengthy silence, Nosh spoke. "We owe you a great debt. There is much in your story that we recognize in ourselves." The being's countenance softened and he looked at each alien face in the gathered assembly.

"My fervent wish is that you will take this gift and learn from it. You have much to ponder. Hopefully, we will talk again in the days to come." He started to turn away, paused and turned back. "But, be cautious. Just as in my society, there will be those in yours that will not wish to hear the message that I have brought you. Be careful how you use your treasure." The light in the dome started to flicker and die. Pire recognized that the being had finished what he had to say.

"Wait ... sir ..." Pire blurted out. "Before you go, I have one more question. Why the book ... the book in the first cylinder ... the one with the strange creatures?"

"Ah, the book. Yes, they are strange aren't they? I suppose I couldn't resist. It was my favorite book as a youth. It is a simple story of great sacrifice and the ultimate triumph of good over evil. Silly I suppose, but perhaps a true portrayal of the vision of the old dream ... the dream of my ancestors." Simon Vargus closed his eyes and bowed his head as the dome went dark.

The stillness in the cavern was almost tangible. Each member of the expedition was mulling over the being's words in their heads. In the span of an hour, their whole universe had changed forever, as had their place in it.

"We must put the machine back in the cylinder and take it with us," Nosh said. "The being in the dome will be an ambassador to our own ruling Council. But we must heed his advice. We must tell no one of the contents of the cylinder or of its message until we can assemble those who need to hear it."

"I agree," Breet said. "There will be many among the High Council who will try and suppress this. I pledge my efforts as head of the House of Breet and a member of that Council to do what I can to protect the cylinder and its message." He paused and looked in the direction of General Somar. "Where do you stand, General? Are you with us?"

Somar-loors was struggling. His Stomari training was still reminding him of his mission, his duty to Takir and Klut, but what he had seen and heard seemed to transcend his narrow instructions. After several minutes of contemplation, he answered. "I have already compromised my mission by aiding you in your quest. I would not have done so if I had not believed it was for the good of our society. The message of the being in the dome has only strengthened that belief. We are headed down the same path as our distance ancestors, yet we have a chance to divert from that path and find a way to lasting peace. I commit myself to that effort. I hereby renounce my membership in the Stomari movement. My troopers may leave me if they so desire, but I will do nothing more to interfere with what I now see as my duty to our planet." Somar-loors glanced in the direction of trooper Fazid who slowly rose and saluted.

"I think you have summed up how we all feel," Nosh said. His gaze settled on Seelar, huddling in the rear of the group, still uneasily eyeing the guardians.

Seelar realized that Nosh was waiting for him to speak. "Oh, certainly," he said nervously. "I've seen the error of my ways ... from now on I'm with you."

"I can say that I will help," Pylo spoke up. "I too had been taken in by the lies and distortions of my leaders." He looked directly at Seelar. "I see for the first time through eyes not blackened by katoc. I believe that the creature is truthful, that he is showing us where our world is headed and I will do what I must to change that future."

"You are welcome, brother," Nosh replied, "...and the rest?" He looked over the other members of the expedition. Each one bowed and nodded in agreement. "We have accomplished a great task, but there is still a great task in front of us. We must bring the message of the cylinder to all of Osstar. Pack up, we will make our way back to the others and then to the ship waiting at the coast. The gods willing, we will be in Prass by spring."

The party heaved their packs and formed up. Fazid and Faaige made a stretcher-like devise to carry the cylinder. With light cones blazing a path through the now compliant guardians, the party began the long trip back across the stone bridge to the comrades that they had left behind, carrying a treasure greater than any had ever imagined.

CHAPTER 37

The return trip was proving less arduous than the trip in. The stone bridge crossing was accomplished without any appreciable trouble, and since the party had marked the proper tunnels on the way, there was no confusion as to the route. Keemass had reluctantly said goodbye to his new found tribe. A small group of the albino apes had escorted the party across the bridge to the first tunnel. Fazid and Faaige were carrying the cylinder, suspended in its new hammock, as if it were some warlord from the feudal era. Spirits were high. The group knew that if they could reach the coast, their ships would be waiting and they would be homeward bound.

They reached the last passageway and traversed its damp, slick interior. Nosh was the first to emerge from the tunnel; he saw several of Breet's troopers and two Faceer sailors standing in the center of the cavern staring at them in silence.

"Not exactly the reception I had envisioned," he said to Pire as the group gathered at the opening of the passageway.

"Hey, Draail," Faaige yelled to one of his compatriots, "look what we've found!" The look on the sailors' face didn't change. It held the same expression that it had when Faaige had first seen him. Faaige was baffled. The party moved forward, perplexed by the lack of enthusiasm shown by their companions. They seemed to be frozen in the middle of the vast room. Nosh had moved to speak to one of Breet's troopers when he heard it ... the sound of a gas rifle being cocked.

"Stay where you are ... all of you!" a sinister voice spoke. From out of the shadows, a large Stoma, dressed in a Stomari uniform that bore the insignia of a General, came into view. At the same time, dozens of armed troopers appeared to reinforce the General's command. "I am General Trios-deenar. You are here on an illegal mission, and in possession of an item that belongs to the High Council. What have you done with General Somar-loors and his troops?" Deenar's troopers were so fixated on Nosh that they didn't see the imposing form of a Stoma emerge from the shadows.

"And I am Breet-Prime, head of the House of Breet and member of the High Council of Osstar. I order you to put down your weapons!"

"I'm sorry, Your Excellency, but I am on direct orders from Takir-Prime, the Head of the High Council. I am to take this party into custody and everyone with it."

"Does that include me as well?" The strong command voice of General Somar-loors rang out across the great room. "Lower your weapons!" The troopers instinctively obeyed.

"General Somar! Are you all right?"

"I have lost many brave troops, but I believe that the price may have been worth it."

"Then you have secured the item that Takir seeks."

"The item is secure. Now we must get it back to Prass." Pire felt his heart sink. Had it all been a deceit?

"And these criminals," Deenar continued, "do we bind them?"

"No," Somar-loors replied. "They are cold and tired; I don't think that they will be uncooperative." He turned his back to General Deenar and gave Nosh a wink. "You won't be, will you?"

"We will cooperate," Nosh replied.

The party was rounded up and herded in the direction of the cave opening. At the mouth of the cavern, they came upon the Narros and their sleds as well as the hot sleds General Deenar and his troops had used.

"We have a sled for you and your assistant here," General Deenar said, pointing to one of the extra sleds that his party had brought.

"No thank you, General," Somar-loors replied. "I will take a Narros sled and these three prisoners as well as the cylinder." General Somar motioned toward Nosh, Pire and Steera. General Deenar looked confused. "Remember General, I was sent on this mission before you were involved. I mean to complete it successfully."

Deenar didn't like the idea of letting the cylinder out of his sight, but he didn't want to anger an officer of the caliber of Somar-loors. "Very well, sir. But I would like to stay along side you in my sled ... for security's sake."

"That won't be necessary, General. Besides, those noisy smokers you have will only distract my animals. Pack those three in the sled and load that cylinder. We have to get moving if we are to make the coast in a day." Deenar gave way. His troopers loaded Nosh, Pire and Steera into one of the sleds and put the cylinder on top of them. Pire barely had room to wiggle his toes, but he did not complain. Somar-loors straddled the two rear runners and gave a tug on the guide lines mimicking what he had seen the sledders do. Somewhat to his surprise, the animals bolted forward and headed out the front entrance to the cave before the others could even start up their sleds. General Somar yelled back at General Deenar as his sled and its contents careened down the face of the mountain. "Meet me at the coast as soon as you can. If you're not there in time for the tide, we will leave without you!" A few moments later, he disappeared behind a curtain of snow.

General Deenar shouted to the others. "You heard the General, get these prisoners on board and get going. The weather is getting worse and we have a ship to catch." The rest of the expedition loaded into the spare sleds and the entourage poured out of the caverns of Aldor and into the blinding snow that hung like a dense curtain between them and the coast.

A s soon as they were a safe distance from the cave entrance, General Somar leaned over and shouted above the roar of the wind.

"Are you all right in there?" Nosh rose up as best he could with the bulk of the cylinder jammed against his legs.

"Yes ... just what exactly are you up to?"

"Trying to save the mission," he yelled back.

"Do you know how to drive one of these things?" Pire asked, having extracted himself from beneath the cylinder.

"Believe it or not, I once had experience with Narros...on a hunting expedition to the Mororall Mountains."

"Once?" Steera broke in, trying to get Pire's foot off of her face.

"I didn't exactly drive the sled, but I learned some interesting things about Narros."

"What do you mean?" Pire yelled. The sled seemed to pick up speed.

"They're homers," Somar-loors shouted. "They can smell their pens from miles away. General Deenar and his troop will be guessing as to the whereabouts of their tragoone, but these brutes will take us straight to their pens. You did have them aboard your tragoone didn't you?"

"Very clever, General," Steera said admiringly. "Yes we had them aboard our ship, but it wasn't a tragoone, it was a cargo steamer."

"No matter, once they get the scent they should head toward it."

"But what if the ship hasn't returned?"

"I'm sure that Tomar Leet will have our steamer waiting somewhere near where it left us," Pire shouted at Steera even though she was only a few inches from him.

"Tomar Leet?" Somar-loors repeated. "I keep hearing that name. It's familiar to me, but I can't place it."

"I'm sure that is exactly how Leet would want it," Nosh chuckled, leaving General Somar with his mystery for the time being.

The snow and wind had picked up considerably, but the Narros pushed on, snorting the white, feathery stuff from their nostrils every few strides. General Somar was now just another passenger, holding firmly onto the control runners of the sled. Nosh handed General Somar a light cone, which gave some illumination in the blinding white of the storm. The sled swerved precariously between chasms and snow banks. The lead Narro sniffed the air, lunging decisively first this direction and then that.

After almost three hours on their erratic course, the lead Narro let out a great yelp and the others joined in the excitement. The sled lurched forward and picked up speed. General Somar thought

that he saw a grey shape in the distance and a muffled cry floated through the blanket of snow. The Narros were now pulling so
hard on the reins that they could be heard stretching and moaning
against the harnesses. General Somar saw it—a large smoke stack
silhouetted darkly against the grey/white sky.

"They've found it!" he cried. "Bless the gods and these furry
beasts; I think we have made it!" Steera kissed Pire and gave Nosh
a peck on the cheek as well.

A group of sailors was huddled at the boarding ramp when
the sled arrived. Two of them immediately grabbed the reins of
the Narros and began to unhook them from the sled. General Somar pulled the hood of his parka back and the sailors froze in their
places. One of them reached for a gas rifle that was sitting on a bale
of feed and clumsily cocked it and pointed it at General Somar.

"No need for that," Steera said as she and Pire emerged from
under the cylinder, "he's with us." The sailors looked at one another incredulously, and turned their attentions back to the Narros.
The captain of the vessel descended the ramp and addressed Steera.

"We hope that the expedition went well. We are re-supplied
and await your instructions." Some of the other sailors were looking for the other members of the expedition.

"All has not gone as planned. We were intercepted by a troop
of Stomari. I'm afraid that they have taken many of our company
prisoner. We managed to escape with the help of General Somar-
loors."

"General Somar helped you?"

"Yes I did." Somar-loors stood in front of the crew in his Stomari uniform. "In a few hours another group will be arriving at
the coast. We do not want to be here when it does. We carry a very
valuable item that they will do anything to retrieve. We must make
haste. Do you have a radio on board?"

"Yes," the captain's expression changed again as Nosh pulled
himself out from under the thick blankets of the cargo compartment.

"He's with us as well," Steera said.

The captain shook his head and turned to re-embark. "I trust that there is nothing else hidden beneath that blanket," he said, speaking back over his shoulder. Nosh laughed to himself and thought it a pity that they had had to leave Keemass behind.

The steamer belched thick, black smoke as it churned its way out of the icy harbor toward the open sea. The snow was still roaring around them and icy waves were smacking at the thick, wooden sides of the lumbering ship. About twenty minutes out, a muffled cry came from the observation post.

"Tragoone ... twenty points to swoonson!"

Anchored far out from the natural harbor, a tragoone bobbed in the strong waves, staying off-shore to avoid the converging currents and treacherous ice. Nosh and General Somar knew whose it was. They also knew that they had likely been seen. After consultation with Nosh and General Somar, Steera instructed the captain to steam west through the Sea of Storms towards the Outer Passage. The consensus was that as soon as General Deenar reported what had happened, an all-out search would be initiated. The Stomari would most likely be looking north and east, thinking it to be a Faceer Ka abduction, and expecting them to try and reach the equatorial region with their captives. Their plan now was to try and make port at Braccar.

"I know that Tomar Leet has good friends among the Alliance," Nosh said, looking over the navigational map that had been spread out on the top of a hold cover. "We should be able to make our final plans from there."

"Why don't we just contact this 'Leet' by radio?" Somar-loors asked.

"I would advise against it," Nosh replied. "General Deenar may be confused by all that is happening, but I doubt that Takir or Klut will be. As soon as Deenar contacts them to report that you and the cylinder are missing, they will conclude that it is a conspiracy and pour everything they have into the search ... including monitoring radio transmissions. From now on, until we reach Braccar, we must become a Gahaal ... a phantom ship."

Pire pulled his parka up as protection against the cold wind and looked out on the grey, swirling, featureless water. *If ever a place was created for a Gahaal,* he thought, *this was it.*

CHAPTER 38

The tragoone was waiting for General Deenar when his beleaguered party finally arrived, but General Somar-loors and his captives were not on it. The trip back to the coast had been costly for the General. He had lost two more sleds to a crevice and two others had simply disappeared into the mist and snow. As well as his own soldiers, two Faceer villagers and one of the contingent of Stoma troopers that were with the captured party were also lost. Takir was furious when General Deenar admitted that he had let the cylinder out of his sight; and when he told him about Nosh, his worst fears were confirmed. Alerts were sent out across Osstar to be on the lookout for a steamer with a strange cargo. Coastal patrols from the Houses of Trios and Druk were tripled, and those of the House of Breet were restricted to the waters surrounding Orial.

As Nosh had predicted, the search was concentrated around the Inner Passage and the Sea of Aldor. Klut was convinced that the conspirators were headed for the Equatorial Region and the safety of their jungle hideouts. What Klut did not know was that, from the very heart of their operational center, other instructions were being issued.

Leet didn't know all the details, but he had gleaned some information from the communications between Headquarters and General Deenar. The members of the expedition had been captured, but a small group had managed to escape with the cylinder. He knew that word of the search for them would spread, and that a bounty would be on their heads, a bounty large enough to attract every pirate and brigand from the west of Osstar. He could not employ normal lines of communications, as he was sure that Takir and Klut were monitoring all broadcasts. It was time to use one of his most trusted and most covert assistants. He would leave for Orial at once to meet with allies, and dispatch his trusted messenger to Braccar. The Alliance may well be their last hope. Above all, the cylinder must remain in their possession.

The steamer hugged the northwest coast of the South Polar Region until it ran out of land. It then headed north into the mouth of the Outer Passage east of Sunar, the Southern Island that was home to the House of Somar. General Somar-loors knew the timing and the patterns of the sea patrols in-and-around the main port city of Sunar. Keeping to the middle of the passage, the steamer was able to avoid sea traffic, with the exception of a brief appearance by a Stoma fishing boat. The word had not spread to the common merchants as of yet.

General Somar's plan was to head west through the narrow Prait-Andorna Passage and make for the Olange Strait between the Equatorial Island of Luceria and Kloose (one of the Islands of the Unincorporated Territories), thus bypassing the Narial and Morate Straits. He knew that these Straits would be buzzing with ships at word of their escape. Since there was no major city on either the northern coast of Sunar or the southern coast of Andorna, the steamer would be able to travel in the daytime and make shore for supplies in the evening. Nosh was counting on Leet and his ability to have someone at the right place at the right time. He was trusting General Somar to get them to Braccar on the southern coast of the Upper Midlands. The rest would be left to Leet and the gods.

General Deenar was beside himself. He was angry at the weather, at the extra baggage of prisoners, but mostly he was angry with himself for letting the cylinder slip through his fingers. His new orders were to drop the prisoners off at Su-prass, to the custody of the House of Loors, then take his brigade to Durrass and refit for a possible strike on the remnants of the Faceer Ka in the Equatorial Region. Headquarters had speculated that the cylinder, and the fugitives who took it, were in league with the Faceer Ka. Deenar didn't buy it. General Somar might have his own agenda but to throw in with the Faceer Ka, that was a thin premise at best. At the moment, however, his career was hanging by an even thinner thread and not following orders would most likely end it.

He stood on the deck of the tragoone and watched the pilot dodge the ice flows in the harbor as they made their way into the Sea of Storms and then eastward into the calmer waters of the Sea of Aldor. Suprass was only two full days sailing away and, shed of his burden of prisoners; he would waste no time in getting to Durrass and a possible shot at redemption for his blunder at the Pole.

The two day journey passed uneventfully with the exception of a brief encounter with a tragoone from the House of Gleer on patrol southeast of Broll. The ship-to-ship radio communications established Deenar' identity, although he was guarded about his cargo even with these presumed allies. Word of a renegade ship had been sent out from Central Headquarters, but there were no instructions as to what to do with it if found. It appeared that Takir and Klut were now uncertain as to the loyalties of any of the other Houses.

The great ship headed into the Sea of Dosomiel towards the harbor at Suprass, tacking against the unfavorable winds. The weather was warming, and the heat from Zenos grew as Rebal continued its long elliptical journey around it with Osstar in tow. Springtime was coming to the planet.

The captain's head shot out of the pilot house door as a cry went up from the lookout.

"Tragoone to swoonson!"

The captain was joined by General Deenar on the observation deck as the radio operator tried to raise the ship. There was no reply.

"Try another frequency," the captain commanded.

"Here ... let me see that," General Deenar said, pushing the radio operator aside. He turned the dials of the device and switched several switches. The receiver crackled to life.

"Turn-to!" the voice on the other end of the line said, "turn-to and prepare to be boarded."

"This is General Trios-takir-deenar."

"General Deenar ... thank the gods! We have been searching for you. Stay on your present course, and we will come alongside." The captain issued an order to the pilot to maintain course and speed, and within minutes, a huge tragoone bearing the insignia of the House of Takir pulled alongside. A contingent of Stomari troopers accompanied their officer across the wide, wooden boarding ramp onto the deck of the ship. An officer approached and saluted. "Major Takir-trios-sood, at your service."

"So, Major," General Deenar began, "You've come to escort us into Suprass."

"No, sir," the major replied. "I've come to transfer the prisoners to my ship and take them straightway to Prass for interrogation."

"But those weren't my orders," Deenar protested. "I was told to take them to Suprass before moving on to the Equatorial Region."

"Well, my orders come from Takir himself. I am to take these prisoners in for interrogation. I would imagine that Takir felt it too risky to unload them in the port, and also this will save you time in your journey to Jaakar."

Deenar felt an uneasiness growing within him. There was something wrong about all this. He had not mentioned Jaakar. If these soldiers from the House of Takir really knew his mission, they would have known that Durrass, and not Jaakar, was his destination. He turned quickly to the captain. "Call the crew on deck!" Before the captain could respond, he was wrestled down by one of the troopers and a large, meaty hand clasped around his mouth.

"Sorry about this, General. You will not be harmed." Major Sood motioned to the trooper to get the General quickly inside the pilot house and out of sight of the ships crew. The captain was also gagged and taken inside. One of the officers of the guard approached the opening to the hold and called to the sailor guarding it to bring the prisoners out. Looking for his captain, but not seeing him, the sailor complied with the armed Takir trooper's request.

The remnants of the various Polar expeditions spilled onto the deck. In a brusque tone, the officer told them to line up as he eyed them one-by-one. His gaze settled on an impressive looking Stoma in a black cape and winter tunic.

"You will come with me." He moved down the line and came to another Stoma. Glancing down at his feet for a moment, his gaze returned to the Stoma's face. "And the crippled one ... you come as well." He continued on, pulling Riatt and Diell out of the line. "This group will come with me. Take the rest and load them into the hold."

"What about the ape?" a trooper yelled.

They said everyone; I had no instructions about apes. Put him in the hold with the others." The remaining prisoners were taken across the ramp to the hold of the Takir tragoone.

The officer marched the selected group into the pilot house on the main deck of the Takir ship. Major Sood hurried across the ramp and had his crew cast off as quickly as possible. Once clear of the Trios tragoone, he spoke to his pilot.

"It will be a few minutes before they realize what has happened. Set the new course we discussed, I have a meeting to attend in the captain's quarters." The tragoone, flying the battle flag of the House of Takir, moved out into the Sea of Dosomiel. The winds picked up. The great, white sails billowed and the ship picked up speed heading due west, leaving the tragoone of General Deenar wallowing in the calm sea without a captain to set its course.

Major Sood entered the outside chamber of the captain's quarters and stood, looking at the two Stoma and two Faceer sitting along the wooden wall.

"Do you have any idea who I am?" Breet said, using a command voice.

"I do," the major replied, taking Breet somewhat by surprise. Something seemed strangely familiar about the officer.

"Do I know you?" Breet asked. "Have we served together before?" Before the major could answer, the door to the inner chamber opened and two guards ushered the group inside. At a large table sat a figure, completely covered in a heavy hooded robe of the type worn by the priests of the temple of Leeth. It was garb seldom seen outside the temple.

"What is this?" Druk-tasis whispered to Riatt. "Are we to be converted to the priesthood?"

"Perhaps you should be," the robed figure shot back. "It's only by the grace of the gods that you are here and still alive ... the gods and a few smart Stoma females."

"Tarsa!" Breet rushed to pull back the heavy hood and reveal the smiling face of his beloved wife.

"I decided to keep you alive," she laughed. "I'm far too old to be breaking in a new mate."

"But how? When?"

"We'll have time to talk on the journey home." She turned to the guards. "Tear the Takir insignia off your uniforms and lower their flags. Unfurl the colors of The House of Breet. Let our people know that their leader is coming home!"

Breet watched with pride as the guards rushed off to carry out their orders. "What a female I have!"

"So," Tarsa continued, "were you surprised?"

"Surprised would hardly describe it," Breet answered.

"Well you weren't as surprised as the captain of Takir's flagship when he found himself flung half-naked into his own hold."

"But how did you know that we had been taken prisoner in the first place, or what ship we would be on?"

"The janitor," Tarsa said with a smile.

"I might have known," Druk-tasis said. "And how is my old companion and confidant?"

"He is well as you will see soon enough."

"He is coming to meet us?"

"He will be at the dock in Orial when we arrive."

"Things must be moving quickly to dislodge Tomar Leet from his stuffed office chair.

"Hopefully they are moving at our pace and not that of Takir and Klut. We have you, but the others and their cargo are, at the moment, unaccounted for."

"I had almost forgotten about Pire, Steera and Nosh," Diell admitted. "And they have General Somar with them ... I'm still not sure that I trust him."

"Neither is Leet," Tarsa answered.

"Nosh trusted him," Riatt spoke up, "and if Nosh says he is to be trusted then that's good enough for me."

"I pray that you are right, my friend," Breet said. "I sensed a sincerity about him that I liked, and I think that Pire trusted him as well. We can't all be mistaken."

"At any rate, it's out of our hands for the moment," Tarsa said. "We must return to Orial and plan our next move. For now I recommend that you rest and eat. I trust that you haven't eaten since your capture."

Tarsa and her husband made their way back to her private quarters where she spent several hours listening to his tale of the expedition and telling him of a momentous event being planned at Orial. Later that evening, they gathered on the rolling deck, discussing their theories on the creature in the glass dome, and watching the lights of the little fishing villages on the coast of the Lower Midlands flicker as they sailed by. For the moment at least, they were heading to Orial and safety.

It was well past Mid-Rebal when the ship cleared the jetty of land that marked the opening of the Narial Strait and headed north toward the harbor at Orial. Druk-tasis was standing on the foredeck with Diell, cupping his hands around his eyes as if he had distance glasses. Suddenly, a sight caught him that caused him to draw in his breath.

"What is it?" Diell asked excitedly.

"I'm not sure. It looks like ships ... hundreds of ships!"

"Oh, we're doomed. It's Takir's fleet; they've found us out!"

Soon, the crew members were pouring onto the deck to see the sight. Tarsa and Breet-Prime joined them, standing arm-in-arm on the foredeck, waving to the ships. Diell and Druk could now see that the decks of the ships were lined with sailors and crews of all sorts, and that they were waving and shouting. The hiss of electric cannon split the air around them as they turned to enter the harbor. Diell could make out what looked to be thousands of residents of the city lining the entire wharf area.

"Quite a welcome home," Riatt said as he joined Druk and Diell.

"Impressive," was all that Druk could say as the ship neared the main dock amidst thunderous cheers.

In the center of the dock a space had been cleared and a large platform had been constructed. Tales about the journey into the Caverns of Aldor, and of the mysterious object found there were already spreading. The crowd cheered at the sight of Breet, Tarsa and the brave members of the expeditions. Druk recognized several of the others assembled. To his surprise, the heads of the Houses of Denoth, Klat, Nomes and Seer were seated around the podium. In the middle of it all, fumbling with his spectacles, was Tomar Leet.

"Something big must be happening," Druk shouted to Riatt over the din.

"I think we're about to find out," Diell shouted back.

The group made its way across the wooden gangway and onto the platform greeting citizens and dignitaries as they moved to their assigned seats. Breet-Prime approached the microphone, which had been placed in the middle of the platform. He waited a few more minutes, and then motioned for the crowd to quiet down.

He began to speak, "Citizens of Osstar, members of the Great Houses, colleagues and friends. I am overwhelmed by this outpouring of your affection. Surely, no being has ever been more blessed than the one chosen to be the leader of such a citizenry — and husband to such a female." Breet pulled Tarsa close to him on the platform. "Without her, I would still be a prisoner of the Old Guard. Without her, we would not be seeing what we are seeing ... an assembly of the best of our beloved world. It is Tarsa who has brought us to this moment, and it will be Tarsa who will speak for me."

The crowd reacted enthusiastically as Breet threw hundreds of years of Stoma tradition to the winds and led Tarsa to the microphone. She hesitated. Looking back over her shoulder at her husband and the members of the Great Houses assembled behind her, she remembered her upbringing, her youthful training on the responsibilities of a Stoma female and later as wife to the head of a Great House. "This is a new day," she thought. "How better to begin it?"

She turned back to the crowd and began to speak. "We are not assembled here to revel in our achievements," she began. "We are here to signal the beginning of a new day on Osstar, a day when violence as a means of diplomacy is rejected, a day when the Old Order gives way to the New, and a day we begin to tap the potential that is present in all of Osstar's inhabitants, for the good of all. I see in front of me not Stoma or Faceer, but citizens of a new world ... a world that has been forever altered by the expedition to Aldor. But there is work to do. The members of the expedition have made a great discovery that will change our world forever, but that discovery is still not safe from the forces of hatred and violence. We must recover this treasure and present it to all Osstarians. For this task we will need a leader of great courage and vision, someone that we can all follow with pride." Denoth-Prime and Seer-Prime were squirming in their oversized chairs, each thinking that they were about to be handed the charge. "I now turn the mission and the tasks ahead over to the new leader of our movement—Tomar Leet!"

If the Stoma in the audience were surprised at the choice, the Faceer were absolutely astounded. Allowing Tarsa to speak for the head of a Great House was a break with tradition, but this was a total smashing of it. A stunned silence enveloped the crowd. A worried look crossed Breet-Prime's face. Perhaps this was too much, too fast. No Faceer had ever been allowed even to participate in such an important undertaking—to lead it was revolutionary.

Tarsa beckoned Leet to join her at the podium. He rose slowly, reluctantly from his chair and stood in front of the thousands of disbelieving Osstarians, dwarfed by the tall microphone. He adjusted his spectacles and tugged at his ill-fitting tunic. His head swiveled back and forth as he gauged the enormity of the crowd. A nearby soldier placed a small wooden box in front of the microphone. Leet climbed up on it and, leaning his head forward, spoke slowly, almost apologetically.

"I fear that my position as head janitor at Central Headquarters has been put in great jeopardy."

Tarsa smiled. Breet-Prime and the rest of the Stoma leaders let out a collective laugh, and the crowd quickly followed, Stoma and Faceer alike.

"You have chosen well," Breet said to Tarsa as they watched the obvious delight of the crowd.

"I am honored by these great leaders and their trust in so humble a servant. We have all struggled long and hard to see this day ... to see our two species come together in the cause of peace and justice. There have been many sacrifices and there will be more to make, but there is also great hope for the future. These brave travelers have brought back a wondrous gift from the gods. A gift that we hope will be a bridge to a brighter future for us all—Faceer and Stoma alike. But there are still forces that will do all in their power to prevent it. These forces must be isolated and purged from all positions of authority. I have made arrangements that I hope will secure this treasure and, when it is recovered, we will present it to the inhabitants of Osstar so that they can decide for themselves the best path to follow.

I am calling for the formation of a Grand Council of Osstar to be convened in Prameel. This Council will consist of those leaders of the Great Houses who wish to attend, a group of Faceer leaders chosen by our local councils, and at least one other member who will serve as an ambassador at large. My friends, our world is at a crossroads. Where we go from here will determine the future of both of our species. I pledge all my strength and effort to make it a future of peace and cooperation."

Leet bowed and turned back to his chair. The crowd applauded. Tarsa's gamble had paid off. Now, if one small phantom steamer could be found in the vast Seas of Osstar, the future Leet described might just come to pass.

CHAPTER 39

"It can't be!" Takir pounded his meaty fist on the polished top of his desk. "I'll have that idiot, Deenar's head on a cotaan pole."

Klut hated to be the bearer of bad news, especially to Takir. "It may be worse still."

"What do you mean?"

"Not only have the conspirators been rescued, but there are reports of several members of the High Council leaving their Houses within the last few days. My sources inside the House of Denoth say that Denoth-Prime left for Orial several days ago, amidst great secrecy."

"Orial! Blast that Breet traitor! Do we have any report on the location of the cylinder?"

"I've sent every available ship to the South Equatorial Sea to guard the Narial Strait and the approaches to Jaakar. If they try and reform with the Faceer Ka in the Equatorial Region we'll have them."

"And what makes you so sure that they're headed for the Equatorial Region?"

"It is the only area outside of the Circular Continent still controlled by the Faceer Ka."

"What about an area controlled by no one," Takir snarled.

"Controlled by no one?"

"Yes, like the Unincorporated Territory. Has it occurred to you that these little worms have outsmarted us at every turn? Perhaps they suspect that we will be looking for them in the Equatorial Region ... the only region that they still control?"

The sarcasm in Takir's voice was toxic. A frown distorted Klut's thick brow. "I could redirect some of our ships..." Klut was cut off in mid sentence.

"By the time you do, they will be halfway across Osstar. I took it upon myself to direct two of my own tragoones to Luceriot. I think our friends will try and slip past us via the western route through the Olange Strait. When they do, they will get a surprise. I will teach them to steal my flagship. It was no 'accident' that made me head of the High Council of Osstar."

"I will dispatch several ships to Luceriot to provide assistance," Klut said submissively.

"You'll do nothing of the sort." Takir snapped back. "I don't want any of your clumsy maneuvers giving us away. I don't think the Faceer are that smart; I think that someone in our very midst has been relaying information. That is why I have done away with all the Faceer aides here at headquarters. From now on, everyone will be informed of orders on a need-to-know basis ... and that means everyone." Takir lowered his chin and stared up at Klut through his thick brow. Klut, still smarting from the "accident" comment, needed no further instruction. He snapped to attention, wheeled about and made his way quickly out of Takir's office.

Pire brushed a seedge fly away from his flask of keera water. It was one of the first of the spring season, so the small inlet where the steamer had moored was not yet teeming with them. They were almost to the western end of Andorna where they would turn north and make for the Olange Strait. So far, they had seen no one in the Prait-Andorna Passage.

"We'll wait until Rebal-wane tomorrow and make for the Strait," Nosh said, getting an assenting nod from Somar-loors. It's a bit early in the season for commercial fishing boats, but I would still like the cover of twinight for the trip across the open ocean. Steera noticed one of the crew members approaching her. From his attire, she knew that he was one of the villagers from Romass that had been replaced on the expedition by a sledder.

"Pardon," he said in a low tone. "I was just wondering if you have any news of my friend."

"And who is your friend?"

"His name is Deelus. He wasn't much of a sailor, and I know that he didn't like the cold at all, but he's the best friend I have."

Steera hadn't had much time to think of those they had left behind at the South Pole. Deelus had been with her when she discovered Seelar, and had been in the cavern when they were all introduced to Simon Vargus. She thought also of Druk-tasis and Riatt, but most of all, her thoughts turned to Diell. She had watched as he had grown up right before her eyes. She couldn't stomach the thought of him suffering in the hold of some Stomari prison ship. The words found their way out of her mouth involuntarily. They came more to comfort her than the villager. "I'm sure they are fine. The Stomari won't want a planet-wide incident on their hands, so I am sure that they will be well treated." The villager walked away with a look of sadness on his face. Steera had done a poor job of convincing him.

Rebal-wane came with its cool pinkish-red light and with it, the strong tidal flows of Osstar. The steamer moved away from the shore out into the open waters of the Prait-Andorna Ocean. The captain called for full steam from the engine room, and the steamer plowed its way through the choppy waters toward the Olange Strait that split the islands of Luceria and Kloose and connected the Prait-Andorna Ocean to the North Equatorial Sea.

The passage was proceeding peaceful when a cry from the observation deck snapped all on board to attention. To the west were two tragoones. It was unclear if they had spotted the steamer, but Nosh and Somar-loors were taking no chances.

"Hard to anchorage!" Nosh called to the pilot. "Head south!"

"Have they seen us?" Pire asked, breathless from rushing up from below decks. His questioned was answered by the roar of an electric cannon and the explosion of a shell just ten yards off the swoonson jib.

"Evasive maneuvers!" Somar-loors yelled to the pilot. The steamer started a zigzag course back toward the waters between Kloose and Andorna and the South Equatorial Sea. Unfortunately for them, the wind had picked up and was blowing directly at them. The sails of the tragoones were full to bursting, and they were practically flying over the water.

"They're gaining on us!" Steera shouted. The unidentified tragoones had made up ten lengths on the steamer. The second shot from their cannon exploded just a few yards behind them.

"Can we get more speed?" Somar-loors asked the captain.

"I've already got her to the maximum," he replied. "Just pray that the wind changes, that's all that can save us now." Somar-loors knew that he was right. The ships were close enough now to make out the Takir emblem even in the half-light of Rebal-wane. It was only left to pour on the steam and hope for a miracle. Two more shells exploded to either side of the steamer. The high wind was a mixed blessing. The tragoones were moving at a fantastic speed, but the angle of the deck made it difficult for the gunners to take good aim at their target.

Nosh and Somar-loors stood watching on the fore deck, helpless to do anything about their plight. Then, Nosh noticed that one of the tragoones seemed to be falling back. Somar-loors saw it too. The wind hadn't changed, if anything it had gotten even stronger. Both watched as the second tragoone also slowed and turned to the north. Then they heard it, the sound of cannon fire from another direction. Nosh grabbed a pair of distance glasses from a nearby sailor and looked north. Heading directly for the Takir ships were four battle sloops of Faceer design, firing as they came. The sloops were more lightly armed than the massive tragoones, but were more agile and maneuverable. They quickly surrounded the larger vessels and proceeded to decimate their sails. Too crippled to continue their pursuit, the tragoones made an about face and headed back toward the open ocean. The battle sloops made no effort to follow, but instead turned and headed in the direction of the steamer.

"Well, that eliminates one problem," General Somar said approaching Nosh.

"Yes, but who are our new benefactors? I hope we haven't simply traded viaal for cather-cats."

There were no insignia flying from any of the sloops. They were in unfamiliar waters in the South Equatorial Sea, somewhere south of Kloose and due west (he reckoned) from Triosie the home city of the House of Trios.

"I can't tell if they are Stoma or Faceer," Somar-loors said.

"I suppose it doesn't make much difference now. They're faster than the tragoones, so we should know in a few minutes." As the sloops drew nearer, they could make out the insignia on the small flags flying from the foremast. It was like none that Nosh had ever seen, but Somar-loors recognized it.

"They're Tyage raiders," Somar-loors said with no emotion.

"Is that bad?" Pire asked.

"They're not known for their hospitality," Somar said, dryly. "Yet, they are motivated by profit, so perhaps a deal can be struck."

The leader of the raiding party stood on the foredeck and called to the pilot of the steamer. "Heave to!" The pilot looked in the direction of Nosh and Somar-loors.

"Do as he asks," Nosh said. The ships were quickly lashed side-by-side with priot vine ropes and twelve armed Faceer crossed the ramp onto the deck of the steamer. The leader of the group approached Somar-loors, but his attention was quickly turned to Nosh. The others gathered round Nosh and stared as if he were an attraction at a roadside carnival.

"What do you desire of us?" Somar-loors asked, moving to place himself in-between Nosh and the raiders.

The Faceer ignored him. "You are the one they call Nosh?" he asked still looking at him intently.

"I am," Nosh answered, calmly.

"You will follow us."

"Where are we headed?" the pilot asked.

"We will travel through the Morate Strait to Tyage."

"But the Morate Strait is treacherous," the pilot complained, "... pirates and bandits."

The leader smiled, "Pirates and bandits! I see no pirates or bandits here." He looked around at his smiling companions. "These are the most peaceful waters on Osstar ... especially when you have four battle sloops escorting you." The message was clear—they were going to Tyage.

"We would be pleased to follow you, and thank you for helping us with those two tragoones," Nosh said. The leader again stared at Nosh as if he was surprised that he was articulate.

"Yes," he snorted. "Well, a few Stoma tragoones don't worry us very much. Make ready to sail....or steam as the case may be." He turned and made his way back across the ramp and onto his own ship with the armed guard close behind. The steamer took a position in the middle of the four sloops.

"So what does this all mean?" Steera asked. "Are we saved or sunk?"

"Hard to guess," Nosh replied. "At least we're still alive. That's always a positive." Pire laughed and patted Nosh on the back, mimicking the affection he showed for the Zerrit. Zenos was returning to the eastern sky, and in the distance they could just make out a large mass of land.

"Must be the Unincorporated Territory," Somar-loors remarked. "We'll be in Tyage by Mid-Rebal." The thought of that was not altogether comforting.

The harbor at Tyage was wide enough for four battle sloops and a steamer—but just barely. The news of the battle had spread, and the shore was lined with curious spectators as the flotilla made its way to the main dock. The sloops made way for the steamer and let it dock first, mooring directly in front of a large warehouse on the waterfront. Nosh had taken the precaution of wearing a hooded parka—it proved unnecessary. A squadron of Security Troopers lined the dock and blocked the view of the onlookers. Inside the warehouse, the troopers were dismissed and the ship's crew was taken into another room. Nosh, Pire, Steera and Somar-loors were left standing in the dim light of the main storage area. As their eyes began to adjust to the light, a voice spoke from out of the darkness.

"Sit it down, there," it said. A squad of Security Troopers carrying a large object entered from their right. Nosh immediately recognized the object they were carrying as the cylinder. The Troopers placed it in front of the group and exited the room. From out of the shadows emerged a stocky Faceer with a pair of large round spectacles dangling from a taanar-hide cord around his neck. He reached for them as he neared the cylinder and placed them on his face, studying the strange object. "So, this is what the fuss is all about. It doesn't look like much to me." He ran his hand over the smooth surface and fidgeted with both ends. "They say that it's hollow ... that there's something in it. Know anything about that?" Nosh and the rest were becoming nervous. The Faceer's tone was sugary-sweet, but there was a dark undertone to it that hinted of violence.

Several figures entered the room from a side doorway and made their way to the cylinder. The old Faceer looked up, his leathery face contorting into a smile as if he were expecting them. "Ah, my friends, you are just in time to examine your prize."

The new group took a position on one side of the cylinder. Steera could see a few of their faces. They were Faceer. The insignia on one of the party's tunics seemed familiar. She recognized it as the same one that was on their steamer. They were members of the Braccar Alliance.

"You'll find that it is in perfect condition. I trust you have the final payment." The leader of the party from Braccar moved closer to the cylinder and examined it, his back turned to Steera. She sensed something familiar about him.

"You'll receive final payment when we are safely at Braccar." That voice, she knew that she had heard it before. The old Faceer huffed at the Braccar leader's reluctance to pay. He had done business with Tyage before.

The Braccar party lifted the cylinder and started out of the warehouse, making their way through the same doorway. Pire and the rest waited for someone to tell them where to go. Finally, the old Faceer noticed them standing there.

"Well, get going. You're part of the deal, although for the life of me I can't figure out why."

Nosh's party nearly ran over each other trying to follow the Braccar representatives out of the warehouse. They were led to a covered docking facility where a Faceer schooner was moored not more than fifty yards from the warehouse. Once again, the transit was made beyond the curious eyes of the local populace. Herded quickly onto the schooner, they were stowed amidships, sharing small but comfortable quarters with the cylinder. Food and water for both Stoma and Faceer had been provided. Soon, they felt the slip of the water under the schooner as it skated over the smooth harbor waters.

The party was just making itself comfortable and enjoying the first good cup of chee they had had in a while when two Braccar security troopers entered and bade them follow. They were led back up on deck and then into the large pilot room of the schooner. Several sailors were busy with their duties.

One Faceer was standing at the rear of the cabin with his back toward the group, looking anxiously out over the water. Without turning he addressed them. "You have cost quite a bit ... you and your little present." Steera was certain she knew the voice now. "Which one of you is the one called Nosh?" The Faceer turned as Nosh was throwing off his hood. He was momentarily silent. "Pardon my impolite behavior, but while I have heard stories of you for years, I have never seen one of your kind before." He turned to Steera. "Still bandying the name of Klut about?"

"Ras!"

"Your servant," he answered, bowing slightly as Faceer to Faceer.

Pire was caught by surprise. "Do you know him?"

"We've met. He is the head retainer of my old family mentor..." Steera couldn't bear to say the name.

"... Klut!" Pire said, finishing the sentence. "So, we've come all this way to be purchased like greel calves at an auction."

"How did you find us?" Steera asked.

"I have a very good source of information. Most people think he's an old fool, but I know better."

Steera was dejected. "So, I suppose that you spied on him for your master just as you helped Klut spy on me."

Ras smiled. "As a matter of fact you are correct, only you have it backwards."

"What do you mean?"

"I spy on Klut for my master. I have been in his service for many years. His name is Tomar Leet." Ras watched the expressions on their faces change as his words sank in. He threw his head back and let out a mighty laugh.

"Thanks be to the gods," Somar-loors said prayerfully.

Steera turned to Pire. "Ras was the one that got me in to see Klut about going on the polar expedition ... but what about the transmitter? Did you know about that as well?"

"I must admit that your presence on the expedition was Klut's doing. My task was to get Nubin Pire to the North Polar Station to help Druk-tasis. After you interjected yourself into the proceedings, I encouraged your presence in order to keep the expedition on track. The transmitter was Klut's idea. Or, I suspect, one of Dr. Lateer's informants. We can thank the gods that he hid it on you. It allowed us to track you to the Equatorial Camp, and relay our instructions to Nosh."

Somar-loors completed the story, "And subsequently, it became the instrument that allowed us to find the third cylinder." Ras glared suspiciously at the Stomari General.

"What do you mean?"

"It is a long tale, my friend," Nosh said. "I am sure that someone will set down a proper account of it all when we have accomplished our mission. What is our destination?"

"Braccar," Ras replied.

"I knew it." Nosh beamed with pride at his deductive ability.

"I wouldn't start to celebrate just yet," Ras cautioned. "We still have to make it there in one piece." He put his distance glasses to his eyes and grunted as two fully-armed Stoma battle tragoones came into view and took up positions flanking the schooner. "There they are, right on schedule."

Somar-loors was looking out the porthole at the great ships. "They're flying my colors!"

"The House of Somar has agreed to provide security for our trip to Braccar. Many things have changed on Osstar of late ... many things." Ras seemed to relax at the sight of the powerful escort.

"And now my friends, I invite you to a special dinner in my quarters where, if we are very lucky, we will be entertained by the best Sonnage singer this side of the Caverns of Aldor."

There were no further attacks on the party. Three pirate skiffs had briefly appeared as they exited the Morate Strait and entered the North Equatorial Sea west of Braccar, but, seeing the two tragoones, they returned to their lairs to await a less "prickly" prey. The cool breeze spawned by the staddich kept the schooner and its escort moving steadily towards the great harbor at Braccar.

Pire's arm had fallen asleep, pinned, as it was, under Steera. She lay in semi-sleep stasis. He nudged her just enough to free it and get to his feet in the cramped cabin. Now that he had her back, he vowed never again to complain about any minor inconvenience that she might cause him. He made his way on deck just as Rebal was returning to the eastern sky. Nosh was already there, sitting with his back against the main mast. Pire sat down next to him.

"Couldn't sleep either?" Pire asked.

"No, I suppose not." He sat for a moment looking at Pire, his face aglow with the light of the Osstarian dawn. He thought of all that they had gone through these many months. How long had it been? Spring was fading when the Zerrits had taken Pire to the caverns and it was fast approaching. He worked up the courage to ask the question that had been on his mind. "Do you feel it?"

Pire knew what he was asking. "Yes, I think I do," he replied.

"It's been hard, dangerous and often disappointing, yet somehow I hate to see it end."

"I know. I miss my little house in the Northern Islands. I miss my job, my lab at the institute, and yet somehow all that seems so unimportant now."

Nosh leaned back and gazed up at the disappearing stars. "Steera's beautiful," he said. "She's the mirror image of my mother ... at least the mother in my picture. Faeed told me about her. She was wiry and athletically built, possessing great strength, yet as soft and giving as a coola with her chicks. Few female Faceer can survive that birth process, you know." Pire remained silent and let Nosh talk. "When the Faceer Ka killed Faeed, my last tie with my mother was cut. I hated them for it. I hated all Faceer for a while, but I finally came to the realization that I couldn't hate Faceer and still love my mother. I lost the last vestiges of that hatred when I saw Steera in the cavern." Pire put his arm as far around Nosh's broad shoulder as he could.

"That's one thing we share in common, friend. I was watching her sleep tonight. In the light from the lamp in the cabin she looked like one of the mountain spirits that the Veertal paint on their houses ... a face as soft as snow and as sweet as a little greel. You know, maybe I am ready to give up the life of an adventurer."

Nosh laughed. "I must confess something to you." He looked Pire directly in the face. "I don't know if I am up to all this. Although I have had contact with the outside since I was a child, I've lived my life in isolation. Sometimes I hated the Stoma and sometimes the Faceer. Mostly, I hated myself. I felt like a freak, sequestered in my cavern citadel with my 'people.' Now I face the prospect of playing a role in the future of Osstar, and I am fearful almost beyond my limit to cope."

"We all have fears to conquer," Pire said gently. "When I am fearful, I think of the ones I love and try and be brave for them. You are a part of those thoughts."

"There are still adventures ahead," Nosh said. "But we can hope that they will leave us at least some time for those loved ones." The conversation closed without an ending. Both leaned back against the mast and let the early light of Rebal warm them. For a while at least, all was quiet on Osstar.

CHAPTER 40

Nosh and Pire awoke from their brief stasis to the sound of electric cannon fire. It was almost mid-Rebal and Zenos had joined it in the pink sky. Pire ducked under a piece of sailcloth that was lying on the deck and peeked out. Nosh was standing at full height, stretching his neck to see out over the rolling foredeck. The cannon sounds grew louder. The passengers and crew spilled out onto the deck.

Pire crawled reluctantly from under his cover and stood with Somar-loors, Nosh and Steera on the deck. Vessels of all sizes and descriptions surrounded their ship. Their decks were crowded with Faceer and Stoma, cheering and waving Osstarian flags as well as the flags of the Great Houses, and the arms of the Faceer clans. The three vessels had to slow considerably to keep from ramming the smaller boats. Slowly, the boats made way and the three ships sailed into the great harbor at Braccar.

A huge platform had been constructed on the main dock, extending out into the harbor at least 20 yards. It was swarming with Stoma and Faceer in many different uniforms and tunics. The warm spring breeze caught the colored cloths of the banners of the Great Houses lining the podium, causing them to wave an enthusiastic greeting to the returning heroes.

"What in the name of Tupo's bell is this?"

"It looks as if we were expected," Ras said, joining them on deck.

"You knew about this?" Nosh asked.

"Well, it is a bit more of a crowd than I expected."

"It looks as if half of Osstar is here," Pire said. Nosh started to hurry below decks, but Ras caught him.

"No need to hide any longer my friend. They know you are with us." Nosh was nervous. He had known all of his life that this day would come.

The two tragoones broke off in mid-harbor, and the schooner sailed the rest of the way alone. At the dock, the crowds had to be forced back behind a large mooring rope. The party crossed the ramp and onto the platform greeted by Breet-Prime and Tarsa. The embraces were long and heartfelt.

"You made it out!" Somar-loors grabbed Breet's hand as that of an old friend.

"We were rescued, as were you, by our venerable Faceer bene-factor." Steera caught sight of Leet and nearly leapt at him.

"Here ... here ... young female," Leet chastised her all the while smiling broadly. "You'll break an old fellow in two."

"So this is, Leet," Somar-loors said, extending his hand. "I had heard so many miraculous tales about you that I had half-expected it to be you when the Being appeared in the glass dome."

"Being ... glass dome? I assure you sir that you vastly overesti-mate me. But I will take the hand of the great General Somar-loors, and am overjoyed that it is extended in friendship." Somar smiled and took Leet's small furry hand in his.

"And the others?" Steera asked. "What of the others?"

"All here for the most part," Leet said. "Unfortunately we lost a few." Steera's eyes scanned the crowd at the podium. On it were the sailors, sledders and villagers that had made up the South Po-lar expedition. There, to her distaste, was a bedraggled Seelar, and to her delight, a jubilant Deelus. Standing next to him, walking in her direction, were Riatt and Druk-tasis. Pire rushed to greet them. Nosh, still partly covered by a hooded tunic, took off in another direction altogether. Steera was still searching the crowd. Surely nothing had happened to him, she thought. Finally, at the rear of the throng she spied a smallish Faceer struggling with something on his tunic. She ran in his direction and reached Diell just as he was getting his button fastened. The impact of Steera's enthusiastic hug undid the fastener.

"Winds of Aldor! I've been trying to get that blasted thing but-toned for twenty minutes."

Steera grabbed him in a massive hug that almost threw him to the deck. "You little broog, since when is a button more important than me."

Diell hugged back as hard as he could. "Isn't it wonderful? Nine of the Great Houses have broken from the Council and joined us, even that pompous Loors-Prime is here ... and Tomar Leet, the leader of it all."

"Leet ... a Faceer the head of such an undertaking!

"You'll know all about it in a few minutes. Leet is scheduled to address the Alliance." Diell took Steera's arm and they made their way back to the podium. Druk and Riatt ushered them to prominent seats behind the dais.

The crowd had quieted. Tomar Leet finished his greetings and mounted the dais to the microphone. In front of him, upright on a metal table, sat the cylinder. It was giving off a radiant, red/orange light in the bright sky.

Leet stood looking at it for a moment and then, waving to quiet the crowd, began: "Citizens of Osstar, you see before you the hope of our civilization. This is the great treasure that these brave beings have risked their very lives to wrest from the grasp of the Stomari and the Faceer Ka. It is our profound belief that its message will help guide us all to a better future. In five days, at Prass, we will convene the first Grand Council of Osstar. As I speak, delegates from every end of the planet and every walk of life—both Faceer and Stoma—are being notified." Leet scanned the podium for a familiar figure. "In her generosity, and perhaps against her better judgment, Tarsa Breet has appointed me head of this Alliance. This, by our tradition (actually, a Stoma tradition), gives me the honor of selecting who will serve as leader of the new Council. I take this opportunity to appoint him now, and to introduce you to the finest being that I have ever encountered. His name is, Nosh ... I pray that you will bid him welcome."

Leet stepped down as the crowd quieted in anticipation. He made his way to the rear of the podium where an uneasy Nosh was waiting. "Speak from the heart, my friend. It's always been the strongest part of your anatomy, and the one most like both Faceer and Stoma."

Nosh moved to the microphone and threw back his hood. A dead silence fell over the gathering. After a moment there were some gasps, and even a few shrieks from the younger Faceer and Stoma. An audible mumble swelled through the crowd. Nosh was at a loss for words.

Leet sensed the awkward position. He wondered if he had forced him in front of the public too soon. He had known Nosh for a long time and had forgotten his first reaction to the half-Stoma, half-Faceer creature. The crowd continued to stare at Nosh, and he at them. The situation was becoming tense.

Then, as if the gods themselves had intervened, the unexpected happened. Nosh leaned into the microphone, putting his mouth almost directly on it. He looked directly at the front row of the crowd and in his deepest voice said ... "BOO!"

The word reverberated from the speakers on either side of the podium and through the anxious crowd. At first, the throng didn't react, but those on the podium did. They started to laugh. A titter turned into a gale of laughter. The crowd joined in, slowly at first, building as the tension was relieved, until it drowned out the sound from the podium. As Nosh stood in front of them, nodding in approval, his Stoma traits became more pronounced to the Stoma in the audience and his Faceer traits likewise to the Faceer. The huge chasm between them narrowed and a sense of calm returned. Finally, Nosh began to speak, this time in a more serious tone.

"If I appear a freak, I can only apologize for frightening you. My ancestry is divided along lines that lead to everyone here. I did not ask to come into this world. I was given life by my Faceer mother and my Stoma father. Yet, it was not who bore me, but those who raised me that I represent today. I was raised by you — all of you ..." Nosh waved his long, sinewy hands in the direction of the crowd. "In my self-imposed exile, I read. I read everything I could find, and I came to love the culture of both of our species. I loved the nobility of the great Stoma leaders who so graciously made room on their planet for the Faceer. I admired the tolerance and patience of the great Faceer scientists and poets who suppressed their own ambitions to benefit their people. Those you see before you are not the only beings that have made sacrifices for a brighter future. Many others are not with us today. They lie dead at the North Polar Station, at the Equator, or in the blinding snows of Aldor or — to our great shame — in a little village in the Layard Mountains. But we are not here to dredge up the past. We are here to look to the future. This cylinder contains a wondrous gift from an ancient civilization. For us, if we heed its wisdom, the gift could be a new Osstar, a better Osstar. If we choose to ignore that gift and continue down the path we are now on, I fear that that future will be bloody and bleak. We have much to do. There will be those that will perceive this cylinder as a threat. They will use all of their power to try and silence or distort its message. We must commit ourselves — here and now — to the truth, and to the path of peace."

Nosh stood silent for several moments, looking out across the crowd. He thought it strange to be speaking so easily in front of such a gathering. Now, at this place, surrounded by his new friends, he had accepted his destiny, the destiny his father and mentor Faaige had prepared him for in the heart of the jungle. "Sons and daughters of Somar-dyzid," he said, evoking the name of the greatest Stoma philosopher. "Sons and daughters of Ouyard Marzz," he spoke the name of the first great Faceer scientist. "Son and daughters of Osstar, are you with me?"

The crowd rose as one. A great cheer filled the crisp, spring air. Stoma and Faceer from across Osstar embraced. Those on the podium rushed to congratulate Nosh.

Leet sat quietly in his chair and smiled a very contented smile. His long years of waiting and watching, of planning and maneuvering, had not been wasted. His beloved planet, it seemed, was coming of age.

Chapter 41

There were no banners or cheering crowds lining the streets of Prass on the day of the first Grand Council meeting. Breet and the others had pressured Takir's administration to allow the use of the main meeting hall, but Takir was not to be present. He had issued a terse statement welcoming the delegates and pledging to listen to any suggestions they might have regarding the improvement of conditions on Osstar, and regretting that matters of State would prevent his and Klut's attendance. Most of the civil servants (who were now mainly relatives of either Takir or Klut or their friends in the House of Trios) had also found excuses to be away from work that day.

The absence of the head of the High Council was no deterrence to the gathered delegates. They had been arriving all week from distant parts of the planet. Their make up was as diverse as the many subcultures of Osstar, and represented the best and brightest of each. The assembly room had been expanded to accommodate the larger council. In all, some seventy-five delegates had been selected and invited to attend.

Not all of the heads of the Stoma Houses had been selected and some higher Faceer functionaries within the central government had also been omitted, but each Stoma House was represented by at least one delegate. The chairs (constructed in a uniform size designed to fit both Faceer and Stoma) were arranged in a great circle around a small central platform, each row elevated above the previous so that all could see the object in the center.

On the platform sat the crystal dome. The delegates buzzed around it excitedly, running their hands over its smooth exterior, punching and poking it here and there. When all were assembled, a voice over the loudspeaker system asked them to take their seats.

Nosh mounted the dais and spoke.

"This is indeed an historic day for our planet. We are gathered here to discuss the future of our government and our own destiny, and we have a unique being to assist us—a gift from the past to the future you might say. Although many stories have been told of late about the discovery of the cylinders, they have been based, for the most part, on hearsay and conjecture. I would now like to introduce two scientists who have seen the contents of the cylinders firsthand, and have broken the ancient code sent to us from the stars, Nubin Pire and Dya-Klut...." Nosh caught himself. He feared he had made a diplomatic error attaching the Stoma House name, in the old Veertal tradition, especially the name of Klut.

Steera came to his rescue. "Dya-Klut Steera," she said, as she and Pire took the stage to polite applause. "My family was proud of its association with the great House of Klut. I know that there are delegates here today that bear that name. If we are to move into the future, we must get past such pettiness." Nosh smiled and touched Steera's cheek as he gave up the dais.

Pire spoke first. "I have heard the tales, as I know you have, of the fantastic events in our lives in the past year or so. I'm here to affirm that a few of them actually happened." The delegates laughed. "The object that you see in front of you represents the culmination of those adventures. It is the end product of much danger, toil and sacrifice. I will not bore you with the retelling of the adventure we had in retrieving it. I hope that it will soon be out in print so that you might know the entire story, and make the author rich in the process." Steera swatted at Pire playfully. "But, as fantastic as the story of the discovery of the cylinders is, it pales in comparison to what you are about to see. I ask you to welcome a friend from far away."

Pire nodded to Nosh who reached around the rear of the dome, running his hand over the small indentation. The delegates leaned forward to get a better look. The machine began to vibrate and the dome filled with a smoky, pink light that then altered to blue, and finally to a soft, clear white. In the center of the dome, the figure of Simon Vargus appeared. He stood for a moment, as if he were merely a three dimensional statuette under a glass dome, then walked forward to address them.

"Friends..." The alien figure in the crystal dome spoke in perfect Osstarian. The delegates sat, enchanted. Simon Vargus walked around inside the dome and studied their faces. He was obviously pleased with what he was seeing. "My good friends," he continued. "I hope that you have made yourselves comfortable. We have much to discuss."

Thus began the first meeting of the Grand Council of Osstar, presided over by a half-breed outcast and featuring an alien in a crystal dome. It was Simon Vargus though, who ultimately held the greatest fascination for the delegates. He talked, asked questions and listened as if he were alive and standing before them. As time passed, they became more at ease with the strange creature and the conversation became more animated. The dome finally went dark some three and a half hours later, but the delegates continued their discussions until hunger and fatigue finally got the better of them.

Nosh took the podium. "Friends," he began, using the same form of the word Simon Vargus had used. "We have much to absorb and much to think about. I believe that we should recess and return tomorrow at Rebal-rise to continue our discussions. But, to make sure that we do this the honest and impartial way, I would ask to see an indication by the lifting of hands as to who agrees with this proposed course of action." Every delegate raised his or her hand in agreement. This simple gesture represented the first vote taken by a unified political body in Osstar's long history.

For the next several days, the meetings were long and intense. On each occasion, Simon Vargus was conjured from his domed machine and consulted. While some minor bickering broke out, spurred by past grievances and perceived wrongs done, for the most part it was highly productive.

Takir, Klut and Trios had all stayed away. The rumor was that they were having their own meeting at Amiel to plot their strategy, but it was obvious from the reports of the media that the Alliance was growing in popularity on Osstar. There had been no reports of sabotage by the Faceer Ka or abductions by the Stomari. No longer believed to be a threat, a subdued Seelar had been allowed to leave Braccar and make his way home as best he could. He was still stinging from the fact that he had not been asked to be a delegate to the Council but that his subordinate, Pylo had.

Diell and Riatt had also been appointed as delegates, Diell being the youngest on the Council. Druk-tasis as well as Somar-loors, and Trooper Fazid were other members of the expedition that were honored with a delegate positions. After three more days of deliberations, the Grand Council announced that it would hold a public meeting in Prass the next day to be carried by both radio and telecommunications to all corners of Osstar.

The subsequent dawn brought a Luceriot, but the delegates skipped the usual breakfast celebration to attend to business. The entire Grand Council assembled on a large platform that had been constructed on the south end of the main government building. Remnants of the damage from the suicide bombing could still be seen on the side of the building. Some thought had been given to moving the location due to the visual broadcasts that would be made, but Nosh felt that the sight of the damage would serve as a reminder of the violence that was spawned by the old order.

Setting on a large table in front of the podium were the crystal dome of Simon Vargus and many of the items recovered from the other two cylinders, including one of the discs, the talking book and the original book from the first cylinder. The items had been open to inspection by the delegates before the meeting was called to order. The original book — with the picture of the winged creature — had drawn the most attention.

The time came, and the video technicians motioned that the broadcast had begun. Nosh, Tomar Leet and Tarsa Breet moved to take their positions on the podium.

Tarsa was the first to speak. "My fellow Osstarians... as you know, what is being called the Grand Council of Osstar has been meeting for these last few days. The delegates, which have been selected from among you all, represent the future of Osstar. We have been shown many wondrous things during our deliberations, revealed to us by a miraculous being sent from a small planet that once existed in the orbit of our own star, Zenos. In the days to come, the delegates assembled here will be returning to their homes across Osstar, sharing with you what they have learned. The message they will be carrying — the message of the cylinder — is one of peace and good will. We ask that you listen to them with an open mind and an open heart. I now turn the proceedings over to Tomar Leet for the results of the Grand Council's deliberations." Tarsa waited for Leet to reach the microphone before returning to her seat. Leet, in a show of respect, waited until she was seated before he began to speak.

Leet pushed his spectacles down on the rim of his tiny nose and gave a disparaging look at the video camera pointed at his face. He wasted no time with formalities. "The Grand Council of Osstar makes the following declarations: First, and with the approval of two thirds of its members, the High Council of Osstar is abolished. All duties and authority of the High Council will now pass to its successor in all matters, the Grand Council of Osstar; secondly, by order of the Grand Council, all security forces in the field will be under the authority of the new Commander of the Osstarian defense force General Somar-loors and his second in command, Colonel Riatt." A polite applause tried to spread through the audience, but Leet quickly stifled it. "Please, hold your response until I can get this blasted electronic box out of my face. By order of the Grand Council of Osstar and a unanimous vote of the delegates present, the being known as Nosh shall serve as the first Head of the Grand Council and shall preside over all future meetings. His permanent appointment will be ratified by a vote of all enfranchised inhabitants of Osstar."

This time there was no stifling the enthusiasm. Cheering broke out across the podium and spilled into the assembled crowd. Nosh exchanged places with a grateful Leet and waited for the cheers to die down. Finally, he spoke, looking straight into the camera, giving all of Osstar its first good look at its new leader.

"All those who love peace and planet, I welcome you. I realize that my appearance will be strange to many of you. You have been asked to absorb a lot in the last few weeks. You will be asked to learn even more in the ensuing weeks and months. I know that, spurred by your love of your planet and your family and friends, you will be up to the task. There have been many sacrifices by many of our fellow Osstarians in the last year or two. We must make sure that those sacrifices are not in vain. Behind me, you see the new leaders of Osstar. They are your friends and neighbors, your cousins, aunts and uncles ... your children. Together we will leave behind the old order and build a new one... for all the inhabitants of our world."

Nosh suddenly left the podium, walked over to a small covered compartment adjacent to it and led a figure out of it and back up to the podium. "We are not the only children of Osstar. It is a planet of great diversity of life." Nosh, with some difficulty, boosted his companion up to the camera. Keemass looked confused at all the commotion. A low chant began, started by the members of the delegation who had been on the South Polar expedition.

"Keeemasss...Keeemasss." It started to grow. Keemass recognized his name and joined in, to the amazement of the rest of those assembled. "Keeemasss...Keeemasss."

Nosh let the moment linger, and then led Keemass back to his shelter. "Before I dismiss this assembly, I want to single out a few of those assembled here today for special recognition. We have honored Tomar Leet, Druk-tasis, General Somar-loors and Colonel Riatt and rightfully so. There are also scores of Faceer and Stoma who have put themselves in grave danger, and have even given their lives for the cause of peace. But, there are three Faceer who have been involved in this adventure from the beginning. They have never tired; they have never wavered ... and practically never complained." Nosh looked directly at Diell and smiled. Diell gave a faint grin back. "Please honor three true heroes of Osstar."

Nosh pulled Steera and Pire onto the dais and motioned for Diell to join them. The response from the crowd was loud and long. "I have been directed by the Grand Council to grant you anything you may desire that is within our power to give you," Nosh said. No one was forthcoming so Nosh asked Diell directly. "What is it that a grateful planet can do for you, my young friend?" Diell was so nervous that he couldn't think straight. His only desire at that moment was simply to melt back into the crowd, but he knew that he would have to say something or risk standing there until he did.

He blurted out the only thing that he could think of. "Tarnn cakes," he said, "but not yours, no offense, but ones made by Steera's Aunt Dree." Laughter spread across the podium.

"No offense taken young friend ... so be it," Nosh said, still laughing. "And I hope I can share one with you." Nosh turned to Steera and Pire. "My dear friends, we have gone through much together. Anything we could give you would not be sufficient thanks for all that you have done, nor repayment for all that you have suffered. But still, is there some token we may give that would express our gratitude?"

Steera spoke up. "You have given me all that I ever wanted. Your courage and devotion has returned Pire to me. That is payment enough for my troubles."

Pire thought for a moment and spoke. "I agree with Steera. Her safety was all that I thought of while we were parted, and her return to me was more than I could have ever hoped for ... but there is one thing ... a memento of our adventure. If it pleases the Council, I would like the book that we found in the first cylinder. I remember the awe it inspired in me the first time that I saw it. With Steera's help, I have come a long way in learning the writing and language of the people of the cylinder. I would like the chance to try and read it in the original language." Nosh went to the table on which the artifacts lay, and picked up the book. He returned and handed it to Pire.

"Take this with the heartfelt thanks of the inhabitants of Osstar." Pire took the book fondly in his hands and kissed Steera. Nosh turned for a last time to the microphone. "With that, I declare these proceeding over until the next called meeting of the Grand Council."

The cameras went silent. The delegates stayed and congratulated each other, milling around the platform and studying the objects on the table. Pire and Steera rejoined Diell, Druk and the other members of the great expedition. The city of Prass took on a festival atmosphere in spite of the absence of members of the "old" government.

That evening, Faceer and Stoma sat together in inns and taverns all over the city, and indeed all over the planet and began to rediscover their common roots. Peace, at least for the present, had returned to Osstar.

Pire and Steera walked hand-in-hand, following the twisting bank of Ossgar as the staddich slowly bled through the pink twinight from the Osstarian sky. Their celebrity, gained from their appearance on the broadcasts from Prass, had followed them home to the hills of the Northern Islands. For a week, they had been wined and dined by every official on Preeg, but now the excitement was wearing off enough to allow them some time alone. They walked, for the first time in a long time, without a crowd of well wishers following them every step of the way.

Pire helped Steera across a small footbridge. A low, wooden bench lit by a soft gas globe overlooked a particularly beautiful portion of the stream. They sat down. Pire laid the small bundle that he was carrying on the bench next to him; Steera put her head on his shoulder.

"Will we ever be parted again?" Steera's voice was wistful and somewhat sad. Pire pointed to a spot on a rock next to the stream.

"Look there," he said. Steera could see two tiny insects sitting side-by-side on the rock, as if they were enjoying each other's company. "In the vastness of Osstar, these two little creatures found each other. They were meant to be together, just like you and me. Even if we were parted, I would find you again, just as I did at the caverns."

Steera leaned over and kissed Pire, a long and passionate kiss. Pire spoke quietly. "I have something I want to share with you." He picked up the neatly bound package and unwrapped it. Inside was the book that the Grand Council had presented him at Prass. "Without your help I would have never learned to read this alien tongue. I'm still not sure I can get it right, but I wanted to try. It's a gift to both of us. I would imagine that it's not been read aloud for millions of years."

Pire took the book in his hands and turned it over a few times, finally returning it to its proper position with the elaborate creature gracing the cover. Positioning Steera against his chest, he opened it to the first page and, with his chin over Steera's shoulder, began reading, "In a hole in the ground there lived a hobbit...."

The sky was alight with stars as only a mid-spring staddich sky can be. The sound of the flowing water and the mellow tone of Pire's voice washed over Steera like warm chee. She knew that their lives would never be the same. She knew that their planet would never be the same. But, Ossgar was still flowing and they were together. She looked deeply into Pire's eyes; they were glowing with the color of burnished gallite in the soft lamplight.

"Finish reading to me tomorrow," she said in her softest voice. Pire instantly put the book down and took her in his arms. Tomorrow there would be time enough for other things. Tonight, it was simply time to live.